Praise for

AN ACT OF TREASON

"Intricate, well-crafted . . . Coughlin vividly [portrays] the ethos of combat soldiers."   —*Publishers Weekly*

"The cat-and-mouse game that ensues between the two adversaries will have readers frantically turning pages. Series fans will enjoy the roller-coaster ride, and military-fiction buffs new to the series will find this episode a great place to start."   —*Booklist*

CLEAN KILL
A Sniper Novel

"The pages fly by as Swanson must face his most personal mission yet. The military tactics take a backseat to the characters, creating a strong and compelling narrative. Coughlin and Davis have concocted another winner that should only encourage a growing readership."   —*Booklist*

"Former Marine Coughlin and bestseller Davis combine a well-paced, credible plot with a realistic portrayal of modern combat . . . The climax . . . will leave readers cheering."
—*Publishers Weekly*

DEAD SHOT
A Sniper Novel

"Compelling."   —*Publishers Weekly*

"The [plot] propels the pages forward, but this one isn't all about action: Swanson proves a surprisingly complex character . . . *Dead Shot* suggest[s] a hardware-heavy story that only an armed-services veteran could love. Surprisingly, it's

completely the opposite. Readers will be compelled . . . and will look forward to another Swanson adventure." —*Booklist*

KILL ZONE
A Sniper Novel

"Stunning action, excellent tradecraft, insider politics, and the ring of truth. Just about perfect." —Lee Child

"Tight, suspenseful . . . Here's hoping this is the first of many Swanson novels." —*Booklist*

"A renowned sniper, Coughlin recounts battlefield action with considerable energy." —*The Washington Post*

"The action reaches a furious pitch." —*Publishers Weekly*

SHOOTER
The Autobiography of the Top-Ranked Marine Sniper

"One of the best snipers in the Marine Corps, perhaps the very best. When I asked one of his commanders about his skills, the commander smiled and said, 'I'm just glad he's on our side.'" —Peter Maass, war-correspondent and bestselling author of *Love Thy Neighbor*

"The combat narratives here recount battlefield action with considerable energy . . . A renowned sniper, Coughlin is less concerned with his tally than with the human values of comradeship and love." —*The Washington Post*

"Coughlin is a sniper, perhaps one of the most respected and feared in the Corps, and his memoir, *Shooter*, offers a uniquely intimate look into the life of one trained to live in the shadows . . . some of the most poignant action ever recorded in a modern Marine memoir." —*Seapower* magazine

AN ACT OF TREASON

GUNNERY SGT.
JACK COUGHLIN,
USMC (RET.),

WITH
DONALD A. DAVIS

St. Martin's Paperbacks

This is a work of fiction. All of the characters, organizations, and events portrayed in this novel are either products of the author's imagination or are used fictitiously.

AN ACT OF TREASON

Copyright © 2011 by Jack Coughlin with Donald A. Davis.
Excerpt from *Running the Maze* copyright © 2012 by Jack Coughlin with Donald A. Davis.

All rights reserved.

For information address St. Martin's Press, 175 Fifth Avenue, New York, NY 10010.

Library of Congress Card catalog Number: 2010040379

ISBN: 978-0-312-57265-5

Printed in the United States of America

St. Martin's Press hardcover edition / March 2011
St. Martin's Paperbacks edition / February 2012

St. Martin's Paperbacks are published by St. Martin's Press, 175 Fifth Avenue, New York, NY 10010.

10 9 8 7 6 5 4 3 2 1

For the Troops

1

The two soft-back Humvees belonging to the 116th Infantry Brigade Combat Team of the U.S. Army National Guard were on familiar turf. The stony ridge on which they were perched provided the ten American infantrymen with a feeling of temporary shelter and safety. After several hard hours of rolling on patrol, it was a pleasure for them to call it a day and move back into the previously prepared positions.

Their unit was a cohesive all-Virginia outfit that had trained together for years, and most of the young soldiers were good friends from towns up and down the lush Shenandoah Valley. Four were African Americans, including fireplug-thick Sergeant Javon Anthony. The 116th could trace its lineage all the way back to the famed Stonewall Brigade of the Civil War, but the modern Army thought it politically incorrect to perpetuate that troubled slice of American history. The brigade was placed in the 29th Infantry Division, a move that did away with the old blue-gray arm patch showing a caped General Stonewall Jackson sitting on his horse,

Little Sorrel. The "Stony on a Pony" silhouette was left behind.

Sergeant Anthony really did not care about that. For him, history had narrowed to last week, yesterday, the past hour. Afghanistan had a way of making a man focus only on what was in front of him. He sat in his Humvee, listening to the buzz of the radio traffic and asking himself the question that plagues every leader: *Have I done everything that I can?*

At thirty years of age, the sergeant was the oldest of the group by two years, and he knew each of his soldiers. He had been with them all the way through the recent tour of duty, well into its sixth month. So far, they had been lucky. Nobody had gotten much more than sunburn and scratches as they pulled routine patrol duty; endless and monotonous and dangerous. He was perfectly happy when night came over the mountains and one more day was done and could be crossed off the go-home calendar.

The squad was already in position up on the ridge. It overlooked an Afghan police security checkpoint about fifty meters away on the road below. The rough-looking cops had waved them into the prepared slots, and the leader, a young man, came up for a cigarette and to check on passwords. He wore a *pakol,* the traditional flat Afghan hat, over his black hair, and a mismatched camouflage uniform, with dusty sandals on his feet and an AK-47 slung over the right shoulder. Sergeant Abdul Aref was a tall man whose narrow face was dominated by a hooked nose. He spoke a little English, and his worried eyes indicated that he was just as glad as

Anthony that the Americans had returned to the familiar position every night. That added firepower, so close to the guard post, had helped keep the peace.

It had been a tactical decision to use U.S. troops as reinforcements at checkpoints along the main roads in Afghanistan. The commanders had decided that pulling everyone back into large encampments was a mistake; it simply surrendered the night to the relentless enemy. The continuous presence at set positions, combined with the presence of Afghan security forces, spelled control of an area. Control meant security, and security provided the bridge to establish regular commerce so people could start living without fear again in this devastated country.

So Javon Anthony got his soldiers settled in for the night. The fighting holes were lined with sandbags, as were shallow revetments in which the Humvees could park nose-first. The .50 caliber machine guns were still aboveground, with a complete sweep of the surrounding area. He walked the perimeter, checked the small latrine area a few meters away, and made certain each man knew his role for the coming night, including who would be on sentry duty with the night-vision goggles while the partner slept. He took a final look down at the road checkpoint as the oncoming darkness flooded over the mountains, chasing the fading twilight from the western sky. He saw Sergeant Abdul Aref down at the checkpoint, threw him a casual salute, and got a wave in return.

Satisfied, Anthony picked up the radio handset and called his company headquarters seven miles away to report that his team was settled. "Saber, Saber. This is Saber Three Alpha."

"Saber Three Alpha, this is Saber. Send your traffic."

"Roger. Three Alpha occupied our overwatch position. Situation normal. Three Alpha out."

"Roger."

With that formality, he had done all he could do. Anthony rewarded himself with a moment of relaxation. His eyes were rimmed with red from staring over the sparse landscape all day, hunting signs of potential trouble, and the dirt and sweat had left him grubby and smelly. They would return to camp tomorrow, so there was a shower in his future. He popped a bottle of water, tore open an MRE package, and pretended that it was food. Then he was instantly asleep.

A line of cars, buses, and trucks was waiting to be checked before rolling on, the drivers and passengers using the cool night during which to travel instead of the baking daytime sun. Sergeant Aref watched them through a firing slit in a roadside concrete bunker. A metal bar outside the bunker had to be raised by a guard to allow a vehicle through. The bunker had a small heater powered by a chugging generator outside that would fight the colder air settling down like an icy layer from the high peaks of the White Mountains.

His position guarded a rural road, a small but vital route that connected some of the wheat farms and villages on the Shomali Plains to the main roads. Aref was confident of the position. Concrete barriers, piles of sandbags, and steel poles forced all vehicles to curve slowly in and out, stop and go, as they approached. Big irrigation ditches prevented much off-road movement. Aref folded his hands and blew on them for a puff of warmth.

The steep little single-lane road at the mouth of the Panjshir Valley had been used back when American special operations teams were chasing Osama bin Laden through the valley and into Pakistan, only a dozen miles away. That had given the entire region a mystique among Afghans. Whoever controlled this section of road held a lot more than a piece of dirt: If the Taliban could disrupt traffic here, the villagers might believe Osama would return, this time leading a mighty force to conquer the infidels. Afghans knew from their long, fierce history that eventually they always won, however long it might take and whatever the price.

Aref's men were allowing one vehicle at a time into the cordoned parking space where a final search was done. It was a slow process, and the drivers were growing impatient as the long line of SUVs, private cars, jammed buses, big trucks, and pickups waited to be cleared. Diesel and gasoline engines spewed noxious fumes. Windows were down, and music came from radios. Some drivers and passengers got out of the vehicles to talk while waiting their turn at the gate. Soldiers were gathered around a small fire off to the side, brewing tea.

There was no moon tonight, but the sky was smooth and so clear that stars blinked like little warning lights, although they could not be seen from the checkpoint, where two racks of bright floodlights punched a bright dome in the darkness. Aref checked his wristwatch. Almost one o'clock in the morning. He decided to break up the soldiers around the fire and get them out on perimeter patrol. There was no reason for worry. Tonight seemed no different than any other in the past two weeks. Still, nervousness itched at him just like the rough blanket.

The attack began two hours later when an old cargo truck pulled into the checkpoint, groaning on its springs beneath the weight of boxes of scrap metal covered by a ratty tarpaulin. The driver stared straight ahead, as if lost in thought, then pushed a button to detonate his bomb, a pair of artillery shells that were tamped down beside cans of gasoline. A stolen case of M-84 flash-bang grenades also was in the cargo bed, four containers in the case, and three grenades in each container. The explosion had nothing to contain it, and curtains of sharp and heavy steel fragments whipped across the area, while the instant mixture of the ammonium and magnesium in the grenades temporarily created a world of instant light a thousand times brighter than a welder's torch. The driver was vaporized.

Javon Anthony had been looking the other way through his NVGs but was still knocked silly by the blast. His goggles, which amplified light, were lit up by the flash and temporarily blinded him. He was deafened by the roar, and the ground shook. Fighting the pain in his eyes, he ripped off the goggles and screamed, "Everybody up! Jones and Stewart: Get on those guns. Everybody get sharp. Now!" He shook his head to try to clear his vision, but it was no use. He saw only dancing panels of red and yellow, and felt the wetness of blood coming from his ears.

As soon as the explosion rocked the checkpoint, a rocket-propelled grenade whistled in from behind the Americans and smashed into one of the stationary Humvees, turning it into a flaming pyre. Shadowy men rose from the tangle of irrigation ditches and stormed in firing automatic rifles and more RPGs. The surprised Americans were barely able to react, much less fight.

Down below, the checkpoint had been utterly destroyed, replaced by a smoking crater. Abdul Aref and his entire team were dead, as were the occupants of every vehicle within a hundred-meter radius. Cars and people alike were on fire, strange torches in the night, and a flank of the attacking force veered away from the Americans and ran to the remaining vehicles to inflict even more damage. They fired as they ran, riddling cars and trucks with bullets. Several drivers had managed to get off the road and were killed when they hit a ditch or stopped to turn around. Vehicle after vehicle was destroyed by the rampaging Taliban guerrillas.

More men with an entirely different mission overran the American position.

At first Anthony was shooting blind and couldn't hear any of the rounds being fired. His vision and hearing slowly returned, and then he picked up the hard hammering of the machine gun of the remaining Humvee.

Johnson screamed curses, then disappeared in the blast of an RPG.

Javon Anthony tried to gather his wits. From all around and below, the sergeant could hear the groaning of wounded men, some of them screaming in agony. First things first. "I need a head count!" he yelled, still hugging the dirt. Only three voices called out. Then another RPG zipped overhead, exploding some distance away, and shadows became men with guns, right on top of him. He shot one.

Anthony crawled over to where Jake Henderson was still moving and shooting. Together, their combined fire made the attack temporarily falter around their fighting hole.

"You hit?"

"Naw. I was asleep in the bottom of the hole."

"Who else is still alive?"

"I heard Eddie Wilson over there to the right," said Henderson, rapidly changing to a fresh magazine.

"Wilson!" Anthony called out. "Wilson! Where the fuck are you?"

Eddie Wilson did not answer. Then an RPG round blew up on the edge of the fighting hole, and Jake Henderson and Javon Anthony were both knocked unconscious. The attackers checked to see if the two Americans were still alive, and when their pulses were found to be strong, both were dragged away to become prisoners.

Part of the Taliban unit that hit the Americans was a snatch-and-grab team with a unique mission. While the others carried out the actual fighting, they used the chaos to cover their advance to the edge of the main group. One young American soldier was sprawled helplessly on his back. Looking directly at the checkpoint at the moment of the explosion, he had been thrown over by the concussion and was clawing at his eyes and screaming in pain. His partner had barely seen the Taliban soldiers before the raiders shot him in the head.

Strong hands grabbed Eddie Wilson, and a fist punched him hard in the stomach to make him lose his wind. Then he was hauled from the fighting hole and pulled into the muck of the big irrigation ditch.

They threw him down face-first into the slime and bound his wrists with plastic flex-ties, then used more strong plastic loops to secure his ankles. Eddie Wilson tried to kick one of the men but was punched hard in the kidneys. The commandos bent him painfully backward and tied his ankles to his wrists. He could hear the firing of small arms and some distant explosions, but he was helpless.

His captors rolled him over so his face came out of the mud, and he sucked in a deep breath. A pinpoint of light flashed on in the ditch. He recognized it as a cell phone.

Wilson was bowed backward with his neck fully exposed. He shouted again and cursed with impotent fury when a strong hand grabbed his forehead and held it steady. Two muscular legs locked around his waist.

He heard the two men speaking calmly to each other. Then a bright flashlight was clicked on and the beam shone directly into his eyes. He yelled, "Sarge! Anybody! Help me! Javon, where are y'all?"

The kidnapper behind him reached out, and in his hand the American saw the shining blade of a huge knife. "No! *No!*" Wilson yelled, trying to thrash his way free, his eyes widening in fear. *"Mama! Help me!"*

The Taliban fighter spun the thick blade and yanked it hard against the lower neck of the screaming, struggling soldier. A bloody crimson gap followed the edge of the knife, the wound yawning wider as the blade moved relentlessly onward. A thick fountain of blood spewed out as the terrorist slowly worked on the tendons, the veins, and finally the spinal cord. Eddie's terrorized screams had been reduced to pitiful whimpers and then only gurgles as his head was sawed off. When the body fell away, the still-beating heart continued pushing out quarts of thick blood, and the Taliban fighter lifted up the American's head and bleeding neck, turning the face toward the cell phone camera being held rock steady by his partner. Eddie Wilson's final expression was a grotesque contortion of agony, shock, disbelief, and surprise. Then the flashlight clicked off, and the two men ran for safety, leaving the American soldier in pieces behind them.

Javon Anthony's entire squad had been wiped out. Seven were killed in the fighting, Wilson tortured and murdered on the spot, while Anthony and Henderson were heading into a brutal captivity.

Two days later, the gruesome little movie was available on the Internet. Terrorists no longer had to rely on

Al Jazeera or any specific journalist for publicity. They could post whatever they wanted directly to the entire world, and the horrible images of the death of the young American soldier spread like a pandemic virus throughout the electronic universe, impossible to stop.

2

Ghedi Sayid rolled the trackball up to the menu, clicked, and opened a new screen on the LCD color monitor of the radar mounted in the bridge of the *Asad,* about a hundred miles east of the Somali coast. The computer designated about two dozen fishing boats all around him, tattered and worn dhows working their nets. Sayid had waited patiently as an inquisitive Italian navy frigate paused briefly to visually examine the fishing fleet. All they had seen was fishermen, fishing, as they had done in these waters for centuries, so the warship steamed away due south. The *Asad,* the Somali word for "lion," was the mother ship that coordinated the boats and stowed the catch. The blip that represented the Italian frigate was no longer even on his screen, which meant that it was now beyond the one-hundred-mile range of the Kelvin Hughes radar. Too far to help.

Meanwhile, his target, the catch for the day, was cruising ever closer. There was too much haze to see it, but radar did not lie. A heavy sweat stained Sayid's lightweight shirt, which stuck to him like a hot rag when he leaned back in the chair on the bridge. The sun was directly overhead, cooking the shimmering air off the coast of Somalia's northeastern Puntland region. Members of the crew silently went about their jobs, waiting for their leader to make a decision.

The radar did not lie, but neither did the weather report. Ghedi Sayid recognized that the blistering heat was just too still and that the dark line hanging low on the horizon was the first skirmishing thundercloud of a major storm. The barometer was falling, and the satellites were showing the clouds gathering in a circular pattern. A monsoon was coming. The fishermen had been calling on the radio about heading in, but he had resisted, denying permission. That meant they would have to race for port in heavy seas if this operation was not carried out soon, and some of the smaller boats might be lost because their sides were so low to the water.

The leather-skinned Somali sighed, but no one detected it. He had been planning to take such a prize for a long time. After the international navies increased their presence off the Somali coast to prevent the hijackings for ransoms of cargo-carrying ships, Sayid gave up those attacks. All battlefields evolve, even small ones on open water, and he believed that he had come up with an answer that would change things and make the overall effort worthwhile.

A luxury yacht, a large and coddled ship that would have people aboard who were so rich that they would probably be carrying a million dollars just in spending money, was coming his way, almost asking to be stolen.

He could kidnap a few of the big names off such a yacht and hide them deep in Somalia, and the ransoms would be astronomical. He was confident in his meticulous planning. All he had to do was beat the storm, outwit the naval vessels of several countries, boldly board and capture or kill everybody on the yacht, then sink the boat. It would change the paradigm of the way business was done in the hijacking trade. Ghedi Sayid would set the bloody example that luxury yachts were no longer off-limits.

He scrolled and clicked, and the picture of a handsome white yacht flashed onto his screen. British flag and owned by a billionaire industrialist. The man would either be aboard himself or would quickly pay to save his crewmen and any guests who were captured. Sayid bit his lip in anticipation. He dialed a number on his cell phone, which sent a coded message to a six-man crew standing by on the coast near the city of Eyl. The men there scrambled into a speedboat, fired up a big Mercury outboard engine, and raced off toward a designated intercept position.

Taking the Zeiss binoculars from a cushioned case, Sayid stepped to the wing of the bridge, careful not to touch the scalding metal with his bare skin. He focused along the axis where the yacht should soon appear. Speaking quietly, he said, "Well, *Vagabond*. Welcome to Pirate's Alley."

"Sir! It looks like we have a bite." The calm, clipped voice of the young man seated before an array of screens in the command center of the *Vagabond* drew the immediate attention of the yacht's owner, Sir Geoffrey Cornwell.

"Put it on screen two, if you please." Cornwell activated a lever at his right hand to propel his wheelchair around for better viewing. The image of a small fast boat trailing a V of white wakes came into view. "Range?"

"Twenty-five miles, sir. Speed of thirty knots. It has been on a straight intercept course since leaving Eyl."

"Very well," Sir Jeff said. "Mr. Styles. Please drop the Bird in closer to confirm who and what is aboard. Is there anything else around?"

The technician worked a toggle, and a few miles away, a tiny aircraft not much larger than a toy swooped into a low circle to allow its onboard television camera to zoom in on the pirate speedboat. "Nothing else in that threat area, sir. A fishing fleet lies off to the east. The nearest warship is the Italian frigate *Espero,* which is departing the zone."

Sir Jeff smiled broadly. "Then we shall now launch the Snake, if you please."

"Aye, sir."

"Are you sure this thing is going to work?" Kyle Swanson leaned onto the back of Jeff's wheelchair.

"I have no doubt of it, Gunnery Sergeant. Our Bird and Snake shall not fail."

Swanson felt a slight *ka-chunk* beneath his deck shoes as somewhere below the waterline of the *Vagabond* a pair of doors slid apart and a flexible black object ten feet in length slithered out of the hull and swam away. "Just in case, I'm going to get a long rifle. We don't want them closing to within RPG range."

"Confusion to our enemies!" Jeff was in an almost playful mood.

Swanson left the amidships inner sanctum that was Sir Jeff's electronic playground. He had not seen the old man so animated for two months. Although still unable to walk, Jeff was hollering naval orders like Nelson or Hornblower or Lucky Jack Aubrey as he orchestrated the first field test of their revolutionary laser-guided torpedo.

Not long ago, the *Vagabond* had been more of a floating hospital ward, with Swanson and Cornwell as its only patients. Sir Jeff had been badly wounded when terrorists blew apart his castle in Scotland as part of a plan to overthrow the government of Saudi Arabia and steal its nuclear weapons. Swanson was wounded while tracking down the mastermind behind the attacks. The two old friends had spent weeks in recovery and painful physical therapy. Kyle was feeling back to normal, but Jeff had a long way yet to go.

Sir Jeff had retired as a colonel from the elite British Special Air Service Regiment and had gone into private business, where he discovered an unexpected ability to sniff out opportunity, then extraordinary success. He was already wealthy by the time he met Kyle Swanson, the top sniper in the U.S. Marine Corps, years ago. The quiet, solid young Marine had been loaned to him by the Pentagon as a technical adviser to help create a world-class sniper rifle they called Excalibur, the same as King Arthur's mythical sword. The weapon proved so revolutionary that Sir Jeff was now regarded as a visionary leader in designing military technology and new weapons.

With Kyle's real-world advice from today's battlefields, he and Jeff were able to think ahead to what would be needed for victory in the future. The SAS colonel had named his entire holding company Excalibur Enterprises Ltd., had become a billionaire with many financial interests, and along the way had made Swanson a major shareholder with a blind trust. The Pentagon, which was their biggest customer, blessed the deal, although Kyle could not control the funds or touch the money while still on active duty.

It was nice knowing that he was a millionaire, but the money did not matter to Kyle as much as how the professional rapport, working relationship, and mutual respect had led to a strong friendship with Sir Jeff and his wife, Lady Patricia Cornwell. He considered them to be the parents he never really had. Wherever they were became Kyle's home.

In idle times, Swanson and Cornwell always spent hours brainstorming ideas for new weapons. They agreed that this was a new age for one of the oldest and most specialized military professions, the sniper, in all his forms. The ability to take out single targets with great precision had overcome the need to obliterate entire armies with massive attacks. During their recuperation from the Saudi business, they spent hours throwing ideas around, and from that stew had emerged the concept of the Bird and Snake. The overhead drone had locked onto the pirate boat and was steering the laser-guided torpedo that was now swimming in the water.

The *Vagabond* had been changed during the process from being virtually a floating hospital into a unique command-and-control vessel with Sir Jeff, in his wheelchair, being the spider at the center of an inconspicuous web. Normally, the yacht could be a playground, but it was no stranger to being used to facilitate American and British special operations. The placid face of the yacht never changed, just its guts and capabilities.

Kyle Swanson was at the rail on the port side of the main deck, his hands lightly holding their first creation, the Excalibur sniper rifle. A weapon of extraordinary accuracy with a scope of pure magic, it already was raising the standards for precision combat. He felt a slight tingle of pre-battle nerves, and hoped that he would get a couple of shots at the pirates. He no longer needed medicine; he needed some action.

Aboard the *Asad,* Ghedi Sayid gave the signal that began the second phase of his operation, and the fishing fleet broke loose from its normal cluster around the mother ship and fanned into a long line across the projected path of the oncoming yacht. The white vessel was unaware of any threat and was maintaining a straight course. Sayid knew that when the approaching speedboat was spotted, the yacht's captain would finally recognize the danger and go to full speed to run away from the immediate threat. That would lead him directly toward the line of fishing boats.

Sayid was a pirate, a seaman, a terrorist, and a technology geek who allowed the computers and electronics to help him predict what was going to happen. He believed in the old Somali saying *Aqoon la'aani waa iftiin la'aan*—Being without knowledge is to be without light. That was why he had remained so successful in such a risky business.

"Put our boats in the water," Sayid commanded. A crane on the deck whined into life, and within five minutes two inflatable Zodiacs were pulled from the hold, with Yamaha F250B outboard motors already attached. When they were lowered, a squad of six pirates scrambled into each boat but did not cast off. Only when the yacht made its fateful turn toward the fishing fleet would the Zodiacs tear out of their hiding place behind the *Asad* and close in from the sides. The yacht, surrounded, would either surrender or be sunk.

It was just a matter of waiting a few more minutes now. Sayid went back to the computer and the radar. Nothing had changed.

Sir Jeff tapped his fingers and stared at the video being transmitted back to the *Vagabond* in real time from the circling Bird, the lightweight spy vehicle that was no bigger than a seagull. The pictures showed men with guns and rocket-propelled grenades crouched forward in the speedboat. No doubt about it. "Light them up, Mr. Styles."

"Aye, aye, sir." Styles pressed a button that signaled the Bird to activate its laser beam and lock onto the heat of the straining outboard engines. "Laser on."

"Feed it to the Snake."

"Aye, sir. Snake confirms."

On deck, Kyle Swanson had the Excalibur out of its protective sheath and resting on a stack of folded pads as he lay sprawled in the prone position, locked and loaded, eye to the scope. He could clearly see the small boat churning through the dark waters. Still too far for a shot.

The Snake had been wiggling into position since leaving the *Vagabond,* trailing a hair-thin aerial that picked up the signals from the circling Bird. When it reached a point directly ahead of the oncoming pirate boat, it slowed its little battery-powered motor to a minimum speed, adjusted for buoyancy, and hovered almost motionless just beneath the surface of the water. Two small compartments on its back opened, and a pair of round canisters floated up. Then the Snake powered up again and swam away to a safe distance. The canisters popped up just as the boat roared overhead.

There was a brilliant flash of white light and a series of thudding explosions, and the speedboat was suddenly covered with a thick veil of smoke. The cloud turned a brilliant orange, and a sticky mist fell over the men and the vessel, accompanied by a horrible stench that made the pirates double over, coughing, trying to draw fresh air into their lungs. The man piloting the boat swerved erratically to get free from the stinking fog and slowed his power, not knowing what had happened. One man had jumped overboard in fright and was screaming for help.

"Ha!" yelped Sir Jeff. "Finish it now, Mister Syles!"

"Aye, sir."

The Snake went on the hunt again, slithering fast and silent until it came directly beneath the now-stationary target. Another canister popped free and erupted into a fireworks show worthy of a Chinese New Year celebration, and the remaining pirates thought they were being swept into the spirit world as sparkles, machine-gun-fast detonations, and blinks of flame rose from the water around them. The Snake itself then rammed into the spinning propeller, tangled into it, and self-destructed with a small charge.

Through his sniper scope, Swanson saw the back of the boat rise out of the water when it was blown off. Then the craft flipped over and the rest of the men were hurled into the water.

"Bridge. We are done. Let's go home." Sir Jeff rolled from his control panel to a broad window and watched with pleasure as the pirates flailed in the water and their destroyed attack boat sank. The *Vagabond* accelerated into a high-speed turn, went to full speed, and departed the area the way it had come, with its proud, sharp bow cutting through the waves, almost as if mocking the pirates being left behind.

In the distance, Ghedi Sayid wiped sweat from his brow, his eyes wide in disbelief. His entire plan had evaporated in an instant. He'd thought he had all the knowledge that he needed, but realized that he had greatly underestimated his opponent. Now a new set of questions arose to bedevil him. Could he outrun that Italian frigate that was sure to return and investigate the disturbance? Could he beat the approaching storm?

Would his men trust him anymore, or would he be dead tomorrow, with some other captain stepping forward to capitalize on his failure? He barked a string of orders to get things in motion, then sat down hard in his chair, with no idea what had just happened.

3

GILGOT
PAKISTAN

Javon Anthony could see the dim dawn sky. His wrists and ankles were tied with tape, and his arms were stretched and bound behind him, but he was neither blindfolded nor gagged. He lay in the open bed of a Toyota pickup truck, his breath ragged and raspy, as the vehicle jolted along a rutted track. Anthony groaned and shifted position to get more comfortable. Jake Henderson lay beside him. A bearded man sitting on the edge of the truck bed noticed the sergeant was awake and kicked Anthony in the head and on the shoulders. The kicks were vicious but without much power, since the man wore leather sandals and not boots. Sergeant Anthony moaned and rolled with the impact and decided to at least pretend to be unconscious again. He wanted water. That could wait. He heard the guard laugh as he delivered a final kick.

The stutter of gunfire and joyful yells shook him fully awake an hour later. The guard was standing now, shooting his AK-47 into the empty sky. Other rifles and pistols joined the shooting, and the cheering grew.

Anthony could not sit up but could see the edges of some buildings. The guard reached down and, with a call of delight, swept up a young boy who had stretched out his hand. The kid landed nimbly in the truck. He was about ten years old, and his eyes opened wide when he saw the sprawled forms of Anthony and Henderson. "Hallo?" he asked with a grin, poking Anthony in the thigh with a finger. "Hallo?" Then the boy spat in the sergeant's face. The glob of wetness splattered on his forehead.

The truck slowed and came to a stop. Anthony heard the mutter and clatter of an approaching crowd as people came to the vehicle and looked into the back, a sea of hostile faces. The kid stood up and pointed at the bound soldiers. "Hallo!" he blurted out, using the only English word he knew. The phrase rippled back until the whole mob was chanting in unison as if giving a football cheer. *Hallo . . . Hallo . . . Hallo!* They understood that the word meant the Americans had arrived. A few men reached in and punched Anthony. The truck began rocking on its tired springs, and a few rocks sailed into the bed and rattled against the metal.

The tailgate dropped with a clatter, and hands grabbed Anthony's ankles and pulled him out of the truck, hurling him to the hard dirt and knocking the wind from him. Anthony gasped, trying to suck in some air while being mauled. He thought his life was about to end in being torn apart by a screaming mob, but more guards arrived and pushed the civilians away. They stood him up on wobbly legs. A moment later, both he and Jake Henderson were hauled away by the guards. They were dragged up a slight incline for about a hundred yards, then propelled through a large door and into a small mud-walled building with a dirt floor. The door slammed shut and was locked. Outside, down the hill, the mob howled in derision, "Hallo!"

The name of Muhammed Waleed was known far beyond his mountain camp in Waziristan. He had spent his entire life battling the enemies of Pakistan and Islam. Now in his fifties, he had ascended from being a naive but extremely bright product of the madrasah, or religious school, in his hometown to being an outstanding college student in France and then to fighting his bloody way upward to take over leadership of the Taliban. Though it had been on the verge of extinction after the American-led coalition threw it out of Afghanistan, Waleed had created a safe haven in the mountains of Pakistan and reorganized the force, unit by unit, and brought it back to strength, ready to fight again, and no longer just in Afghanistan. It seemed that his fierce eyes could see everywhere.

Waleed had learned of the arrival of the two American prisoners almost as soon as the trucks had threaded through the rugged border from Afghanistan and entered the long valley that emptied into Pakistan's tribal areas, the desolate Waziristan. When the trip terminated at the village of Gilgot, they were still out on the high plain, about eight miles from the border and the same distance from the major town of Wana. That was only fifty miles from his stronghold. Waleed had given advance approval of the raid and the murder of the

American solider, but the kidnapping of the other two took him by surprise. Bringing the Americans back into Pakistan represented a threat to his overall plans. They should have been killed in Afghanistan, where open conflict raged.

The United States could be counted on to apply immense pressure for the government in Islamabad to rescue and retrieve those soldiers. Waleed summoned his advisers, the council of longtime comrades he called the Wise Ones, and asked, "What should we do about this situation in Gilgot?"

"Once more, the instigator was Fariq, nephew of Mustafa Khan, the village headman," replied one senior counselor. "He led the attack team into Afghanistan and helped capture the Americans. For unknown reasons, he decided to keep them alive and bring them home. His proud uncle now plans to honor him with a celebration."

"Fariq is an ambitious boy," observed Waleed.

"Very ambitious," agreed the counselor. "Perhaps too much so."

"I believe those American prisoners will not survive long in Gilgot. That will certainly draw more attention to this area by the Americans and the other Crusader countries. The prisoners could be of better value to us in the future."

"Yes, Leader. On your word, we can go and take them. It would be no trouble."

Waleed crossed his arms and lowered his head until his bushy beard pressed against his chest while he thought things through. "We need to keep Mustafa Kahn happy, too. He safeguards the area well for us. Please let him know that I send him congratulations and the blessings of Allah, the most merciful, for having such a brave young fighter in his family. Offer him twenty-five thousand American dollars for the soldiers."

"He will not accept that amount."

"Let him set a price, then. The main thing is to keep the Americans safe until they can be put to a maximum use. Spilling their blood in Gilgot would be a useless gesture to satisfy the pride of a headstrong youngster. Be quick about this."

The Wise One was correct. The offer was made and rejected, but instead of a counteroffer, there came a polite invitation to the esteemed Muhammed Waleed to attend the celebration in two days' time and personally meet the warrior nephew, Fariq. Not accepting the deal was a veiled insult to the authority of the Leader.

"Inshallah," said Waleed. God's will. He had everyone leave the room because he wanted some time alone to pray to Allah for guidance—and to make a private call to a very old comrade.

Jake Henderson was a good-looking kid from Petersburg, Virginia, who had been considered a hound dog in high school for the way he had always sniffed after the girls. He liked women, and women liked him. Being in the Army had not changed the broad smile on his chiseled face. The touch of a woman, just the *idea* of the touch of a woman, usually propelled Jake into high gear. For the only time in his life, two women were pawing his skin, laughing, and he was scared to death.

"What are they doin', Javon? Why they bathin' me and not you?"

Sergeant Anthony shook his head. "Guess you stink more," he said, feeling that something awful was in store.

Both men had been regularly beaten by guards for the past two days, more out of sheer brutality than to elicit information, and had expected another dose of fists and feet when the door had opened and two women carried in buckets of water and folds of cloth. Two guards accompanied them and hauled Jake to his feet, then sliced away the twisted tape that bound him and stood back to let the women work. All had dour smiles as they pushed him to stand in the middle of a square of oilskin. Then one woman used a pair of scissors to cut away the soiled uniform and his filthy underwear. Their boots had been taken the first day, and now Henderson's stinking socks were removed. All of the discarded clothes were thrown into a corner, leaving Jake stark naked.

The women soaped and bathed him, scrubbing away the caked-on dirt with a bar of soap that smelled of flowers. A bucket of water doused his head, and the scissors came back to trim his hair and beard. Henderson stood as still as possible, but the chill of the water made him start to shiver. As the younger of the women shampooed his hair, the older one carefully cleaned the dirt from beneath his nails. As she bent to do his toes, her eyes roamed to his penis, which was shriveled almost to invisibility, as if it were trying to hide. She said something in her language, and the guards laughed; then the younger woman used soap and water in and around his crotch, allowing her fingers to rest longer than necessary on the penis. Instead of sexual attraction, Jake's only feeling was one of horror. He whimpered, and the older woman made soothing *tut-tut* sounds and told the younger one to stop playing with the prisoner. Big towels were used to thoroughly dry him, and a sweet-smelling oil was massaged deep into the aching muscles.

Javon Anthony finally began to understand. The morning had been filled with noise outside their hut, even music and laughter lifted from the town square at the foot of the hill. When the door opened, he caught glimpses of the square, where colorful thin banners waved atop tall poles. As the hours had passed, he watched the crowd grow in the town square, and traveling merchants selling items at stalls. The guards were cheerful.

The younger woman needed several trips to gather the discarded clothes and cleansing items, and Jake Henderson was given a pair of new white jockey shorts before a guard clamped on handcuffs. This time, they put him in a chair, as if trying to keep him clean, and secured him tightly.

At a small bench beside the door, the older woman unwrapped a dark roll of cloth and exposed three long knives of varying sizes. One was a broad butcher-style blade, while the second was a long serrated knife that ended in a perfect point, for use in cutting joints. The third was slender and slightly curved with a tiny hook on the end, which was used for detail work in skinning animals. "They're going to cut off my dick and balls!"

Henderson screamed to Javon and started urgently thrashing in the chair.

The woman picked up the biggest blade and moved to Jake's right side, putting her palm against the simple red tattoo on his bicep, the word "Jen," short for Jennifer, his fiancée. At a nod, both guards seized him, and she placed the shining sharp edge against his flesh and rocked it gently, top and bottom, then side and side, cutting a rectangle around the tattoo. The slices barely broke the skin and caused little pain and only a thin trace of blood. The younger woman stepped forward and pressed a small cloth on the wound to dry it while the elder returned to the bench and exchanged blades. She held up the little knife with the hook and examined it in the sunlight that streamed through the window before returning to work. With the guards struggling to hold the victim steady, she hooked a corner of the opened skin and peeled it toward her, slid the blade beneath the tiny flap, and pressed the ribbon of flesh against the steel with her thumb. With a slow pull, she ripped the rectangle away from the fatty membrane beneath while Jake Henderson screamed in agony and genuine terror. His eyes were huge. "Javon! They're going to skin me alive!"

The woman held up the piece of skin like a prize and dangled the tattoo before Jake's eyes. Satisfied with her work, she said something, and the younger woman rushed forward again and applied ointment and a thick bandage. Remarkably little blood oozed from the wound. The older woman had returned to the bench and slowly wiped, polished, and sharpened her knives before rolling them up and tying a knot in the small leather strap that held the bundle together.

Outside, Javon Anthony could hear the merriment increasing as he prayed for his friend, who remained tied to the chair, mumbling incoherently, sounding like he was going mad with fear.

The door opened, and six of the terrorists who had taken them prisoner came inside, laughing with a fat man with a thick gray beard. The old man approached Jake Henderson and bent forward, hands on knees. He spoke with a thick accent. "Hallo, American. I am Mustafa Khan, the leader of defense forces in this area. In a few minutes, we will be called to the town square. I shall walk down the path beside my nephew, the courageous Fariq, who led this especially trained team of strong fighters in Afghanistan. People have come from all around to pay them honor today for their deeds on the battlefield. Then we will bring you to the square, and Fariq will personally give you over to the women as a symbol of his victory. It will be quite a sight. Afterward, we shall have a feast."

"Fight them, Jake! Fight back!" Anthony screamed, somehow lurching up from the floor, only to be knocked back down again by the guards. "Fight the bastards! You goat-fuckers are all dead men! Hurt him like that again and the United States will destroy this fucking dirty village, and I'll see you in hell!"

Mustafa Kahn walked over and slapped his cheek hard. "Your time will come, black man. Just not today. Be patient."

* * *

The previous day, the United States had unexpectedly received information on the captives from a very reliable source, and early that morning an unmanned Predator robot plane had been launched to carry out a reprisal raid. The aircraft coasted without detection into a circular pattern nine thousand feet above the village of Gilgot, too high to be heard, and its controllers back at Bagram Air Base in Afghanistan scanned the target zone with an infrared camera. Clear shots of the cluster of buildings came onto the command screen in real time and confirmed the nugget of information, that an American was to be sacrificed during a celebration honoring the terrorists who had kidnapped two soldiers and slain a third. The camera also provided a close-up picture of the small building where the prisoners reportedly were being held.

With that confirmation, the order was given without a second thought. Two Hellfire air-to-ground missiles slid off the rails beneath the drone. Pushed by solid-propellant rocket motors, they tore away on flights of their own, homing in along the invisible path of a reflected laser beam.

The Hellfires appeared seemingly from nowhere in the clear sky and crashed into the center of the village, and the twin impacts of their twenty-pound blast-augmented warheads exploded almost simultaneously with terrifying thunder. The hut on the hill saved the lives of those inside, but the small building seemed to leap on its foundation when it was socked by a gigantic concussion wave, then a shower of debris. Mustafa Kahn struggled to the door in time to see a huge and pulsing orange-red fireball consuming his village. .

Behind him came the maniacal laugh of Sergeant Javon Anthony, who was rolling from side to side. "Told ya, motherfucker! Tried to warn your stupid ass. There goes your fucking party. Big storm headed over the mountains, straight for this shithole, and you and your pissant nephew gonna die hard!" The laughing continued until the guards beat him unconscious.

Warlord Mustafa Kahn would never learn how his village had been discovered as the hiding place of the prisoners. He staggered among the bodies, hearing the cries of the injured and seeing the devastation spreading from the big crater on the northern edge of the square. He had failed to protect his people, the worst thing that could happen to a tribal leader. He did not want a follow-up missile strike, which would either kill him outright or ignite a rebellion that eventually would have children kicking his severed head around like a ball. Even while Kahn spoke the usual promise that Allah would take the ultimate revenge on the Americans, he was regarding his nephew and his friends as objects worthy only of his scorn, filthy things that had brought doom to Gilgot. The six young fighters were transformed into a commodity. Mustafa Kahn believed he had sacrificed enough to show them honor and protect his own dignity. Now they had to go.

He reestablished contact with the esteemed Taliban chieftain Muhammed Waleed to say that he would welcome a price of twenty-five thousand dollars for each American soldier in his possession, and that he would throw in the half-dozen brave heroes who had captured them as a bonus. The deal was accepted, and three highly polished SUVs arrived that night to whisk away all of the men, who had been traded like a herd of camels. The young fighters were glad to leave Gilgot with their own skins intact.

Mustafa Kahn finally could relax, count the money, and consider the overall episode to have been a profitable venture. He had long been eyeing a beautiful falcon whose owner and trainer was asking about twenty-five thousand dollars for the graceful bird. Now he could buy the falcon, share about ten thousand dollars among the villagers who lost family members in the missile attack, and still have another fifteen thousand left over. He also had curried favor with the powerful Muhammed Waleed, the leader of the Taliban.

4

CIA Director Bartlett Geneen and his luncheon guest remained politely silent while Filipino servants in white tunics and creased black trousers set a table in his office with regular china instead of the elite tableware used to impress politicians. When the stewards left, the two men nibbled quietly on vegetable salads and small servings of jumbo shrimp sautéed in a light mustard sauce. They had known each other for a long time and would tend to business in its turn.

Geneen was a carryover from the previous administration of President Mark Tracy and had been reappointed by the new president, Graham Russell. The director had spent his entire professional life remaining studiously nonpolitical in the intelligence world. From his point of view, it did not matter who was sitting in the White House, for he served the office, not the man. Geneen gave unvarnished advice, heavy on facts, and stayed out of the line of political fire. He had other people do that kind of thing. One of them was sitting across the table.

The long battle with America's changing foes over

the years had drawn deep lines of worry in Geneen's sharp, emaciated face, and his white hair was almost entirely gone. Age made no difference in his determination to keep the nation as safe as possible.

His guest at this 12:30 P.M. lunch was another CIA veteran, James Monroe Hall, a special assistant to the deputy director of operations. Hall was calm and sipped some iced tea, waiting for Geneen to speak.

"Jim, this beheading thing and the capture of our two soldiers poses a problem for us," the director said.

"Tough call for the new president," Hall agreed in a neutral tone.

"President Graham cannot let this atrocity go unpunished," Geneen repeated. "To do so would make him appear soft on terrorism. He is furious about the incident."

Hall shrugged his shoulders and spread butter on a tiny triangle of toast. "With all due respect, the bottom line is that all ten men in that squad were volunteers, and this Wilson boy is only the latest single casualty in a dirty war that has cost thousands of American lives. He died doing his job. They screwed up by parking in exactly the same place every night. Now the squad leader and another soldier are gone. A terrible development." He paused, dabbed his lips, and drank a little water.

"I see fault here with everybody in the command structure who allowed that practice of keeping in the same position night after night, at least all the way up to the battalion level. They made it too easy for an ambush, bypassing established defensive protocol. It was a snafu, but shit happens in war." He had laid out facts and not ventured any suggestion.

The CIA director picked up the remote control for a large flat-screen television that was set into the wall of his office. He clicked a couple of times with no result. "I hate these things," he said, continuing to punch buttons. The machine finally flickered to life, and with another click the terrible pictures of Eddie Wilson being murdered came onto the screen. "Jim, the public relations fallout from this gruesome torture has been extraordinary—an evil and macabre execution that has gone all over the Internet and has received millions of hits. The Muslim crazies are crowing about death to all Americans, and our own crazies here at home are demanding that the president nuke somebody."

"Turn it off. I've already seen it about a hundred times, and it still disturbs me," said Hall. "Gruesome, yes; tragic, yes; but the soldier's death really changes nothing. The kidnappers, however, are slick. Our best guess is that they were not killed by that Predator strike in Pakistan. We were too hot for revenge, pumping in those Hellfires without really having eyes on the exact target. The Pakis up in that village there claim we wiped out a wedding party, and they paraded the usual corpses of some dead kids. I call bullshit on that, but the strike unquestionably made this bad situation even worse. Now the Pakistani government, with more than enough problems at present, has to pretend to be outraged with America."

Geneen speared a prawn with a toothpick. "Which

is why I asked you by for lunch today, Jim. I need some alternatives."

"I have no crystal ball, Director. Our sources say that our kidnapped soldiers were in the village at the time the Predator came in, but they have now been moved, as have the kidnappers. We do not know where."

The CIA leader watched Jim Hall carefully, almost able to see the wheels turning behind those brilliant blue eyes. "Options?"

"Several, I should think," said Hall. "Another highly visible hit with a Predator or a cruise missile could send the message that this thing isn't over, no matter how much the Pakis complain, but it would create a further mess. Big explosions always do. Or we could pay someone a bunch of money to have these bad dudes killed for us, but that would not send the proper message of our determination and strength. Best option is to stage a precision black operation with a low probability of further collateral damage."

Geneen walked to one of the bulletproof windows in his office, turned, and examined Jim Hall, the assassin at sunset. Hall would turn sixty-two soon but looked ten years younger. Twenty-four years in the Marines and another two decades with the CIA. He was slim for his age, still held a military posture at six feet tall, and was in superb physical condition. His nails were manicured, the hair trimmed, and the shave perfect on tanned skin: a well-groomed killer. "You already have something in mind, don't you?"

"Yes, Director. I have been looking at it since I heard

about the Predator screwup. We have to do a precision strike now, something close-in and absolutely certain."

"Nothing is absolute."

A grin slid across Hall's face. "This might be. We send in two of the best snipers available, spend some money to set up the tangos, and then our guys blow them away."

"What about the prisoners?"

Hall shook his head. "A separate issue at this point. We cannot rescue them without making a large military footprint. The Predator apparently accomplished one good thing in getting these boys moved away from the badlands and farther along the food chain of responsibility. Our agency can try to locate them through covert sources, but we cannot mount a major rescue operation. However, we can sure as hell punish the kidnappers, which will motivate the Pakistanis to turn them over in a political settlement."

Bart Geneen had been thinking along those same lines. There was a limit to what even the CIA could do. "Have you chosen the snipers?"

Jim Hall placed a folder on the white tablecloth, flipped it open, and handed a head-and-shoulders photograph to the director. "Kyle Swanson is one of them. He ran that Palace of Death thing in Iran and other dicey assignments for that Task Force Trident special ops group. He's the whole package. Gotta be on the team."

"I know Swanson. He is very good. But why not just use the SEALs or perhaps some FBI sharpshooters?"

"We want to keep this under our control. Swanson would report to the CIA field agent in charge of the operation."

"So your second sniper choice is one of ours?"

"Me." Hall looked at the director with a steady gaze. "I want to go in for this one."

Geneen scoffed. "No, Jim. You run the op from here."

"Bart, I will be retiring in three months. I want to go out at the top of my game, not sitting behind a desk half a world away from the action. I may be a step slower, but there is nothing wrong with my shooting skill, and I have the personal contacts over there. Besides, I helped train Kyle Swanson. We can work together almost without words. There would be no learning curve for a new partnership."

Geneen mulled it over in silence. Hall wanted a last job that was a big task worthy of his skills and would carry the stamp of finality for a veteran agent. He deserved the chance. "Then go do it," Geneen said, extending his hand across the table to shake with his prized operator. "Good luck, Jim. Remember. The president does not want any more collateral damage. Nor do I."

"That will not be a problem. I'll have a brief for you in a couple of days. It may get expensive."

"For this one, money is no problem. If I have to blow a hole in the federal budget, so be it. I will give you the authorization."

Hall walked away from the director's office with his usual confident stride. Before reaching his own door, he stuck his head into the office of his deputy, Lauren

Carson. "Find a Marine sniper named Kyle Swanson and get him assigned to us for temporary duty."

She jotted the name on a pad. "All right. Where is he?"

Jim Hall was on the move again and called back over his shoulder, "Could be anywhere. Let me know when you get him."

5

WAZIRISTAN

Pakistan seldom held a stable government for very long. Its politics held great rewards but even greater risks. Once again its people stood at the precipice of chaos. Muhammed Waleed believed it was his turn to seize power.

In the Arabian Sea port city of Karachi, street bonfires painted the sky in orange and yellow. Farther up the Indus River, the mayor of hilly Hyderabad was assassinated. Students were marching in Rawalpindi and Quetta. Public workers were striking in various cities throughout the Punjab. Order was slipping away, and the democratically elected government in Islamabad was unable to bring stability.

Muhammed Waleed had created a masterpiece of simmering chaos. He had spent years slowly weaning the competing elements of the Taliban away from their love of senseless violence in hopes of forming a permanent political movement. He decided to name his fledgling party the Bright Path, words that meant almost anything a follower wanted to believe, always viewing it as a better future. Fighting without obtaining political gain was both costly and pointless. Their extremist founders had come from the Afghans who defeated the Russians, but their days in power lasted only five years, from 1996 to 2001. During that time they accomplished little beyond having the rest of the world regard them as savages. Their downfall was inevitable, sped along by backing terror groups, mistreating their own citizens, and being unable to form a popular government.

Muhammed Waleed was determined not to make similar mistakes in Pakistan, and his support was growing almost by the day. The Muslim clerics were siding with him because of his pious religious beliefs. Al-Qaeda, far from being an ally, fell into line; Pakistan offered them benign shelter at a time when they would otherwise have no home. The warlords gave him support because he was one of them, and easily the smartest and most powerful. Young people were drawn to his magnetic speeches and sermons about how tomorrow would belong to them. The media was cultivated to present him as an exciting new face in pragmatic Islamic politics, and the Bright Path as the party of the future. Power brokers knew the dire results of openly opposing him, such as having one's family slaughtered, and were taking a neutral position. The president of Pakistan had become almost a prisoner in his own office, and his government was weak.

The overall result was that Waleed's Bright Path had seeped out of the traditional mountain redoubts of the tribal warlords and Taliban hideouts and was extending its control the way a rude and uninvited guest might take over a man's home.

As much as he would like to believe that the Pakistani military was a tired machine with a skipping heart, Waleed knew that it was stronger and better equipped than ever. It was ready to defend the government, up to the unknown point at which one of the generals or colonels changed his mind and staged a coup of his own.

The vaunted secret police known as the ISI was waiting to see how it all turned out, for they would work with whoever held power.

Even for a man like Waleed, a warrior with a vision, it was difficult to imagine the power he might soon wield. A combined force of the Taliban, the Pakistani military, and the secret police, allied with al-Qaeda and other terrorism organizations, everyone fired with the zeal of Muslim fundamentalism, would present an incredible front. It would not be merely a new regional regime. A truly united Pakistan and its arsenal of Islamic bombs would be a nuclear superpower.

Waleed forced himself back to reality. It was not done yet, and many matters called for his personal attention, for the Taliban was still developing the chain of command and even a routine bureaucracy that would allow him to delegate authority. The American prisoners had fallen into his hands like apples from a tree, a gift from Allah, praise be unto his name. There must be a purpose, one that he just did not yet fully understand, although an idea was forming.

He was satisfied that he had gotten the best of the deal with Mustafa Kahn, the impudent warlord who had not immediately grasped Waleed's wish that he surrender the prisoners without incident. So there was a bit of revenge to be had, a message to warlords less powerful than Waleed. He sighed with exasperation, for he was juggling a lot of balls and could not afford to drop a single one. He did not need this problem.

"Take me to them," Waleed said, walking from his living quarters. A pair of guards led him a quarter mile down a dusty street and into a dirt yard bordered by a mud fence. Six men were kneeling on the ground in a row, facing to the east, toward Mecca and Medina. A guard holding an AK-47 stood at each end of the row. Waleed walked down the line and patted each man's head, giving them a fatherly touch and muttering words of comfort.

His voice was gentle and rhythmic. Waleed had long ago learned to speak just above a whisper so people had to strain to hear his words. "Which two of you slew the American soldier in Afghanistan?" he asked.

"I did, Leader," said one in the middle, and the man kneeling next to him echoed the answer. "And I, Leader."

"Please, stand," Waleed said, and the guards helped the men to their feet. "Free them." The blindfolds and wrist restraints were removed. "You did well and followed your instructions perfectly. Your obedience shines as an example to other fighters. Thank you." He rested a hand on their shoulders, each in turn, then motioned for them to leave.

"Now, which of you is the brave Fariq, whose uncle is my friend, Mustafa Kahn of Gilgot?"

"I am Fariq, my Leader." The man on the left end raised his head, proud that Waleed knew his family.

Muhammed Waleed tapped Fariq and a man on the other end. "Take those two and put them against the wall." The guards jerked the men upright and forced them out of line, then shoved them to the wall until their faces were ground against hard rocks embedded in the tall fence. Waleed took the AK-47 from one of the guards and racked the bolt to be certain it was loaded. The safety was off; the firing selector was on automatic.

"All four of you disobeyed your instructions. Nobody told you to bring back prisoners." Waleed's voice began to rise from the normal quietness, and the change was frightening. "You should have killed them on the spot. Instead, you dragged them back to our home ground, caused the destruction of one of our villages, and have left me to clean up your mess. I will not tolerate such disobedience."

He pointed the weapon and pulled the trigger, holding down firmly on the stock to keep the aim true. Fariq and the man beside him pitched forward, their bodies flopping into the thirsty dirt that soaked up the blood as Waleed kept pounding them, ripping through an entire magazine of bullets. He gave the automatic rifle back to its owner, walked to the final two fighters at the wall, and personally removed their blindfolds. "You men were misled by that incompetent Fariq, and Allah has granted you a second chance at life. This time you will do better. I will have a new task for you that will earn you the right to honorably rejoin the Bright Path. Do you understand this?"

"Yes, Leader."

"Yes, Leader."

Waleed patted each on the shoulder again and said, "Good boys." He went back to his office. Fariq was buried that night in barren ground far away.

WESTERN PAKISTAN

"Where are we, Javon? Where they taking us? What are they going to do to us now?" Jake Henderson was bewildered.

"Be still, Jake. Still and quiet." Sergeant Anthony was trying to figure out those same questions.

Henderson was too nervous to listen. So much had happened during the past twenty-four hours that his nerves were stretched tight and his pulse raced. One minute they were getting ready to flay him alive, then there was the big explosion, then they were beaten some more, then they were out of the village, driven away in a comfortable SUV under minimal guard. "Why did they untie us? How come those Talibans that grabbed us are gone? Who are these new guys?"

"Jake, if I could answer any of those questions for you, I would. All I know for certain is that we are both still alive and unharmed."

"I was harmed. Bitch cut off my tattoo." Jake's fingers touched the clean bandage around his bicep. The arm was still sore, and the vision of the sharp knives played over and over in his mind like a sports highlight reel.

Javon decided to ignore him. The boy would talk until his tongue fell out if he thought anybody would listen. Maybe some silence would chill him a bit. Anthony assessed the moment. No doubt things had changed dramatically for the two of them, but why? He rubbed his wrists. Loose handcuffs bound their hands in front of them, and all other restraints had been removed. They were in the back of a cargo truck, having changed vehicles twice during the night, and were now on a paved road with the sounds of other traffic. A single guard wearing local clothing sat opposite them with a rifle across his knees. He was an old guy with a belly and a big mustache and smoked a cigarette, hardly looking at the Americans after having given them some water and some spicy meat wrapped in what looked like tortillas. No use trying to jump him and escape, for there was nowhere to go. The threatening demeanor of their captors had entirely changed.

"Javon?"

"What is it, Jake?"

"We gonna be all right?"

"Dunno. We're better off now than we were yesterday. Can't tell you about tomorrow." Anthony motioned to the guard, pointing to his own eyes and to the front of the truck. The guard nodded approval, and Javon crawled on his knees to a position just behind the cab and peered through a small window that let him look over the shoulders of the driver and another guard. Far ahead was a sparkle of light, a fat dome of man-made illumination. He got back into his seat.

"What's out there, Sarge? Where we at?"

"God damn, Jake, give it a rest, will you? I think they're taking us into a city. Now shut up and try to sleep."

6

"I have to leave."

"You're not ready."

"A message came in from Washington an hour ago. Jim Hall of the CIA. I've been ordered to report to Bagram."

"I repeat. You're not ready for operational status." Sir Jeff slid his reading glasses down his nose and peered over the steel rims. "Not in Afghanistan or anywhere else."

Kyle drank some coffee. "Running and stamina are the only things that are below par for me right now. I've been exercising for hours every day for weeks but still don't quite have my wind back. Can't do a real five-mile run on a tub like this."

"This tub, as you call it, is a one-hundred-million-dollar yacht. Show some respect. And I know you use the treadmill in the gym."

"Not the same."

"I agree." He smacked the arms of his wheelchair in mock frustration. "I'll be glad to get rid of this damned thing and at least do a mile. Even so, the treadmill is no substitute for a military course."

"No heavy pack, no curves, no rocks underfoot, no obstacles. I jog along, listening to music."

"You're not ready, Kyle. Tell them that."

"I'm ready enough. Get on shore, work out some kinks, get my endurance back up. I'll be ready to kick ass."

Sir Jeff smiled. "Who are you lying to, Kyle—me or yourself? Our friend Jim Hall is putting together a package, and you think there will be time to do some conditioning? No, the CIA, particularly Jim, does not work that way. He will expect everyone, including you, to arrive ready to roll. He will throw you right into the cauldron. My guess is that it will be in Pakistan."

Swanson pushed back the chair and walked to the rectangular window, rubbing a hand along the wainscoting of polished African mahogany. "Ahhh. I'm bored, Jeff."

"I know that. I'm bored, too, but I'm in this wheelchair, you see? Reality is involved, Kyle. Boredom sometimes must be endured. Then there's the quality of your shooting to consider."

"I've been banging skeet on the boat and running bullets through Excalibur at floating targets."

Sir Jeff laughed derisively. "Neither of those is the same as real shooting under battlefield conditions. Another reason that you're not ready. So there is your wind to consider, and also your shooting eye. Tell me truthfully, lad, could you take out a terrorist at four hundred meters today? Five hundred?"

"Yeah. Sure I could. I could have taken down those pirates on that speedboat, except you wanted to play with them instead."

"That was more important. It was a field test of a new weapons system that you helped design and, I shall remind you, will bring you a lot of money in your declining years."

"Still, I could have picked them all off. Sniping ain't exactly rocket science."

"Actually, it is. Maybe even more difficult, because space rockets are not living beings and do not shoot back." Cornwell rolled his chair forward and peered at Swanson with eagle eyes. "You obviously are not sure you're ready at all, and that uncertainty is hardly the correct frame of mind for some world-class combat shooting. By the way, Hall did not ask my opinion, or I would have advised him to find someone else and let you finish your rehabilitation in peace."

"Oh, bullshit, Jeff. How many missions did you refuse just because you had a couple of bumps or bruises? Hell, I know that story of how you had a broken arm and lied and bullied your way aboard a plane for a jump."

"Don't change the subject. That was just a training exercise. Kyle, it is not proper for you to take on a special ops mission just to salve your ego. Not just for a lark. Muck it up and there could be hell to pay."

"I can do this, Jeff."

"Now you're just whining." Sir Jeff stopped talking and unfolded a newspaper with great ceremony, snapping the pages open. "I have said my piece. I shall not allow some common American Marine to turn me into a grumpy old man. Will you still be aboard for breakfast tomorrow?"

Swanson did not look away from the window, just shook his head negatively and continued to watch the passing small, frothy waves. In the fading sun the water was like gold. "The *Ike* is in the area and will send a helo to pick me up about oh nine hundred. From there I take a plane to Bagram."

"Very well, then. I think that I shall wheel off to bed now. Sleep well tonight, son. It has been my experience that you might need the rest. I shall see you tomorrow morning."

Kyle Swanson walked aft along the central corridor of the huge yacht, then up the circular staircase to the main deck, and back again to the broad rear deck. He dropped into a chair and propped his feet up on the lower railing. The *Vagabond* was driving hard to the southwest, churning a good wake that pointed toward the dimming horizon. The place he was sitting was sheltered from the wind. He popped open a small green bottle of cold Perrier water and drank half of it in two long gulps. "Well, fuck me," he muttered.

After the quick, intense fighting in Saudi Arabia, everyone involved was determined to force U.S. Marine Corps Gunnery Sergeant Kyle Swanson to take a long, long break. He needed to recover from some wounds, but also to recover from the mental stress of having had so much work fall on him.

Jim Hall had provided no details about the new package, other than that he looked forward to working with Kyle again. It had to be something unique and special. Knowing Jim, that hint that they would be working together meant they would probably have to kill somebody, sometime, somewhere, in secret. It had to be in Pakistan, Swanson figured. The CIA had made a direct request for him by name, but Kyle knew that he could either accept or pass. He was assigned to Task Force Trident, a covert operations force that operated on a Presidential Finding from the White House. Although hidden inside the Marine Corps, he was occasionally loaned out to other agencies when the task was approved by the Oval Office. Hall would not have even sent the message if he did not have that authorization, or thought Kyle was not up to it. Of all people, he knew that Kyle Swanson lived for these jobs. It was a chance to get back into the game, if Kyle wanted to do so. He did.

For the first time in two weeks, Kyle suddenly wanted a cold beer. He looked at the green bottle; the bubble water tasted pretty good. A small price to pay for staying in shape. Swanson had realized during this recovery period that he had been leaning for a while against the shaky wall of becoming an alcoholic. Then he found that he was also relying on narcotics to ease his pain and help him rest, too easily reaching for the pill bottles for relief. By the sheer force of his will-power, he had entered a rehab program of his own design and turned off those switches in his brain. He had not had a beer or even a glass of wine for three months.

Alcohol also packed on the weight. He missed cold beer the most, but his body was thanking him for kicking the habit. No booze. No smoking. No pills except the required antibiotics. Hard exercise. Excellent diet. He figured that for such sacrifice, a healthier body had better be worth the effort.

His blue-gray eyes swept the darkening sea. One thing that had vanished with the lust for alcohol and the easy-life narcotics was the surprise visits of his old nemesis, a creaky skeletal ghost that he had come to know as the Boatman. Always paddling to the surface in his nightmares, coming to cackle and offer grim predictions about looming and unavoidable catastrophes, the Boatman tried to plant doubts in his mind and remind him that at heart, Kyle Swanson was a cold killer who steadily supplied fresh souls to hell. Being drunk and high usually opened the mental door for the Boatman to drop by. Being clean and sober again, Kyle had not seen the son of a bitch for a long time and did not miss him at all. Good riddance. Still, he had been reduced to drinking bottled water from France.

He closed his eyes and stretched his neck as the freshening breeze from the coming storm whipped around him. The hazy sunlight finally blinked out while crooked bolts of lightning cracked the sky and thunder bowled over the water. The first raindrops came dancing across the deck, and still Kyle sat alone, balancing the bottle on his knee and watching and listening and pondering Jeff's question. *Am I really ready? Will I jeopardize this mission and the lives of others before it all even starts? Can I pull the trigger on a tango at four hundred or use a silenced pistol or even the Gerber knife up close and personal? Am I ready?*

"I am disappointed that you entertain doubts." A shaky voice seemed to rise up to him from the water, where a small craft rode at rest, unmoving in the troubled sea. "I have allowed you enough time off. Get back to work." A little snicker of a giggle trailed on the wind. A tall figure was at a stern oar, the winds not touching the bloodstained black rags that drooped from the skeletal bones. The Boatman was back, his personal omen of deaths yet to come.

"I was hoping never to see you again," Kyle replied into the night storm. "Shit. I'm not even asleep and I can see you out there."

"Look at you! Living a good life on a fancy yacht, and goodness me, developing nonlethal weapons! How can such a thing help me fill my boat?"

"What? You think I work for you? Boatman, you are a raggedy-ass creation of my own mind, sailing around in my brain. You are nothing."

The sardonic, hateful laugh came again. "Wrong. I am everything. I am your today, and I am your tomorrow, the sum of all of your parts. You know when they place the gold coins on your eyes at death, you will be all mine, sitting in this little boat with me ferrying you to the unknown. And that is the one thing, the one place, that you fear: the unknown."

"Go away. You're boring."

The Boatman leaned on his oar, and the little boat shifted position, nose into the waves now, taking the motion of the water. "You will notice that the boat is currently empty of souls. You should have filled it with the corpses of those pirates, and you know it. Excalibur was calling for you to shoot, and you let them live."

Swanson was on his feet, at the railing, staring out at something no one else could have seen. "That was the mission. We accomplished what we intended to do. Everything does not have to end in a bloodbath."

The single crackle of laughter was lost in a boom of thunder that vibrated the big yacht but sounded like a derisive shout from the heavens. "Yes, it does. For you, it must end in blood, and it will not stop until you take your seat in my boat. Enough." There was a flash of face, nothing but white bone and a grinning jaw of sharklike sawteeth. "I just stopped by to welcome you back to our private world. Go hunting now. Bring me fresh souls."

Kyle loosed a primal shout of anger from his gut, grabbed the green bottle, and threw it as far as he could. It splashed into the water far short of the disappearing boat, which blinked out in the big waves as the noise of the storm swallowed the final burst of laughter. He did not care if he was being environmentally unfriendly and perhaps bonking a whale on the head. Fuckin' Boatman. Kyle would do the job with Jim Hall, and that was that. He still had questions, yes, but there was only one way to find the answers.

7

Swanson returned to his cabin, took a quick shower, and slid into the neat bed. He grabbed a Robert B. Parker Western novel to read until he was drowsy enough to sleep, but his mind refused to return to the Old West and its sturdy gunfighters. He kept thinking about the gunfighters of today, and how he had become one. Instead of being a sheriff calling out bad guys to duel in streets outside of saloons, Swanson preferred never to let his quarry get anywhere near him, and also to never know the end was imminent. A well-placed shot from a hide that was hundreds of meters away did the job just fine, and the sniper would then slip away to do the same thing on some other day. Swanson saw no point in standing toe-to-toe and having a quick-draw contest. Too much was uncertain. If he wanted a man dead, he would kill him, which was, after all, the point of the whole thing. It would be good to be working with Jim, someone he had known for many years and whom he trusted without question.

He put the book aside and clicked off the light, feeling the *Vagabond* sweeping through the water and letting it rock him like a baby in a seagoing cradle. If he had ever had a real mentor in the Marine Corps, it was Jim Hall, who spotted something special in Kyle when he was just a pup in training and had groomed him for bigger things.

Soon, sleep came, and with it a remembrance from seventeen years ago, at the sprawling Marine base at Camp Pendleton in California, when Kyle had been young and talented, but with an attitude problem that was driving Jim Hall nuts.

Lance Corporal Swanson slithered through the dirty drainage pipe beneath the wide road. He knew he was going out of bounds, and didn't care. To him, the popular motto of the Marine sniper, "One shot, one kill," was just public relations bullshit. Out here, he steered by a much truer compass, the much more relevant axiom of "If you ain't cheating, you ain't trying; if you are caught cheating, then you ain't trying hard enough."

That was what he was doing right now, cheating, but he was not going to be caught. Swanson had been busting tens, maximum scores in the stalking trials, since he began the phase. Nobody could see the invisible man until he wanted them to, and the instructors were getting pissed at how his success was feeding his already cocky attitude. The youngster was an absolute loner, and he was scoring the max while simultaneously throwing the lesson plan on the trash heap.

"See anything?" Gunnery Sergeant Jim Hall, the non-commissioned officer in charge of the training, had three Marines scanning the scrubby field with powerful binos and spotting scopes. Out in the stalking course were a couple of walkers, who were merely tools for the day's exercise. Since they wandered around a specifically outlined course, they could easily spot any irregularities up close, but they were not allowed to give the spotters help, advice, or information. The spotters had to find something unusual, then guide the walkers onto the students. The walkers just went to where they were told to go. If there was a sniper at that spot, then the student failed.

"Nothing," said one of the spotters.

"Nope."

"Not yet."

Stalking was the hardest phase of the Scout Sniper School and was responsible for a large percentage of the dropouts. That damned boot Swanson was making a mockery of the difficult training. Hall decided to put an end to that.

There were a total of ten stalk sites on the vast military reservation, and this morning, on a thousand-yard course with clearly defined boundaries on each side, he had paired Swanson with a student who was really on the ropes. The kid was a Navy SEAL doing a remediation stalk because of an earlier failure on another course. If he did not make it this time, the guy was gone.

The task was to crawl unseen through the high grass, dotted with occasional big bushes and scrawny trees, and get to within 250 to 200 yards of the spotters, well within shooting range. It would take at least four hours, because progress was extremely slow. The snipers, wearing bulky ghillie suits that matched them perfectly with the foliage, moved so carefully and slowly that they made snails look fast. The spotters at the other end of the course were looking for any changes in the landscape.

Swanson went through the big drainage pipe with ease, ignoring the debris but being careful not to accidentally dislodge a rock that would bump against the metal tube. Any sound was to be avoided. It took him ten minutes. He crawled out into the sunlight with all the speed of a growing bush, and ten minutes later he was almost a part of the large ditch on the east side of the two-lane paved road that marked one of the side boundaries of today's exercise. Life became easier there, and instead of wiggling on his belly, he rose slowly to his hands and knees and moved forward. Another drainage ditch up ahead would bring him out behind the spotters. They could not see him if they were looking the wrong way. He found the pipe, went in, and took a break. He planned to hook out from his hiding place and reenter the course approximately fifty yards from the spotting platform. For now, he had about three hours to kill, so he went to sleep, telling himself not to snore.

"I've got something," one of the spotters called out to Gunny Hall. "Dust plume about six hundred meters out and fifteen meters from the west boundary."

Hall put his binos on the area. Somebody's boot had probably been moved too quickly across a stretch of bare ground. Easy mistake to make. "Put the walkers on it," he ordered, and the radio chatter began.

The walkers moved toward the target, which appeared to be a lump in the ground. It was really one of the sniper candidates. "Bang, you're dead," said the walker. "Motherfucker!" said the young SEAL. This could be his ticket back to the fleet.

Hall checked off the name. "Now find that little son of a bitch Swanson," he snapped to the spotters.

The early morning haze had burned away, and the California sun was promising a hot day, but a slight breeze channeled through the pipe as Swanson lay on his stomach with his chin resting on his folded hands. He was awake again but did not move other than to breathe, not even to take a drink of water; he just lay motionless in one of the only shadows around the entire course. It amused him that Gunny Hall, the spotters, and the walkers were sweating out there.

Even before arriving at the school following basic training at Parris Island, South Carolina, Swanson had started a careful study of the topography of Camp Pendleton. During days off and after hours, when the other Marines were out getting drunk and partying and hunting girls, Kyle was in the local libraries, even on the base itself, and in the offices of the county clerks. He drank not with other Marines but with old Seabees and contractors whose bulldozers and heavy equipment had helped mold Pendleton into one of the largest Marine Corps training bases in the world. Such an ongoing project required hard work by a lot of people, and Kyle found plenty of maps in the public domain and in the hands of people who liked to talk about the area's history. Old guys were better sources of information than the young guys. It was not hard to figure out what was where, all the way from the Pacific coastline inland to the Santa Margarita Mountains, from Oceanside to San Clemente. That wasn't cheating. It was homework.

By the time Scout Sniper School began, Kyle Swanson had an exceptional knowledge of his territory. This morning, he recognized the area of the training exercise as soon as the truck pulled up and parked. There would be four culverts along this two-mile stretch of back road, put in place to protect the area against periodic flash flood overflows from the Santa Margarita River. The large pipes had been laid down in the 1980s, and later reinforced to withstand the increased traffic and the weight of heavier armor and big tanks being hauled on lowboys to different parts of the base.

He made a final equipment check and moved out.

Gunny Hall checked his wristwatch. Half an hour left in the exercise. If Swanson didn't make it to the finish zone by then, he would fail. That would be good. "Anything? Anybody?"

"Negative."

"No."

"Not me."

Hall decided to cheat. Swanson had to be caught this time. He broke the rules and ordered the walkers to report the trainee's position.

In less than a minute, there was a soft crackle of a

radio in his earpiece. "I got him," said a walker. "Northwest corner of the zone. Only about fifty yards from you."

The spotters put their glasses on the area and still saw nothing.

"Go stand on him!" Hall ordered.

The walker solemnly strolled over and put a foot on the immobile back of Kyle Swanson. "Bang," he said. "You're dead."

"Nope," Swanson answered, "but everybody else is."

Swanson shed the bulky ghillie suit and had some water, then was trucked back to the camp. Anger had turned his face red, and his muscles were as tight as banjo strings. Thirty minutes had passed and Kyle was still seething when he was called to see Gunny Hall in the operations tent.

"Stand at ease, Lance Corporal," Hall barked. "I failed you today. Four points. You have one chance to remediate. One chance to pass or fail. Screw up again and you're out."

"Gunny, permission to speak freely?" Swanson asked.

"Permission denied," Hall said with a steely curtness. "I know everything you have to say—that we didn't play fair today, that you've already accumulated enough points to pass the course, that you're better than everybody else out there. Right?"

"Yes, Gunny Hall." Kyle's muscles tightened even more. He wasn't allowed to lay out his side of the story, and there was too much of a rank difference for a fight.

"Now I will tell you where you are fucking up big-time, Marine. I've seen a hundred guys just like you: the loners, the special cases, the 'I don't need anybody else' types. This school ain't about you, Lance Corporal. Stalking is not an individual event."

"It should be," Kyle said before he considered the impact his words would have.

"Nobody said you could speak, asshole. So typical of you, Swanson. Always with an answer even before the question is ever asked. You're willing to do everything we want . . . but you refuse to listen! Now you get my little lecture, and you will by God pay attention." Hall was on his feet, pacing back and forth like a drill sergeant, his hands clasped behind his back and his face contorted with emotion. "Now stand at ease, even sit down if you want to, but for Christ's sake, *listen* to me. Okay?"

Swanson exhaled deeply but remained standing at a rigid parade rest. Hall shook his head at the feeble silent protest.

"Lance Corporal, we lost a good man out there today, that SEAL kid. Why?"

"He fucked up."

"Yes, he did, and because he did, he is gone, out of here, and that is not the friggin' point."

"What is the point then, Gunny? He screwed up and I didn't. Why are you so pissed off at me?"

"Because war is not an individual sport." Hall stopped beside his desk and opened Kyle's personnel folder. "I've wasted some time looking into your background, Swanson, and talked to a couple of shrinks about your kind of personality. It's all there. You're about as special as a cheap Tijuana whore. All the symptoms of a classic loner: Alone as a kid in an orphanage. Alone in school. Even when you played baseball in high school, you were a pitcher, the one individual that everybody else on the team supports. But this is not a place where a loner can excel."

"I seem to be doing okay on my own, Gunny Hall."

"You think so?" Hall sat down in his chair, leaned back, and folded his hands. "Not in this game. The name of the friggin' course is Scout Sniper, you moron. Consider this as a combat situation: A minimum of two men go out together, and if one of them dies, chances are damned good the other one will, too. Scout. Sniper. Personal excellence is mandatory, but it is not enough. Right now I would not want you as a partner."

Kyle blinked, caught by surprise. "Why?"

"Because I could not trust you. You might go off and try to accomplish the mission on your own, leaving your spotter alone. I could not rely on you for help if I was trying for a shot, or trying to escape and evade."

"So I should give myself up to make somebody else look good?" Kyle did not understand this logic.

"No, Swanson. Look, we both know that you cheat and that you succeed. That is good. You are a natural leader, and you really are better than the rest of them, so I expect more from you. Help these other guys, son. Share your skills and your ideas and your methods. Show them how to do what you do. I want you to prove to me and the other instructors that you can be trusted when the crap hits the fan. It's all about trust, Lance Corporal Swanson."

"I can do that."

Hall was finished with the lecture and just grunted and waved the kid away, with no idea if Swanson had listened to a word he had said.

8

Jim Hall was spread out comfortably aboard a Citation Bravo executive jet, the modified Cessna 550 model, sliding through the night sky at four hundred knots and thirty-five thousand feet. He had dropped the facing seat to make a bed, changed into an old Adidas tracksuit for comfort, popped five milligrams of Ambien, lowered a silk mask over his eyes, and stuck the buds of an iPod into his ears. Classical music and the drug would ease him into sleep while they crossed the pond.

The private plane was one of the ghost fleet, special aircraft owned by an Agency front company and used primarily for unique missions such as renditions and paramilitary support. The small, quick plane, with its pair of Pratt & Whitney turbofan engines mounted aft and high, had been to a lot of places, always off the record. It was still bouncing through some air pockets from a storm front that was closing across the East Coast but would rise through the clouds soon. Lauren Carson was across the aisle, wide-awake, to answer the phone if he needed to know anything.

This was style, exactly the way Hall wanted to run the final assignment of his career with the U.S. Central Intelligence Agency. Word had spread that he was about to retire, and even before he left Langley to board the plane at Andrews Air Force Base in Maryland, he had detected the tattered threads of disrespect tangling around his ankles. Invisible shackles. After this, he would be nobody; another old man gone. Somebody else would become the special assistant to the deputy director of operations, and there would be a string of promotions on down the ladder. The CIA was a gigantic bureaucracy. No desk stayed empty very long.

He changed position in the seat and increased the volume of the music to mask the whine of the engines. Like many workers with a lot of years in any industry or business, Hall had become disillusioned with his profession.

The first major puncture in the balloon of faith came with the hard lesson that the shield of anonymity provided to CIA agents was neither impenetrable nor absolute. That idea was knocked for a loop when a political scandal ripped the name and face of one agent out of the shadows. The president of the United States himself had declassified the identity and thrown her to the political and media wolves. The affair actually had made Jim Hall feel a little better, because it proved that he was not the only person running a game in the dangerous jungle known as Washington, D.C. In fact, he figured that he was one of the littler fish. After he assessed how the impact of an agent being outed had spread like a virus through Langley and ruptured so much trust, he decided that it was only prudent for him to prepare for the unexpected; in other words, cover his ass.

Hall was one of the old-timers who had been chosen to help put the trust train back on track and given the rank of special assistant to the DDO. Instead of being a plum assignment, a springboard to an even better position, he viewed it as a sign that he had gone as high as he was going in the Agency. His lack of formal education was given as the reason for the blockade. He had managed to earn an associate's degree from a community college, but that could not compare with bright men and women from the Yales and the Harvards. A lifetime of experience spent in the weeds, learning about the world and risking his life to protect the nation, could not overcome the ivy-covered walls of academia. It grated on him and made him feel inadequate: Which of them could do what he had done? None!

Nevertheless, he had set about the new job with gusto, coming out of the chill of being a spy to craft a very public persona. Jim Hall became the top CIA lobbyist on Capitol Hill, where he was a coveted source of news tidbits for the media hounds, and the go-to guy when deals needed to be struck in cloakrooms of the Capitol concerning the intelligence community and its secrets. He was amply rewarded with limos and unlimited credit cards and girls and fancy restaurants and embassy parties, seats at the Kennedy Center, status, and entrée into the corridors of power, including the White House. He even had the beautiful Lauren Carson around to carry his briefcase. Hiding in plain sight and being highly paid in many ways was a life that Hall enjoyed.

Every once in a while, for a special job, he had to return to his roots for a mission and pick up a weapon or personally guide a black operation. Then the affable Jim Hall would disappear from Washington, and Ms. Carson would explain that he was skiing at his condo at Crested Butte, or fishing in Alaska, or visiting his mother down in Palm Beach. After a few weeks, Hall would reenter the Capitol hive, cheering up everyone with risqué jokes and making his rounds of secret briefings and dropping pro-Agency propaganda to journalists. It was perfect.

Retirement would end that easy access to power and money. He could live out a full life within a protective bubble, mowing his suburban lawn and cooking bratwursts over his propane grill. That held no appeal whatsoever for Jim Hall. There was the option of becoming a real lobbyist for a defense company, but that meant that he would eventually end up as one of the old guys standing alone at the end of the bar at the National Press Club, soup stains on a wrinkled tie, hoping for a conversation about the good old days. Hall had decided to make other arrangements.

Across the narrow aisle, fully alert at a little desk, sat Lauren Carson. She watched Jim settle down and fall asleep so amazingly quickly, as if he had not a care in the world. An old warrior's trait, he had explained; eat and sleep when you can because you don't know how long it will be before the next meal or rest. His chest barely moved, and the slightly parted lips breathed in the cool cabin air.

She had been with him for six years, straight out of the training farm, and admired the tough, quirky guy with the sharp sense of humor. She had no illusions: Jim always looked out for Jim. He always had a plan, was always a couple of steps ahead of everyone else. He was also a liar and some other unsavory things, like being a professional killer, but he was, after all, a veteran field agent of the Central Intelligence Agency. He was a spy, as was she. Another major difference was that Lauren had never killed anyone, not that she objected to the possibility of having to do so.

She felt a tug of regret that it was going to all be over for him, for them, so soon. There was also a twang of guilt because his retirement also represented an opportunity for her. Finally, she would be able to leave the administrative side and take an assignment in a field office abroad to punch that necessary career ticket.

Lauren knew she was ready for field work and would prove that once again in Pakistan. She picked up a phone built into a wall holder and spoke softly to the two pilots up in the flight deck. Nothing of interest. Stay focused.

The two Taliban fighters who were spared at the wall of the execution yard, Makhdoom Ragiq and Mohammad Sial, understood that they were living on borrowed time. They could only trust their future to the will of Allah and the whims of the Leader of the Bright Path. So far, things had worked out well, although in a very strange manner, for while they were safe and being well treated, no one shared information with them.

It was easily determined that they were being contained within a Class A prison near Peshawar, close to the Khyber Pass in the rugged northwest. In the morning light, they were pleased to be able to see the mountains from the windows of their rooms. The domed towers of the Islamia College were to the left. Most of the doors remained open at the prison, and there was plenty of tasty food served by attractive girls who also offered other pleasures.

The open doors did not mean freedom of movement. The pair were told they would remain in the prison while Muhammed Waleed completed his thoughts about how best to employ them. Waleed's representatives also assured the fighters that they were being kept out of sight for their own safety in case of further reprisal attacks by the Americans, and their incarcerations would be brief.

They leaped to their feet when a young man in a tan Western suit, light blue shirt, and matching tie entered their rooms, wearing a small silver falcon, wings outspread, in his lapel. The hunting falcon was the symbol of the Bright Path Party. His beard barely covered his face, as if he shaved frequently.

"Ah, thank you for being here today," the man said in a polite tone. "Please excuse my being late. You both are aware of the need for secrecy and deception in operational situations, so it would be better if you do not know my real name. I am here to represent the Wise Ones." He dipped his head as if in modest apology, then brightened. "You may call me Selim. And please sit down and be comfortable. We have something to discuss."

The room became still as he looked them over—wiry tribal men with smoldering dark eyes, ashamed that their beards had been trimmed and their fingernails cleaned. They were both in Western-style clothing, clearly uncomfortable. "You look perfect," Selim said.

"I am a mountain fighter and would rather blow up a building than wear these clothes," declared Makhdoom Ragiq. The taller, older man, with his mustache and beard cut back, displayed bad teeth within a narrow mouth when he spoke.

Selim shrugged his shoulders. "You both will soon be transferred to lodgings in Islamabad, to a place in which rough mountain fighting clothes would be too different. You have to blend into your surroundings, just as on a battlefield."

"What do you want of us, Selim?" The second man, a short fellow with a moon face, a muscular body, and oily hair, asked the question directly and in a firm voice.

Selim responded with a further helping of praise. "You are both very valuable fighters, and the Leader and the Wise Ones were correct in recommending that I be responsible for you while the Americans are hunting you. I have agreed to keep you safe, but you will have to endure the dreadful ways of the Western world for a little while longer. Then you can go back home, back to your mountains out there, if you so wish. Do you understand?"

The two fighters looked at each other. They were true soldiers and followed orders. Someday, God willing, they would figure out how they had gone so quickly from being battlefield specialists to having to dress and act like infidel tourists. All they knew was that they were kept alive after the fiasco initiated by Fariq, that son of a whore dog. They would do the bidding of the Wise Ones without question, although it was something too complex for them to fathom.

"You brought great honor to our cause by participating in the death mission of the American. It was a daring and courageous act that struck fear into the infidels, Allah be praised. All true Muslims cheer you." He skipped over any mention of the kidnap and Fariq.

"Thank you. But what do you want?"

"We need your services again."

That brought a sense of swift ease to the pair of soldiers. The short man asked, "Where will we do this favor? Will we go back into Afghanistan again?"

"No," Selim answered. "This time it will be right here in Pakistan. You will be housed in an apartment in the best part of Islamabad until you are required to act."

"We need to train our bodies and our spirits, sir," said Makhdoom Ragiq. "We will need details. Many details, to make our plans."

"There is little time. You can exercise in the privacy of the apartment suite. I am personally handling the planning. Once you are in Islamabad, I shall give you the details. Tell me at that time whatever other information you need and it will be provided."

The tall man spoke again. "And when do you want this, this *operation* done?"

"Very soon. Perhaps just a few days. Everything is being arranged. Rest here until I call for you with a car. We will make the trip down to Islamabad together." Selim smiled a final time and left the room as quietly as he had entered.

9

The Citation settled out of the predawn sky, blacked out even on the landing approach into Bagram Air Base. The mottled black-and-gray paint scheme blended seamlessly with the surrounding darkness. Cockpit avionics did most of the heavy work as the control tower cleared a path through all of the air and ground traffic. The plane whispered down onto a concrete runway that was almost ten thousand feet long, rolled to a stop, and scooted in behind a little tractor that guided the humming aircraft plane over to the Special Operations ramp, and then into a secure hangar. All interior lights had been turned off. Big doors rumbled closed, the lights came back on, and the engines shut down.

The ground crews jumped to work, preparing the bird for a quick turnaround. It was not the kind of plane that kept a strict schedule, and this was not a normal airport. This particular Citation was to be ready to go at a moment's notice, with never an official flight plan on record. Everybody who needed to know about it would be advised at the proper time, given what they needed, and no more. Cargo manifests and passenger lists did not exist.

Two crewmen popped the hatch from the inside. They sauntered down the small staircase and walked a short distance from the plane, where they stopped and looked around while stretching their arms, twisting and bending to loosen the muscles that had cramped during the long trip. There were no salutes. The flight line workers gave the air crew no attention: just another couple of pilots.

A man in a dark suit appeared at the top of the stairs, and he reeked of authority. He stood motionless and looked around the vast hangar, but the angular face registered no emotion. It was only a moment of passing interest for the technicians, who did not pause in their jobs of servicing the plane. He was just another of the many VIPs who had passed through this special hangar over the years. Maybe a congressman or somebody. Who cared? A clean SUV cruised to the tip of the wing and stopped.

It was after he came down the stairs that things came to a momentary jarring halt, for a slender, beautiful blonde woman lugging a small bag appeared in the doorway. Now here was a rare and agreeable sight for the grease monkeys, a real live white-skinned leggy American beauty wearing a dark blue pantsuit that emphasized her figure. The noise level fell perceptibly around the hangar. Every workman who had a chance to see her suddenly realized that he had been in Afghanistan too damned long. A dropped crescent wrench clanged against the concrete floor and brought them all back to life again.

An Army officer who had gotten out of the passenger side of the waiting vehicle came to attention and saluted the man, struggling to keep his eyes away from the blonde, wondering if she was also a VIP or just arm candy for the guy in the dark suit. "Welcome to Bagram, sir . . . ma'am," he said. "This vehicle and its driver are yours for the duration of your stay."

"Excellent, Captain," the man growled. He immediately climbed into the backseat of the big black Ford Expedition SUV. He said nothing to the driver, who was expected to already have instructions.

Lauren Carson smiled politely at the captain. She refused his offer of help with her bag, and at the vehicle she bent over slightly, snapped shut the handle and the little wheels, and used both hands to heave the bag into the backseat. The man pulled it in. She climbed in, and the captain closed the door, the darkened windows shutting off the view of her golden hair. The driver turned on the big 5.4L Triton V8 engine and dropped the automatic transmission into gear, and the SUV drove out through a smaller door in the hangar.

While Lauren had diverted attention, the two fliers who had been the first off the plane split up. One headed for a pilots' lounge at the end of the building. The taller man pulled at the rumpled seat of his olive green flight suit, put on a blue Air Force campaign cap bearing the silver eagle of a full colonel, and casually walked out into the breaking dawn. It was getting cold, and the temperature stung his cheeks. An old brown Army Humvee was waiting, and he got inside and shut the cloth door.

The driver looked at him with open contempt. "You're no more an Air Force bird colonel than I'm the Little Mermaid," he said. "In fact, I think you're a goddam spook."

"Well, I'll be damned," the new passenger replied. "That's a pretty smart mouth for a shit-eating Marine to use when talking to his betters." Jim Hall's face split into a grin. "Hello, Kyle. Good to see you again." He reached out a hand.

Kyle Swanson shook hands with his friend, then cranked the Humvee. "Hello, Jimmy. We going to cause some trouble?"

"Oh, yeah, my boy. Bet the farm on that. Now drive."

Lauren Carson had made several trips with her boss to Iraq, but this was her first time in Afghanistan. The huge mountain range that reached into the brightening sky in the east like a huge wall took her breath away. Then she compared that ageless wonder with the military base. Remarkable. It was also huge, a place that was becoming a strange, small city with a first-class airport. The SUV driver had turned the heater on low to fight the chilly morning air. Bagram was five thousand feet above sea level, and snow would soon layer those huge Hindu Kush mountains overlooking the base. The arid peaks would be impassable within a couple of months.

The senior commander at Bagram was a U.S. Army two-star, the top slot of a chain of command that looked like a spider's web more than an efficient flow chart. Other branches of the American armed services were there, and U.S. Air Force planes of all sizes were the predominant feature. Fleets of construction vehicles were busy beneath the racks of bright lights, biting and shaping more land so Bagram could continue to expand. The American war that had started in Afghanistan after 9/11, then shifted to Iraq, then heated up again in Afghanistan was undergoing a new phase as tensions grew in Pakistan. The strategic location of Bagram made it essential to any and all of those efforts.

Lauren felt that the huge base was coiled and tense with an alertness that seemed to her to be beyond the normal military sense of security. Off to her left, an F-15 Strike Eagle roared into the violet sky on tails of blue-white fire, with ribbons of white mist streaming back from the wings that fought for lift in the thin air. It was slung heavy with bombs. This was Afghanistan, not Arkansas, and war was just over the horizon.

Her SUV turned a corner away from a neat street of tentlike buildings and pulled to a halt at a square fortified position from which a helmeted soldier behind a .50 caliber machine gun kept watch as another guard, in a full armored vest and camo battle gear, came forward. The driver rolled down his window, and the guard peered inside. "Identification, please," he said.

The escort officer had collected the military ID cards for himself, the driver, and the man in the dark suit. Lauren handed over the leather wallet containing her CIA creds. The soldier checked them, let his eyes linger for a moment on her face, then returned her badge and the IDs. "Welcome to Bagram, Ms. Carson. They're expecting you inside," he said, then to the driver, "Neil, park over there behind the Hummer."

Lauren put on her game face. "No need for anyone to get out," she told the driver and the escort officer. "I can open a door by myself." The mystery man in the dark suit would stay in the vehicle and be driven to another safe building to complete the deception. He actually was the second member of the Citation's flight crew and just wanted to dump the monkey suit and get a shower, some chow, and some sleep before having to fly again.

Kyle Swanson had driven faster than the SUV, and he and Jim Hall were already standing with coffee mugs in hand and talking when Lauren Carson came through the door. Swanson was seldom surprised by anything, but the moment that his blue-gray eyes met her blues was like the flash of a camera, a frozen moment of unexpected emotion. He sucked in every detail, from her stylish shoes to the small silver necklace and lack of makeup. *She doesn't need makeup*, he thought. *If I was God, I wouldn't change a thing.* Lauren hesitated for only a fraction of a second, caught off balance by her own feelings. Although there was only one other person in the room, it was as if a large crowd had parted to open a path between them, and they both instantly knew in that first glance that their lives were going to be different.

"Kyle, meet Lauren Carson, who runs me and my entire shop like we were a bunch of slaves pulling oars.

Lauren, this is Kyle Swanson, the guy I've told you so much about." Jim Hall could almost see the electricity buzzing between these two. *It's only been three seconds and they already should go get a motel room.*

"Good morning, Ms. Carson. Welcome to Afghanistan." Kyle took a step forward and reached out his hand, and she took it in her own. Her skin was soft, but her grip was firm.

Ordinarily, Lauren could just turn on her blazing Miss Arkansas smile and dazzle a new man with her beauty. This time, she had to fight to keep from blushing. His strength was understated, but obviously he could have broken her hand with anything more than a gentle squeeze. "Thank you, Gunny Swanson. I look forward to working with you." There was a slight southern accent. She intentionally broke the moment and went to the big coffee urn on a table and filled a mug. Black, no sugar. *Now what?* She looked over at Jim, who seemed to be enjoying their discomfort as the initial sizzle came under control.

They all sat down, and Kyle was glad that there was an entire table between himself and this new girl. Woman. *Damn, fool, think of something to say.*

"Well, I finally win," said Jim Hall, breaking the ice for them. "I never lose. Sometimes it just takes longer."

"Win what?" Lauren asked, blowing on the scalding coffee. The pout of her lips was totally sensual to Swanson.

"Yeah," he echoed dumbly. "Win what?"

"Fifteen years ago, mate. Rocket Mountain, when we tried to recruit you."

Lauren reacted with mock surprise and touched her heart with her hand. She turned to face Kyle, and he saw the first glimmer of a smile. "You mean my legendary boss Jim Hall failed an assignment? Amazing. Tell me. Tell me, so I can spread some gossip back at the shop."

"I didn't fail anything. I never lose. You know that."

"Tell me the story and let me be the judge."

Kyle shook his head. He remembered the incident well.

10

Rocket Mountain, a big bump of dirt in the Sierra Nevadas, was part of the Mountain Warfare Training Center outside of Bridgeport, California, and a place with little supervision. Corporal Kyle Swanson had driven up with a dozen other Marines as part of a sniper package to practice high-angle shooting, above-to-below, and cross-compartment shooting from one ridgeline to another. No supervision meant that the rules were loose, and it was more fun to shoot hand grenades than proper targets. About twice a week, that kind of goofing off would start a fire among the fake buildings, and everybody would yell and run down to throw water and dirt on the flames to stop the whole place from burning up. Then the mud fights would start. Things were usually pretty loose up on Rocket Mountain.

Master Sergeant Jim Hall was pulling instructor duty for the course that week because the regular staff guy was on leave. Hall and Swanson had been friends for a long time, and Kyle had gone through Scout Sniper School with Hall riding him like a balky horse, pushing to make him better than everyone else. They had gone nose-to-nose a couple of times, because neither one would back down. That only made them better friends.

Hall was forty-two years old at the time, and Kyle Swanson represented to him the continuation of a tradition, a worthy successor. The boy was an incredible sharpshooter who did everything asked of him on a range and in the classroom and in the field, but also was bright enough to think beyond the moment, with an uncanny sixth sense that could turn a disadvantage into a win. Hall would reluctantly admit, but only to himself, that the young Marine was a prodigy with a sniper rifle.

One Wednesday afternoon, everybody shaped up, cleaned their weapons, policed the area, and dumped trash into the pair of big Dumpsters that squatted beside a storage shed. A truck was grinding up the hill trailing a plume of dust, a visit by the colonel and his sergeant major, coming to check on the training and show the men that the battalion brass cared about them. In the back of the truck were sealed containers of hot chow, straight from the base mess hall, a choice of chop suey or meat loaf and lots of things like broccoli and potatoes, along with cookies and brownies. The colonel knew his men had been roughing it, sleeping outside, choking down MREs for three meals a day, and drinking gallons of water, so the fresh food would be a nice reward.

They set it up on picnic tables and had a good-natured lunch. Then the colonel and the sergeant major watched the snipers blow off a bunch of rounds at steel plates, wrecked cars, and the weather-worn plywood buildings. Finally, the visitors got back into their truck and made the long drive back to the base.

The snipers washed up, changed into civvies, and also drove down the hill. Bridgeport was only twenty minutes away, and every fast-food restaurant had a franchise there, so the Marines seldom ate their MREs. That evening, most of them went to McDonald's, but Hall pulled Swanson away and took him to a quiet Mexican place identified by a neat sign as Alphonso's Restaurant. Most of the customers were seated outside, drinking cold beer on the open patio beneath a sprinkling of little white lights. Kyle liked the fact that many of them were Hispanic, always a signal that a Mexican restaurant served authentic food. Hall went inside. Kyle followed.

A row of high-backed booths lined the far wall, each with long, cushioned seats that were separated by a plastic-topped table. Windows at each booth faced the parking lot, but at the last one, a customer had adjusted the blinds so no one could see in. Overhead lights in the middle of the room did little to brighten that corner. Hall slid into the booth, motioning Kyle to follow.

"This is Morgan," said Hall. The man was slender, with thick dark hair that did not show a sign of gray. No emotion showed in the dark brown eyes as he slowly dipped a fried chip into a cup of red sauce and put it into his mouth and chewed. A dark linen blazer covered a pearl gray golf shirt that had a little sheep figure sewn in gold on the left chest: Brooks Brothers.

No one said anything until the waitress came over, already with three cold Coronas on her tray. She was a beautiful young Hispanic woman, no more than twenty years old, with challenging eyes and a catlike walk, dressed in a denim miniskirt and a loose white blouse worn off her right shoulder. The name Mary was imprinted in black on a white plastic name tag.

"Ah, Maria, we meet again. You are *sooo* pretty today." Hall gave her a big smile.

"You always say that," she said, serving the chilled bottles. "All talk, no action. I think you have a wife and many children somewhere and just like to flirt."

"No. You're the only girl for me in the whole world." Hall laughed. Mary laughed. "Someday we will run off to Las Vegas and get married."

"I have a boyfriend," she said.

"But do you have a telephone number?"

"I will tell your wife if you are unfaithful." She giggled, flipped a hand at him, and walked away.

Kyle sipped his beer. "I didn't know we were joining your friend."

"Business," replied Hall, who instantly turned serious. He took a deep swallow and put his elbows on the table.

"What kind of business are you in, Mr. Morgan?" Kyle asked.

"Just call me Morgan, Corporal Swanson. No mister." The voice was smooth and as easy as the cold cerveza. His posture was a little odd. "What kind of business do you think I'm in?"

Hall stifled a small laugh. Drank his beer.

Swanson took a chip, dipped it, and ate for a moment, studying the man. Then he said, "You don't have the skin color to be from around here, so you don't get much exposure to the sun. No intentional identifying marks, but that scar by your ear shows maybe you once got your scalp peeled back by a bullet or some shrapnel. You carry yourself well, with confidence, so you're probably ex-military, since Jim Hall would not be doing business with someone who wasn't at least a veteran. Your jacket is cut a little full at the left arm, so you have a weapon in a shoulder holster. Something small, but with stopping power. Then there is your choice of this place, the last booth with your back against the wall and the shade drawn. Up there over the window where the blinking sign is advertising Budweiser, you might as well have one pointing directly at you and saying CIA."

"Maybe I'm just on a fishing trip over at the Virginia Lakes." The man's eyes remained steady.

"Your kind buys fish. You don't catch them. No calluses or blisters on your fingers from a running nylon line. The cowboy boots give you a little more height, but they are clean, and your jeans are pressed. Desk man."

Jim Hall finished his beer and held up the empty and waved it at Mary, signaling for another round. "Told you this kid was good."

"I'm a headhunter, Corporal Swanson, a talent scout. Master Sergeant Hall suggested that I come take a look at you, so I went through your records. You are now twenty-one years old with three good years in the Corps, and fast-tracked for sergeant. We wonder if you might be interested in a new career, a better one."

Kyle turned to look at Hall, who shrugged. His bright blue eyes showed he was amused. "Everybody's gotta work somewhere, Kyle. Might as well do some good for your country while you're at it."

"Wait a minute, Jim. Are you saying you're with them?"

"Have been for a while, buddy. The Corps gives me legitimate cover. I really am a master sergeant, but I do other things, too."

"Jim is a very talented man. He thinks that you are," Morgan said.

An uncomfortable silence settled on them as the waitress brought another round. There was another brief round of flirting between Mary and Jim Hall, and she asked if they were ready to order. "Not yet, honey. Give us a few more minutes," he said. Mary slid him a folded matchbook, red and yellow with the restaurant's logo imprinted on it. He flipped it open, laughed softly, and showed it to the other two men. Mary had written her telephone number on the inside.

Kyle resumed. "What would you want from me, Mr. Morgan?"

"Just Morgan."

"Not until I know you better."

"Jim Hall is coming to the end of his Marine Corps career soon, after twenty-four years. He will shift over and join us full-time then. So we need to replace him. Have somebody on standby for special jobs."

"I'm already qualified for that kind of assignment. In fact, I've already done some temporary duty with you guys. That's in the folder, right, Mr. Morgan?"

Morgan glanced around to be sure there were no eavesdroppers. "Not the same thing at all. Those were all military related, Swanson, strictly up and down the chain of command, which always leaves an inevitable paper trail. Your new work with us would be way off the books."

"An assassin." Kyle tightened his lips.

Morgan's eyes did not flinch. "Look, Corporal Swanson. Not everybody has the balls for this. You can get up and walk out of here at any time, and we will just let it all go. This meeting never happened. We will find someone else. Make no mistake, the job will be filled by somebody just as good. You are not the only shooter out there."

Jim Hall spoke again. "The money and side benefits are terrific, too, Kyle. You would be doing almost exactly the same thing that you are doing now. No one in the Marines would ever know the difference."

Morgan continued the sales pitch. "Hall would be your contact. As a friend, you could meet with him in public and people would just see a couple of jarheads having a two-man reunion."

"What about you, Mr. Morgan? Where do you fit into this?"

"Like I said, I'm only a recruiter. You will probably never see me again. What do you think?"

"I think that I'm going over to McDonald's and catch up with the guys." Kyle slid out of the booth.

"You are passing up a good thing here."

"I can get a good burrito somewhere else. See you tomorrow, Jim."

Morgan watched him leave. "You're right, Jim. I want him."

Hall picked up a plastic-covered menu and slid one to Morgan. "Long as he stays in the Marines, we have him on call anyway for regular work. Problem with Kyle is he sees things as right or wrong."

"Naive way of looking at a complex world," said Morgan.

"It ain't all that complex for Swanson. Let's eat."

After Swanson and Hall finished the story, arguing about specific points as they relived the old days, Jim Hall asked Lauren, "Okay, Your Honor. I have won, haven't I? The mature Kyle has surrendered his youthful scruples and is now working for the CIA. He has killed men on missions that the Agency has run, and by doing so has become one of the best assassins in the world. I win on all points."

Kyle's look was sharp and steady. "Bullshit. Even when I do work for you guys, I remain in the military chain of command and act within my orders. I am a professional Marine sniper, not an assassin, so I shoot specific targets, and not innocent people to satisfy some murky political point. Therefore, I still have a scruple, your case sucks, and you lose."

Lauren had eased back in her chair while they spoke, catching the byplay between the veteran warriors. Her arms were folded across her chest, a move that emphasized her breasts. "Sorry, Jim. The way I see it, not much has changed from fifteen years ago. We are running this particular show, so technically Kyle is working for us.

When the job is done, though, we remain spooks, while he goes back to being a Marine."

Jim Hall huffed in mock disappointment and pushed away from the table. "Judge Carson, you are a traitor to your class, and I don't like you anymore."

11

PAKISTAN

Muhammed Waleed squeezed some lemon juice on the *aaloo keema* but could only nibble at the spicy dish of tender beef and soft potato. The tastes of ginger and green peppers tingled, but he was eating for sustenance rather than enjoyment at this meal. Too much was on his mind to really enjoy the dishes that came from the women in the kitchen.

He had spent years working to move Pakistan toward a tipping point, to a precipice at which he could give it a single mighty shove. There had been no real timetable, only the firm conviction that he would reach his goal before he died. Now, without warning, it was spread before him, a gift from Allah, praise be unto his name.

"Is everything ready for your meeting with Jim Hall?" Waleed directed his dark eyes into those of his confident younger son, Selim, who returned the look without hesitation. The interior of the small home with the thick mud walls was cool, despite the heat outside. A few fans churned the still air.

"Yes, Father. The two fighters are safely tucked into the apartment, and the two American soldiers are secluded in a place near the hotel." Selim was not worried about incurring the famous wrath of his father, for he had spent a lifetime obeying every command. The young man's education, war-fighting experience, and religious and political studies were part of his father's careful plan. Over the years, Selim had come to respect the old lion, whose bravery was tempered with wisdom and cunning.

Waleed swatted at a fly that buzzed around the food, then drank from a tall, chilled glass of crushed mango pulp and yogurt. The taste pacified the tanginess of the food. "At first, I did not understand the plan of the Prophet in all of this. It was truly a puzzle. I asked why these people had fallen into my hands."

"I can understand your concern, Father," said the son. "There was no doubt the fighters had carried out the assigned mission to slay and behead the infidel soldier in Afghanistan. Once the awful images found their way to the Internet, the outrage was as expected. It should have stopped there."

"My intent was only to show that our fighting forces remain strong enough in Afghanistan to strike when we see fit." He fell silent again, letting his son continue the line of reasoning.

"Then that irrational Fariq decided on his own to capture the two Americans and bring them back to his village as trophies, a vain and stupid act. The Americans had almost forgotten about the fighting in Afghanistan and Iraq, and now that huge, rich, and powerful country was galvanized to action and was once again united, at least temporarily."

"Only the target was now in Pakistan." Waleed followed with a question. "Was that a bad thing, Selim?"

"Yes, Father. Your problem was obvious. Fariq turned a military scrimmage into a political problem. The Americans wanted vengeance. You had to find a way to bring opportunity out of crisis. A great problem, indeed, and events were being forced upon you."

Waleed chuckled, a deep rumble in his stomach. "Ah. When that fool of a village leader rejected my invitation to buy the prisoners, he did me a favor by narrowing my options. Things became clear just as the slow settling of ripples makes a pool of water as smooth as mirrored glass."

"And you had me contact Jim Hall to provide the coordinates of the village. For a million American dollars."

"Correct." Waleed sat back and put a hand on each knee, ever the teacher. "And what is the lesson to you?"

Selim was dressed casually today, but there was nothing informal about this discussion. "Without question, Fariq deserved to be executed, and the fact that his hometown suffered dearly is on his head. That left you, my father, to deal with the prisoners. Again, you turn to Jim Hall of the CIA. What is that old saying, 'Keep your friends close and your enemies closer'?"

Waleed was nodding vigorously now. "Jim Hall and I have known and worked with each other for many years. He was a field agent when I was directing the supply mules ferrying money, equipment, and information from the CIA to wherever they wanted it to go. But we both recognized that no matter what was going on between America and the Taliban, our friendship could be of immense value in the future. The passing years have proven that we were correct. I hope that you are investing time and effort into grooming your own future sources of intelligence from other countries."

"I am, Father. I thank you for these lessons."

Both men stood, then embraced. "Then back to Islamabad with you, my boy. Rid me of these American prisoners. You have my instructions. Please tell my old friend Jim Hall hello from me and find out what he really wants. I trust you to make it work. Do not use any form of telephone to report back to me."

The son bowed to his father and left the room.

ISLAMABAD
PAKISTAN

"This was an incredibly precise incision," the Pakistani doctor observed after a brisk examination of the wound on Jake Henderson's arm. "Few surgeons could have done any better."

"She cut off my tattoo." Henderson was on clean sheets in a medical clinic. "Sliced the edges and pulled it right off. It hurt like hell."

The doctor was small, with precise and birdlike movements. "Well, I am most certain that it did. Consider yourself lucky, Mr. Henderson. That woman had experience with a blade and apparently also a knowledge of the human body. The damage could have been a lot worse." He applied some salve to the soggy area, bandaged the wound, and gave Jake a shot of antibiotics.

"You seen this kind of thing before, Doc?"

"Yes. Some of the tribal people are quite brutal." He returned his implements into his small case. "However, you are the only survivor."

Javon Anthony spoke from the adjoining bed. "Can you tell us anything about what is going on?"

The doctor moved to him and put on a blood pressure cuff, timed it, then used a stethoscope to listen to his heart and lungs. As he ran his hands over Javon's limbs, he said, "You are a strong and healthy young man, Mr. Anthony. A few bruises, but nothing else is wrong with you. I expected some broken bones."

Javon gave a bitter laugh. "Except for being prisoners and expecting to be killed at any moment."

"You must think us to be monsters."

"Pretty close, Doc. Pretty damned close."

The doctor stood and pushed his hands deep into the pockets of his white coat. "I understand. Really, I do. Just remember that in wars, monsters come in all shapes and sizes and wear all sorts of uniforms."

Anthony let the comment slide. "So where are we? Can you at least tell us that?"

"For the time being, you are in my private clinic on the outskirts of Islamabad. My job was to judge your health and chances of recovery. As I have said, you are both fine. I will tell the people in charge of you that I recommend a full day of rest here. You will remain handcuffed to the beds. I have treated you with respect, so please do not cause a ruckus. Beyond that, I do not know. As God wills."

He checked the handcuffs linked to the metal hospital bed frames, then left the room.

"He spoke good English, for a raghead," said Henderson.

Anthony gave the chain a jerk. It rattled without giving any indication of looseness. "He probably attended medical school in England, Jake. Not everybody over here rides a camel."

"So let's escape!" Henderson swiveled upright and into a sitting position. "Get out of here, Javon. I feel good enough to make a run for it. You tell me what to do and we'll do it."

Anthony pointed over his shoulder with his thumb. "Bet your soul that they have guards right outside the doors and windows, Jake. Compared to what happened to us in the first twenty-four hours after our capture, we have it pretty good right now. Best not to rock this particular boat too hard."

"I don't understand," Henderson said, helping himself to a cup of water on a small bedside table.

"Makes two of us. Listen up: Islamabad is the capital city, which means there are plenty of Americans around town, and an American embassy in the diplomatic quarter. If things suddenly go bad, I want you to try to get there. Never mind me. Just go."

"I won't leave you, Sarge."

"It might be our best hope. I might be able to create

enough of a diversion to help you get away. You reach the embassy and they will know I'm still alive and come get me."

"What kind of diversion?"

Sergeant Anthony rolled slightly to one side and raised his right hand. In it was a glittering sharp scalpel he had stolen from the doctor's bag. Jake Henderson said, "Awwright."

12

Kyle Swanson and Lauren Carson ran at an easy pace, padding along side by side on a track that was part of the base exercise facilities. Hall declined the morning run to make some last-minute arrangements before they all headed over to Islamabad.

Lauren wore a lightweight Washington Redskins jersey, loose black nylon sweatpants, and dirty shoes that were coming apart at the seams from so much use. She did three miles every day. Her hair was tied back in a ponytail that swished as she ran. Kyle was in shorts and a Red Sox T-shirt. He doubted if anyone noticed him.

"CIA agents are supposed to be low-key and invisible. You don't exactly blend in with the woodwork," he joked. "Every guy on the track is going to trip over their own feet staring at you."

She laughed and shook her head, making the ponytail bounce even more. "Can't help that," she said. "Jim taught me to do just the opposite. Since I can't really hide my looks, I play it to my advantage. Being just a pretty dumb blonde is good cover. Nobody takes me seriously."

"Until it's too late."

"Yeah. Men can be pretty dumb." They finished the rest of the first quarter mile in silence, finding a rhythm in the run.

"Well, you are pretty."

Lauren shot him a flinty sideways look, then changed the subject. "Jim says you're rich. So why do you do this work if you have a lot of money?"

Kyle looked over at her with a flash of annoyance. "I live on my Marine salary, Lauren. I was lucky enough to fall in with some good folks, and we did some crucial and timely weapons development. Everything I did had Corps approval. The company has allotted me a small ownership stake and invested all of my shares in a trust. They never even let me see a statement. I don't want to know."

"That doesn't answer the question of why continue with this killing people stuff if you can get out and live in comfort." Their pace was comfortable, and neither was breathing hard.

"I like my job," he said. This was not exactly the kind of conversation he'd had in mind when he asked if she wanted to come along for the jog.

They finished the first mile. "Tracks are boring," she said. "Can we run on the streets?"

"Better not. You attract too much attention. Let's stay in the Spec Ops area."

"I've never killed anyone," she said with a sudden honesty, a serious comment that surprised him. "Does it bother you afterward?"

"You have to deal with it mentally at some point," Swanson replied. "If you ever have to pull a trigger, remember that your target was a danger and posed a threat, sometimes a major threat to others, even to your country. That is not some personal saddle to lug around for the rest of your life."

"How many have you killed, Kyle? Jim says you're the best."

"It isn't a numbers game, or some shooting competition with paper targets, Lauren." His voice was edgy. "I never kept score."

"Humh." They ran around the track again without speaking. Then she said, "Know what I think? I think it *is* some kind of competition for you. Jim says that with Kyle Swanson, what you see is what you get, that you are Mr. Incorruptible because you don't have to care about money, and you don't have to care about right or wrong because you work for that weird Task Force Trident unit that answers only to the president. So what do you care about? You care about being the best, ol' Numero Uno."

Swanson picked up the pace, and so did she. "You are sounding like a psychiatrist with that kind of crap, Agent Carson. Don't try to dissect me."

She ignored his comment. "You're like an NFL line-backer who cannot wait to get into the game. All your senses point you to the action, and only then, with some game-saving tackle at the goal line, only then is Kyle Swanson a happy man. How'd I do?"

"I'm not on your couch, shrink."

She looked over with a teasing grin, reached out with the flat of her hand, and slapped his butt. "Wanna be?"

* * *

Pretty? That's all? He thinks I'm just pretty? Lauren, appropriately yucky and aching after the long run, stomped back to a tentlike VIP barracks for women.

On the plus side, there was a feeling that she might have eventually been able to outdistance Kyle today. Maybe he was still not up to his maximum workout because of that wound he had suffered in Saudi Arabia; he might be still recovering. Perhaps he wasn't Superman after all. That did not mean she was not intrigued by him. That was about the only good thing she could think of at the moment.

She found a private shower stall, shucked off her sweaty clothes, and turned on the hot water. Liberal handfuls of shampoo and conditioner were needed to slosh the clinging dust from her hair. This was one dirty place. She switched the water to a blast of cold.

As Lauren dried off with a thick towel, she found that she was not only miffed at Kyle Swanson, but she was also peeved with Jim Hall. Not long after she went to work at the CIA, they had almost inevitably become lovers, although it did not last a very long time. Neither wanted an office romance to derail a career. They ended it by mutual agreement but over the years had remained close, and they still occasionally slipped between the sheets, comfortable with each other. It wasn't really a *thing,* but now Jim seemed to be pushing her away, making no effort to fight for her, to keep Kyle from making any moves. It was as if Jim were clearing her from his life. If he did not want her around anymore, why didn't he just say so?

She brushed and flossed her teeth, sat on a bench,

and slowly rubbed skin lotion on her hands and body. Why wasn't Kyle being more aggressive? Didn't he find her attractive? In the few hours they had known each other, she had already done everything but plead for some sex. *He thinks I'm just pretty! I was in the Miss America Pageant, for God's sake!* She had an emergency need to go check herself in the long bathroom mirror and was relieved to see that she had not turned into a troll with big zits on her nose.

She slid into a blue bra and panties and a little robe, then spent some time giving her hair some serious brushing, followed by a bit of makeup, staring at her reflection all the while. *Why doesn't anybody want me?* The clean dark suit and gray blouse were waiting in the garment bag, with her low heels, and when she put it all on, she immediately perked up. It was her CIA all-business costume. A little more lip gloss, spinning around to look at the back view, and she declared herself ready to return to the Spec Ops office.

Both of the bastards were there, standing beside a wall map, talking to the two crewmen of the ghost plane. None of them gave her a second glance. She growled a soft order to herself to stop pouting. Men can be such assholes. At least someone had loaded the Mr. Coffee with a fresh packet of Dunkin' Donuts brew, so she poured a mug and walked over to the group. She could pretend to look at maps, too.

Jim Hall finally noticed she was alive. "Wheels up for Islamabad in an hour, Lauren," he said.

"You look nice," said Kyle.

Nice!? That's all?

13

Kyle Swanson, Jim Hall, and Lauren Carson rolled through the wide avenues of the capital city in the comfort of a black SUV, with a CIA driver up front. The air-conditioning flowed with a cool insistence that pleased Lauren, who was handling the logistics for the trip. The laptop in her briefcase was a one-mission personal computer that contained the access codes for a ten-million-dollar blind bank account that had been set up for expenses, probably including bribes, before they left Langley. With details on her mind, she was in full business mode and paid little attention to the men around her, but having come out of the blandness of Bagram, she was surprised at the showcase buildings sliding past them on Ataturk Avenue.

The capital of Pakistan was a metropolis that had been carefully designed to show important foreigners that the country was more than just a collection of dun-colored buildings and tin-shack slums. No doubt there were slums on the outskirts and narrow back roads stacked with filth, but there were few signs of open rebellion or reminders of war. This was a city of diplomacy, of business, of deals.

Jim Hall had been here many times and knew exactly where they were going and what they were going to do, so he just drummed his fingers in time with a tune running through his head.

Swanson had taken the front passenger seat and stayed silent for the entire trip, watchful and wary as he began preparing himself mentally for the job ahead. He would be fighting somewhere in these beautiful streets soon, kill or be killed, and there was no such thing as too much information. Where others saw bright, clean buildings, Kyle Swanson saw the shaded alleys between them and the dark windows that stared back at him like blank eyes.

He and the driver were the only ones carrying weapons. Hall decreed, as a matter of spook protocol, that he and Lauren could not walk into an expensive hotel room to meet a valuable contact with weapons on them.

"Screw that," Swanson said and checked out the .45 ACP pistol that he had requested before leaving Afghanistan. Since they had arrived in the ghost plane, customs officers had given them a quick wave through; then the heavy CIA SUV took them away. Swanson wore jeans, a black T-shirt, and a lightweight tan sports coat. He stuck the pistol into the back of his belt, which forced him to change position in his seat. "What else do we have in this wagon?"

"My personal handgun, a street-sweeper shotgun clamped beneath the front seat, and an Uzi under a panel in the rear. Smoke grenade and extra ammo in the glove box." The driver turned smoothly off Ataturk and onto Aga Khan Road. "Plus, this buggy is pretty much bulletproof. Safe, but lousy on mileage."

He maneuvered slowly through the double blast barrier and came to an easy stop in the broad driveway of the Islamabad Marriott. *Nice address,* Kyle thought. Not far away was the office of Pakistan's president.

Lauren adjusted a sheer black scarf to cover her head in respect for the Muslim tradition, although it did little to conceal her beauty. They entered through tall glass doors and were into the spacious ground-floor lobby, a quiet hive of activity. Diplomats, businessmen, political figures, and hangers-on of various stripes were gathered in clumps around the chairs and sofas on the rich carpets. The faces were all friendly. A plump banker was in a large chair, speaking with a general from some African nation, who was in full gilt dress regalia. On another sofa, a British journalist interviewed a Japanese builder of computers. There was just enough noise in the lobby, with enough occasional laughter coming from the nearby restaurant, to cover the appearance of the three Americans. They were sized up as just another business team in from the States, and although the woman was gorgeous, the men were forgettable. With aimless chatter, they worked their way through the islands of conversation.

Their shoes made no sound as they moved across the thick carpets and knotted rugs, reached the bank of elevators, and went up to a floor of private suites. The hotel staff had made certain that for this one hour, all other rooms along this hallway would be empty of other guests. Hall stopped before the door of Suite One, opened it, and stepped inside.

"My good friend!" Selim stepped forward and extended his hand. "It is good to see you again, Jim Hall. My father sends his best wishes and regrets that he cannot be here today."

Hall shook the hand and gave the younger man a pat on the shoulder. "Selim. You are the very image of your honorable father when he was a young firebrand. It is good to see you, too." He introduced Lauren and Kyle in turn, and the dark-haired Selim was as stylish as a European in acknowledging them.

Swanson broke the mood, sensing trouble. "This is your contact, Jim?"

Hall grinned sheepishly. "Not quite. He represents his father, whom I have known and worked with for years. We cannot be seen together in public, so Selim is our go-between. Good at the job, too."

"Who is the real contact?" Swanson asked.

"You don't need to know that yet," Hall snapped.

"Oh, stow the bullshit, Jim. You specifically brought me in for this job, and I want to know who I am working with. You think I'll put his name on Twitter or blog it or something?"

"Of course not. It's just that his father is a top-level asset, one of my own recruits that I have groomed over the years."

"The name?" asked Kyle. "No use continuing this conversation if you won't tell me."

Selim arched an eyebrow and looked from him to Lauren and then to Jim. "That is not a real problem." He was sure of himself, confident of his work and his ability. "My father is Muhammed Waleed."

"The top dog of the Taliban? We're working with the Taliban?"

"The very one," said Hall. "He will trust only me, and he is a real rainmaker."

Kyle forced himself to keep a neutral look. Friend or not, he would not risk his life just because Jim Hall was engineering a deal with people that Swanson considered the enemy. "I'm more used to killing the Taliban than being nice to them."

"We are quite aware of your reputation, Gunnery Sergeant Swanson. You may return to the battlefield again someday against our fighters and perhaps not be so lucky. But the world is changing, and in Pakistan, the Taliban is a legitimate political party, and my father runs it. Unfortunately, he does not speak for all of the renegade tribal chiefs. Yet."

Hall laughed softly. "It's a new world, Kyle, but it is still the old world in many ways. We are going to kill us a couple of Taliban terrorists while we are in Islamabad, and Selim is going to help us do it. If you don't have the stomach for it, leave now."

"Why don't they just kill these guys themselves and be done with it?" Swanson asked, still irritated.

"Washington wants the word to spread that whoever messes with us is going to get squashed. This is a good target, Kyle; these boys are not a couple of suicide bombers but a highly trained team, and we need to take them out."

Selim was standing with his hands folded in front of him. "We already have them in the city, Gunny Swanson. They will be ready when you are."

Lauren finally spoke. "How will it happen, Selim? You will pick out a spot for our two snipers?"

He laughed, and a smile creased his firm jawline. "No. I pick out the spot for the targets. Jim Hall and the reluctant Gunny Swanson will find their own positions, although I have some recommendations."

"You can guarantee that?"

"Of course. You can depend on good Muslims to always be on time to pray. The people are in a private apartment with a balcony. They have been given beautiful prayer rugs and will come out and prostrate themselves to offer their *maghrib* prayers as the sun goes down. If you don't mind shooting someone in the back while he is talking to God, it should be easy."

Lauren said, "That's pretty cold-blooded."

"Please do not be shocked, Ms. Carson. In this part of the world, we have been doing this sort of thing for a thousand years. Even a prince at prayer in a mosque is not truly safe. You must remember from your studies that we coined the word *hashshashin* . . . assassin."

"Works for me," said Swanson.

"I know," said Selim with coldness, then broke into his relaxed smile. "Now, Jim Hall, you mentioned a price in our last conversation."

Hall pointed to Lauren's bag, and she pulled out the

laptop, took it to a round table, opened the top, and went online through a secure satellite frequency. "A million dollars for each of them."

"Hell of a campaign contribution."

"Shut up and sit down, Kyle. Say the word, Selim, and Lauren will move the money."

Swanson plopped hard into an overstuffed chair, looking sullen, and exhaled loudly. The others quickly ignored him. He was not involved in the talks. Kyle made a show of crossing his legs and adjusting his coat, carefully pulling the .45 ACP out of his belt and placing it beneath his thigh, with the butt facing out. Then he put an arm on each side of the chair, looking like he was resting. The fingers of his right hand were less than eleven inches from the pistol.

Selim leaned against the back of a long sofa. "My father appreciates that, but I believe these people are of more value. It has not been easy to separate them from their friends."

Hall grunted a laugh. "The other part of the payment was getting those missiles to hit that village when he needed them. Took some doing on our part. Missiles cost money, too."

"Still."

"Oh, fine. Okay. Courtesy of the American taxpayer. A million and a half each, for three million dollars total. Will that make the old man happy?"

"Oh yes," Selim said. "Excellent. Exchanging favors of equality leaves neither party indebted to the other."

"An old Arab saying?" asked Lauren.

"No. I just made it up."

"Fine." She looked over at Jim Hall. "That's it, then? Want me to punch the buttons on a three-million dollar transfer of funds to the assigned account?"

"Do it," said Jim Hall. "Let's wrap this baby up."

Lauren's fingers deftly worked the keyboard for about thirty seconds; then she stood back. "Transfer under way. Confirmation of receipt . . . right . . . now. Done."

Selim coughed in his fist. "Excellent. Now, Jim Hall, before we part for the day, my father wishes for me to present you with a very special gift. Please wait for one moment." He went to a door and said something.

They could hear some stirring on the other side; then the portal swung open and a pair of lean, hard-looking men in civilian clothes brought in Sergeant Javon Anthony and Corporal Jake Henderson. As the blindfolds were stripped away and the handcuffs removed, Selim said, "Please take these young men safely back to America."

Kyle was already on his feet and locked in a two-fisted combat stance.

14

"Kyle! Put down that weapon!" yelled Hall, his voice filling the room.

"Not a chance," Swanson snapped back, training the weapon on the two men who had brought in the American soldiers, then ordering Anthony and Henderson, "You guys move behind me!"

"Selim just gave these prisoners back to us!"

"And we are damn straight going to keep them." Ignoring the others, Kyle moved quickly to the guards, spun them roughly and pushed them to the wall. Holding the pistol against each man's kidneys in turn, he gave them a quick pat-down—shoulders, hips, crotch, ankles. No weapons. He backed away. "Come on, Jim. This meeting is over and we're out of here."

"You're overreacting, Kyle." Hall sat down and looked at Selim. "Tell your father that this came as a big surprise."

Selim had hardly blinked at Kyle's protective outburst. He shrugged his shoulders. "Gunny Swanson, you really don't need the weapon. I *want* those men to leave safely. We have gone through a lot to make this happen."

"Your men captured them in the first place, and coldly murdered one of their friends, also an American soldier, in the process. I should believe you now?" Anthony and Henderson stood rooted behind him.

Hall put his palms out toward Kyle. "Okay, okay. Settle down. Give me a second. Keep them all covered if it makes you feel better. Lauren, while you still have that laptop online, transfer another two million to that same account, on my authority. More than worth the price."

She quickly ran the numbers and confirmed the transfer.

"Now, Lauren, you are going to be the hero in all of this. Radio the driver to get our vehicle ready for a fast trip to the U.S. Embassy."

Kyle broke in with a shout, "Jesus Christ, Jim. You just told these people where we're going and how we're going to get there!" The pistol was still firmly pointing at the guards as Kyle mentally processed the security options to egress the hotel. Was someone waiting on the other side of the door? Downstairs? On the streets?

"Just let me finish talking before you start shooting." Jim Hall was having difficulty controlling his own voice because of Kyle's stubborness. He took a deep breath. "Then, Lauren, you escort them down to our vehicle and haul ass out of here. Kyle, why don't you go along and ride shotgun before you have a heart attack. Once they are inside the embassy gates, both of you come back here and meet me."

"You can't stay here in this room alone, Jim. We may just be swapping two prisoners for one."

"Damn it, Kyle! Get it through your thick head that everything is fine here. Selim and I have some business to finish."

"That is true, Gunny Swanson. No one in the Taliban or the Bright Path Party is going to try to stop you." Selim seemed amused.

Lauren packed up her computer and shouldered the bag. "Let's go," she said.

"Leave the computer with me," Hall said. "I may need it." Lauren let the case slide from her shoulder.

"Don't walk in front of my pistol," Kyle said. "Sergeant Anthony, are you able to function?"

"Yeah. Who the hell are you?"

Swanson did not look at him. "Gunnery Sergeant Kyle Swanson. U.S. Marines. You check the door and the hallway. You move first, then Lauren, then Corporal Henderson. I bring up the rear. Jim, I will be back here in no more than two hours. Selim, I wish that I could trust you, but I can't. So I will save any thanks until I get back."

Selim smiled, totally at ease. "Actually, I understand your problem. I will be gone by the time you get back. I see everything I have heard about you is true."

Jake Henderson leaned close to Lauren and whispered, "Who *are* you people?"

"Stay close," she said. From her computer bag, she had pulled a small Heckler & Koch P7M8 pistol. Jake stared. The most beautiful woman he had ever seen was packing 9 mm heat and acting like she knew how to use it.

Then they were out the door.

* * *

Swanson jumped into the lead and ran down the carpeted hallway to the fire exit, his eyes roaming the area for telltale signs that this could be an ambush. He kicked the door open, and they dashed down the concrete staircase, their feet echoing. He called back over his shoulder, "Lauren, change of plan. Radio the driver to pick us up at the delivery entrance. We cannot chance going through the lobby."

Javon Anthony had taken the trail position and kept checking over his shoulder. "Clear back here," he shouted.

"Why didn't we just take the elevator?" Jake asked.

"Keep going. Follow that dude and protect the lady," said Anthony.

They pounded past the third-floor landing and kept going. There was no second floor, just a mezzanine. At the final landing, Kyle made a sharp turn toward the rear of the building and went into a service corridor, pushing by a surprised maid with her cart. He slowed, and they all grouped together as the corridor opened into a large, busy area where numerous staff members were going about their jobs. Sunlight poured through the wide delivery doors, where crates were being unloaded from trucks that had backed up to the loading docks. Swanson kept his pistol tight against his waist, hiding it beneath his sport coat.

"Here comes the car," Lauren said softly, pointing to the right, where the CIA SUV was racing toward them. The driver hit the brakes, and the big vehicle skidded to a sideways stop. All four of them tumbled in through the unlocked doors.

"Get us to the plane and be ready for trouble," said Kyle, pulling his weapon free again. The driver reached into a shoulder holster, withdrew his own Glock semi-automatic pistol, and put it on the seat between them. Swanson turned around. "Sergeant Anthony, there's an Uzi under a panel behind the rear seat. Dig it out and stay back there to watch our six. Henderson, reach beneath the front seat and get the shotgun."

Lauren moved aside so the soldiers could reach the weapons, but she barked at Kyle. "The airport? Hell, no, Kyle. We're supposed to go to the embassy. Why are you acting like this? Jim said everything was okay."

He did not look at her but kept scanning the street and the buildings. "Jim might be wrong. We just did a deal with the Taliban, and they aren't famous for their generosity, nor their hospitality."

"Their women were going to skin me alive," said Jake Henderson, jacking a round into the pump shotgun that had been sawed off at both ends to make it short enough to fit in the vehicle. "I don't trust them neither."

Swanson put on his sunglasses to cut the glare. "Never do what your enemy expects, Lauren. If they have an ambush plan, it would be set between the hotel and the embassy. Unless you want to chance having an IED explode under our asses, we ain't going that way."

"So you want me to take these guys back to Bagram?" What Kyle said made sense. Jim was going to be angry, but she wasn't really needed here any longer.

Getting these boys entirely out of the Middle East and back on U.S. soil as soon as possible was the right play.

"Nope. The ghost plane is at your disposal, and it has aerial refueling capability. You take them all the way back to Washington. While you're flying, have the CIA meet you at Andrews Air Force Base under a full security alert."

"I'm worried about Jim's reaction. He's my boss, you know." The computations whirred in her head. Swanson did not seem tense at all, but rationally reaching decisions that made total sense.

"No sweat. If he pulls any chain-of-command crap, tell him that I put you under temporary duty orders. Until you are in Washington, you've been drafted by Task Force Trident, and our authority comes from the White House."

"You can do that?"

"Oh, yeah." He flipped out a small green notebook and scribbled a telephone number on it. "And take this, Lauren. If the Agency people give you problems over this, call that number. It's a private and secure connection directly into Trident. They will supply whatever backup you need."

Javon Anthony never took his eyes from the windows as the SUV sped down a wide boulevard. The light-weight submachine gun with its stock folded and a full thirty-two-round magazine in place rested easily in his hands, locked and loaded. He had listened intently to the snippets of conversation, and it was obvious that the Marine was in charge. Anthony said to Swanson,

"Listen, man, we're just a couple of Virginia boys who have been through a lot in the past week, and right now, I'm confused as hell. How about letting us in on what the hell is happening?"

15

Selim and Jim Hall were in the comfortable chairs of the hotel suite, sipping glasses of Tennessee bourbon from a flask that Hall had brought along. Both Taliban guards had been dismissed and the four Americans were racing to escape. "I think they probably went out to the airport to put those soldiers on our plane," Hall said. "Swanson would never go to the embassy after I mentioned it to you. Which is why I did it, and he reacted just like I thought he would. I know his moves. It gives us some extra time for our private talk.

"First, I want to thank you for giving up the prisoners. That leverage will be useful. And I want to return that favor immediately." He emptied the glass in a final deep swallow, put it on the glass-topped table, and leaned forward with his elbows on his knees. "I do not know if your father has informed you of this, but I have decided to go into business on my own, Selim. You are my first customer."

Selim flinched in surprise. He grasped for a response. Nothing worthy of the situation came to his lips. Jim Hall turning traitor? Selim's father had said nothing of this, but Hall and the old man had been communicating in secret ways for many years, and Selim was just one channel. They had already made some kind of deal.

"You have been with the Central Intelligence Agency for a very long time." Selim said it as a statement, no more than conversation between two friends. "In your capitalist system, such a lifetime of excellent service should guarantee you a good pension. Enough to see you through your old age, correct?" In the distance, there was the sudden rapid burp of submachine gun fire, followed by the pops of pistols. "Somebody apparently tried to run a roadblock out at the edge of the city," Selim observed.

Hall laughed. "Probably Kyle causing trouble. Hope nobody was hurt. Anyway, a government pension would never be enough for me. I have to give up more than money—my access, too. No more White House dinners, no more invitations from rich guys for salmon fishing trips in Alaska, no more pretty young girls furnished with my suites in Las Vegas. No more excitement. And actually retiring from the CIA is impossible. They always keep track of you and your finances and your friends. For the rest of my life, some agent will be showing up at my front door to snoop. Telephones bugged, e-mails read. The secret life does not let you just quit. I need money and lots of it to pay for the kind of golden years I have in mind."

Selim steepled his fingers in thought. "Just to be sure that I have heard you correctly, Jim Hall. Again, please. You are telling me that you are going to be a traitor to your country?"

"Yes."

"And what is it that you are selling?"

"Everything in the store. Twenty years, off and on, with the CIA, and another twenty-four in the Marines. You guys want secrets? I've got them."

Selim involuntarily sucked in his breath. The size of this betrayal was beyond measure. "The Americans will surely come after you with everything they've got."

"Not if they believe I am dead."

"So our, hmm, this *situation* tomorrow will mark your exit from the American government service."

Hall poured refills from the flask again and had a long drink, letting the bourbon sooth his nerves. He was not uncomfortable, because he had carefully thought out his position and now had everyone in the government fooled. His entire life was about to change, and there would be no going back. Of course he was nervous. Once the feeling was identified, he dealt with the emotion and cast it away. Hall steadied himself and began the pitch to close the deal.

"Your father did me a great service today. When those Americans get back to Washington, everyone at Langley will be singing my praises. Then will come the news of my sad death in a very public way, and I will become a CIA legend—the agent who sacrificed himself on a final mission to rescue American prisoners and kill terrorists. Now I will repay your favor with one of my own."

"What?" Selim was fascinated at the man's audacity. It might work! He was offering the Taliban access to some of the innermost secrets of America's best intelligence-gathering apparatus. The Bright Path Party could come to power if it knew what the CIA possessed concerning the opposition party members. That was why he had been sent here. His father wanted him to secure that situation.

"You remember what Swanson said just before he left us a little while ago? About how I might be just trading two prisoners for one? Well, he was right. In addition to the extra two million dollars I signed over, I'm going to give you Kyle Swanson, America's best covert killer. All I want is a little help for a clean escape."

Selim just stared silently for a full minute, his dark eyes searching for any sign of hesitancy or a trap. He decided to act. "Then we have a deal, Jim Hall."

"Outstanding. Now, let's go look at the apartment where you have set up our new targets. After I see that, I will be able to give final instructions."

"Listen to the children." Mohammed Sial sighed contentedly from the apartment balcony as the voices of hundreds of boys and young men in the madrasah across the street chanted the soothing words of the Koran. His round face beamed with pride.

Makhdoom Ragiq, his tall and taciturn partner, came out and leaned on the low balustrade. The madrasah was a two-story building with an ornate front intricately laced with green, blue, and white tiles and crowned with small towers and minarets. A pair of large doors stood open. Both men had been schooled in the stern madrasahs that dominated all education in the

Northwest Frontier. "I think the government has too much influence in these schools in Islamabad. They are too liberal."

Sial ignored him. Ragiq could find fault in anything. "Just let your soul feel the words," he coaxed.

Ragiq snorted and let his gaze roam away from the school. "They are learning the alphabet and reading the same verse over and over. Nothing more." He pointed to the walled compound adjacent to the madrasah. "What do you think is going on over there?"

There was a grinding of truck gears in the broad courtyard, and the shouts of workmen intermingled with the students reading next door. The laborers shoved and stacked boxes against the fence that bordered the school. A forklift balancing three large crates on its twin steel tongues wiggled into a narrow place and raised its load, settled it, then backed away. Racks of lights had been wheeled into place so the work could continue at night. Uniformed soldiers were on the walls, working on the defenses. Stacking the crates against the walls left the center of the camp open for normal operations.

"I don't know. It's just a small army camp," answered Sial. "They probably are stockpiling weapons and materiel, getting ready for when the political problems worsen and the fighting comes here."

"Then let us hope we can speed that time along. I hate this place." His dark eyes took in the entire area. It bespoke wealth and prosperity and Western influences that challenged basic Muslim beliefs. European women walked on the sidewalks with their heads uncovered. Islamabad was a cesspool.

Makhdoom Ragiq tapped a Gauloise cigarette from a blue pack and took his time lighting it. Smoke rolled from his mouth and out into the open air, and he inhaled deeply, sucking the flavor into his lungs, then blew it all out again. It was a vice, but no man is perfect, particularly someone like himself. The sleeves of his white shirt were rolled up to his elbows, and the ugly puckered indentation of a bullet wound on his left forearm was a reminder of how often he had cheated death, the last time only a few days ago in the execution yard. The rest of his life was probably going to be short, and he did not intend to worry about having a cigarette. Tobacco would not kill him.

They turned at the sound of someone entering the room behind them. The young Taliban envoy, Selim, called a friendly greeting and motioned them back inside as he removed his suit jacket and handed it to a servant. "The time is close, my friends. Our informants have penetrated the last major obstacle, and I can now tell you more of your mission."

Sial and Ragiq sat side by side on a long sofa. *Finally.* "Who?" asked Sial.

"The president of Pakistan," he said. "The death of the president at this moment will throw Pakistan into chaos."

Ragiq inhaled his cigarette again, ignoring the displeasure of his host. "Impossible. He has the army on his side, and the security police are everywhere. I am surprised you would even mention this."

"Are you refusing the assignment?" Selim's voice was chilly.

"No. It is suicidal, but that is unimportant. We will never even get close."

"Circular protection," agreed the other fighter. "Rings upon rings. If the government of this country has learned anything from its history, it is that the president and leading political figures must always be considered a target of assassins." Mohammed Sial had once been a schoolteacher and knew of such things. The list of the slain leaders was long. "It is a difficult tactical problem, to say the least."

Selim let a smile slide back onto his face. "As I have said before, we are taking care of that. There will be an opportunity, an opening, at a critical moment, and then we shall strike. All you will have to do is put a pistol in his ribs and fire."

Sial said, "There is no plan for us to escape the scene, I assume."

"Of course there is. A mob will be jostling around specifically to provide shelter for you. Within a minute after you kill the president, you will be wearing different clothes and have new identities. Within five minutes, you will be safe and headed back here. From here, back to the mountains within an hour."

"Then anyone could do this job?" Sial asked.

"No. It takes experience and dedication and skill. As fighters, you have all of those assets." Selim unknotted his silk tie. "It will happen in two days, but tomorrow I have a pleasant surprise. An early reward." He knew that they were both skeptical of the mission, but his next words would let them think of something else.

"The Taliban and the Bright Path Party have a great

deal of influence with the local mosques, and the clerics have given permission for both of you to address the students at the local madrasah. The emotional impact of those young men meeting true frontline fighters will be of great help in inspiring new recruits."

Fond memories of his own schoolteaching days came flooding back to Sial. "Yes!" he said, clapping his hands. "Wonderful idea. I remember when fighters came to our own classroom when I was a boy. I have never forgotten them."

For once, Makhdoom Ragiq did not automatically disagree. At least it would get them out of this apartment for a while. Then there was the possibility of imminent action. His muscles began to feel loose. "When do we do this meeting?"

"Tomorrow evening," Selim replied. "The students have dinner at seven o'clock, then evening prayers. Immediately afterward, when all is ready, someone from the madrasah will come over here to escort you. You will have two hours among them, with tight security to keep you safe. We have bigger things in mind for you, my friends, but I promise that this will be an evening the boys will never forget."

16

"Got carried away a little while ago, in my opinion," said Jim Hall. "I had it under control."

"The mission changed up in that room, Jim. The terrorists became a secondary issue as soon as those boys were paraded into the room."

"No doubt. No doubt. I wanted a clean sweep, both the prisoners and the terrorists. Selim was the key. I know him and have worked with his father for years. I knew it was not a double-cross."

"You can trust the Taliban if you want to. Not me."

"We have to make deals in this world, Kyle. That's the way geopolitics operates. Diplomats in the salon, people like me in the shadows. Anyway, what's done is done. I'm glad they are in the air and out of here, too."

They were walking in a park, a strangely green and grassy section that had been grown and cultivated just for the purpose of looking pretty. Tall palms threw long and skinny shadows as the sun settled in the west. During the cooler night, a sprinkler system fed the manicured scenery from pumps in an underground man-made reservoir of some of the city's recycled water.

"Selim showed me around the area while you were gone. Look up there." He pointed to a tall apartment building. "Third floor, corner apartment nearest to us. That's where the tangos will be."

Kyle saw a spacious terrace lined with ornamental iron rails. It was about waist high, and beyond it was an open set of French doors.

Jim Hall pulled out a small notebook and flipped to a folded page. "Sun goes down tomorrow, September 30, at nineteen twenty hours. The Muslims use dusk as the marker, not the exact minute on the clock, but the loudspeakers will be calling everyone to prayer. That's when we take them."

Kyle remained silent as he studied the position. "If the targets come out like your Taliban buddy promises."

His friend laughed and gave a big smile. "Guaranteed. These assholes will be out here on their knees, facing away from us, and touching their heads to their rugs to offer their *maghrib* prayers as the sun goes down."

Swanson began to walk toward the building, and Hall fell in beside him. "Where will our hides be?"

Hall put away the notebook and put his hands in his pockets to avoid pointing. Lights were coming on in almost every apartment, and men and women of many nationalities were emerging from the buildings and into the park to enjoy the cooling evening air.

"Right behind us is another apartment building. You will be on the fourth floor, firing from the corner window with the blue curtains. There is an open view of the terrace from there, looking down, and the railing should not be a factor. Selim has made certain the place will be vacant for this entire week, so you will be alone. He offered to furnish a spotter, but I decided that probably would not work out very well after your attitude attack this afternoon."

Swanson made a quick check, mentally measuring the angle while they stepped off the distance. "Working with the Talibs again?"

"Don't start with me, Kyle. It is what it is, and you're in for the whole ride. Now, I will be two blocks straight ahead, on the top floor of that office building. Also a slight downward shot."

Swanson remained quiet for a while. Pausing at the building where the targets were staying, they both stopped and visually checked the shooting hide locations again. The sightlines were unobstructed. He noticed the tiled front of a madrasah across the street and heard what sounded like construction going on nearby. "What's all the noise?" Would herds of trucks and laborers be wandering about tomorrow and perhaps interfere with the assignment?

"There's a small army camp on the far side of the wall. They've been busy stockpiling weapons and materiel in case the political problems worsen and the fighting reaches Islamabad. Could very well happen. They stay pretty much in the compound and should not be a problem for us. I think that all their noise will probably even cover our shots."

Swanson thought about that. Once again, Hall was correct and was moving the mission along exactly the way Swanson himself probably would have laid it out. He had not been in on this planning, however. On a usual mission, he would have been the man in charge—the cool and confident special operator who could count split seconds in his head and stay a minute ahead of reality, dealing with any crisis with a cold and unflappable demeanor because he knew everything about the mission, and what was going on around him at all times. He had surrendered that. Swanson could hardly remember a time when his world had not been framed in a sniper scope, and Jim Hall was his mentor, almost a brother, one of the few men on whom Kyle could depend either in a bar fight or on the battlefield. Sometimes, you just had to let go.

"Everything sounds good. Let's get some dinner, then come back and check those positions after dark. If everything is still cool, we can move in with our gear."

The two snipers turned and walked back toward the hotel. "What about afterward?"

"The egress plan is pretty sweet. Selim will have a vehicle standing by for each of us, with a driver and a cop in each one to get us through any blockades or protest groups that may be in the streets. Yours will have a blue pennant on the front fender, and mine will have a gold one. We drive straight out to a C-130 cargo bird that is kindly being provided through the courtesy of the Pakistani air force. The plane will be warmed up and ready to go." Hall snapped his fingers and grinned. "Shoot and scoot, pal. Bad guys dead and we're back at Bagram in time for a late dinner."

"If your Taliban buddy comes through, which is a

pretty big *if*. Nothing ever goes according to plan," said Swanson.

"Oh, be quiet. You're boring me. It will work," said Jim Hall. "Trust me."

That was the issue that was chewing at Swanson, and it continued to gnaw on him after night fell, like a dog with a bone. After dinner, he collected the dark blue North Face backpack and a black airline suitcase from the hotel luggage room, popped out the wheels and pulled up the handle, and trundled lazily over to the apartment building. A doorman in a plain brown uniform greeted him, having been alerted that he would be a guest for a single night in the apartment of an Australian couple, Mr. and Mrs. Derek Williams, who were on vacation. Mr. Williams had made the arrangements by telephone earlier in the day.

Kyle unlocked the door and turned on the lights room by room as he walked through the spacious apartment to be sure that he was alone. In the kitchen, he laid the suitcase on a polished round kitchen table made of maple and opened it. Inside the padded compartments was a disassembled Accuracy International AW covert sniper rifle, complete with a folding stock, a flash suppressor, a bipod, a pair of ten-shot magazines, and a box of twenty rounds of 7.62×51 mm cartridges. He loaded the magazines, put the weapon together, and spent time cleaning it, still mulling the questions that would have no final answers until tomorrow. As Jim Hall had said, he was in for the full ride.

He emptied the contents of his backpack on the table and got ready to take a shower, then lights out. Beside his toothbrush was his satellite phone, a secure link back to the Special Ops headquarters at Bagram. He made a call and identified himself by code, then asked to be connected to the Task Force Trident hut and soon heard the twangy voice of Staff Sergeant Travis Stone.

"Hey, boss," Stone said.

"Is Rawls there with you?" Swanson asked.

"Yeah. You want him?"

"No. You can pass the word. This is a quick job. I need both of you on it ASAP."

"Doin' what?"

"Guarding an embassy," Swanson said and then laid out what he wanted them to do.

17

Master Sergeant Malcolm K. Turnbridge looked like a Marine. The dress blue trousers had a red stripe down each leg, and the starched khaki shirt held sharp creases, several rows of ribbons, and six stripes on each sleeve. The tie was perfectly knotted, and his shined shoes gleamed in the fluorescent lighting, as did the polished black bill of his white cover, which lay on a nearby file cabinet in his office. The overall effect reflected the old Corps recruiting pitch of wanting a few good men: The two jokers standing before him were not them.

"Staff Sergeants Rawls and Stone reporting, Master Sergeant," said the tall African American, who had the build of a basketball player and wore a faded red Texas Tech T-shirt. "I'm Rawls," he said. The smaller guy looked like a rat with a flare of long red hair. "I'm Stone," he said. His T-shirt was black with pink lettering that read I AM VICTORIA'S SECRET. They both wore old blue jeans and tired sneakers.

"Welcome aboard, boys," said Turnbridge, taking the oversized manila folders from them. "Botha you will get your hairs cut immediately and be totally squared away before setting foot in the public areas of my embassy. That clear? Lookin' like that, how are you even in the Marines, much less staff sergeants?"

Rawls gave a big smile. "Sorry about the sloppy look, Master Sergeant. We just received the orders last night over at Bagram, and they put us on the first plane to Islamabad this morning."

Stone also grinned. "Six weeks temporary embassy security with you guys instead of sweating in Afghanistan? Real chow instead of MREs? Clean sheets? American women to look at? Sweet!"

Turnbridge grunted with approval and immediately cut the boys some slack. He once had been an infantry sergeant himself before being ordered into what was then called the Marine Security Guard Battalion, and he showed all of the correct badges and ribbons to prove it. "Awright. I didn't ask for help, but things are getting kind of tense around here, and I don't mind plussing up with a couple of experienced men. Have a seat and let's see what we got here." He thumbed open the flaps and pulled out the paperwork.

The orders were computer printouts and were routine and straightforward, with all of the appropriate squares filled in, and signed by the colonel who headed the Marine Corps Embassy Security Group based back in Quantico, Virginia. The colonel oversaw the postings of Marine guards at U.S. embassies around the globe. Master Sergeant Turnbridge, in charge of the Islamabad detachment, went through the papers fast and found no irregularities. "Okay. I'll take you over to the Marine House and introduce you. You'll like the duty here because the embassy civilians treat us like pets. The other guys will probably make you newbies do the grocery run downtown today as part of the usual initiation." He put the orders in a desk drawer and reached for his cover.

"Not quite yet, Master Sergeant Turnbridge," said Rawls. "We have some other hand-carried orders as well."

Turnbridge, halfway out of his chair, paused at Rawls's comment and plopped back down. "I knew this was too good to be true."

Looking serious, Rawls held out a sealed white envelope. There was no smile on the little guy's face anymore, either. The envelope was marked TOP SECRET. EYES ONLY. DETACHMENT COMMANDER. ISLAMABAD. Turnbridge ripped it open along one edge and unfolded a single sheet of paper.

The new men were to be accepted as part of the Marine detachment but were not under the control of the master sergeant, and no questions were to be asked. He was to provide all requested support, including arms. It was signed by the president of the United States.

Turnbridge folded the letter and returned it. "I'm not comfortable with this, Staff Sergeant Rawls," he said. "I believe it may put my men and the embassy at risk. This is a sensitive post. Also, since we are talking of orders from outside normal channels, I have to point out that I work for the ambassador here."

Travis Stone interrupted. "And the ambassador works for the State Department, and the secretary of state works for the president. So here we are."

"In other words, I just shut up and do what I'm told, huh?" The man's face reddened as embarrassment and anger crept into his tightly controlled demeanor.

"I know this puts you between a rock and a hard place, Top, and no offense is intended. We just had to get here in a hurry for a special job, and someone decided this was the quickest way." Rawls paused. "We won't be here long."

"And when we leave, we won't be coming back," added Stone. "Like Staff Sergeant Rawls, I don't like big-footing anybody, but we don't write orders."

Master Sergeant Turnbridge calmed down. "Okay. Okay. Just burned my ass for a moment there. The orders are legitimate, so although I don't have much to offer other than cover, my armory is open to you. I'll furnish whatever you need. We can go pick it out now, get the serial numbers, and you can sign it out."

"Sorry, but we cannot do that, either, Master Sergeant. We don't sign for things. We just get stuff and are not supposed to bring it back. When we go, we're gone."

"My name is on that inventory list. I'm responsible for it!" said Turnbridge.

"Right. After we pick out what we need, you just send a classified message to the man whose name is on those orders, and he will erase all traces of those weapons from your Serialized Inventory List. It will be as if they were never here. Then they will be replaced with identical weapons carrying the proper paperwork."

Turnbridge rubbed the prickly hair on his scalp. "Ain't that some shit. You know, boys, I've been around the Corps for a long time, and the only people I know of who can operate like that aren't even from Force Recon. We talking Task Force Trident here?"

Darren Rawls and Travis Stone just looked at him. "What kind of groceries you want?" Stone asked.

18

CIA Director Bartlett Geneen arrived at the White House at two o'clock on Wednesday morning to personally brief President Graham Russell in the Oval Office. The only other person in the room was the president's chief of staff, Robert Patterson, a popular former congressman who had been with Russell since their days as football teammates at the College of William & Mary in Williamsburg, Virginia. Patterson was a fierce protector of his friend and possessed a pit-bull, take-no-prisoners political temperament. The lights were subdued against the white walls, and small flames threw a soft glow from the fireplace. This was not the routine Presidential Daily Brief, which a ranking Agency official would deliver later in the day, but the president had wanted a final talk with Geneen before going to bed after the surprising release of the American captives.

"That was a slick piece of work, Bart," said Bobby Patterson, shaking the CIA director's hand as soon as he entered the Oval Office. "Congratulations."

The president, sleeves rolled up, also gave him a warm welcome. "Have you spoken with the soldiers?"

"No, sir," Geneen said. "We put them straight into Walter Reed Hospital out in Bethesda for thorough medical checkups. One has a bad cut on his arm, but other than that, there is only some bruising. We let them telephone their families, and that was how the news leaked."

"Nothing but good," said Patterson. "Other than allowing some family members in to see them, *excellent* photo op, by the way, it would be good to keep them under wraps and away from the press for a little while."

Geneen nodded in agreement, the old spymaster already a step ahead. He knew how to orchestrate such events. "Of course. We will begin the full debriefing only after they are recovered. That will be a couple of days."

Patterson softly clapped his hands. "Nothing but good."

"How about the agents who were involved? Does this change anything on the strike against the terrorists who killed the other boy?" The president was clearly anxious to be kept up to speed with the pending assassinations.

"I spoke with the agent who brought them back, a bright young woman named Lauren Carson, and she says everything was in place for the hit when she left. We have had no word from the strike unit about any postponement. So we can assume it is still on."

"That would make it quite a haul," said President Russell. "Get both prisoners back and take out the terrorists who killed our soldier."

"Yes, sir, it would. The situation is under control for now, and it is only noon over in Islamabad, so nothing is going to happen for a while. It would be a good time for you to catch a few hours' sleep. Go ahead. I will be spending the night in the Situation Room to monitor events from there."

Russell yawned in a reflex to the mere mention of some sleep. He was exhausted. He had been in office for less than a year, his long days dominated by the economy, which was slogging through a recession. There had been some slight increase in the gross national product during the past month, and the stock market had a solid upward bump, but the prisoner release would overshadow everything for at least two news cycles. He welcomed anything that would keep the news positive. "Yeah. I'm tired. What about you, Bobby?"

"I'll stay with Bart. Good night, Mr. President."

Patterson and Geneen walked down to the White House mess for some late coffee or an early breakfast. Scrambled eggs and fresh blueberry muffins, with a side of grits for Patterson, were on their plates when they settled in at a corner table. Unlike a regular cafeteria, the mess kept cooking all the time, for there were staff members coming in around the clock, and if the president suddenly decided he wanted a tuna salad topped with four-inch slices of coconut and olives stuffed with walnuts, he could have it. After two o'clock in the morning, though, even this place was unusually quiet.

"You think the Middle East will ever cool off?" Patterson asked the director.

Geneen looked up owlishly. "You mean will they ever settle down and live a Western-style existence like us? No. There's really no solution for that tinderbox. Our goals have to be limited to keeping Israel alive and safe, sustaining the region's oil production, blocking terrorism where we can, and preventing nuclear-tipped missiles from flying around. That's the best we can hope for in our lifetimes."

The chief of staff chewed his muffin and drank some coffee. "Defusing these incidents one at a time is like trying to drain a swamp with an eyedropper. Hard to measure progress. At least we're doing something by keeping the fight focused over there."

"Look, Bobby, I've been in this game for a long time, and I have seen incredible turnarounds in other countries that began small. We encourage the good guys. Tonight we take a couple more of the bad ones off the board. That cannot hurt our interests."

Patterson smoothed his napkin. "It will be a surgical strike, right? You trust these guys. No collateral damage. The Predator was a mistake."

Bartlett Geneen let that pass. He did not need to let Bobby Patterson know that it was the CIA call to let that one fly based on Jim Hall's contact from his old source. The Predator led directly to the release of the prisoners. "I know them both. They are the best at what they do, but there is a risk-reward situation in everything we do. I feel good about this one. I really do. It will rattle the cages of every fanatical leader by sending the message that he might be the next one in the scope of a long rifle."

Patterson finished his coffee. He had another job to do today. Let the spooks do what they do, but he was also charged with keeping the president politically safe. The prisoner release was an unexpected bonus. He would build on that if the snipers picked up these scalps.

ISLAMABAD
1600 HOURS

Kyle Swanson and Jim Hall were hunched over a small plastic-topped table that was covered with equipment and papers, combing over the final details of the coming shoot. Outside, the heat of the day was waning as the sun drifted lower in the western sky. Swanson was ready, but Hall had spent the night at the hotel. He appeared rested, alert, eager.

"Selim gave me these two pictures of the targets. They're pretty grainy because they were taken with a cellular phone, but there is enough definition to identify them when we see them." Hall slid the photographs across to Swanson.

Kyle studied them carefully. "They sure don't look like mountain men. Look at the clothes and the background. They are comfortable, which means they are getting a bit lazy. Outside of the battle zone, they obviously have lost their edge."

"Good for our side," Hall said. "Selim is more than holding up his end of the bargain."

"If he's not lying to us." Kyle dropped the pictures

and looked out the window to where the daylight was a thick orange color and losing its strength.

"Not the first time we've had to kill people without a formal introduction."

Swanson would have preferred an exact, specific time to pull the trigger. The sun would take a while to vanish, which was a concern. The longer it took, the longer Kyle and Hall would be exposed to being discovered. He put his strong binos to his eyes and studied the balcony where his targets were to appear. No one was out there now, but a man who looked like a servant had been out for a few minutes and was now moving around inside, cleaning and preparing a table. "I've got a good view from here. How about your position?"

"Same kind of unobstructed clear view. We're good to go. I better get on over there now, so I can settle down. We can do a final comm check then, and shut down outside radios." Hall picked up the little suitcase that contained his own Accuracy International AW. "Good hunting, pal."

"Yeah. Compensate for the downward angle on the shot. See you after work."

"Right. And you remember on egress that your dark SUV with the blue flag on the bumper will roll up downstairs just as the sun is sinking. There will be a driver at the wheel, and one man as a lookout."

"Got it."

"Good, then. Let's do it. Piece of cake."

19

Through a wrinkle in the world's time zones, Pakistan was ten hours ahead of Washington. Seven o'clock at night on September 30 in Pakistan would be 9:00 A.M. the same day in Washington and the headquarters of Task Force Trident. Not that it made any difference. When a covert operation was in progress, the office was always manned and available to support whoever was in the field.

In a city of vast bureaucracies and in a building that possessed endless chains of command, Trident was tiny by design, with only five people in the entire organization. It could pull together from any branch of service whatever forces were required to plus up for an operation, and had first call on a four-platoon Marine special operations company for its immediate needs. The tightness of the core group kept things simple.

While Swanson was in Pakistan, the remaining four members of the team had pulled rotating eight-hour shifts at the Pentagon. Rank made little difference behind the thick closed door with the big lock that required fingerprint and retina scans to open.

Master Gunnery Sergeant O. O. Dawkins, a Force Recon legend known as Double-Oh, was Trident's administrative chief and had finished the overnight shift that started at midnight. He was relieved at 0800 by Navy Lieutenant Commander Benton Freedman, Trident's unkempt but brilliant communications officer and the resident computer geek.

"No change in mission status," Dawkins told Freedman. "The timeline is holding. Only thing is that the White House keeps calling for updates."

"What did you tell them?"

Dawkins smiled, and big, bright even teeth shone in his square jaw. "That they had the wrong number. We are a logistics unit designing new Meals, Ready to Eat packets. Let the general handle those people. We say nothing."

"We were not required by the previous administration to provide ongoing oversight of an operation to anyone," Freedman said. "That would risk exposing..." Gunnery Sergeant Swanson would not be... not."

"No," Dawkins answered. "...into the computers, ...akfast and fresh coffee.

Once Freedman was... Trident's operations officer, Double-Oh left to... had arrived, although she was By the time ...noon shift. The commander, Major, S...ley Middleton, was at his desk. Everyna... be on deck when the strike took place in

Summers was sipping coffee from a thick white mug and wearing a slim headset that was tuned to the encrypted channel the field operatives would use after the job was done. She glanced at Dawkins when the big Marine came back, but said nothing. Summers was concentrating on just listening, although there was nothing coming through the headset.

Freedman remained at his computer console, rapidly scanning through other frequencies and trolling for information from multitudes of possible sources. He had been tagged "the Wizard" by other midshipmen when his technical genius had been recognized at the U.S. Naval Academy, and the nickname stuck with him during his two tours aboard nuclear attack submarines. When Middleton created Task Force Trident and drafted him for duty, that nickname was changed to "the Lizard," or just Liz, because saying "Wizard" did not adequately bust his balls, Marine-style. He might be a genius, but he was still a squid.

Digital clocks tracked the time, counting down on both sides of the world. Dawkins settled into a chair. He had been out on the sharp end of these missions too many times to

"They gone nervous.

The Lizard just question. The radios at his head to acknowledge the the field would be free field so the snipers in somewhere would try to mold so the situation at the last time that somebody, what was actually happening on d micromanage would reestablish contact when he was knowing son

Double-Oh carefully put his spit-shined black shoes on the desk, leaned back, and was instantly asleep.

Makhdoom Ragiq waited patiently while Mohammad Sial finished the lavish meal that had been spread for them by the servants, who had withdrawn to the kitchen. His eyes roamed the spacious apartment. Only to himself would he admit that he had come to enjoy the comfort of the place over the past few days. A warm and comfortable bed, and the delicious food, the cleanliness, and the subtle rhythm of the city beyond the window had been more like a vacation for him than a place in which to prepare for a combat assignment.

Siad dipped some bread in the hot sauce and gobbled it down, followed by a gulp of pure water from a clear pitcher on the table. "I know what you are thinking, my friend," he said. "You are thinking that you like this place and that it will be hard to return to the mountains."

"I have enjoyed the comforts, yes. I have not forgotten our mission. We are fighting men, Mohammed. We will die on some frozen hilltop in the name of Allah, killing infidels. So there is nothing wrong with having a few moments of enjoyment."

"You feel guilty about taking such simple pleasures. Well, my friend, in just a little while, we will be surrounded by admiring students at the madrasah, and we will leave them spellbound with stories of how we have carried the banner."

The dour, tall man actually laughed a little and passed his hand over the bowls and dishes between them. "I think we ate better than they did tonight."

The final flare of the late afternoon gleamed like gold through the open French doors. "It is almost time for prayers," he said. "Let's go outside."

Staff Sergeant Travis Stone was at the wheel of a black Land Rover Defender parked three blocks away, with the strong engine idling. Darren Rawls was in the passenger seat, giving a final check to the equipment they had taken from the U.S. Embassy: day- and night-vision gear, pistols, walkie-talkies and secure phones, and three of the little A-3s, the renovated M-16s with little scopes. A few bottles of water were in the SUV, but no food had been brought.

This trip was to be short and sweet. Both had small buds in their ears and were waiting for Kyle Swanson to take the shot, then to call them, using the code phrase "Dunkin' Donuts." By the time Swanson reached the pickup point, Stone and Rawls would be there. Maybe sixty seconds at the most.

About twenty miles beyond the city limits, a special operations heavy-lift CH-53E Super Stallion was circling over a safe area. The Marines would call for it to come get them as they raced out of Islamabad.

"Sun's going down," said Rawls.

Stone cocked the wheel to one side and eased out of his parking space. "Let's go get our boy."

Kyle Swanson studied the faces of the men through his scope. Those were the faces in the photographs. "Shooter Two. Confirming these are the targets. Are you on scope?"

"Roger." The voice of Jim Hall came back over the headset. Hall had his big rifle resting on its bipod, tilted down. He also could see the targets plainly. At first, he thought the taller man was wearing a bulletproof vest, but on closer examination, he saw it was just a woolen vest beneath the buttoned suit coat. "I have them," he said.

Around the city, the big sun was going down in a blaze, and Muslims were ready for the evening prayer. The two men on the balcony shifted over to a pair of beautiful mats that had been laid out for them and went to their knees, side by side, solemn and lost in their own thoughts of how much God had blessed their lives.

"Target One in position," said Kyle. "Shooter One on target."

"Target Two is in positon. Shooter Two on target," answered Hall.

"Roger." It was exactly as they had rehearsed. Kyle would take the target on the right, Hall the target on the left. "Stand by for my count," Swanson said. He was waiting to hear the start of the call, so the targets would bend forward and become immobile. Any shot before that might be affected by their sudden movement forward.

The loudspeakers that were placed throughout the city began the song for the faithful—*Allahu Akbar*. Allah is the greatest.

"Four," Kyle said. "Three . . . Two . . . One . . . Fire."

Their rifles barked at exactly the same time, and the bullets slammed into the unsuspecting Taliban fighters. The cheerful Mohammad Sial and the reserved

Makhdoom Ragiq were hurled forward on the balcony by the twin impacts, their heads destroyed, but their hearts still pumping blood.

Kyle pulled a cell phone from his vest and punched a speed-dial number.

"Dunkin' Donuts," answered Staff Sergeant Darren Rawls.

"Mission accomplished. Need a pickup," Kyle said.

Rawls snapped a button on the side of his big wristwatch and logged in the exact time of the call—19:19:14 hours. "On the way. Black Land Rover Defender coming up on your three o'clock."

"Now!" cried Selim Waleed and launched his own attack to capture U.S. Marine sniper Kyle Swanson.

20

Jim Hall had planted small blocks of C-4 explosive along the edge of the roof where he had been hiding, and as soon as he took the shot, he pressed a button on a small box that he had placed beside him. A digital screen came to life, activating a countdown. He had two minutes.

Hall raced down the long emergency staircase in his building, with his right hand gripping the descending metal railing to help him sail around the tight corners. He hit the ground floor at full speed and rammed out through a fire door, where the promised SUV with the gold flag on its fender was waiting. A huge man with bowling-ball muscles held open the rear door. There was no expression on his face.

Hall dove inside, and the big vehicle surged away from the curb with Hall flat on his back in the rear seat, hidden behind the tinted windows. "Get us out of here! Go!" he yelled.

They had not traveled more than a block when the explosives detonated in a series of sudden booms. Fire flashed, and a rising cloud of dirty smoke spread across the roof and curled upward as the entire upper corner of the building blew out with a crashing roar.

Kyle Swanson had no intention of following any escape route the Taliban had helped plan. When Hall had left him earlier, Kyle had spent some time pushing and pulling furniture and appliances across the only doorway into the apartment. The refrigerator, the dresser, the sofa, a toppled bookcase, and other heavy items were barricaded against the inward-opening door.

His hide was far back in the shadows of the living room, and as soon as he saw his target collapse, Swanson bolted down a narrow hallway and into the bedroom, which had a terrace of its own. The gathering darkness worked in his favor. He jumped lightly over the rail and stepped easily to the steel fire-escape ladder that stretched from the ground floor to the roof and was painted the same shade as the cream-colored building. Kyle headed for the roof.

Behind him, he heard thudding against the barricaded door to the living room, followed by shouts and finally by three short bursts of automatic weapons fire. Bullets might damage the refrigerator, but they would not get the pursuers through that door.

He reached the roof and spider-dropped to a crouch. Clear. They had expected him to go out through the front door. Instead, he was heading across the rooftops of two adjoining buildings and would take the fire ladder down the rear of the more distant one.

Swanson had started to run when the C-4 erupted a few blocks away. He froze in his tracks, turning in time to see the wall of the apartment house blow apart. He made an involuntary lurch toward the dying building because he knew his friend Jim Hall was trapped up there. Hall had trusted the Taliban once too often, and now he was dead. The options rolled through his mind in a few seconds. The CIA veteran, if he was somehow still alive, knew procedure; he knew the location of safe houses and where to get help. There was nothing Kyle could do to help Hall. Swanson's own mission was done, and he had to get out before the security forces flooded the area.

He ran hard, his shoes grabbing traction, and leaped over a small railing that separated the two buildings.

The big, boxy Land Rover jumped the sidewalk as it rounded the final corner and came to a screaming halt, one side crashing into a parked car. The entire palm-lined boulevard was sealed off, and cars of various security agencies were slashing in from all sides without regard for pedestrians or civilian motorists. Police in black armor and helmets were throwing a ring around the entire block and plunging into every building.

Travis Stone threw the Land Rover into reverse and flattened a parked motor scooter as he made a sharp three-point turn. Police were watching, and he jammed down the gas pedal and barreled away.

Darren Rawls called out to Swanson on the radio, ignoring routine procedures. "Get out of there, boss. Abandon the plan. Cops and soldiers all over the place down here. Streets are all blocked, and they are hitting every building. We can't reach you."

Kyle stopped loping across the final roof, edged to the side, and peered down. Vehicles were coming in for blocks all around. Men with guns were closing in. Flashlights were cutting lines of light through the gloom. He heard a yell behind him as a couple of policemen made it to the roof of his hide building and spotted him. "You guys egress," he said. "I'm gone."

"Roger that. We'll hold the Taxi One Four at the assigned grid for as long as we can. Go, boss. Go."

WASHINGTON, D.C.

Master Gunny O. O. Dawkins did the arithmetic in his head. Two minutes would be required from the time of the triggers being pulled to getting the shooters out of the buildings and into their cars. About another nineteen mikes to weave through the city streets and reach the countryside, then another five to the landing zone. That meant a total of twenty-six minutes just for them to reach the helicopter. The clock now read only zero-plus-five. There was no need to get nervous. Everything that could be done had been done. Now all they could do was wait and see.

The Task Force Trident office remained quiet except for the hum of the Lizard's computers. Waiting for a team to come up on the net precluded idle banter. Like a baseball team remaining quiet if a pitcher has a chance for a no-hitter, there was a superstition among special operators that talking too much might jinx the mission.

The silence was broken when a telephone buzzed on

the desk of Major General Brad Middleton and the caller identification showed it was the White House chief of staff. "Patterson," the general grunted, "this is the second time you've called in the last five minutes. Quit bothering us. I will let you know when we hear anything. Do not call back."

This new guy at the White House, Bobby Patterson, apparently thought that because he worked for the commander in chief, he was also an expert on war and covert operations. Asshole had never even been in the service. Fuck him.

Swanson was trapped like a rat in a maze, as the actual terrain dictated his movement. There was only one way to go. The edges of the building corralled him right and left, and the cops were coming up the ladder. He pulled out his .45 ACP, fired a single shot for some harassing fire to make them take cover, and took off for the next roof.

This time he had to jump a narrow alley and took it in full stride, leaping into space and landing with a hard hit and shoulder roll. He noticed that despite his own shot, the cops were not firing back, although they were still chasing him. More of them had reached the roof. That meant their radios were working and they were calling up reinforcements to flood the area. He couldn't stay on top, and there was no time for analysis or strategy or even fright; just a rush of instant decisions, each built flimsily on the previous one. He trusted his instincts and training, determined not to meekly hold up his hands and quit.

A rooftop entry cubicle loomed on his right, and he grabbed the handle and threw it wide. See a doorway, hit it. Empty. He started down the stairs but heard the shouts and the boot stomps of men entering the bottom of the stairwell. The door to the third floor was at hand, and he ducked through.

A carpeted hallway stretched the length of the expensive residential building. It was neat and wide, with only two facing doorways on either side of the single elevator in the middle to serve the apartments at each end. Fat potted palms huddled beneath framed artwork, the fanned fronts brushing the ceiling.

Kyle needed a diversion to confuse the men chasing him. Using the butt of his pistol as a hammer, he crushed the lights at his end of the hallway, and it fell into a gray dimness just as the soft chime of the elevator bell rang. Kyle kicked open a door, hard enough to break the lock, then ducked behind the nearest broad potted palm.

Two security men wearing black coveralls and body armor dashed out when the elevator doors parted, immediately breaking toward the dark area. When they saw the door sagging open, both of them rushed into the apartment with weapons drawn instead of one providing cover for the other.

Kyle came in right behind them, pulling the door closed as he passed it, and silently counting off the passing seconds in his head. *One* . . . He punched his shoulder hard into the back of the officer directly before him, using the man as a battering ram and their forward momentum to knock down the front man. *Three* . . .

Swanson reached over the head of the man he had pushed and grabbed him by the rim of the helmet, jerking the head backward to expose the neck. With his left hand maintaining the leverage, Kyle swung his right hand and pistol up and smashed the muzzle and barrel into the man's larynx, crushing it. *Six . . .*

He did not want to shoot either man, and did not want them to have time to shoot at him. If they died, so be it, but he could not afford a single gunshot that could bring in the reinforcements. If that happened, Kyle wouldn't stand a chance. He dropped the body of the man he had just killed and slammed into the second one with a rear choke hold. Right forearm around the throat, clasp left hand with the right, and lean back to trap his air. *Nine . . .* Swanson squeezed with all of his might. The man was in such pain and shock that he clawed at Kyle's arm with both hands, trying to get air instead of working to bring a weapon to bear. Finally the man fell limp. Kyle started a new count, holding his victim tight and continuing the unrelenting squeeze until he reached the number seven.

He eased the body to the floor and plopped down between them and caught his own breath. Nineteen seconds from start to finish. He looked at the door, which had shut tight, and listened for noise in the hallway. Nothing was happening.

Swanson got back to work and quickly stripped both bodies and pulled on a black jumpsuit, a black vest, a black helmet over a black roll-down mask, an equipment belt, and a set of big goggles. Being of average size himself, the first man's boots were a good fit. He dragged the bodies into the bedroom and stuffed them between the bed and the wall. With an AK-47 grasped in both hands, Kyle Swanson charged back into the hallway, then into the stairwell to merge with the throng of men who were hunting him.

Selim Waleed would wait no longer. Everything was in the timing tonight, and he had allowed two minutes for the capture of the Marine sniper. It should have been a simple task but took a bad turn when the police reported the Marine had not been in the apartment. They were chasing him.

At the two-minute mark, Selim heard the explosion and looked out from his own apartment in time to watch the upper floor of the building where Jim Hall had been hiding disappear with sharp blasts and coiling smoke. Fire was already rising through that wreckage. That jarred him back to reality. He could wait no longer. Plans change. It did not matter whether Hall or the Marine or Taliban fighters or students studying the Koran or cops or soldiers were alive when overturning the government was the true goal. Anyone could be sacrificed. At four minutes, with still no report of a capture, he grabbed his cell phone and dialed number by number, then punched the SEND button.

For a moment, time seemed to stand still in the beautiful city of Islamabad. Soldiers on rooftops, people in the streets and in their homes and businesses, or on their knees at prayer, paused as their brains processed sudden new information that something dangerous was happening.

Waleed's signal was received by a detonator planted among the boxes and crates of ammunition stacked in the big yard next to the crowded madrasah, and a spark jumped to complete a firing circuit. The jagged high hill of explosives erupted, and as the old sun disappeared for the night of September 30, a volcanic new sun of fire and destruction rose in the heart of the city.

21

Cops, security personnel, and soldiers swarmed, throwing a cordon around the apartment block. Blockades of police cars with flashing light bars sealed the streets, and officers yelled directions to their men going into the buildings. Swanson swam easily against the tide, moving with the self-confidence of someone on a specific mission, just another uniform, and nobody stopped him. Every second counted. Just being out of the building did not mean he was safe, although it improved the odds.

He needed wheels. Beyond the first line of policemen guarding the inner perimeters were clusters of official cars that had parked haphazardly and been abandoned along the street. Chances were good that if the lights were blinking, some anxious driver would have left the motor running in his excitement to join the hunt. Ironically, Kyle realized that he was moving toward the same building where his targets had been standing on the balcony. Swanson methodically worked his way along the line of cars, placing his palm on the hood of each in turn to detect the vibration of an engine. The third one. An iron gray Nissan sedan with no insignia had been abandoned with its red and blue lights still winking brightly behind the grill. A disciplined officer would have shut down and locked the vehicle, but this one had not done so. Kyle knew his chances had just improved remarkably. Once through the cordon of cops, Kyle could drive like hell to reach the helicopter.

Swanson ducked into the driver's seat and tossed his AK-47 into the passenger compartment. He closed the door and snapped the lock shut, and an automatic seat belt harness strapped across his chest. With one hand on the steering wheel, he glanced down to find the gear lever and shifted it into reverse. He looked in the rear-view mirror. Clear. He gunned the accelerator.

In the next heartbeat, the entire car was snatched from the ground by a monstrous blow and twirled into the air like a toy by a scalding cyclone of superheated air. *It's not just the car that's flying, it's me!* A gigantic explosion had erupted less than a block away and was flattening and destroying everything in its path. Cops and people tumbled, walls were crushed, cars were flung about, and tall palm trees were shorn off at their roots. Big chunks of concrete became deadly boulders of shrapnel.

The Nissan completely overturned while airborne, then corkscrewed back to earth, whipped by the concussion. It crashed once back onto the street, bounced, and rolled over twice more while skidding a hundred feet before coming to rest with a half-dozen other cars that were stacking against a building.

Kyle Swanson was unconscious, hanging upside

down, suspended by the seat belt, and supported by inflated air bags. He never heard the explosions that rolled over him.

The SUV that was carrying Jim Hall of the CIA also overturned when the concussion wave snatched it, and slid in a cascade of sparks on its side as debris smacked it like an unending barrage of mortar shells. A length of steel rod punched through the front window and stabbed the driver through the head.

The other agent in the car was dazed and groaned in pain. He could function. The man put his arms against the door that was now over his head and pushed with weightlifter strength until it popped free, then levered himself out of the wreckage.

Instead of disappearing in the chaos, running away to find safety, the agent turned back to the vehicle. He called out in broken English, "You alive?"

"Yeah," Hall shouted. "Help me out of here." He had been hurled against the seats and was torqued into a tight corner, trapped by twisted metal.

"I am coming." The large man ignored the blood streaming down his own face and put his big muscles back to work, hurling away chunks of material and digging with his bare hands. The explosions thundered. He found the American at the bottom of the car, twisted and caught in a corner. The agent needed leverage. He squeezed into the backseat, put his feet against the front seat and his back against the rear, and pushed hard and steadily. There was strong resistance, but he continued to push, grunting with effort, and felt some give. Then came a sharp snap as a weakened metal strut broke, and the rear seat catapulted backward.

Hall felt the pressure ease against him. "That's it." He could move again. He squirmed up and grabbed the man's beefy hand. The Taliban agent clamped onto his wrist and hauled him free. Hall stood and wiped his face. Around him lay a wrecked moonscape, and more explosions were rocking the area every minute. "Thanks, big guy. I owe you one. You know a way out of here?"

"Yes. Follow." The big man was breathing hard, still bleeding from his nose and both ears and from a corner of his mouth. Hall guessed there was some internal damage, probably to the lungs, but said nothing. They dodged around a fallen tree and ran for safety.

The blast lifted the fleeing Land Rover several feet into the air, as if it had been picked up by an angry child, while the momentum kept it moving forward, flying until the extreme weight of the vehicle pulled it back down. Staff Sergeant Travis Stone was slammed against the door, with his head ricocheting off the window, and he saw stars as he fought the steering wheel. The armored SUV bounced down hard, swerved onto a sidewalk, and clipped a wall. The strong engine howled as Stone gunned it. Darren Rawls, holding on with both hands, stared back wide-eyed at the carnage in their wake. "Jesus H. Christ," he muttered.

Entire apartment buildings were cascading down in a slow landslide of concrete and glass and metal. On the street, cars overturned, the sidewalks buckled, and other walls crumpled, then fell, and a hundred fires bloomed. Bodies lay in the street, and wounded people struggled to get away from a deadly hail that began to fall when the storehouse of antitank rockets and mortar shells ignited and spun without direction into other parts of the city. The missiles blasted into private homes, businesses, public parks, foreign embassy compounds, and hotels with equal savagery. A jagged piece of black metal blew directly over the hood of the Land Rover and sliced into a parked truck like a giant arrow. Stone kept his foot hard on the accelerator and roared on toward the edge of the city, dodging fires and wreckage. The newly dark sky boiled in crimson orange. Ruptured underground water mains spouted like fountains. Tidal waves of scalding air were being sucked through the streets, feeding the developing firestorm.

"What happened back there?" Stone yelled. "What the fuck, man?"

"Next left!" shouted Rawls, and Stone threw the Land Rover into a screeching ninety-degree turn. Loud booms jarred the area like an unending earthquake and shook their teeth. Debris banged against the vehicle like a hailstorm.

"Taxi One Four, Taxi One Four. This is Trident Two Two," Rawls shouted into his radio, trying to keep his voice calm. He felt wetness on his face as blood streamed from his ears due to the blast. He wiped it away as best he could.

The answer came back immediately from the CH-53E helicopter. "Trident Two Two, this is Taxi One Four. Send your traffic."

"Roger, Taxi, Trident six mikes out." Rawls estimated they were about six minutes from the landing zone.

"Roger, Trident. Six mikes. We are heading in now." The helicopter heeled out of its long turn and began a straight-in descent to prearranged coordinates. The spectacle of the explosions and fire could be easily seen from the sky, a carnival of chaos.

"Kyle was right," Stone said, fighting the wheel. "It was a setup." A curtain of dirty ash had caught up with them and was drifting down, so he activated the windshield wipers. The air conditioner was going full blast as a filter.

"We'll worry about that later. Just keep going." Rawls scanned the sky as the SUV charged forward over everything in its path.

"Taxi One Four. Taxi One Four. This is Trident Two Two. One mike out, approaching from the south in a black Land Rover."

"Roger, Trident. I have a visual on you."

The huge helicopter dropped out of the night like a fast-moving monstrous shadow, then flared at the last moment, throwing up its own curtain of dirt, dust, and debris. The rear ramp was already down, and a gunner was strapped in behind a .50 caliber machine gun, watching them.

Stone killed the headlights and stopped about twenty-five meters away, and he and Rawls jumped out.

"Setting the timer to two minutes!" shouted Rawls as he tossed an incendiary grenade into the Land Rover to totally destroy the vehicle, their DNA, and any other trace of its use. They ran around the gunner, and the whine of the helicopter's big GE engines immediately increased. Travis Stone held up two fingers to denote the correct count of the people coming aboard, then twirled the fingers in a circle. The crew chief nodded and spoke into his microphone.

The helicopter lifted away and bent into a fast, climbing turn. Stone and Rawls knelt on the metal floor and looked out of the square ramp opening, holding on to supports as the horizon tilted. There was a bright flash when the incendiary bomb detonated in the backseat of the Land Rover.

It was nothing more than a firecracker compared with the inferno back in Islamabad, where trails of rockets still sizzled through the sky, delayed secondary detonations were still rocking buildings, and fires were out of control, burning fiercely and unchecked. Their faces were orange and red with the reflection.

"I better call home," said Rawls, staggering into a seat and signaling the crew chief for a helmet with a radio.

"Yeah, you better," his partner agreed. In a softer voice, Stone whispered, "Good luck, Kyle."

Darren Rawls went to an emergency frequency to report back directly to Task Force Trident headquarters in Washington. The signal bounced off a couple of satellites, went through the trapdoor of a global financial network's interoffice data stream, and was routed into Trident's private comm setup. "Trident Lizard, Trident Lizard. This is Trident Two Two. Come in."

In the Pentagon, Lieutenant Commander Freedman saw a flashing code on his computer screen to alert him to the incoming traffic at the same time his headset came alive. He threw up a hand and snapped his fingers to get the attention of the others. Middleton, Summers, and Dawkins stopped what they were doing and hurried to his side. "Trident Two Two. This is Trident Lizard. Send your traffic."

The signal was weak but clear. "Be advised Bounty Hunter confirmed mission accomplished at exactly nineteen nineteen fourteen hours. Mission compromised. Shooters attacked. Bounty Hunter is trying to exfiltrate under heavy pursuit. Attached partner missing, status unknown. Subsequent massive explosion of unknown origin is causing extensive damage downtown. We are aboard Taxi One Four. Standing by for orders."

General Middleton switched to the frequency. "This is Trident Six. Roger your transmission. Authorize Gunrunner for you, effective immediately. Out." Gunrunner was a contingency plan that would let the helicopter take the two special operators to join a routine mission that was already in progress in Afghanistan. Retroactive paperwork would show that Stone and Rawls had never been in Islamabad at all.

"Sir! Look at this!" The Lizard's voice was rising in alarm. He had been scouring the live feeds from Pakistan, and his screen was suddenly busy with images of destruction, fires, collapsed buildings, and dead men, dismembered women, and bleeding children. Cameras shook as explosions continued to cook off in Islamabad, rocking the photojournalists. The Lizard, who never cursed, spoke for them all. "What the fuck is happening over there?"

Double-Oh stood back and rubbed his square jaw in thought. He spoke in a calm voice, weighing possibilities and options. Nothing would be gained by panic on this end. "We have only that brief report from Staff S'arnt Rawls, and now these early news feeds. Not much to act on, General. Gunrunner takes care of our boys on the bird, but they apparently never actually linked up with Kyle. He provided the time check to confirm the shoot."

"Replay the call, Liz." Major Sybelle Summers wanted to hear what had been said once again. Did they miss anything? There was obvious stress in the voice of the unflappable veteran operator Darren Rawls. *Mission compromised. Shooters attacked.*

"We might not know exactly what happened, but it's obvious that somebody is trying to kill our guy," she said. "That's good enough for me. It was a setup."

"I agree, Major, but there's no proof." Dawkins heard a telephone buzz and picked up the receiver.

General Middleton glowered at the screens, as if he could change things through sheer willpower. "I will need to speak to the president. Liz, put in a call to the White House and tell them I'm coming over."

"No need for that, sir," said Dawkins. "That was his chief of staff again. He seems upset. Your presence has been requested."

22

His world flickered, a grainy old movie, hard to see. Kyle Swanson opened his eyes. He could smell smoke, hear screams, taste dirt, and see rubble. It was a struggle to breathe. The sniper thought for an instant that he was tied up, but as his senses focused, he found that he could move his arms, although they were entangled in some sort of sturdy fabric. His chest was tightly held, but his feet were free. Bits of memory returned, slowly at first, and then faster, accentuated by the hellish landscape before his eyes. He was upside down in a vehicle, and a seat harness was holding him firmly in place. The other material was only air bags that had filled on impact, then deflated. Kyle worked his fingers to the buckle of the belt, snapped it open, and fell onto his head. The combination of wearing the helmet, the goggles, and body armor and being held securely inside the car by the web of safety belts and air bags had saved his life. Getting his feet into a firm position, he gave a strong heave of his shoulders and levered himself out through the destroyed windshield, rolled out from beneath the car, and came to his knees, hands on thighs, back straight, head up, trying to breathe in a place where there was no fresh air. He had a headache that seemed ready to split his skull.

The big goggles were safe windows to another world, and he brushed a glove over them to clean the lens. He was inside a thick, pulsing stew of smoke and pulverized concrete, dirt turned to dust and particles of civilization that had been blown to bits. The shifting, boiling cloud was everywhere, climbing the walls, channeling like a wave through the streets, scouring the ground with a savage wind.

My God, it's 9/11!! I'm at Ground Zero!! Swanson shook his head hard to clear it. *No, that can't be. I'm in Islamabad. Something has happened. I need air.* Another memory of 9/11 came to him. *This cloud is poison, and if I eat it or breathe it, I die. Think, dammit, think!*

The car. It had saved him once, and maybe the little gray sedan had another miracle. Swanson staggered to his feet, coughing hard, and felt his way along the overturned vehicle until he found the line of the trunk. It was crumpled from the rollover and subsequent impacts. Kyle grabbed the edge and yanked down hard, but there was no movement. Still locked. He pulled his pistol and fired twice, knocking the latch apart, and a gap appeared along the trunk line. He holstered the weapon and pushed down on the lid again. *Please be there!*

Despite its size, the Nissan was a police vehicle, which meant that it would be equipped to have a support role in emergency situations such as accidents and riots. When the trunk lid popped open, a large black nylon emergency kit spilled out at his feet, and Kyle tore open the lid. He burrowed through the contents until he found a smaller soft-pack container; unzipping it, he pulled out an old-style hooded gas mask with built-in lenses and a large round air filter on the left side. Although it was probably meant to protect the wearer against tear gas used against mobs, it was the same familiar M-40 full-face type that Kyle had used during desert sandstorms.

Also in the emergency kit was a plastic six-pack of sealed water bottles, and he tore one free, unscrewed the top, and sloshed the liquid over his face and eyes, drank a mouthful, and spat out streams of mud. He did it again, then took a deep hydrating drink that still tasted like dirt. He used a fingertip to clean his nostrils, then opened the straps on the mask while huffing out a couple of breaths to clear his lungs as much as possible. With a swipe of his hand, he got rid of his helmet and goggles and slipped into the mask. The protective hood fell around his shoulders, and when the straps were pulled tight, the rubberized mask sealed to his face. He could breathe again. Kyle put the helmet back on, leaned back against the wreckage, and sat down hard, sucking the filtered air deep, letting life flood back into his body.

23

THE WHITE HOUSE

Bartlett Geneen was among the most secretive of men and did not explain to White House Chief of Staff Bobby Patterson the dangers of an outsider becoming so closely involved with a covert operation. *A moth drawn to a flame.* In fact, Geneen was pleased that Patterson had wanted to be in on the blow-by-blow action as the dual hits took place in Pakistan.

It was important for the CIA director to have the eager Patterson witness an assassination as it happened, for it provided automatic White House cover. Task Force Trident, which provided the second shooter in this operation, possessed a signed Top Secret Presidential Directive for its authorization, which made Kyle Swanson immune from blowback. The CIA had no such protection, but Patterson could not dump blame on the Agency if he was in on the operation, and thereby giving it tacit presidential approval.

That was the true reason why he was in the Situation Room and not back at his office over in Langley. For any regular mission, Geneen would not have watched the event at all.

As the magic moment had approached, Geneen and Patterson were in comfortable gray swivel chairs on opposite sides of a rectangular table of polished wood in a small office adjacent to the main Situation Room conference area. The times in six different cities were shining in red numbers near the ceiling of one wall—7:20 P.M. in Pakistan. A pair of large plasma television screens dominated one of the whisper walls, and each man had a laptop computer and a multichannel telephone on the desk before him. Patterson was constantly working the phone, calling Trident headquarters over in the Pentagon and growing angrier each time his inquiries were rebuffed. Geneen could have warned him that spooks don't tolerate last-minute meddling, which is why they shut down comms just before taking action. The director chose to let the chief of staff discover that unpleasant fact for himself. *Rookie mistake.*

Just outside the door was the large National Security Council watch center, which was always fully staffed by experts who kept their fingers and eyes on the pulse of the world. All the technology and talent that was immediately available created a comfortable and mistaken feeling that everything was always under control. Supervisors slaved to maximize the level of alertness.

When the sun went down in Islamabad and two snipers fired their weapons, the NSC watch shift had a satellite overhead with a fuzzy but live infrared view as the operation quickly fell apart. Bobby Patterson was stunned. The multiple views were being thrown onto the plasma screens, which seemed to put him right in the middle of things. The distant and indistinct satellite views soon gave way to an avalanche of news reports and cell phone transmissions. American diplomats and intelligence agents in Islamabad popped up on quadrants of the screens to be in direct contact with the NSC. It seemed the conference room was filled with giant, disembodied talking heads. They all reported the same thing: explosions and fires rocking Islamabad.

Patterson grimly picked up a handset to call the Residence and alert President Russell. Then he would contact that irritating general at Task Force Trident and get his two-star butt over here for a royal chewing.

Geneen used the distraction to slip into one of the privacy telephone booths built into a whisper wall. The curved door slid smoothly closed behind him, and he pressed a button to immediately frost the transparent glass. He stood casually, leaning against the wall, and punched in a coded number.

A few silent moments passed as the encrypted connection was made to a cellular telephone carried in the shirt pocket of his counterpart in the Pakistani intelligence service. General Nawaz Zaman of the ISI looked at the caller identification on his screen, the one-word code "Football." He pressed the telephone to his ear and answered, "Soccer." The intelligence chiefs of the United States and Pakistan were speaking directly with each other, bypassing the labyrinth of subordinates. Such communications channels were never closed but seldom used. To prevent an overreaction and clear the field for Kyle Swanson and Jim Hall to operate, Geneen had deemed it prudent to inform the ISI chief in advance of the planned strike on the Taliban terrorists in Islamabad. Zaman had agreed that he had no reason to stop it. Now something had gone wrong.

"My friend," said Geneen. "What is happening?"

General Zaman exhaled loudly enough for the sudden gust of breath to sound like a typhoon on the amplified connection. "You have blown up my city, Football! Your people have caused us more damage on this one evening than the Taliban has in a year."

Geneen suddenly wanted a cigarette, although he had not smoked for twenty years. "Do not jump to conclusions, Soccer. Are you sure that our people were the cause?"

"No. It is too early to establish exactly what happened." The sound of another explosion banged over the cell phone. "There goes another one. A lot of dead and injured civilians and military are out there tonight. Have you heard from your people?"

"No. Nothing yet, and that's the truth," Geneen said. "What are you going to do?"

Zaman was slow to answer, thinking it through. "My only choice is to report to our president now. This disaster may force him to declare martial law. We have few options. I also have to dispatch ISI agents to investigate."

"I understand. Let's stay in close touch, Soccer. And brace yourself. The FBI will want in on this investigation."

"I shall do my best."

Geneen hung up the telephone and walked back to the conference room in time to hear a red-faced Bobby

Patterson on the telephone to the Pentagon, demanding that General Brad Middleton get to the White House. Right now.

Major General Bradley Middleton was in no mood to be bawled out by a politician. Bobby Patterson, who had returned to his magnificent office from the National Security Council side room, was not expecting to be chastised himself. "How dare you summon me away from my command post in the middle of an ongoing crisis!" The general's voice had the sound of tumbling boulders, and his eyes were of stone. His driver had brought him over with siren and lights, and Middleton had bounded up the familiar steps of the White House after the usual entry checks by the uniformed Secret Service.

Patterson was standing behind his desk but hesitated in the face of Middleton's obvious fury. He glanced nervously over to CIA Director Bart Geneen, who was standing with his hands behind his back. Geneen and Middleton did not exchange greetings, but the director chuckled to himself. He was on the general's side on this one.

"I want an immediate personal report from you to give to the president." Patterson's voice, rising slightly in tone. Tentative.

"Okay." Middleton crossed his arms over his broad chest. "We took down a pair of tangos in Islamabad, as ordered. Anything else?"

"What about the explosions?"

"What about them?"

The chief of staff blinked. "General Middleton, the

collateral damage accompanying this mission was supposed to be minimal. That was the purpose of the entire operation."

"No. The purpose was to kill the terrorists who had butchered an American soldier. We did that."

"Then the capital city of Pakistan is rocked by explosions! The president is not happy with this."

The general finally looked to Geneen, who shrugged, then back to Patterson. "And you think that the CIA-Trident shooters were responsible? Have you the slightest shred of evidence to back up that idiotic claim?"

Patterson sat in the big, soft office chair and pulled it up to his desk. He picked up an envelope. "Not yet. But your boy Swanson has a reputation for doing this kind of damage."

Geneen coughed quietly into his fist to interrupt. "We have not heard from Jim Hall, General. You have anything from Swanson?"

"No. Last we heard, Kyle was being chased by a lot of cops." The general did not mention the message from the exfil team of Rawls and Stone that the mission was apparently compromised. *Never answer questions that have not been asked.*

Patterson tapped the envelope on his neat, polished desk, his mood shifting. "You have to admit, however, General Middleton, that Swanson is capable of igniting this holocaust."

"Well, he could not have caused it with a single bullet, that's for sure. It takes time to organize something of the magnitude we are seeing over there, a massive set of explosions. Anyway, that isn't Swanson's style. Bart?"

"I agree. Same with Hall. No one shot could have caused something like that to erupt." Geneen sat down carefully and crossed his ankles. He had been through many such meetings in his career. Patterson was injecting politics into the mix. *Cover your ass.* "What's in that envelope that you are so nervously tapping?"

Patterson started, almost as if having forgotten that he even had the envelope in his hand. Then he held it up by one end and gave it a slight wave. "Mr. Director, General Middleton, before coming in for this meeting, I removed this from the Oval Office private safe. It is the presidential finding that authorizes the clandestine unit known as Task Force Trident. As of today, Trident ceases to exist."

Bending slightly to his left, Patterson fed the envelope and the document it contained into a government cross-pattern paper shredder. The quiet buzz sounded like a drill. "You're out of business, General."

"That is the act of a goddam coward, Patterson. Kyle Swanson and Jim Hall went into enemy territory with valid orders to fight this country's enemies. They may have paid the price with their lives. Now you are abandoning them? I demand to speak personally to the president."

"That is impossible. The decision has been made."

"By who? You?"

Bartlett Geneen was appraising the deteriorating situation. He did not like what he was seeing. "This is uncalled for, Bobby. The general is right. We do not abandon our agents."

"We are not abandoning anyone, Bart. We are disbanding a rogue covert operation within the American military establishment. It was an idea that once had merit but has devolved into being a dangerous tumor. Trident is gone. The CIA is now in total charge of getting those men out."

Middleton reached into the breast pocket of his uniform jacket and pulled out an envelope of his own. He tossed it onto the desk. "I always thought you were just another political snake, Patterson, and not the brightest one in the woodpile. Now I know why you were only a one-term congressman. You've got no balls. Here's my resignation. Leave my people alone."

Bobby Patterson picked up the envelope and shoved that one also into the shredder. "Negative, General. Your resignation is not accepted. You remain in the military chain of command, and the president remains your commander in chief. I suggest that you return to the Pentagon now and close up shop. You and your Trident people are on indefinite leave, pending reassignment."

"Bullshit. I work for the president. Not you. I have my own copy of that finding you just shredded, so don't start trying to rearrange history. I and the members of my team will follow the signed or verbal orders of my commander in chief. Until I hear directly from him, then, fuck you." Middleton stalked from the room.

Bart Geneen said, "Bobby, you are playing a very dangerous game."

"Don't be so melodramatic, Director."

"And what happens to Middleton and Trident?"

"He got off easy. I just want him on the sidelines for a while. I considered having him arrested as a national security risk. Remember the Patriot Act? We could have them all held without charges, without lawyers, without trial, and at an undisclosed location for as long as we wish. You, of all people, should remember the good old days of rendition, secret prisons, and enhanced interrogation techniques. You guys created this whole apparatus yourselves, and it is still on the books. Reasons don't matter when national security is involved."

"You consider Brad Middleton to be a national security risk?" Geneen reined himself in from making a more intemperate remark. "Really. That is absurd."

Patterson kept his face a blank mask. "I do, Mr. Director. You do not need to know anything more than that." He paused and made himself hold the stare of the older man, although it was like looking into the cold eyes of a cobra. "Your job is to unravel this mess, so I guess you had better get back over to Langley and get busy."

"Does President Russell know what you're up to?"

"Good day, Mr. Director."

24

The early reports showed a butcher's bill that was moderate, in the opinion of Selim Waleed. He had anticipated more, although the sixty-eight dead and two hundred and twelve wounded, many of them seriously, was certainly a satisfactory early outcome. That toll would undoubtedly rise substantially as hospitals reported throughout the day and emergency crews arrived to sift through the wreckage. The capital city still sizzled from the explosions and fire and vibrated with the pitiful cries of the victims.

Waleed had created a whirlwind of uncertainty and violence. Now he had to steer it. The Taliban Wise Ones were swearing they were not responsible. Fundamentalist Muslim fanatics announced that the disaster was not caused by a suicide attack. The elected government condemned it as a terrorist attack by political opponents. The thinly stretched Pakistani army went to a higher state of alert, considering it to be an attack on one of their installations. The Pakistani secret police, the ISI, were in full crackdown mode.

Then Waleed's agents spread the news that the

explosions came immediately after two famous Taliban fighters had been assassinated while at prayers. That further insulated the Bright Path Party from suspicion of any involvement. Beyond that announcement, Selim Waleed remained silent while the country fell into what he hoped would be a final fracture.

Antigovernment demonstrators surged into the streets of other cities, unsure of whom to blame. They blamed everyone, even each other. Fighting broke out between rival mobs, and police responded with more violence as the foreign news media covered it all.

The only thing that was out of balance was the escape of the American Marine. Somehow, Swanson had evaded the trap.

"You were supposed to capture him, Selim, but you wanted the cops to grab him. Amateurs don't beat professionals in this game." Jim Hall was sprawled on a sofa, a large ball of ice wrapped in a soft blue towel resting on his swollen left eye.

Waleed pulled a bottle of Scotch from a cabinet and poured each of them a drink. It was a taste he had acquired while serving at the embassy in London. Drinking spirits was against his religion, but he was a pragmatic man and needed a drink. "He won't get far." There was a significant pause. "You knew nothing about what he was going to do?"

Hall sat up, took the offered glass, and removed the ice pack so he could drink. The entire left side of his face was purple and black, with a few stitches from a doctor holding together a ragged cut below the eye. He had already taken a shower and put on clean clothes.

Even with the doc's painkillers, Hall had a raging headache. "When I left him, the plan was still on track. He must have changed it at the last minute and didn't tell me."

"So he did not trust you after all?"

"Swanson was my friend. He saw something he didn't like, maybe some of your boys made some noise, and he changed the plan. He did not have to wait around for me because the plan was always for us to make separate escapes."

Selim finished his drink, put the bottle down, and sat across from Hall. "Things have changed, then."

"Not really. You get your revolution started, and will be able to blame Washington for the assassinations and explosions. I get out of your fair country, to become a gentleman of leisure."

The eyes of Selim Waleed hardened. "True, you have done as you promised. Perhaps a new deal is required at this point, Jim Hall. You have many secrets of your government, and you are willing to sell them. What is to stop me from just taking you captive and wringing that information out of you, one bit at a time? Don't forget where you are."

"Jesus Christ," Hall said as he lifted the ice roll onto his face again and leaned back. "Don't you think I covered that possibility before I ever left home to come over here?" He laughed aloud and poured himself another drink. "Don't be stupid, boy. You and your father are some of those secrets! I have arranged a specific time at which I must do a certain thing, in a certain way, at a certain time and in a certain place. If I fail to show up and perform exactly as planned, then information about every meeting you and your father have ever had with me, your meddling in the affairs of other countries, and your plotting here at home will be given to your enemies. Pictures, recordings, documents. You cannot afford to risk that."

Selim's face remained placid, but some muscles in his jaw were pulling his mouth into a frown. "Extortion."

"Insurance," countered Hall. "Anyway, you did not tell me that you were going to blow up half of Islamabad while I was still in the area. You almost killed me with that damned play. So let's just call it even. I'll take off first thing tomorrow morning."

"I think not," Waleed said.

Hall paused for a moment. His head hurt. Time to change gears. "I can change your mind. Is that big guy that pulled me out of the car still around? Let me ask him a couple of questions about the team that was supposed to pick up Swanson."

"He is already being questioned in another room."

"Mine are a different kind of questions. Would you please bring him in here? At any rate, I want to thank him for saving my life."

Waleed was curious. He called for the agent, who came in, still shaken from the earlier action. His face also was bruised, but he managed a small smile when he saw Jim Hall rise and approach, holding out his left hand in a friendly greeting. The right hand held the ice.

Hall had rolled the ice tightly in the towel and twisted it into a solid ball. In a quick move, he uncoiled like a spring out of his relaxed position and smashed the unsuspecting Taliban agent in the face. It was nothing sophisticated, just an old-school straight-on unexpected beating. The force of the hurtling mass of cold cubes had the effect of a large hammer, and the first blow broke both the nose and the jawbone. As the muscular agent staggered, Hall hit him twice more, grabbed his collar, and flung him facedown on the floor. He flipped the towel out once, and the ice flew away in a spray of chunks. Hall wrapped the cold, thick, wet cloth around the stunned man's face, shoved a knee in his back, and yanked hard on the towel. The spine snapped with a loud, grating noise, and the body sprawled limp on the carpet.

Hall stripped out the .38 caliber snub-nosed revolver from a soft holster on the agent's belt, leaped from the corpse, and smashed the heel of his open hand into the chest of Selim Waleed. He rammed the short barrel into Waleed's ear, grabbed him by the throat, and pushed the young man hard, choking him even more.

"This is the other reason that you cannot and should not keep me here, Selim. Never forget how I cut my teeth in this game. I kill people, and I fucking own you and your daddy in more ways than you could possibly know. Show me that you understand that right now or I blow your Talib brains all over this pretty carpet."

Selim was terrified as he looked into the amazingly lifeless eyes of his co-conspirator. *He would do it!* Waleed shook his head rapidly to agree because he could barely breathe, much less speak.

Hall eased his grip, and an instant smile replaced the rocklike immobility of the bruised face. He tossed the pistol aside. "You okay?"

Waleed was aflame with anger but buried it inside. "I am fine," he said. He poured himself a final drink to gain some time gathering his wits. "Are you prepared to proceed?"

"Let's do it. Bring in the doctor."

25

Go! Get out! Where's Jim? Escape and evade. No way Hall could have survived that explosion. Up, Swanson. Quit dogging it! Move your ass out of here. Where did I get this AK-47?

Kyle's mind buzzed as the shock slowly wore off. He was grinding his teeth. The destruction spread before him like an enormous smoldering blanket. He shut his eyes, then reopened them, and things had not changed. The hood and mask had become a shield, and he was looking through his private window out onto a circle of hell.

A shadow ran by him. A man, running for his life . . . or toward something. Other movement. From the images taking form around him, Swanson began to piece together a logical pattern. He had made the kill shot, then he got out of the apartment and was chased cross the roof, then the car, then *boom,* and he didn't remember anything after that until now. Waking after a dream, a period during which his body had accomplished things his mind could not recall.

Leaning against the overturned car, he did a personal inventory and was convinced that somehow he had just come through this thing without any broken bones. He could breathe. He was wearing body armor. The AK-47 with its folding stock had fallen out of the trunk of the car. Yes. The emergency kit. The memory was coming back, and with it, the knowledge that he was still in great danger.

He forced himself to his feet and grabbed the black nylon emergency bag that lay beside him. It would contain medical supplies and saline solutions and water, maybe even some dried food, and it could all help him escape. The AK looked ready to go, if need be.

Putting his priorities in order took a few more moments as he stood, wobbling. *What about Jim?* Swanson oriented himself until he was facing down the boulevard, directly across the crater. Loose ammo was still cooking off, zipping randomly around and ricocheting off obstacles. The building where Jim Hall had been perched was nothing but an empty shell, with the entire front wall collapsed. Fire raked the remains. It was a Marine thing, to never leave a buddy on the battlefield. This time a rescue, even of a body, was impossible. Jim Hall had to be dead in that mess. Bodies were strewn everywhere. Ashes to ashes.

The wail of approaching sirens registered as his hearing returned, and he could hear people yelling. Screams. Cries. It was time to move. His first few steps were halting and zombie-like, but then the well-trained muscles reacted. Kyle Swanson began to walk away.

* * *

The pirated outfit he wore provided cover for hiding in plain sight. Swanson looked no different than any of the other cops, soldiers, and emergency personnel in the area. Many were stunned, just like him, and hobbled around aimlessly. Help was coming from all points, though, and the beams of flashing bright lights slashed through the hanging curtain of smoke and debris. The new arrivals were geared up for the emergency, and their hoods and hazmat suits lent even more credence to Kyle's disguise.

He was on the opposite side of the city from the only allies he could count on, the Marine Guard at the U.S. Embassy in the diplomatic quarter. They were on the eastern edge of Islamabad, but if he could get some more wheels, maybe he could reach the Kashmir Highway or Fourth Avenue or the big Rawal Lake and vector in from there. Remaining exposed in this critical situation would not work. Kyle decided to reach the embassy compound first and worry about the questions later.

Swanson stepped out of the street as a fire engine howled past; then he turned a corner to start a long loop around the stricken area. He had tunnel vision now, his entire sphere of existence beneath the protective hood, and a severely limited view through the goggles. He could hear his breath as the air was sucked through the filter. With every step, he felt stronger, more energetic, more aware. Uniformed men were hurrying everywhere, and no one gave him a second glance, the boxy emergency kit strapped over his shoulder adding to his appearance as a first responder.

He was jogging now, making progress, sweeping his

eyes over the terrain to look for threats and opportunities. He never saw the arm that tripped him and sent him sprawling on the ground. Swanson yanked his AK-47 semiautomatic rifle into position, rolled over, and pointed it. About three feet from the end of the barrel sat a child, a little girl no more than six years old, with a bloody cut above her ear, a filthy and torn black dress and ripped leggings, and tears of mud cutting through the grime on her cheeks. Her eyes were huge, but she was not staring at him. Her full attention was on a woman who lay facedown beside her, unconscious and partially covered by a pile of loose rubble. The child was crying and pulling on the arm of her mother.

Kyle registered the thought *No threat* and scrambled to his feet. This was not his problem. He was a trained killer, not a humanitarian aid worker. He had to leave. Now.

The woman coughed, and a small cloud of dust rose from her mouth. The little girl quit pulling the arm and jumped to the woman, brushing some hair away from the face and crying out a name. *Not my problem, dammit!* He hesitated, then turned his back on them and started to jog away again.

He stopped and looked back. The little girl finally gave him a heartbroken glance. Swanson stopped, turned, and walked back. *Okay. Just a minute to get this sorted out. Just do this one thing, quick, then I'm outta here.*

Swanson knelt beside her. She was in shock. He opened the nylon bag to get at the equipment, doused a large gauze pad with water, and gave her face a quick and gentle wipedown. She hardly knew he was there and continued pawing at her mother. Kyle began to whisper comforting sounds as he used another pad to clean away the blood above her ear. The ear bleeds a lot when it is cut, and that was the problem here. No scalp wound, just smeared blood. "Move over a little bit, honey. I'm here to help you. Let me look at Mommy," he said softly, nudging in close but not forcing the child to release her grip. She gave way. He handed her the rest of the bottle of water, and she made a choice, reached for it, and drank it all. "Good girl," he said.

The woman's dark eyes were open, fluttering, and she gasped for breath. Kyle checked her for major wounds, found none, and opened her mouth to clear the airway. She was coughing up phlegm and dirt, which meant that she was able to breathe, but she was totally disoriented. He felt safe speaking English because the hood of the mask muffled the sounds. Just soothing tones. "I got you now. You're going to be okay. Just relax. Your daughter is fine, too."

Standing up again, he began clearing away the spill of rubble that entrapped her. "Hold on, lady. I've got to move this stuff." Rocks and sticks and small chunks of concrete and dirt had been swept into a pile over her. She lay only a few steps from the front wall of an apartment house, which was heavily damaged, as if chewed by some monster. Still, it was a distance away from the explosion, and the main force of the blast had missed them as it was channeled elsewhere. The woman stirred, and when he cleared her legs, he saw a broken bone protruding through the flesh. "Damn," he said. He pulled the emergency kit over and dug out a small web belt with a buckle that quickly became a tourniquet around her thigh to stop the bleeding. She began to groan as consciousness returned, and Kyle used a couple of small sticks in the debris to fashion a crude splint.

He found another bottle of water and splashed her face, wiping away the grime with broad strokes. "There. That should hold you until help arrives." She blinked at the touch of cool water, and her daughter launched from beside Kyle and grabbed her mother in a tight hug. They smothered each other with love, but the woman suddenly tried to sit up and looked around wildly. She stared at the collapsed doorway that she apparently had just stepped from at the time of the explosion and screamed a name Kyle could not understand and began pointing, continuing to scream.

Somebody else! There's another kid there! Swanson dove away from the woman and frantically began to throw away debris that led back into the building's entry corridor. Suddenly, someone else, a young policeman, appeared at his side, also digging away at the obstacle. Behind them, Kyle heard someone talking to the woman, and several more uniformed men gathered and joined the search. *Pull away now! Let them do it!* He was about to release and go when his hand brushed flesh and he saw the hand of another child. He let out a shout, and the other men gathered to dig.

They had him free within thirty seconds, a boy who seemed about ten years old. The child was hauled out and laid beside the mother. Kyle stepped back, but the other men seemed frozen by the sight of the body. *Do CPR! Somebody get down there!* No one moved. Swanson went to his knees and pulled off his dirty gloves to clear the kid's airways, levering out some wads of dirt. He felt a faint pulse. When he looked up, the others were only watching. He nodded to them to take over. One soldier lit a cigarette. The mother screamed. The daughter cried.

If I do this, I will have to remove the hood and expose myself. Right now, none of them realize that I'm an American. Why doesn't someone get on this kid? It's not that hard. He made his decision, stood up, and slowly began to retreat. The rest of them began to drift away. The boy was dead, and there were other people needing help. Live people.

A hand grabbed his, and he looked down. The woman had her daughter wrapped in an arm and was clinging to Kyle with all the strength she could muster. She called loudly to him, *"Please!* Please help my son!"

At the sound of the English language, the other men stopped in their tracks and looked back at the mother, the little girl, the unconscious boy, and the man in the gas mask. Swanson knew it was over. The disguise was ruined. Fight or flight, now . . . or stay and help.

"Okay," he said, dropping his helmet, peeling back the hood and goggles, and throwing them away. "I'll do what I can." The men were moving closer, forming a circle. "Tell them to stand back while I help the boy," he told the woman, and she barked at the others. Kyle rummaged around in the nylon kit again, grabbed the CPR kit, and tore it open to reach the little plastic dome and tube. He positioned the mask over the boy's face, tightened the elastic strap for a snug fit, and began the process of resuscitation, alternating blowing into the tube and massaging the chest with powerful pressure from his crossed hands.

Time became irrelevant as he repeated the process, time and again, pausing only to feel the pulse. Something was blocking the passage. He pulled off the mask and rolled the boy over, hauling the child against his own chest and wrapping his arms around him. Once, twice, he pulled in suddenly and hard in the Heimlich maneuver, then a third time, and the boy gagged with a deathly sour groan and vomited a stream of mucus and dirt and a couple of small stones.

Swanson laid him down again and resumed the CPR, and within a minute the kid's eyes clicked open, dark and surprised, and he started hauling in air to fill his lungs. The woman screamed in wonderment and grabbed the boy in a tight hug, calling to Kyle, "Thank you! Thank you! Thank you!" Swanson sat back on his heels, exhausted. Several of the men clapped their hands and patted him on the back.

Kyle slowly raised his hands and placed the palms on his head. It was a new game now, back to being a Marine. Take a deep breath, stare directly ahead without expression, make no sound, and act totally unafraid. They were going to do whatever they were going to do, and if he had to die in this place, so be it. They would never see him scared.

It took only a moment before someone knocked him on the head with a rifle butt and he toppled over, seeing flashes of colors in the pain. They would be brave now and close in as a pack to have their fun, so cover up. He

brought his ankles and knees together hard, ducked his
head into his arms, and rolled into a tight ball as the
first kicks slammed into his kidneys and back, then
more rifle strikes pounded his arms and legs and head,
and cuts opened and blood flew out and there was a lot
of unintelligible noise and the woman screamed some
more, her pleas keening over the curses of the men who
were blaming him for everything that had happened on
that awful day, and Swanson could do nothing but take
the beating and let it all flow over him. He kept hoping
for the black sea of unconsciousness but could not find it.

26

Janetta Jones adjusted the red-rimmed glasses that perched near the tip of her nose. A thin African American woman with twenty years in the CIA administrative branch, she was a pleasant co-worker but slow to warm up to others. Everybody in the building was that way, so it had come as a surprise to her when she became friends with Lauren Carson. She wanted to buy Lauren a drink and have some girl talk. She was surprised when she found Lauren sitting at her desk with her head in her hands, looking lost.

Jones went into the office, closing the door behind her. "Are you okay, Lauren? You should be celebrating, girlfriend. Letter of commendation going in your file for bringing those prisoners back is a big deal. I'm buying you a drink tonight."

Carson pushed herself up straight, opened a desk drawer, and pulled out a small mirror. "I look like crap," she said. The eyes were serious.

"Right," Janetta said. "Most normal women would sell their favorite shoes to look as good as you do on your worst day. What's going on?"

Lauren dropped the mirror back and closed the drawer. Time for some major cosmetics. "I've just been summoned for an emergency internal review. Since I've already been debriefed about the prisoners, I guess it has to be about those explosions in Pakistan. No word from the team that went in yet. I don't know anything about what happened over there."

Janetta Jones had been around the Agency too long to try to dig for details. Jim Hall was probably involved in it somehow. Man about to retire goes off on a secret mission and gets himself involved in a crisis. Lauren, being his deputy, could catch some fallout. Then there was the emotional component. Lauren cared about Jim, and their affair had been no secret. It was impossible to keep that kind of secret within the walls of the CIA. "We're in a risky business," she observed.

Lauren was happy that Janetta had come in. The woman was almost an oracle, a walking encyclopedia of internal CIA mechanics.

"Just routine, so don't worry about it. I've seen it many a time before. Many a time," Jones said in a slow, soft voice. "I'm sure that it is just a SODD investigation. When something bad happens almost anywhere in the world, the CIA is usually held responsible until we can prove Some Other Dudes Did It. Getting blamed for everything is as much a part of this building as the elevators and the stones. Just who we are. What time is your interview?"

"Tomorrow morning. Meanwhile, I was told to make sure that the door to Jim's office is locked and that a special team will be sent along to secure and seal it until we hear from him. Nobody goes inside."

Janetta smiled. "So let's go do that. I'll witness for you. Then you go fix your face and we'll get out of here and go chase men."

Lauren stepped from behind her desk, picked up her purse, and glanced sideways at the glass window to check her reflection. "I'm a mess."

Janetta Jones rolled her eyes and turned away. "Yeah. Hideous. I'll make you an appointment with one of the company's plastic surgeons."

ISLAMABAD

General Nawaz Zaman of the Pakistani intelligence service said, "We have captured an American assassin and killed his partner." Then he tapped the spent embers from his cigar in an ashtray on his desk. The smoke coiled gray above it. His round face remained calm, but his eyes drilled into those of Daniel Silver, the SAC, or special agent in charge, of the U.S. Federal Bureau of Investigation's huge office in Islamabad.

Silver carefully measured his response. He had been so tightly focused on the massive explosions that had rocked the city that he had heard nothing of this. "I do not understand, General."

"It is simple, Special Agent Silver. Your country decided to come across the Afghan border once again without authorization in pursuit of the Taliban." He pointed out the window of his office. "Look and see what you have caused."

"That is an absurd accusation, sir."

"Perhaps, but it is also true." The general opened a file on his desk. "The man we have captured has been identified as Kyle Swanson, apparently a United States Marine sharpshooter of some renown. The dead one has not yet been identified." His eyes rose again to stare at Silver.

The FBI agent felt sweat beneath his armpits. "How do you know all of this?"

That brought a gruff laugh from Zaman. "Do you believe that you are the only investigators here? This is my country, Special Agent Silver, and we have put everything we have into finding out what happened here yesterday and what caused it. Our techniques can be quite different than your American standards, particularly in the wake of such an atrocity. We are quite comprehensive, and have numerous sources."

"Well, General, all I can say right now is that I am completely baffled by your statement, and completely unaware of any involvement by my country."

"Then let me give this file to you. From the rubble of an apartment house, we recovered two bodies with gunshot wounds to their heads. They were a pair of Taliban gunmen, according to our people. Some local police apparently heard the shots, just before the explosions, pursued this man Swanson, and eventually captured him."

Silver rubbed his knees, a sign of nervousness. "We want to interview him."

"Naturally. Have someone from your embassy contact the Foreign Office to arrange it." The ISI official slowly pulled on the cigar.

"No, General. I mean we need to talk to him right now, to begin our own investigation."

Zaman shook his head. "That is not possible."

"You refuse my request?"

"Not at all. I just want you to go through proper channels, Special Agent Silver. Enough of the cowboy stuff, doing whatever you want to and whenever you want to do it in our country. The government of Pakistan will cooperate, and in the proper manner. Meanwhile, Swanson stays where he is, in our protective custody."

"I will protest this with the ambassador."

Zaman waved away the complaint. "Fine. Meanwhile, if you want to do something productive, take a look at that envelope in the file. We have been unable to identify Swanson's accomplice. Police were closing in on him when the explosions began, and he was blown apart and buried. One of the officers managed to reach what was left of the body before fire consumed everything. He thought fast enough to use his knife and shear off a sample that should help identification through DNA and international police databases. We would appreciate the FBI putting its computers to work to help on this particular front, since we are overwhelmed at the moment."

Silver opened the big folder and found a smaller envelope, sealed, with something lumpy inside. He tore open the flap and removed a square, transparent ziplock bag. Inside was a human finger.

* * *

Jim Hall stood before the huge window in the spacious living room of the Royal Ocean Suite of the Jumeirah Beach Hotel, on the coast of Dubai. Maroon curtains flanked the impressive view of the water and the white yachts, while thin, sheer curtains cut the glare. His hand hurt.

He had flown from Islamabad International on a nonstop Emirates flight and, with his German passport, cleared customs on both ends without a problem. The customs officer in Dubai asked about the bandaged left hand and was satisfied with the explanation that much of his hand had been crushed by a falling stone in Islamabad, and then a finger had to be amputated, which was verified by a doctor's statement. A waiting limousine delivered him to the beautiful hotel.

Once in the huge suite, some 2,325 square feet of luxury, Hall took a shower, and paused while changing the bandage to examine the wound. The amputation had been clean, although after the finger was off, the edges of the severed digit were chopped and caked with dirt to make it look like an amateur job. With the mild sedatives, he had not felt much discomfort at the time, but as the anesthetic wore off, the pain visited. The doctor did a good job. Keep it clean and give it time to heal. He opened a bottle of pills and chewed two, washing them down with water. Then he used the gauze and tape to bandage it up again.

Retrieving his PDA from the pocket of the sports jacket he had worn on the trip, Hall slid into the armless gray chair before a table of shining light wood and opened the laptop computer that Lauren had left behind.

The hotel offered wireless Internet connections, and in less than a minute he was logged on to his account. The bank routing numbers that he kept on the PDA were pecked carefully into the appropriate formats, using only his right hand. His days of ten-finger typing were over, he thought.

One by one, he opened various accounts in various banks and investment houses, answered security questions, and used his right index finger like a spear to force the computer to do its job. He did not have to speak to a human during the entire process, which took less than thirty minutes. By then, he had cleared out every account he had ever established for the CIA, secret holding pens in which tens of millions of dollars had been stored to pay for covert operations over the years and never returned, although the funds technically had still been under CIA control.

No longer. Jim Hall emptied them all that afternoon, as if shaking a giant trash can of cash, and moved the money to new accounts under new names in new places that protected the identity of their investors. After receiving confirmations and safely logging those combinations of letters and numbers back into the PDA, he scrubbed and destroyed the computer hard drive. He shut the lid, walked to the window, and looked at the pretty people on the pretty boats on the pretty water. He was now one of them. Jim Hall was rich, and he did not miss his finger at all.

27

Kyle Swanson sat with his back propped against a stone wall, blindfolded and with his hands cuffed behind him. His ankles were bound together. Spots of wetness told him where he had been bleeding, but the cuts were insignificant. The boys out in the street had taken their own sweet time bringing him to a headquarters area. Once inside, the rifle butts and kicks had given way to slaps and being jerked around and dragged across a smooth linoleum floor. There was still an odor of smoke in the air. It had taken them long enough to catch him, Kyle thought with satisfaction. If he had just kept going and not helped that woman and her kids, who knows? He might be back at Bagram by now, having a cold soda. Didn't work out that way, but he was glad that he had stopped to save those lives. It was rare in his line of work to actually have an opportunity to do something good for someone else.

Now that they had grabbed him, Kyle knew he would be moved up the chain of command and out of the reach of the maddened soldiers on the street. He presented his captors with a problem, and killing him would not really solve anything. Swanson rotated his neck to get some relief from the tight muscles. A thin band of light showed beneath the blindfold, but he could not see anything. That, plus the smooth floor, indicated that he was probably secluded in an office somewhere, or an interrogation room, and not in some prison cell. Questioning would follow. Worrying would do no good, and wondering what might happen next would only lead to nightmare speculations. Shakespeare had written long ago that "present fears are less than horrible imaginings." Stay calm. Wait. Give the Pakis time to figure out who he is and what to do with him.

It did not take long. He heard the door open and boots stepping across the linoleum. Two sets of hands stood him up and removed the handcuffs and the blindfold, leaving the ankles hobbled. The room was small and rectangular, with an enclosed toilet area at one end. Kyle blinked in the sudden light, but it wasn't really bright, certainly not interrogation room bright. "Bathroom?" he asked. The two guards helped him move to the toilet and stood outside the open door while he urinated. He washed his hands and glanced into the mirror covering a small medicine cabinet. Filthy. Without asking, he left the water running and washed his face, too, sluicing the water into his aching eyes. Then he hobbled back out, and they put him in an ordinary folding metal chair.

Sitting three feet away was a bearded man in clergy robes, about forty years old, with dark eyes and dark skin, and a second man stood nearby, older, dressed in a suit. The second man spoke in clipped English. "This man is a revered imam in our city," he said. "His name will not be disclosed, but he has something to say to you."

Kyle kept his hands in his lap and watched carefully.

The cleric spoke in a low and slow voice that was choked with emotion. "I do not know who you are, other than that you are a soldier. And it is best for everyone that you do not know my name." The translation was brief, and Kyle nodded that he understood.

"Today, on this miserable day, Allah, praise be unto his name, held you in his palm, soldier. I do not know if you had anything to do with all of the destruction that has befallen us, but I suspect that you do, in some way. To determine that is the duty of others." The translation was made. Kyle was baffled and remained silent.

The imam pulled on his robes and paused, studying Kyle's face and torn wounds. "On this day on which so many people have died, you risked your own life to save my son, my daughter, and my wife. I came to this place to express my personal appreciation." Another burst of translation.

This time Kyle managed a small, embarrassed smile. "Are they okay? Did the boy pull through?" The translator worked rapidly and the conversation came faster, almost as if he were not present.

"Yes," replied the imam. "Once the obstruction was cleared from his throat and he started breathing, he recovered rapidly. My wife has a broken leg and two broken ribs. The girl needed some stitches to close her head wound, but she, too, is fine."

"I'm glad about that, sir."

"The other soldiers explained to me what you did. You are a very brave man. Your actions led directly to your capture."

"It was the right thing to do," Swanson said. "Given the same circumstances, I would do it again. Thank you for coming to see me."

The imam rose swiftly, and the robes fell smoothly into place. His posture was firm, as if he were used to carrying authority. "May Allah bestow his blessings and protection upon you, soldier. We will not meet again. While you remain in our country, as a prisoner or whatever your status, you will be treated well. You need not fear for your life. But when you leave, do not return."

Kyle also stood, somewhat unsteadily. Favor for a favor. "My thanks, sir."

The imam turned and left the room without another glance.

The interpreter went behind him, closed the door, and returned to where Kyle was standing. With the quickness of a snake, he slapped Swanson hard across the left cheek and sent him reeling back against and then over the chair and onto the floor. The cuffs went back onto his wrists, and he was roughly shoved back into the chair.

ALEXANDRIA, VIRGINIA

Lauren Carson awoke in the upstairs bedroom of her small town house on the fringe of Old Town Alexandria, a tight redbrick building that she had spent money and time to decorate just for her. The rooms were small but colorful and comfortable, and everything in the place was precise and so exact that when her alarm clock buzzed, the Mr. Coffee turned on and a Bose CD player smoothed into a Chet Baker album. The morning was good. She got into her sweats, drank some orange juice straight from the bottle, and then went for a run.

She would do only three miles this morning, for although there was no real hurry to get to work, she could not stand the feeling of being so cut off from information. No word from either Kyle or from Jim, the disaster in Islamabad—so much she did not know.

Back at the condo, she showered and hurried through her makeup, then pulled a freshly laundered dark blue pantsuit and a snowy white blouse from her closet. Comfortable black shoes with low heels. Credentials and weapon in her purse. Ten minutes later, she was in her Honda, sipping a Starbucks mocha latte and driving to CIA headquarters in Langley. The first thing on her schedule today was the SODD meeting to again go over the role she had played in Pakistan. That would be easy, because she had played no real role at all. Everything had happened around her, as if she had been at the end of a whipping rope, snapped by events. She wanted them to bring her up to date when the meeting was over. The idea of becoming a field agent in her next Agency posting, getting close to the excitement and action, had an inexplicable and undeniable attraction after helping Kyle get the American soldiers to safety. Lauren planned to suggest that she be sent back over to

Pakistan. At least she was friends with both of the major players in this drama, and both Jim and Kyle would accept her help before that of a CIA agent they did not know.

She walked into the small meeting room filled with confidence. Two men and one woman were already seated around a table, waiting for her, and another male agent had opened the door, then closed it behind her and took a seat beside it. Curious. None of the others rose, and their eyes were guarded.

"Have a seat, Ms. Carson," the man on the right directed. "I am Mel Langdon from the Department of Operations, and with me are Jack Pathurst from the Office of Security and Mia Kim from the Financial Department." When he stated "for the record" the date and time and place of the interview, Lauren had changed her mind about the nature of this meeting. It was being recorded. One thing she had learned from Jim Hall was that there are times to keep your mouth shut, and this seemed to fit that description.

"We are following up today on the previous statements you have made concerning your most recent trip to Pakistan," Langdon opened.

"My *only* trip to Pakistan," she corrected him.

There was a quick blink of his eyes and all friendliness was gone. "You reported that under the direction of Agent Hall, you transferred funds while you were in Islamabad, is that correct?"

"Yes. The account was set up for this specific purpose. We disbursed a total of five million dollars of the ten million authorized."

"And you countersigned the creation of the account?"

"Yes. Agent Hall was primary and I was secondary. There was nothing out of the ordinary on establishing and operating it. A standard covert account."

The agent from the Office of Security, Pathurst, spoke for the first time. "And how were the funds distributed? Personal check? Cash on the barrelhead?"

Lauren kept her temper, although they were playing with her. "I accessed and transferred the funds electronically."

"Does that mean that you used a computer?"

"Yes. My laptop, a Mac Pro."

"So you say that it was your laptop? That computer was your personal property, Agent Carson?" Pathurst was digging like a terrier for some subject she did not know.

"Agency issued in my name," she said. "I have used it for two years, and no, I never surfed for porn or went on eBay with it. It was used only for Agency business."

Pathurst's grim mouth twitched. The internal affairs man was unamused. "Do you have it in your possession now?"

"We covered all of this in the earlier interview," she said. "It hasn't changed. When Gunny Swanson and I escorted the American prisoners out of the hotel room, Agent Hall asked me to leave the computer behind. He is my boss, so I let him keep it."

"So the answer is no; you did not bring that Mac back with you."

It was a statement. Lauren was trying to keep her

wits together. "Are you people doing an inventory check? So I left behind a computer with my boss that cannot be used, or even accessed, by non-Agency personnel, at his request. That's what this is all about? You want me to buy a replacement?"

Ms. Kim, who had been silent from the start, glanced at a yellow legal pad. "No. We don't care about the computer itself. But we are curious about the funds. Ten million dollars was authorized. You confirm that you personally transferred five million of that amount while on the mission. Correct?"

"Yes."

"Then where is the remaining five million dollars, Agent Carson? That account now shows a zero balance, and was closed yesterday."

Lauren was startled by the announcement. "That would be unusual, but not impossible. Agent Hall would finish the accounting process personally after a mission was completed. Normally, he would wait until he was back at his desk here so he could put together a complete report. Ask him."

Mel Langdon shook his head. "We would love to, Ms. Carson, but Jim Hall is dead. He was killed in the explosions in Islamabad. The FBI gave us DNA and fingerprint confirmation overnight. Hall won't be confirming your story."

"Jim's dead?" The news was like a punch. "How? When?"

"Later," said Pathurst. "Stay with telling us about your computer."

"Ask Kyle Swanson, then."

"Swanson has been captured and is being held prisoner in Pakistan, and the two rescued soldiers have no recollection of seeing any computer at all."

Kim spoke. "You had the computer in Islamabad. You had all of the access and account codes. You claim that Jim Hall took it from you, but have no proof, not even a receipt of property transfer. And the account was cleaned out after your only alibi was killed."

"A receipt of property transfer?" Lauren's voice rose. "We were pulling a couple of American captives to safety from the Taliban in a hotel room and you think I should have taken time to jot out a transfer receipt and have Jim Hall sign it?"

"We think you should have followed established procedure," Ms. Kim said. "Now five million dollars has gone missing. It was last in your possession, you cannot explain what has happened, and your computer is conveniently missing."

"Yesterday I get a letter of commendation in my file and today you think I'm a thief, selling out my country to make a few bucks?"

Pathurst made a tent of his fingers and touched them to his chin. "We make no accusations whatsoever, Agent Carson. We wanted to alert you that an investigation is under way of all aspects of the mission to Pakistan. We have one agent dead, another American shooter in a Pakistani prison, an encrypted company computer missing, and five million dollars gone. Deserves an investigation, wouldn't you agree?"

"Of course." Lauren reined herself in. She wanted to shout and tell them how stupid they all were, but her training made her shut up. "My earlier statements stand, and I will cooperate in any way."

The man from the Security Office leaned forward on his elbows. "Good. That's what we wanted to hear from you. But pending completion of the investigation, you will be taking two weeks of authorized leave time, starting immediately. You will give our teams access to all of your personal data, computers, and accounts, as well as permission to search your home, vehicle, and personal possessions. Believe me, Agent Carson, full cooperation is the only way to go on this. Clear it up and get you back to work as soon as possible."

"The leave begins immediately?"

"Yes. Don't go back to your office. It has been sealed." Pathurst closed his folder. "Good day, Agent Carson. We'll be in touch."

28

The man who had been translating came close and spat in Kyle's face. Swanson flinched as the drool hit his right cheek and dripped down. Then came another slap, rocking him to the side. There was a chuff of quiet laughter from one of the guards. "You worthless dog. I would like to cut off your head and put it on a skewer! I am the warden here, but in my own prison, I am being given orders by outsiders. I am as handcuffed as you."

Kyle bent his head down to his chest and whispered, "Tough shit, asshole."

"What did you say? What did you just say?" the warden shouted. His facial muscles working with anger, he grabbed Kyle by the hair and yanked his head straight. Swanson lobbed a gob of spit right into his face.

"I called you an asshole."

The warden jumped back in disgust, and one of the guards popped Kyle on the ear. This time Swanson rolled to the floor and pulled his legs to his chest as if curling into a fetal position. The guard advanced, and when he transferred his weight to his left foot, Kyle

kicked out hard with both feet and caught him just below the left knee. The bone snapped, and as the guard
fell, Swanson whipped up and drove a shoulder into the
second guard, who bounced off the wall with the wind
knocked out of him.

In doing so, he had turned his back on the warden,
giving the man time to hit an alarm button. The door
flew open, and more guards poured inside and quickly
pinned Swanson to the floor. The warden grabbed a
riot baton from one of them and moved toward the immobile American, his whole body shaking with fury.

Kyle closed his eyes and prepared to take the strike,
but it never came.

From the doorway, someone uttered the quiet order
of *"No!"* and Kyle saw the imam standing there, with
his dark eyes freezing the warden in his tracks. "Dis-
obey me again and it will mean your life." The voice
was cold and lifeless and certain.

The warden dropped the baton on the floor, wiped
the phlegm from his face with a sleeve, and panted as if
he had just run a mile. He fell back into his chair. "Very
well. So be it," he said to the imam. "There will be no
problem, Excellency." He spoke to the guards. "Put that
piece of filth in the cell. At least his partner was killed.
We can let the politicians deal with this one."

Kyle was hauled down an interior stairwell to a corridor of dank concrete. A row of four metal doors was on
each side of the central access hallway. He was pushed
into the little cell at the right rear by a quartet of guards.

They wasted a lot of time uncuffing his wrists and untying his feet before backing out carefully while keeping him at gunpoint, ready for another attack.

In the dim light, Swanson had ignored them in order to take a good look at his new home and take some mental snapshots. Everything that had happened in the room upstairs was now irrelevant; that was history. What he could do in the next few moments was critical to survival. There was no exterior window, so he set the door as the root of a mental map-clock that he instantly created in his head. If his back was to the door, then he was at the six o'clock position, facing the rest of the clock. Directly across at twelve, rivulets of water seeped down the rear wall and fed into a puddle along the edge. To the right of the door, along the three o'clock wall, a dirty and thin mattress lay on the floor, with a set of thin tie-up trousers and a pullover tunic folded on it. A bucket was in the most distant corner, to be used for his waste. The nine o'clock wall was blank concrete, scribbled and scratched by earlier prisoners.

The door slammed shut and a lock fell into place, followed by a sliding sound of metal across metal as a narrow gap was closed just above the floor—the food slot. Darkness enveloped everything, and the place reeked of death; men who had been imprisoned in this place before him had died here.

Swanson found the mattress, lay down, and closed his eyes. He had things to do but was totally exhausted after the long hours of planning, action, and capture. If they weren't planning on beating him anymore, at least he could get some rest. Just a catnap. *Hell of a day,* he thought and was instantly asleep.

ALEXANDRIA, VIRGINIA

Jack Pathurst from the CIA Office of Security turned up the collar of his dark blue windbreaker and pulled down the blue baseball cap against a drizzle of rain that was giving the entire D.C. area a good soaking. The trees were not in their autumn colors yet, and the water emphasized the healthy green of the landscaping around the redbrick town house complex in which Lauren Carson lived alone. He would direct the search today, and if he turned up anything suspicious, anything at all, he would burn Agent Carson to the ground. Pathurst had neither tolerance nor sympathy for renegade agents.

Using the key that she had provided, the Security operative opened the white front door. He held the crew behind him outside until he did a walkthrough on his own. He wanted to see it fresh, before his locusts moved in to graze and tear it apart. The first impression was not that the place was neat, which it was, which would be typical of her southern upbringing; it was that the condo was a perfect match for Carson's rank and salary. There was nothing showy, nothing to indicate that she had been on the take. Most rogues spend large; why else steal?

The place echoed as he walked through the living room. No animals, reptiles, or fish. Family pictures on a small mantelpiece above a miniature fireplace. He peered back through the fresh white curtains at his people who were waiting in the rain, then stepped into the kitchen. Tight quarters, small refrigerator, standard apartment over-and-under microwave and stove. The cabinets were of light pine. Everything was dusted and clean. Enough fruit was in a bowl to cover the bottom, and the fridge was almost bare, but for some bottled water and a container of fettucine mixed with Parmesan. Nothing to sour or go rotten, an indication that she did not eat here much. He reminded himself to look for restaurant receipts.

Up the stairs, white railing and soft carpet, to a pale yellow bedroom and bath combination that occupied the entire narrow second floor. Two slender windows with white trim and matching shades pulled down an exact matching distance. There was gloom outside the glass, and rainwater trickling down it, but inside, an easy scent of potpourri and the colors created warmth. Bed made. Clothes in order, folded on shelves or hanging in a neat row. Even the damned shoes were lined up in matched pairs or in hanging plastic sheaths. Neutral colors for all furniture. The kind of place you would live comfortable and leave just as easily. Typical Agency anal-compulsive personality, he thought.

A couple of books were on a bedside table—a thick biography of Thomas Jefferson and a paperback romance novel. A blank legal pad and a couple of pens lay atop her personal computer, the corners squared. The computer was not in sleep mode but had been turned off. How neat can you be?

He opened the drawers of the dresser. Nothing out of the ordinary. No condoms or birth control devices, and no sign of a boyfriend. Oddly, he thought, there were few personal pictures of Carson. A beautiful woman usually has to be reminded that she is beautiful, if only by herself. Had she moved beyond that? Confidence as a professional.

The apartment did not talk to him. It was bland, lower middle class, and totally average in every way. Pathurst trotted back downstairs and set free the search teams. *Well, Ms. Carson, let the games begin.* Things were too right here. Nobody lived with such perfection. There was gold in here. Pathurst could smell it.

ISLAMABAD

Kyle was walking up to the back screen door at Flo's Hot Dogs, a low building of weathered wood in Cape Neddick, Maine. He had been going there for so long that they knew him, and he never had to wait in the long line of tourists that wound out the front door. He peered inside. The counter was busy, and steam rose from the kettles. When he called out a greeting, a welcoming shout came back. "Hey, Kyle. How many today?"

"Two guys with me, so make it seven dogs, sauce and mayo on all of them."

"You got 'em."

The first time he had gone to Flo's had been with other kids from the orphanage, aboard a rattling old school bus from the summer camp. As Kyle grew up, the little out-of-the-way restaurant remained a summertime standard for him. As a surfer and as a Marine, he always brought his pals to eat there, usually just as an excuse for returning himself. He regarded those early visits as his only really good childhood memories.

The food came out stacked in folded cardboard boxes, each hot dog wrapped in a napkin. The buns were large with square bottoms, and the steamed dogs had crisp outer skins and were coated with Flo's relish, the recipe for which was a secret right up there with McDonald's special sauce and the Coca-Cola formula. He washed them down with two small cartons of chocolate milk.

He and his friends would sit at one of the few plank tables outside beneath the big trees, with their surfboards sticking out of their cars like wooden sails and the sharp wind blowing through the shade, the sure sign of a New England fall. Best hot dogs in the world. Some kinda good, as they said around Cape Neddick.

The dream vanished in an instant when little feet ran halfway across his chest and stopped. Kyle jerked awake, angry that it had been ruined just as he was enjoying the exploding flavors. A rat was checking him out. He swatted it hard, and the furry body thunked against the concrete wall with a squeal of pain. The water in the cell drew the rats, and he heard them running around the space, alert to the foreign presence and sniffing to determine whether it was threat or food.

He came to a sitting position on the mattress. At least his captors had let him keep the boots, which meant that his toes would not be bitten. He found the pajamas and stood to change into them, then sat down again, shifting slightly to be in the corner. Rats ran around.

Time was passing, and he did not know how much because the catnap that he had wanted had turned into a deep slumber. While he awoke refreshed, he had lost track of the one thing he most desperately wanted to keep a hold on. Still, he had things to do.

The smelly cell was completely blacked out, but he had already reconstructed it in his mind, so light was not an imperative need. He got up and walked clockwise all the way around the room, feeling the wall with his fingertips. Okay, back at the door again. Feel it. Give it a little shove. It was rusty but strong, and when he checked the hinges, he was able to confirm the initial memory. Because the corridor outside was so narrow, the cell door opened inward and to the right. *If I scramble over there and get behind it when I hear them unlocking it, I can use it as a battering ram against whoever comes through first.* Swanson measured it in hand-widths and then stood against it and put his hand atop his head, slowly raising it to the top edge. He was five-nine, so the door was about six and a half feet high, and no more than three feet wide.

Then he paced off the cell, side to side, corner to corner, and logged it all away on the checkerboard that he was assembling in his brain.

29

Major General Brad Middleton arrived back at his office with a full head of steam, as if he were looking for a wall to smash through, and muttering many unkind things about former congressman Bobby Patterson, the president's chief of staff. He marched directly to the E-Ring and the office of General Hank Turner, the chairman of the Joint Chiefs and the former head of the Marine Special Operations Command. Turner was waiting in the big, sunlit office along with Admiral Ted Johnson, the chief of naval operations, and General Buck Manchester, the Marine chief, who was technically Middleton's boss. A rainbow of flags on poles was displayed behind them. Middleton saluted.

"The White House is throwing us under the bus," the Task Force Trident commander declared after being told to be at ease and take a chair. "Bobby Patterson shredded the presidential directive that authorizes Trident and has put the CIA in charge of sorting out the Pakistan mess."

The other generals traded glances. "Does the president know about this?" asked Admiral Johnson.

"I honestly don't know. Patterson sets the agenda over there, and he would not answer that question."

Turner was pacing the room. "What do you think, Admiral?"

"Sounds like Patterson is using the opportunity as another attempt to screw the military."

"Buck? You've got a PhD in international relations. How do you read it?"

"It is moving much too fast for precipitate action of any sort, General," replied the Marine chief. He had a question, too. "Brad, were there any witnesses to this exchange between the two of you?"

"Yessir. CIA Director Geneen was right there. As usual, he was quiet as a tomb."

Hank Turner was a thoughtful man, and he walked around his office listening to his subordinates discuss the problem. He occasionally would drop a question. He stopped pacing, and the others turned. "One thing, Brad. What's this crap about you resigning?"

"I offered to step aside rather than let Trident go down the tubes. Patterson refused. He wants to keep me in the military chain of command, and therefore silent on the situation. As if I would talk to the press."

"Well, at least he did one thing right. I'm not going to let you resign either."

Middleton scratched his crew-cut hair. "All right, sir."

General Turner resumed pacing, ticking off items on his fingers as he spoke. "We know that Jim Hall was killed. FBI confirmation on that. Kyle Swanson is a prisoner. Again, an FBI confirmation. Bobby Patterson has hit the panic button. The CIA is taking control of what started off as a covert military operation, thereby cutting us out of the loop. My final question to you, Brad, is: Did Swanson spark off those explosions?"

"Absolutely not, sir."

Admiral Johnson stroked his chin as he considered the situation. "How can you say that with any certainty?"

"Sir, we know exactly, repeat *exactly,* the time that Swanson pulled the trigger. He reported in just after he did it. His job after that was to escape and evade, which he would have done in utmost silence. The man moves like a shadow, Admiral. He may have set a booby trap to delay pursuit and misdirect attention, but nothing that would be guaranteed to bring the entire Pakistani army and police force down on his head. On top of that, the explosions did not begin until almost five minutes after he pulled the trigger on the tango. Our men on the scene said that dozens of uniforms were chasing Swanson by then. This is not the kind of thing he would do, particularly when it would cause so many civilian casualties."

General Manchester also had been soaking in the unfolding situation, mulling the possibilities. "I agree. Blowing up something that big is not what any Marine sniper would do on a mission."

"Nor a SEAL Team," added the admiral. "Just because they *can* do it does not mean they *would* do it."

Hank Turner made up his mind. "We are kind of stuck between a rock and a hard place for right now, until we see what the Pakistanis do with Swanson. I intend to meet personally with the president about Patterson, an unelected bureaucrat, intervening in the chain of command. Meanwhile, General Middleton, you get back to work."

"Any instructions, sir?"

"Yeah, Brad. Support our man in the field."

ISLAMABAD

Once, over a pitcher of beer at the Stumps, a little tavern outside of 29 Palms, California, Jim Hall had allowed that Albert Einstein had truly been a pretty smart old duck. "Albert was trying to explain his Theory of Relativity to some dumb-ass, probably some Air Force fighter jock," Hall said, "so he dreams up a comparison. Sit with a nice girl for two hours, and it only seems like a minute. But if your ass hits a hot stove for a minute, you're going to think it is two hours. Albert was talking relativity, but he nailed the way a sniper has to think about time. No highs, no lows. Just smooth it all out. Slow is smooth, and smooth is fast. Remember that, young Skywalker, and you will do well."

Kyle Swanson recalled the conversation as he pushed through a set of isometric exercises in his prison cell and tried to figure out the time. The hit on the tango happened just as the sun went down, then all of the other stuff happened, and that had soaked up more hours. He figured the entire night had passed, but with the unknown factor of how long he had slept, he could not be certain.

Another rat ventured onto his thigh, and enough was enough. Games were a good way of passing idle time. Snipers and spotters even played games while on a mission. He picked up the adventuresome rat with his bare hands, wrung the neck, and tossed the worthless carcass to its friends on the far side of the cell.

"Nothing happens eighty-five percent of the time on a mission," he told the rats quietly. "So you have to amuse yourself to stay awake. That's why we play games. Layin' there, just keeping watch on the target for hour after hour, gets pretty damned boring. So I say to the other guy, 'Let's spot dogs,' and then I find a dog and the spotter has to match me. Then we do the goats and the other animals. And women. Always checking out the women. But it's more than just a game because it keeps you vigilant and tuned in, you understand?"

While he explained what was happening, Kyle tied a sleeve of his discarded uniform shirt into a tight knot at the cuff and began using it occasionally to snap the curious rodents. Sometimes he hit them, sometimes he didn't, but they sensed the danger and hugged the far wall and the trickling water. "Everybody stake out a place," Kyle said, "and stay there. I'm the biggest and meanest alpha rat you guys have ever seen, so keep the hell out of my way."

He was thinking that if worse came to worst, they could be a food source. And there was the dripping water on the wall. He could last for a while in here. Smooth out the time.

WASHINGTON, D.C.

This was not what Lauren Carson had expected when she called the secret telephone number that Kyle had slipped to her while they were spiriting the captured soldiers away in Islamabad. When a gruff voice announced that she had reached the 179th MRE Research, Development, and Tasting Brigade, she thought she had the wrong number, but when she mentioned the name of Kyle Swanson, the tone of the voice changed immediately. "Hold while I get his boss." The crisp voice of a woman came on the telephone next, carrying the slightest hint of urgency. Lauren identified herself as being the CIA agent who was with Swanson in Pakistan.

"Do not say your name on this connection," stated the strong voice. "Did anything change recently in your personnel file?"

"Yes," Lauren replied. "It was confidential, and I can't talk about it."

"A letter of commendation for the extraction of the two captives."

Lauren paused. Whoever this was had access to her personal CIA file. "I'm in some trouble, and Kyle said I should call this number if I ever needed help. I need help, and I cannot very well come to any office at the Pentagon. I think someone may be following me."

"From your shop?"

"Yes. Can we meet somewhere?"

There was a pause. Then the woman said, "Drive out to Tysons Corner in McLean. I will meet you at Burgers and Burgers. Order something and grab a table. Soon as you can make it."

"Wait! How will I recognize you?"

"You won't. But I have your picture right in front of me, and the latest driver's license photo. I think I can pick you out of a crowd. I will be there in about an hour."

"What's your name?"

"Tysons Corner. One hour." The call terminated.

Lauren kept her eyes moving to the mirrors as she drove around Washington on busy Route 495, the Capital Beltway. She saw a lot of cars, vans, and trucks of every description but nothing that lingered as possible followers. Since the Silver Line of the Metro was still under construction and did not reach the expansive shopping complex, some sort of car would be required to keep her under surveillance. Or, she thought, a truck, a motorcycle, helicopter, airplane, or satellite. *Getting paranoid, girl?*

By the time she found a parking place, looked at guides to the many different stores and shops in the regional supermall, and hiked to the hamburger cookery, the hour was almost up. She went to the counter and ordered a cheeseburger, and was surprised at how all of the cooks and servers yelled at each other and even across the restaurant to call out orders. No microphones, just shouts. Combine that with the conversation of the customers, who also had to talk loudly in order to be heard over the bawling of the crew in the candy-striped shirts, and you had a place with the noise level of a small indoor football stadium. People who had put in orders and were waiting for the food stood around idly reading or just killing time. Lauren found a napkin and took a handful of peanuts from a bucket, then sat at a small table. She looked at her watch. An hour and five minutes had passed.

Her number was shouted, and she went to pick up the order. Another woman was sitting at the table, nibbling a peanut, when she returned. Jet black hair cut just below the collar, lithe, with piercing dark blue eyes. Tight black jeans and sneaks, and a dark, overlong Abercrombie & Fitch T-shirt. "We spoke. Let's go," the woman said. "Dump the greaseburger on the way out or your hips will pay the price."

Lauren left with the stranger, who casually guided her to the nearest exit in silence. A midsized motor home was at the curb, with its diesel engine purring. The sandy brown and cream paint scheme was faded and unwashed, and the right rear had a big dent; altogether, it was the epitome of a worn old road warrior needing some serious restoration work and better care. The woman opened the door, and they both climbed in. The vehicle was moving before the door was shut.

"Okay now, Agent Carson. Welcome aboard," the stranger said. "I'm Major Sybelle Summers, the Trident ops officer. That big guy at the wheel is Master Gunny Dawkins, and this little geek with the Coke-bottle glasses is Lieutenant Commander Freedman, our intel chief.

What's going on?" Both of the men wore blue jeans, with loose shirts hanging over their beltlines.

Lauren wasted no time. She took one of the comfortable swivel seats and faced Summers. "We have to help Kyle."

"We intend to," replied Summers, with a smile that did not reach her eyes. "What do you have in mind?"

Lauren looked around at the traffic and realized the RV was doing a slow loop of the perimeter roads around the supermall. "Do you think we're being followed? Can anyone overhear our conversation?"

"No, you're not being followed, Agent Carson. Commander Freedman was in the burger joint when you arrived, I was watching from the security office, and our driver was roaming the area. Nothing suspicious. And no one is listening because we have jamming devices and shielding in this old buggy. Now talk to me, Lauren. Kyle Swanson is our buddy, part of our team. Tell us what we can do to help you." Summers had decided to go the personal route, and it worked.

To Lauren Carson, Major Summers was both very competent and believable. Once she decided to trust them, the words came out in a rush: the Islamabad experience with Jim Hall and the Taliban politician, Kyle's stern behavior in changing the entire mission on the spot to get the soldiers out, the unexpected catastrophic explosions, and then the start of the CIA inquisition and her two weeks of mandatory leave.

"A serious discrepancy has already turned up in their internal investigation. A covert bank account was cleaned out yesterday, five million dollars, based upon codes and commands known only to myself and Jim Hall. I didn't do it, so that means that Jim did! The problem is it happened after Jim supposedly was killed. They have to blame somebody, and pointing the finger at a corpse doesn't work. So they are leaving me to be the scapegoat."

"The withdrawal came after the fact," said Freedman, just to be sure of the point.

"Yes." Lauren opened her purse. "Here's the zinger. That was hardly the only covert account to which my old boss Jim Hall had access. He had worked for the Agency for many years, and I know of at least twenty others because he had my name on those, too. Jim never actually returned money to the general funds, and the Agency watchdogs knew it. It was already authorized and approved through proper channels, so if a couple of million was needed for some really off-the-books operation, Jim could supply it. Untraceable, with no questions asked."

The RV continued its journey to nowhere. The parking lot at Tysons Corner could handle 165,000 vehicles, and traffic was always coming and going. Perfect civilian cover. Sybelle looked at Freedman. This CIA agent's story, wrapped with their own timeline about how Swanson could not have been responsible for the explosions, seemed to jell. "We also think it was a setup. Your superior, Jim Hall, is feeding both you and Kyle to the wolves."

A stricken look came across Lauren Carson's face. "I'm going to be friggin' executed," she said. "I'm a loose end. Kyle is the only one I can really trust, because

he knows Jim Hall even better than I do." She unfolded a
sheet of paper that listed the series of financial institu-
tions and account numbers that she had culled from another computer workstation before leaving Langley.
"I've got this information, but getting into those systems
for confirmation and status reports is beyond my technical ability. The Agency has people who do just that kind
of thing all the time."

"So do we," Summers told her. "Lizard, do your
thing."

Lieutenant Commander Freedman spread his fingers,
like a concert pianist warming up, and ran both hands
through his thick black hair. He opened the wooden
cabinets along the left side of the RV and tossed out several bags of dry cereal. With the touch of what looked
like a light switch, the plywood backing and single shelf
folded forward to reveal a multiscreen computer center.
Green dots of light indicated the power source was on.
"Let me give it a try," he said, adjusting a rolling chair
into position.

ISLAMABAD

This was as boring as sketching. Kyle hated drawing—
going into a target zone prior to a main assault and
sketching everything around in complete detail in a
little notebook. The observations would be molded into
the other intel gathered by other means, and the attack
would proceed. Drone airplanes and their sharp cameras had taken over a chunk of that overall task, but

airplanes, by definition, stay in the air. Men on the ground bring a much different perspective. A pilot twiddling a joystick hundreds of miles away to guide a drone would never have the same outlook. It just took so much time, being completely hidden and still except for drawing and measuring things with lasers before you could go kill somebody. Some of the same techniques of waiting could be applied to enduring the passing time in a prison.

He popped the shirt knot twice, but without enthusiasm, just to keep the rats on their toes and awake and alert and fearful. He spoke to them. "There was this one time, guys, talk about being bored, I crawled into an abandoned building about six hundred yards from the actual home of this dude who was the big leader of a rebel force in an African country. Can't tell you which one. Sorry about that, but it's classified. Stayed there forty-eight hours, clicking away pictures with my Nikonos and narrating on the radio about who came, who left, their tendencies, how much security they had, when they slept, you guys know, the usual stuff. The guy thought he was safe, but I was living in his front yard . . ."

There was a sound outside the door, and Swanson stopped his conversation with the rodents. He had been expecting it, sooner or later, so his heart did not go into overdrive. With a squeal of metal, the grate at the bottom of the door slid open, and a plastic plate with some food and tea was passed through. The bluish green light in that brief moment was from the fluorescent lights in the long hall, which told him nothing. The grate was left open, so he was expected to eat and return the plate, two beverage containers, and plastic fork.

None of the rats had a watch. He had asked them. Now his jailers had provided the start of a feeding pattern, allowing his internal time to click to zero. Swanson began counting seconds, adjusting his thoughts to let the silent little metronome in his brain begin twitching back and forth on such a regular basis that he could do two things at once. When he picked up the plate to determine which meal of the day it was, he gave a soft laugh. No problem; it was breakfast, of a sort. The imam had been at work again, determined that Swanson would have familiar food, and Kyle thought that might have been a mistake. Instead of a regular large Pakistani breakfast, the cook had tried to prepare an American meal. Swanson had been given runny scrambled eggs, a couple of slices of charred toast slathered with honey, and a cup of sweet black tea and milk. No matter. This was survival, and he ate it all, while at the same time using a prong of the plastic fork to punch a little hole in his shirt. Then he pushed the plastic and paper back through the hole. Someone picked it up and closed the grate.

Darkness again, only this time with a difference. He worked on his timeline, his boring, tedious, glorious timeline. More than just a count, it gave him something to do, something to think about to keep his psyche engaged. The count was already up to almost ten minutes, piling higher second by second. The strike had been at evening prayers on Tuesday, so this was Wednesday morning, breakfast time. Sixty seconds to a minute. Three thousand six hundred seconds to an hour.

Swanson's fingers had already widened the hole he had punctured in the tunic, and when the hour mark passed, he made a small rip along one edge. The shirt was now a physical clock. He could keep time, counting down to the next feeding time. It was a routine that he could do for days if necessary.

He leaned back against the wall with a sigh, gently touching the rip. One hour. There was no such thing as an indefinite mission. Each operation had an end time, and a purpose. This didn't.

30

Crisp morning light slanted through the blinds covering the bullet- and soundproof windows in the private interview room on the second floor of the CIA headquarters. Despite the glare, the faces of the three investigators on the Agent Lauren Carson case were dark, betraying their emotions. Jack Pathurst, the internal investigator from the Office of Security, had a muscle twitching in his jaw. Mia Kim from Finance had a pursed mouth, as if she had eaten something sour. Team leader Mel Langdon of the Department of Operations adjusted his rimless glasses and looked over the report one more time.

"She has not returned to her home since our meeting yesterday?" Langdon asked Pathurst.

"No." He did not say that there was nothing for her to return to. His searchers had torn the place apart— stripped out the insulation in the attic and pulled up the floorboards, sliced apart the stuffed furniture, tore down cabinets, and took out drains. In the wall of the bedroom, behind the headboard of the bed, they had found a half million dollars in cash, along with a gun and a fake passport. Pathurst edged close to the table and propped his elbows on it, resting his chin on his fists and just staring at the others for a few moments. "She has to know that we found her hidden stash, so she won't be going back." Jack Pathurst enjoyed his job. "I am afraid we fucked this up."

Langdon exhaled heavily. "And all you found was a plastic trash bag filled with money, a gun, and fake ID? That was a little convenient, don't you think? Carson was trained as a CIA agent, and you believe she would leave her getaway pack where you could find it so easily?"

"The point is, Mel, that we *did* find it. And we're still looking through her personal records. If she has more out there, we will get that, too."

Mia Kim cleared her throat before speaking. "We also discovered that bank account in Argentina that we traced directly back to Agent Carson. There is no question about the identity of the person who has sole access to it. It belongs to her."

Pathurst asked, "How much is in it?"

"Another half million, plus or minus," Kim said.

"That's another fact, Mel. Not a guess."

"And also pretty easy to find. Sloppy work, and Agent Carson is not a sloppy person."

Langdon was gliding through the motions, certain that this was going to be off of his desk soon and over to the lawyers for prosecution. He wanted to be right before passing it along. No blowback. "Nevertheless, just what you have uncovered thus far gives us enough to throw the book at her. Her career here is over, and she probably is facing a prison term. She has to know that."

"Agreed," said Pathurst. "The sooner we arrest her, the better."

Langdon did not want to take the final step. "Jack, I have been conducting internal investigations for many years, and we have to be careful. I'm not ready to file charges."

"Mel, dammit, we are CIA and we don't have to file anything! I say we should pick her up right away. Carson knows what can happen, just how deep we can make someone disappear. Faced with a grind of enhanced interrogation at some third world hellhole, she'll fold in a minute."

Mia Kim broke in. One hand rested on the arm of her chair, and she was gently tapping the table with her other fingers. Nervous energy. "Jack, I also don't like sudden gifts from the angels when doing an investigation: sacks of money and phony bank accounts. We should have had to unravel a lot more fronts and dodges before getting to that point. No doubt that she is involved in something, but we don't know what, or whether she knows anything about it."

Jack Pathurst examined them both with curiosity rather than alarm. The normal reaction should have at least been some outrage, but Langdon and Kim were dithering. "All the more reason to get her in here. I have agents checking area hotels and motels because she had to spend the night somewhere. I need your permission before asking for police help. We can have every cop on the streets looking for her within an hour."

"That risks going public," Langdon said. "Not a good idea."

"Mel, I can get this girl. She's just a beauty queen, not a real field agent. She is out there on her own and without resources. I will get her and throw her down a well until she tells us what we need to know. There is no downside to snapping up one of our own agents. I don't understand why you are hesitating."

Langdon pushed away from the table and stood, shoving his hands into his pockets. "It doesn't pass the smell test, Jack. You're wrong to think of Lauren Carson as just a pretty face. She's tenacious and very smart. She has already proven that, because you do not have her in custody already. Carson saw an opportunity to get away yesterday after that first meeting, and she snapped it up."

Pathurst remained silent. It was true. He had been concentrating on the search rather than being ready to take Carson off the street. She should have been considered guilty until proven innocent, not the other way around, but she had walked out on authorized leave, with no one following her. Now she was gone.

"No matter what the situation, Carson has answers or at least information that we need. We cannot ignore the facts," Kim said. "We need her to talk. I don't like it, but Jack is right."

"I know. I know." Langdon picked up the papers. This was turning into a serious situation, and Carson was right in the middle of it all. "Very well, Jack. Go find her. Use whatever you need, but keep it quiet. Word gets out, and there will be sexy pictures of her wearing a tiara all over the TV, and she will be identified as a rogue CIA agent forever."

ISLAMABAD

Kyle Swanson was startled by new noises outside his prison door. Not the normal pattern that preceded the usual feeding and waste disposal, but the scuffle of multiple boots and voices made dull and distant by the concrete and steel. He rose from the mattress, straightened his outfit, turned to the wall, and shielded his eyes as a key was inserted in the lock and turned. The burst of light still hit him like a thrown rock.

Then came some yelling, and strong hands grabbed his biceps and legs. He did not resist. Handcuffs and leg irons were put in place. He kept his eyes tightly shut against the harsh light when they spun him around and someone shined a bright beam directly into his face. An order was snapped, and the unseen hands pulled him forward, his stumbling steps measured exactly by the length of the ankle chain. Swanson went with the motion. The air in the tunnel hallway was fetid, but almost fresh in comparison with the stale odor of his cell, where there was no circulation. Hot and stuffy in the day and cold at night. He heard the metallic racking of a guard cocking a pistol. They were taking no chances with him.

At the staircase, the guards on each side lifted him up so his toes could catch the next higher step, then repeated the process sixteen times until they reached the landing that led into the main floor of the prison. Kyle opened his eyes during the climb and allowed the dungeon shadows to help adjust his sight for the onslaught of light he knew was coming. His breath was slow and measured, and his pulse was normal.

Through one door, across a room, then another door, and he recognized being back in the warden's suite of offices. The warden stood beside a window, taking obvious pleasure in observing the filthy condition of his prisoner.

Another man rose from a chair when Swanson was brought in. He was tall and fit, with neat gray hair and a lightweight blue suit with a striped tie. *Every inch a diplomat,* Kyle thought, realizing his own garments were ragged and his body stank. He had not had a bath since being captured.

When the man spoke, it was with a flat Ohio accent. "Please leave us alone for a while, Warden. And please remove the restraints."

"You may have all of the time you need, Mr. Riles, but the restraints remain in place. This man is very dangerous."

"Not to me."

"To everyone," the warden insisted, leading his men from the room. "Do not be too long."

Alone with Kyle in the room, the American spoke. "Let me help you to a chair, Gunny Swanson. Get you a glass of water? My God, man, you look terrible."

"Thanks," Kyle said, drinking the clean, clear water in a couple of gulps and holding out the glass for a refill, which he also drained. "Who are you? State?"

"Yes." He fished out a wallet with his State Department identification. "Dean Riles, deputy chief of mission. We have been battling to get to see you since the capture, but the Pakistani government has been dragging its heels because of the damage in Islamabad."

"I had nothing to do with those explosions," Kyle said. "I promise that it came as as much of a surprise to me as anyone."

Riles sucked in a breath. "Still, it has been awful. The government is still reeling, but somehow it is holding on despite the unrest throughout the country. Now, how have they been treating you? Your shirt is in rags."

"Three hots and a cot, sir. Not really, but I've been through worse. Solitary confinement in a basement cell with no light or heat. There have been no beatings because I apparently have an influential friend." Swanson let his gaze wander around the room and to the warden's desk. A digital clock told him it was a little before noon, just about what he had guessed. He could start counting again when he went back downstairs.

"Your friend has worked hard in your behalf. That brings me to the second reason for my visit today." Riles opened his leather briefcase and took out a file. "Good news and bad news, really bad news, I fear, Gunny, but the only deal that is open to us."

Swanson liked this quiet and studious man. Obviously Ivy League by education, probably a good lawyer who decided to embark on a course of public service while he was still a young man. Most likely an old-school diplomat who had seen many a tight negotiation in his time. If he said the deal was the best, it probably was.

"There has been a hard bargain made, with the upside being that the Pakistani government doesn't want you around. Therefore, a team from the Diplomatic Security Service will come over here at noon tomorrow, remove you from this prison, and take you to the embassy. Another twenty-four hours, Gunny. Can you do that?"

"Yes, sir. I can do that."

Riles used his hand to flatten a typed document on the desk. "Now for the bad news. You are being charged with violating Article 118 of the Uniform Code of Military Justice, specifically with unpremeditated murder. There are twelve specific charges, but that number probably will grow." Riles looked at Swanson straight. "The maximum punishment will be directed by a military tribunal, and such punishment may include dishonorable discharge, forfeiture of all pay and allowances, and confinement for life."

Swanson thought hard. "Not a death penalty?"

"That was part of the bargaining, son. No death penalty. You will be held in Fort Leavenworth, but the court-martial will be held at Camp Pendleton. At least we get you out of here and back in the USA, and you will have a fair trial, with a good lawyer. It's the best I could do under the circumstances."

Swanson slumped in the chair, mentally swinging between despair and happiness. He looked at Riles and gave a grim smile. "Okay, sir. Better than a piano wire around the neck some night over here. Thanks."

Riles was on his feet. "I look forward to seeing you at the embassy tomorrow, Gunny. Get you cleaned up and some decent food and we can talk about this in more detail, with a temporary defense attorney present. Is there anything else I can do for you before I leave today?"

Swanson actually let out a little laugh. "Actually, there is. Downstairs I have to pee and crap in a bucket. I sure would like a trip to the warden's bathroom before you call them back. I can waddle over there and will leave the door open. Won't take but a minute, and I'd like to wash out my eyes, too."

Riles started putting away the papers and strapping up his briefcase while Swanson made his slow way to the bathroom, closing the door slightly with his elbow. Moving to the toilet, he quickly scanned the small room, and when he finished urinating, he flushed and moved to the sink and turned on the water. A mirrored medicine cabinet was above it, and Kyle pulled it open and discovered a treasure chest of possibilities. He quickly grabbed a small roll of dental floss that he could keep in the palm of his hand and tucked a blue-handled plastic safety razor into the waistband of his trousers.

31

Jim Hall told the taxi driver that waited at the front door of the beachfront hotel to drive him to the Burj Dubai mall. He wanted to buy several pairs of comfortable gloves that would serve until he could have some hand-crafted to disguise his missing finger. The sharp pain of having it severed was only a memory, and he was already exercising as if the digit were still there. He settled back into the soft seat and let the strong air conditioner flow while he watched the passing landscape.

So this is what is going to happen to the entire Middle East when the black gold runs out. Dubai was the second largest of the seven sheikdoms in the United Arab Emirates, but most of its oil wealth was controlled in Abu Dhabi, the capital of the federation. That had compromised the funds needed to pay for Dubai's grandiose desires, so the city-state had concentrated instead on becoming an international trade and financial center, with the underpinning of real estate development, most of it through companies owned by the government. When the global banking and real estate markets utterly collapsed in the first decade of the twenty-first century, little Dubai was left with billions and billions of dollars' worth of debt. It had taken years just to stabilize the economy, and even today apartment buildings, office complexes, avenues of private homes, and resort hotels stood unfinished in the desert sun.

In addition, sticking up in the middle of the desolation like a toothpick in the dirt stood the world's tallest tower, the Burj Dubai, 2,717 feet high. Somehow the billionaires and the state would not let the project fail, as if national survival were at stake. Soon enough, the one being built over in Saudi Arabia would make the Burj Dubai look small in comparison, but Hall did not care.

The taxi let him off at one of the many entrances to the supermall attached to the tower, and Hall spent a couple of pleasant hours wandering around the shops. He found some gloves, watched the skaters gliding along the improbable giant indoor ice rink, visited the aquarium, and then drifted into the tower itself, stopping in the lavish lobby to read the long list of tenants. The energy consulting firm of Baker Harris & Associates occupied the entire seventh floor. It was a CIA front company that posed as a legitimate business, analyzing myriad amounts of energy data and production for clients while also trolling for intelligence nuggets for the Agency. Standing in the lobby, he dialed the business number on his cellular phone.

"Baker Harris and Associates," came the greeting in English, the universal language of business. "How may I help you?" The answer was bland, giving away nothing.

"Connect me with Margaret Dunston's office, please."

"One moment." A pause, a click, and a ring.

"Margaret Dunston's office. This is Malia. May I help you?"

"Hello, Malia. I'm Preston James, a reporter for the *Wall Street Journal*. We're putting together a story on the Dubai recovery efforts, and I wonder if Ms. Dunston might be able to give me a few minutes right now for an interview. I understand it is inconvenient and short notice, but I just happen to be in the tower and another interview canceled. Could you ask, please?"

"Oh, Mr. James, I'm so sorry. She is just starting an important luncheon meeting, and the rest of the day is packed full. Her schedule is absolutely jammed. I know she will be sorry not to be interviewed for your story, so if you leave me your . . . Hello? *Hello?*"

Jim Hall had hung up in her ear. All he had wanted was confirmation that covert CIA operative Maggie Dunston was in her office today. Which meant she would be returning home tonight. Where he would be waiting, just like in the old days.

A few hours later, in the sluggish dead heat of the afternoon, Hall strolled into her exclusive apartment building and directly to the elevator. The doorman gave him no more than a glance of attention because he looked vaguely familiar and walked as if he belonged in this exclusive enclave of foreigners. In the elevator, he punched twelve and got off on the exact floor of her apartment, making no attempt to cover his approach. He wanted people to remember this visit. Her door was the third on the right along the carpeted corridor and made of shining oak, not more secure metal. He knocked, not expecting an answer because he was sure Maggie still lived alone. He already had the key he had stolen two years ago in his hand, and it fit perfectly. A quick turn and the lock opened and he was inside, with the door closed and locked. Silent but for the hum of the central air-conditioning.

Margaret Dunston had been a project of his for years, starting when he was first assembling his plan of escaping the clutches of the CIA and getting rich. He had mentored her, courted and bedded her, made friends with her gray cat with the blue eyes, Sapphire, and stolen her apartment key.

The place was dim because she kept the blinds and curtains closed to deflect the heat. He peeked through the window coverings and once again saw the impressive view, beautiful if you liked flat land. The Burj Dubai Tower could not be seen from this angle. He let the drapes fall closed again. If she happened to glance up on the way home, they would seem undisturbed.

The furniture was expensive, and the apartment was well kept but not extremely neat. A big flat-screen television on a low black table dominated the main wall, and a built-in cabinet next to it contained a rack of home theater controls. A matched sofa and love seat combination faced it. Fashion magazines lay on a table, and there were plenty of CDs around, mostly light jazz. On the wall were a few pictures of her family back in California.

He found Sapphire sitting in the hallway to his right, head cocked, staring, tail twitching and curious. She seemed to recognize him, and as he went farther into the apartment, she followed and got her ears scratched. Hall turned down the air conditioner as low as it would go. Maggie used a spare bedroom as her office, and Hall went to her desk, sat down, called up the word processing program on her computer, and wrote his confession, printing it out on the laserjet printer and folding it neatly into an envelope, which he licked and sealed. Again, he did not care about leaving fingerprints or DNA samples. The more the better.

Then he went into the main bedroom. The queen-sized bed had not been made that morning, as if Maggie had been in a hurry. A few articles of clothing and a towel were in a pile outside the bathroom door. Jim Hall stripped off his own clothes and laid them neatly over a chair because this job was going to be messy. It was getting colder in the apartment by the time he adjusted the bedspread and settled in for a nap before she got home. Everything he needed was in the kitchen. Before he fell asleep, he felt Sapphire jump onto the bed and fold into a ball behind his knees, purring.

Maggie breezed in through the front door just a few minutes before eight, locked it, and stood still for a moment, shivering as the chill hit her. From his position beside the kitchen door, Jim Hall saw her plainly: medium height, with a good figure and a face constantly refreshed by makeup. Her hair was dark brown and cut long, swept back over her shoulders. *Ah, Maggie, you've lost some weight,* he thought. *Good times.*

Sapphire was on the couch, awake and still, the eyes

locked on Maggie, who smiled when she saw the cat. "Hey, girl. Cold in here," she said and walked straight over to the digital thermostat on the wall. She leaned close to read it, and Hall materialized silently behind her, swinging the twelve-inch cast-iron frying pan down hard. It slammed just above her ear, and he drove a shoulder into her spine, smashing her into the wall, breaking her nose on the stiff plastic housing of the thermostat. She collapsed with a whimpering moan, her head feeling like it was exploding.

Hall did not want to really hurt Maggie; he just needed her dead. He smashed her head twice more with the heavy pan and, on the final blow, heard her skull crack. She was totally unconscious, dying from the brain and spinal injuries, and he knelt beside her for a moment to catch his breath. Not long—he had to get to work while the heart was still pumping; it was important. A lot of blood would spew out to help make the scene as gruesome as possible for investigators.

Standing up and taking three strides back to the breakfast bar in the kitchen, he silently put the heavy, bloodstained frying pan into the sink and lifted a long, sharp cutting knife from a wooden stand on the counter.

Then he worked methodically, pulling multiple deep wounds across major arteries. The thick purple blood fountained out and splashed the walls as well as the floor and his body. Slashing and disfiguring facial cuts were necessary, too, and he also sliced off the eyelids. Those enchanting brown eyes were staring up at the ceiling, seeing nothing. Changing to a cleaver, he chopped off her little finger. With a dishcloth dunked in her blood, he wrote on one of the white walls, following with a huge exclamation point: CIA SPY!

When the work was done, he went to the bathroom, closed the door, and took a scalding hot shower because he had been working out there naked except for an over-sized gray sweatshirt he had found in her closet. The steam wrapped him comfortably, and he soaped and washed carefully, particularly under the nails and in every bodily crevice, shampooing twice.

Jim Hall dressed quickly. The frigid air-conditioning was to keep her body chilled and prevent quick decay, but *damn* it was cold. He laid the envelope addressed to the CIA station chief on the living room table, gave Sapphire a final rub, and left the apartment, locking the door behind him.

32

White House Chief of Staff Bobby Patterson felt like he was juggling live hand grenades. Everything involved in the mess in Pakistan seemed to trail right back to his desk. President Russell, his friend of many years, had just chewed him out and threatened to fire him for using poor judgment and overstepping his authority. "Put a lid on this thing, Bobby," the president had ordered.

Patterson summoned a Town Car to go out to the CIA and talk it over with Director Bart Geneen, whom he counted as an ally in the political battle. On the way there, Patterson remained silent, ignoring the monuments and lines of trees beyond the tinted windows as he considered options and political risks. If he did not exert strong control, things could spin even further out of hand, and that would mean his job. The black car wound smoothly off the Beltway and into the woods outside Langley, and once he was through the extraordinary security apparatus at the front gate, a sense of privacy and secrecy seemed to drift upon him like a silent blanket of snow. It felt good. The car proceeded along a shaded lane, past the parking lots and right up to the front entrance of shining glass and polished marble. He was met by an escort who gave him a VIP visitor's clip-on tag, then led the way through the inner courtyard. Patterson, lost in his own puzzles, ignored the statue to the code-breakers of World War II, the famed Kryptos sculptured fountain that contained its own enigmatic 865-character cipher. The two men entered the holiest of holy places for secrecy; imbedded along one wall was a galaxy of bright stars, each representing a fallen operative. The stars bore no names, for the anonymity of the agents lived on beyond their lives, truly unsung heroes. If one's name became known, enemy intelligence services would pounce on everyone who ever had anything to do with the exposed agent. These men and women carried their secrets beyond their graves.

Patterson's confidence grew with every step. With all of the professionals on this big campus and the billions of dollars of support, he felt fresh wind pushing his sails. He had given the job to the right people. All things would be set right. His decision to let the CIA be the lead dog in investigating the devastating terrorist attack in Pakistan was a good one. The Agency could not afford to fail any more than Patterson.

Then, instead of going to the office of Director Geneen, the escort veered into a basement conference room, a drab place in which pastel colors did nothing to dispel its blandness. *Underground at the CIA: How about this for security?* Waiting for him was Mel Langdon, the director of operations, who motioned the chief of staff to a chair beside a worn oblong wood table that bore circular stains left by coffee cups and water glasses. A bulletin board and a white grease board were filled with documents and writing, and scraps of loose paper littered the dreary carpet. *Work is done in this place*, Patterson thought, *and Langdon is the officer who handles the hard decisions.*

"I hope you brought along your thinking cap, Mr. Patterson. We have a few problems."

Bobby Patterson closed his eyes and sighed. *Now what?* "Where's the director?"

"Unavailable." Langdon's response was curt and to the point. "Our principals should not be directly involved with this so they can maintain deniability. That's why you and I are relegated to this room in the basement, a couple of high-level flunkies doing the devil's deeds, far out of sight."

Not meeting with the director came as a direct slap in the face for Patterson. *Has word already leaked that I'm in trouble?* Bobby Patterson shrugged his shoulders, adjusted his suit coat, and covered his embarrassment at the impolite response. "Let's go from the top. What's up?"

"Do you remember our shooter who was killed in the Pakistan strike? Jim Hall?"

Patterson did. "FBI identified the corpse, right?"

"No. They never actually saw the body. They worked from a print from a severed finger and DNA from bloodstains, all supplied by the Pakis, and came up with the positive identity."

"Well? He's dead. So what?"

"He's not dead, and he's gone rogue." Langdon

worked a panel of buttons, and a viewing screen un-
rolled from a hidden reel in the ceiling, the room lights
dimmed, and a series of PowerPoint slides began. The
butchered body of a woman in a pool of blood. The
words CIA SPY! scrawled on a white wall above her.

"My God! Who is that?

"Her name is Margaret Dunston, and she was one of
ours. She worked in Dubai for Baker Harris and Associates, a company that we set up to maintain surveillance and exert some control in the oil industry, and a
pretty expensive piece of work with a lot of years of
development invested. This is Jim Hall's way of telling
us that he has blown the entire Baker Harris show, a
whole network."

The pictures now changed to a dirt courtyard in some
unidentified, barren place. Close-ups of the bruised and
broken faces of two men standing against a wall, then
the camera pulling back to show a line of other men facing them, holding AK-47s at the ready. The next picture
was of the rifles being fired, and the last, the victims
slumped over dead. "Two more of our agents, local
talent this time, who had infiltrated the Taliban in the
Northwest Frontier. Hall claims to have sold them out to
an old friend of his, Muhammed Waleed."

"The Taliban warlord in Waziristan?"

"The same," said Langdon. "He left a letter at the
scene of the murder of the woman in Dubai, confessing
everything. He wants a deal."

"We can't deal with a man like that," Patterson said.
"He's a terrorist himself!"

Langdon turned the lights back up and the gruesome pictures vanished, but the screen stayed down. "Like I said earlier, Bobby. We're doing the devil's deeds here today. We are backed into a corner and pretty much have to give him what he wants. The man is a walking encyclopedia of Agency secrets. He could cripple us."

"Then what does he want? A pardon?"

Langdon replied. "He wants very little. He has stolen a few million dollars from a covert account and plans to go find somewhere quiet to retire in leisure. We wipe that from the books. He instructs that we pay him off with another million dollars a year for the next ten years through covert channels. Petty cash. Mostly, he does not want to be looking over his shoulder for a CIA-paid hit squad. In return, Jim Hall proposes that if we leave him alone—just keep pretending that he really is dead—then he will leave us alone, and our other networks and agents remain operational and safe."

Patterson rubbed his hands together. "Are you willing to do that?"

"It actually is a small price. Yes, we can send somebody out to get him in a few years, but it might be better just to cut him loose rather than take the chance of failure. My recommendation would be to back off and let him go. After all, as he mentions, he also supplied us with two patsies to take the fall for Pakistan. Jim Hall was a very thorough agent."

Bobby Patterson was absorbing the troubling information and admitted that it made a weird kind of sense. A rogue agent silenced and two people to blame for the Pakistan troubles. "What about those others?"

"First, we have Agent Lauren Carson, who was Jim

Hall's assistant." Mel Langdon worked his slide show again and a series of photos of a beautiful young woman walked across the screen. "She was under suspicion almost from the start, primarily for helping him steal the money, and now she has cut and run. We found evidence of her apparent guilt, so our top investigator is running a search for her and is confident that she will be in custody within a few hours. Once we have Carson, we take our own sweet time to convict her in a secret court, and send her to a secure prison within our private system. We impose a total press blackout on Carson, because the news vultures would love to run stories of the beauty queen spymistress. Unfortunately, she is also CIA, and we don't want that connection known." A final picture of the smiling woman lingered on the screen, then disappeared in a shower of pixels, just as the real Lauren Carson was about to do.

Patterson realized that he was sweating, despite the air-conditioning. He had been in many negotiations in his life, but this was literally life-and-death material. Sending an attractive young woman to a prison cell for the rest of her life while letting a real killer go free was hard to swallow. "What about the other person that Hall claims to have set up for Pakistan? I assume that would be the Marine sniper?"

"Yes." A few photos of Kyle Swanson came onto the screen, and he was never smiling. His eyes, in each picture, no matter how informal, carried a flash of predator. "That one is a done deal. We got the Paki government to agree to turn him over if we filed a pack of murder charges against him. We pick him up from prison tomorrow and fly him back to the States. Gunny Swanson will be secured in Fort Leavenworth. Once in, he won't be coming out. He will suffer a fatal mishap before he ever faces a military tribunal."

Bobby Patterson saw the symmetry as the noose was pulled tight on Kyle Swanson. President Russell had sided with the generals and come down hard on Patterson for overstepping his bounds in the flap about Task Force Trident. "So this renegade Marine sniper from Task Force Trident will become the face of this disaster in Pakistan, murdering innocent people and all?"

Mel Langdon brought the lights back up for a final time and found Patterson looking more comfortable than he did when he had first entered the room. *Sold him.* "Yes. An out-of-control covert operative goes nuts, takes the fall, and the little secret military group that runs him will be abolished. The White House and the CIA cannot be held responsible that he was not trained and handled properly."

Patterson thought quietly as he mulled the situation. A photograph of Kyle Swanson lingered on the screen, as if staring at him with that icy and unrelenting glare. *The man is afraid of nothing,* thought Patterson. "How do we wrap it up?"

"Lauren Carson is as good as caught," Langdon replied with confidence. "The sniper is already in custody. All we have to do is post a coded answer on a phony Facebook account that Jim Hall can access from any Wi-Fi computer or PDA, anywhere in the world, and he goes away."

"What could go wrong?" Bobby Patterson asked. It

was more hope than question. *The end is in sight!* Put a lid on this thing, the president had said. The White House chief of staff breathed a sigh of relief.

"Nothing," said the CIA director of operations.

"Okay," said Patterson. "Send the Facebook message and we're done."

33

Kyle Swanson worked slowly in his cell, doing what he had to do, whether or not he liked it. He was facing a stretch of unknown duration at the United States Disciplinary Barracks in Fort Leavenworth, Kansas, a hard-time military prison. And he was not naive. A prisoner does not have to be officially sentenced to death in order to die when the immense forces of the intelligence world want him dead.

"It's kind of funny, when you think about it," Swanson told the rats as he took a seat on his mattress and prepared to get to work. "It wasn't that long ago, back when I rescued General Middleton from his kidnappers, that they buried me with full honors at Arlington Cemetery because they wanted me to disappear and do even more work for them. Now it looks like I'm heading for an unmarked grave in the Leavenworth cemetery, branded as a traitor. Hell of a thing, boys."

He picked at the end of the dental floss and measured out a string that encircled his waist, plus a few inches, then used the built-in metal tab to cut it. Swanson was sitting with his legs crossed and laid the strip carefully before him, memorizing it with his fingers. A skittering sound was heard nearby. "You damned rats stay over there," he ordered. "Don't fuck with my dental floss."

The State Department guy said he would be picked up from this prison tomorrow at noon, which meant Americans would take him into custody. He did not want to kill any Americans to break free after he was pulled out of this cell, but he also did not want to reach Leavenworth in irons. He would only have one chance. He strung out another length of floss, cut it, laid it beside the first.

If he could pick the right moment and overpower one of them, then he could grab the pistol the man was certain to be carrying and take control of the situation. He could escape, but that would make him a white boy on the run in Pakistan, wanted for murder by his own government. Not good, but the options were few.

Strip after strip of dental floss was measured and cut, then laid out. He could not go to the helpful imam, because while the man might be honor-bound to help, he had also exposed himself enough for Kyle's sake. Another visit might doom him, no matter what his rank in the government or religious establishment. "You know, rats, I made a big choice back there during the explosions. I've seen women and kids die before, lots of them, and I could have walked on by without a second thought. But no, not this time. I essentially went against all of my training and experience and gave myself up for those kids." He paused for a long moment. "I don't even know why I did it. People die in wars all the time. It wasn't my job. But here I am with you guys in a dark cell, and your futures are brighter than mine. Hell of a thing."

When the roll of floss was emptied, Kyle flipped the plastic holder to a back corner of the cell. Leaning forward at the waist, he pressed his palms against the multiple strands and began to slowly roll them back and forth on the floor a few times to tangle the thread, then tied knots in one end to stabilize it, put it back on the floor, and rolled it some more. Satisfied at last, he tied off the other end. A single strand of dental floss was useless, but twenty strips woven together made a perfectly satisfactory garrote. Many little strings can tie down a giant, as Gulliver discovered among the tiny Lilliputians. Swanson stood and wrapped the gathered string around his waist like a belt, then secured it with a light tie, one end dipping lower than the other. His waist measured thirty inches, which allowed plenty of room for him to wrap the ends around each fist a couple of times and use the excess in the middle as a choking weapon.

To kill an American guard would really make him guilty of murder, though, just as he was charged. Beating them up was one thing, but not an outright death. If it could be avoided.

He was being treated like an HVT, a high-value target, so security was going to be tight. How many guys? Putting on new handcuffs would supply a moment of freedom, but would it be enough? A thousand questions surged through his mind.

Swanson used both hands to snap the twin-blade top off of the plastic razor. The molding was so close to the edge of the blades that they were useless as anything but a small tool, and it popped easily at the slim elbow where the handle bent toward the face. Now he had a piece of plastic about five inches long, not even as big around as his middle finger. Still. Possible.

Jesus, I don't want to kill anybody tomorrow. I don't want to have to kill anybody.

He made the decision on the spot, an internal choice. He could resist, fight, try to immobilize the guards, and push it right up to the edge. However, if it came to deadly force, Swanson decided that this time he would take that punishment himself rather than kill other Americans who had done him no harm. "Life is simpler behind a trigger in a sniper hide," he told the rats. "This humanity stuff is complex. Actually, it kind of sucks."

Holding the lower part of the handle firmly, he placed his index finger against the broken edge, positioned it at an angle on the rough concrete floor, and gently bore down on it, careful not to break the thick part. In slow, persistent strokes, Swanson began sanding away the plastic edge, stopping after every dozen strokes to feel the result. The concrete peeled away the plastic like rough sandpaper. Within a half hour, he had sharpened the lightweight handle into a jail-type shiv, a makeshift stabbing knife that could be deadly if he had to use it.

He then tied it on the longer string hanging from the garrote knot and hid it beneath his trousers. Since he had been in prison for days, it was doubtful that he would be searched.

Fifty-eight. Fifty-nine. Sixty. His internal clock told him that another hour had passed. He made another rip in the shirt, then settled back against the wall and tried not to think too much because he was not happy with the conclusions that kept coming back like little nightmares, the same thing over and over. He would do what he had to do. Leavenworth was not an acceptable option. Maybe death was the more viable possibility.

34

There was movement in the corridor, and Kyle Swanson detected it, felt the certainty, before he heard any boots. A subtle shift in air pressure, the cessation of the rhythmic movement by the rats, or just an overall alertness, something. He snapped awake. It was too early. His fingers counted the recent tears. It was only about six o'clock, around dawn in the outside world. He checked his weapons, then stood, spread his arms, and yawned.

By the time the guard detail arrived at his door and he heard the rattle of the keys, Swanson was stretching his muscles and calming his mind. He had no real plan for escape, other than being determined never to set foot in Fort Leavenworth's military prison. Stay in the moment, he reminded himself. Something had changed in the schedule, but he would not dwell on it. Thinking of too many possibilities could bog down the brain when it needed to be concentrating. Breathe easy. Stay loose. He did a few toe stands, lifting his heels as far as possible, rolled his shoulders and his head from side to side. The familiar pre-battle calmness settled on his nerves, and in the darkness Swanson's world slowed down and his senses sharpened. Looking into a corner to protect his eyes, Kyle could actually *see* a few rats. They were crouched, fearful, mystified.

The door creaked open, and he closed his eyes tight, then slowly opened them again in a squint. The light from the hallway blazed in, creating silhouettes of the four-man guard detail. Kyle extended his wrists, and two turnkeys clapped on the cuffs and ankle restraints while the other two protected them with rifles. Since he was leaving, they really expected no trouble from him, and he did not plan to give them any . . . unless he had to. " 'Bye, rats," Swanson said and moved his left foot the length of the chain, then his right. A guard took each elbow, partially carrying him.

Working together, it took only a few minutes for Swanson and his caravan of prison guards to climb the stairs and get into the office of the warden. It was bathed in the muted golden glow of the new morning, allowing Swanson to confirm this transfer was about six hours ahead of schedule.

The dark-haired warden gave him a hateful look, rose from behind his desk, and silently herded his guards from the room through one of its two doors, leaving with them and closing the door behind him. He said not a word.

Two lithe men with fair skin and short haircuts were standing casually beside the other office door. Kyle recognized the military bearing immediately and his heart sank. They radiated confidence and ability and would not be easily surprised or overcome. The embassy had sent professionals. At a nod from the leader, his companion took three quick strides and stood in between the two closed doors, facing them at a forty-five-degree angle to each. He unbuttoned his coat to expose a large pistol, pulled the weapon free, and took up a combat stance.

The other man sauntered toward Kyle, smiling as he approached. "G'day, mate," he said. "That big bloke over there is S'arnt Jimmy Todd, and I'm S'arnt Colin Moore of the Australian SAS. Sir Geoffrey Cornwell sends his compliments and requests the pleasure of your company."

"*Jeff?* Sir Jeff sent you?"

"Yes, mate. He wanted me to tell you 'Haggis.'"

"Haggis never sounded so good," Kyle responded. "Haggis," an odd concoction that passed for food in Scotland, was Jeff's private code word for "All is well." A wave of relief hit Swanson so hard that he staggered, but he was easily held up by Moore.

"You have some interesting friends. Now that's enough words until we get you out of here. Be still while I get rid of the restraints. Got to put some of our own cuffs on you for a little while, just for show, in case anybody sneaks a peek." Moore was already working with a set of keys, and the handcuffs fell free. In ten more seconds, the leg irons were off. Moore popped open a set of shiny cuffs and looped them softly around Kyle's wrists but did not lock them. From an ankle holster, Moore removed a small .38 caliber revolver and handed it to Kyle.

"Cross your hands and hold those cuffs so they don't

slip off, and put that weapon where you can reach it," he said. Swanson stuffed the little pistol into his waist-band and covered it with the ragged shirt.

Moore then opened his sports coat wide enough to rest his right hand on the butt of his Walther 7.65 mm PPK in a belt holster at his hip. "We are ready to move here, Jimmy."

"Very well." The voice was soft, emotionless. "I'll follow you two."

The large room outside was empty when they left the warden's office, although there were cups on some of the desks. A smoking cigarette balanced on the rim of an ashtray. No one barred their way. In a twenty-four-hour prison that never closes, not a guard was in sight.

Colin Moore walked in front, moving with the smoothness of a cat while his gaze swept every desk, chair, window, closet, and corner. After days of incar-ceration, Kyle's muscles would not respond to the quick pace, and even the dim light was like staring into bright headlights. He could not see worth a damn with eyes long tuned to complete darkness. He heard the skip-slide footsteps of Jimmy Todd behind him, moving forward while facing the rear. The door of the elevator stood open at the end of the room, a chair blocking it from closing. Moore threw it aside and guided Swanson in, leaning him against a wall. Todd backed in, still with his gun pointed at the vacant space.

Moore punched a button, and the door hissed closed. He removed his own weapon as the descent began. "Down to the loading area, mate. Hang in there."

"That place will be swarming with cops," Kyle said, drawing air down deep into his lungs. "If they are going to jump us, this will be the perfect ambush spot."

"No worries. I think they're all on a tea break for a few minutes."

With a jolt, the elevator stopped moving, and as the door began to open, both SAS commandos had their guns at the ready, with Kyle leaning against one wall. No one was there to stop them.

They went out, moving faster. Moore and Todd flanked the stumbling Swanson. A large white SUV was parked beside the loading dock, with its motor running. As they piled in, Kyle saw a small Uzi submachine gun waiting on the backseat. He grabbed it.

"Go!" Colin Moore barked when the doors were closed, his voice loud in the confined space. The SUV lurched into motion and headed away from the prison, soon to be lost in the morning traffic.

Kyle dropped the handcuffs. "Thanks, guys. I buy the next round," he said and passed out, totally spent.

"No worries," said Moore, taking away the Uzi.

At a window on the top floor of a nearby building, General Nawaz Zaman of the Pakistani intelligence service inhaled a long draft from his cigarette as he watched the white van merge into the growing traffic and fade from view around a corner. "He's gone, without a shot being fired," he said. "Good."

"The Americans are going to be furious," said the tall warden, sitting in a folding chair, legs and arms crossed.

Zaman shook his head, and his jowls moved with

the motion of a broad smile. "It makes no difference. Somehow the prisoner, a very clever and highly trained assassin, escaped during the night. The breakfast tray was slid into his cell as usual and was discovered to be untouched when the guards went to fetch him at noon. I shall pretend outrage and invite the FBI to assist in the investigation."

"You should have let my men beat the prisoner as punishment before we turned him loose." The warden's lean face was in a pout. His comment was directed to the third man in the room, the helpful imam whose family had been saved by Kyle Swanson.

The religious leader said, "Warden, this was a matter of my personal honor. I consider that man to have been a guest in my home, and the traditions of Allah, his name be praised, demand that I protect him, with my own life if necessary. Were we still living in some village, everyone would be required to protect him. You know that. Anyway, you accepted the offered money, so why do you continue to challenge me?"

"He blew up half of our city!"

"No, he did not. You know nothing. All that man did was shoot a worthless Taliban and then get snared in a web of fate," said General Nawaz Zaman, focusing on the warden, the geniality gone. "Why do you speak at all? These things are beyond your understanding. If you utter so much as a whisper about this matter, even in your sleep, you will take his place in the prison."

The general then flicked his cigarette through the open window. Dawn was giving over to a beautifully bright day.

35

Only when Jim Hall received the anonymous Facebook message as he had demanded from the Central Intelligence Agency did he realize that his plan had actually worked! He had beaten the system. He had blackmailed the CIA and had gotten away with a forever get-out-of-jail-free card. He went down to the hotel bar and ordered a solitary, celebratory drink, feeling a long-sought sense of transformation, and without a second thought about selling out Kyle Swanson and Lauren Carson.

He played with the ice cubes and picked his teeth with the little plastic sword that speared two olives in the martini. New clothes were a must. He could buy whatever he wanted in the exclusive shops in Dubai, but why bother? It would be more fun, a better experience, to go to the source for his threads. Hand-sewn shoes from a British craftsman, custom-made suits from the best tailors of Europe, fitted shirts in Italy, with money no object. Jim Hall liked that idea.

The message had arrived during the night, and Hall left Dubai the following day, bound for Charles de Gaulle

Airport in Paris with a first-class seat aboard Qatar Airways. He used a backup passport that allowed him to use another name for customs and legal paperwork, but he did not worry about fingerprints or facial recognition software or retina scans. It did not matter if the authorities tracked him, because there would always be an asterisk on his file that would guarantee that he would not be molested. They would do nothing, and eventually give up.

In Paris, he rested, had a nice lunch, and then purchased a tuxedo from a designer's studio shop, along with matching black dress shoes, polished to a bright sheen. A stylish haircut at a salon set him back two hundred and fifty dollars. The following day, a high-speed train whisked him south to the Principality of Monaco, the money-soaked independent state snuggled between the mountains and the Mediterranean on the French Riviera. A memory of the beautiful Princess Grace and her fairy-tale romance flitted through his thoughts. Like Grace, he was going to be living the dream.

That evening, the dream would feature Jim Hall as James Bond, and he believed he fit the part better than some of the movie stars who had played the role. Not as good as Sean Connery, but better than most of the others. After all, he was a real spy. He strolled that night along the Golden Square that led to Le Grand Casino de Monte-Carlo, where master craftsmen had created an ornate castle on the outside and a perfection of polished stonework within. He caught a glimpse of himself in his tux and thought he looked good. He moved with ease through the corridors, ignoring the Salle des

Amériques, where rich rubes from the States came to play familiar Las Vegas games such as craps. Smiling at the genteel segregation of the Americans from the more cosmopolitan European casino atmosphere, Hall decided to speak only French that night. At a gilded private room for serious gamblers, he paid an additional entry fee and stepped inside.

A waiter in a short white jacket and dark trousers appeared at Hall's shoulder as he sat down at the roulette table, and Jim ordered a double martini on the rocks, with olives. A thick slab of one-hundred-dollar bills from his new wallet was exchanged for chips.

He let play continue while he tasted his drink and made himself comfortable. The women were gorgeous in colorful gowns, with diamonds at their ears and throats, and the men wore upscale suits, dinner jackets, or tuxedoes. A slender brunette with long hair over her bare shoulders and a low-necked gown the rich purple color of ripe plums was checking him out from the far end of the table. Hall smiled at her.

Hall placed his bet, ten thousand dollars, on red, for a single spin of the wheel. He did so because he had always wanted to do that once in his life. He did so because he *could*. It did not matter whether he won or lost, it was just fulfilling a whim, and automatically earned him the respect of everyone at the table. He was a player. Hall watched the little ball clatter around the spinning wheel until it slowed and finally caught in a slot. Red! The goddess of gambling was showing him respect. He had won. The ten thousand became twenty thousand, and he let it ride for another spin, when he won again and the money became forty thousand dollars.

That was enough showing off. He stacked the beautiful chips into small towers of colorful plastic and settled down to play for only a thousand per spin for a while. Win some, lose some, and the brunette had taken the seat next to him and placed warm fingertips along his thigh.

Jim Hall knew it was going to go on being this way. He would enjoy his new life in Europe, travel the high roads in Asia and South America, and never have to return to those sandy and hot wastes in the Middle East. A final favor had to be repaid, but that would not happen in Pakistan. Then, out.

PAKISTAN

The father and the son were sharing a small meal, eating quietly until they were done, and the women left them alone. It was not very hot outside, and there was already fresh snow on the highest ridges. For mountain dwellers, it was time to be certain they had acquired everything they needed before the passes were clogged by snow and ice so thick that even a mule could not traverse a path.

Muhammed Waleed, the strongest warlord in the Taliban badlands, was proud of Selim. The attack in Islamabad had brought a horrendous toll of death and destruction, and it was all being blamed on an American Marine assassin, who had now escaped from custody.

"You have accomplished an important task, my son, and you did so brilliantly."

"Thank you, Father. I felt the hand of the Prophet upon me during the entire operation. All praise be unto him."

The older man adjusted his robes. The weather had been hot only a few days before, but now there was a faint chill in the early afternoon air. "How do you read the government's situation at this point?"

Selim gave his father a frank look. "I admit that I was surprised that they did not crumble after the Islamabad incident. The president did not impose martial law, which I had anticipated."

"Perhaps he held back because of all of the foreign presence in the city. The diplomats would have reported back to their capitals that he had panicked. He would not want that."

"Yes," agreed Selim. "Well, no matter. Confidence in his administration was already being shaken by the riots elsewhere, and now, as I read it, the president is hanging on by no more than a slender thread. The generals may not follow his call for any harsh crackdown on the people, and the secret police continue to play their own game."

The Taliban leader laughed. "Ah, our old friend General Nawaz Zaman. That fox even keeps secrets from himself. He will not intervene in our plans if the price is correct and he is left in power when we take over."

"He has been useful," Selim replied. "When the bribe offer was made by the British billionaire for the escape of the Marine, Zaman arranged everything and

kept me informed. As a prisoner, the Marine represented nothing but diplomatic and media problems in
the future. It is best that he is gone. We have all washed
our hands of him. Let Kyle Swanson be a problem elsewhere. Here, he was a distraction that we did not need
at this important time."

"And the condition of our political arm, the Bright
Path Party?"

Selim's dark eyes almost glowed. "Strong and ready.
That is why I have come. It is almost time, Father. You
must leave this place very soon and prepare to step into
public view."

"I think it is still too early, my son." There was a
hint of warning in the statement.

"Please allow me to explain my thinking, Father. I
would never presume to know as much as you, nor to
instruct you in the proper thing to do."

"Speak."

"The leaders of the Western countries are showing
great concern about the situation in Pakistan. I have
learned that the president of Pakistan will be invited to
meet the leaders of major European countries and reas-
sure them."

"Where?"

"That has not yet been decided. The United Nations,
The Hague, Washington, London, Paris. All are possible, and it makes little difference for our next steps. He
will not return from the trip, and his government will
collapse."

Waleed got to his feet and walked to the main
window. People in the village below were content and

working. Soon he would be ruling the entire nation, out in the open. The other Taliban warlords would fall in line or face his wrath. The West would be forced to accept him.

Selim continued, "The president will be killed while he is away, and you will step forth as the candidate of the Bright Path Party to be elected and bring stability and peace to Pakistan. There will be a token opposition candidate, but anyone else seeking the office would find that life will be very, very difficult."

"And Jim Hall does the job, wherever it may be?"

"Yes, Father. I have already set him in motion."

36

Commander Stacey Thomas, captain of HMS *Iron Duke,* led the boarding party himself, somewhat chagrined at having been ordered to stop and search the sparkling yacht of Sir Geoffrey Cornwell. The Type 23 frigate of the Royal Navy rode easily in the deep waters, parallel to and only 150 yards off the port side of the white pleasure vessel *Vagabond,* which had been ordered over the radio to heave to.

Awaiting him on deck was Cornwell, the legendary former SAS colonel, now an international businessman. Cornwell was casually dressed, and, although he was still confined to a wheelchair from his injuries in a terrorist attack, his welcome was warm and friendly. No sign of animosity for being confronted by the military. That came as a relief for Commander Thomas, who did not want to make an enemy of this influential man.

"Welcome aboard, Commander Thomas," Sir Jeff said, extending his hand. "Allow me to introduce my wife, Lady Patricia." An elegant woman in a casual blue and white deck outfit, with a white scarf around her neck, gave a cheerful smile.

The naval officer saluted, then accepted the offered handshakes. "Thank you, Sir Geoffrey. Lady Patricia. I am terribly sorry for this intrusion."

Cornwell waved away the apology. "You have your orders, sir, so why get all bothered with legalities when what you seek is not here? Come and join me at that table beneath the deck awning while your lads conduct a thorough search. They may have the run of the ship. My crew will help if asked. It is important to clear this up as soon as possible."

Stacey Thomas issued the command, and the five armed commandos spread fore and aft, scaling ladders and descending belowdecks. The entire crew of the *Vagabond* stayed together on the bridge for ease of identification. There was more polite chitchat; then Commander Thomas said, "May I get to the point, sir?"

"Certainly. Some tea first?"

"Not at the moment, sir. Perhaps some other time, when things are not as tense."

"Then let me answer your question before you ask: No, we have neither seen nor heard from Kyle Swanson. I was delighted to learn that he had escaped from custody in Pakistan, for we—Pat and I—will never believe Kyle is guilty, or even capable, of mass murder."

"That would be simply impossible, Commander," said Lady Pat in a pleasant voice. "Kyle is always very particular about whom he shoots." She removed a small gold case that snapped brightly in the sun, took out a slender cigar, and lit it. She blew the smoke away from them.

"Kyle is also a very bright and resourceful boy, Commander Thomas. He knows that Pat and I would automatically be viewed as having a hand in protecting him. And that would be true . . . if he had asked, which he has not. He will not turn to us for help."

"May I ask, then, why the *Vagabond* is out here? I do not doubt your word, but this yacht would provide a valuable refuge for a fugitive."

Sir Jeff slid a notebook filled with diagrams and photos in plastic sleeves across the table to the commander. "This is one of the latest projects. We call it the Bird and Snake, and it is designed to be a low-cost and pinpoint weapon against pirates. So we are conducting some sea tests. It is a Top Secret project, sir, so I must trust you to keep it confidential, other than for need-to-know personnel."

The sailors were emerging from belowdecks and reporting nothing unusual. The cabins and workspaces were all clear; the engine room, galley, and communications shack were in order. All personnel on the bridge had proper identification and valid passports, and there was no evidence that Kyle Swanson had been aboard.

"I can have my captain show you the Bird and Snake setup we have below, if you wish. Our computer hard drives contain proprietary data that I should not release to you without a proper court order. Nevertheless, we would welcome an electronics technician with proper security clearances to come aboard and review the contents, should you so desire. He would have to sign a separate and stringent government nondisclosure form, of course."

Commander Thomas checked his men. All five were ready to return to the *Iron Duke*. "No, Sir Geoffrey, that will not be necessary," he said. "The Americans are running this manhunt, not us. I imagine we were tasked to this irksome duty just as a warning that they are covering all angles."

"Naturally," said Sir Jeff. "Well, then, sir, it was nice to meet you and watch your team work. I always enjoy seeing the operations of a well-trained unit." He smiled. "Have a pleasant voyage, and do not hesitate to notify us if you need us again. We remain at the queen's service."

"Thank you, sir," Thomas said, giving another salute. "Good day, Lady Patricia." The boarding team returned down the side staircase to the inflatable speedboat and shoved off as soon as Thomas was seated.

"Nice enough chap," observed Jeff as the boat sped away. He stayed at the table with Pat, drinking tea and nibbling an apple pastry as they watched the big frigate haul the inflatable boat back aboard, then slowly pull away, gaining speed as it went. He turned to the *Vagabond*'s captain, William Styles, and said, "Bring them up."

Two figures with underwater breathing gear treaded water in the silent twilight world about twenty feet directly below the hull of the *Vagabond,* their rising air bubbles unnoticeable at the bow, where the water was rippled by gentle swells moving against the boat. For Kyle and Lauren, swimming together, the grumpy loud noise of the British frigate getting under way meant their watery exile was about over, unless some

Royal Navy sailors had been left on board, which was very unlikely.

Treading water for thirty minutes, with weight belts and big flippers, was easy for both of them. Lauren Carson had been diving for years on vacations and had been on a swim team as a kid, and she held her position with no trouble. She looked through her face mask at Kyle, about ten feet away. His military training in underwater warfare and his passion for surfing had left him with an effortless stroke, and he appeared as a virtually stationary silhouette in the water, breathing easily. She thought about how normal people paid good money for scuba diving trips in the sunny Med.

As the noisy engines of the frigate faded, Kyle held up two fingers, estimating they would remain down for only about two more minutes. For security, they had not carried radios when they had changed quickly and gone into the water at the approach of the naval vessel. All signals were made by hand.

She could see the plain, bright surface above, and the dark sleek shadow of the yacht that had been her home for the past two days. Kyle had arrived yesterday. Two international fugitives from justice, hunted by every intelligence service in the world, and they were catching tans and eating well. It was not like she had imagined.

Another sound reached her, a sudden dull *thunk,* as a set of doors in the bottom of the *Vagabond* opened. Kyle immediately kicked toward the new rectangle of light, Lauren followed, and they broke the surface in the oblong launching well of a weapon she had never before seen, something called a Snake. Crewmen helped them up and took off the vests, tanks, and other gear and handed them big towels. "Sir Geoffrey asks that you join him in the main salon as soon as you have changed," said a young woman, trying not to stare at their bodies. Miss Carson was perfectly shaped and toned, while Mr. Swanson bore numerous scars. She had heard tales about this American, a familiar figure aboard the vessel who was a business associate and close friend of Sir Jeff and a deadly sniper for the United States Marines. As he stood nearly naked in his baggy shorts, the jagged marks on his flesh bore out the truth of those stories.

Lauren, in a T-shirt and blue shorts, was already with Pat and Jeff in the spacious cabin when Kyle joined them. He flopped into a chair and popped open a chilled bottle of water. "Man, it's good to be here. Even dodging the Royal Navy is a lot more fun than being locked in that damned cell."

"I dare say," agreed Jeff. "Keeping you out of another prison is going to be difficult." Reading glasses were balanced precariously on his nose. "The visit by that frigate was a close-run thing. Next time, we might not have the advantage of seeing them coming twenty miles off."

"They won't give up, will they?" Lauren's voice was low. Her legs were crossed, and a sandal dangled from her toes.

"No, they won't," said Kyle.

"So, what do we do? Just keep running?" Her eyes were bright and watery as she considered the enormity of the opposing forces. Navy ships? Satellites? Paratroopers?

Lady Pat went to the bar, poured a stiff dose of whisky, and handed her the glass. "Drink up, Lauren. It will steady you a bit. It is understandable for you to be nervous."

Lauren tasted the amber liquid and then drank deeply. "I'm a wreck, and the rest of you don't even look very concerned."

"Well, dear, we've been through much worse," Pat said, getting a drink for herself.

"Lauren, there is a big difference," Kyle said, "between running away from something and running toward something. There is absolutely no way that we can evade capture for any extended length of time. Sooner or later, the odds will catch up with us. So we cannot just remain static. We have to be aggressive, and careful."

"True." Jeff rolled his wheelchair closer to her and leaned forward, resting on his elbows. "Never you fear, young lady. We will get you out of this jam."

Kyle locked his hands behind his head and worked his neck muscles around.

Lauren thought that he looked incredibly fit after such a short recuperation time. A bit of freedom and sunshine and getting out of prison was all he had really needed. Now he was eating like a horse and sleeping soundly. He showed no sign of being worried. "Do you have more magic up your sleeve, Jeff?" she asked. "Like bribing Kyle's way out of prison?"

"Ha! I didn't use my money. I used his!"

"But Pat said that you paid a half million dollars."

"Came right out of Kyle's shares. A little accounting sleight-of-hand, but any trace will indicate that he arranged the deal himself."

"You have that kind of money?" Lauren stared at Swanson.

"I guess. Never use it."

"So we aren't totally broke when we have to run?"

"No," said Pat. "He is a major shareholder and will be a part owner of our entire business some day when he leaves the Marines. Meanwhile, his earnings are secured away in trust accounts and other financial vehicles. But quite a bit of it has been made liquid and available at the moment."

Jeff rolled over and tossed some loose papers into Kyle's lap. "The CIA is being clumsy with their internal communications. Lieutenant Commander Freedman in Trident is keeping tabs on them. First, he discovered that Jim Hall is still alive, and now he can confirm that Hall is making a very strange deal. The Agency will leave him alone and he will leave them alone. Slaughtered a poor woman in Dubai and took down an important network there, and yet they have agreed."

Lauren stood abruptly and crossed her arms as she stalked to the long side window and looked out. "They give him a free pass but are coming after us! That's not fair!"

"Fairness has nothing to do with it, dear girl."

"And they still haven't figured out how much money he has stolen over the years. They don't know the half of it."

"We will let them know at the appropriate time,"

said Jeff, "but let's deal with the here and now." He turned to Kyle. "You cannot stay aboard the *Vagabond* much longer. They will have our communications strictly monitored and will keep the yacht under surveillance. It's too dangerous."

Kyle nodded. "Yeah. I agree. We need to get off the boat if we want to find Jim and take him down. That will make all of the troubles go away."

Lauren turned toward them, and this time tears were on her cheeks. "How? Jim knows what he's doing, and he was a great field agent."

Kyle rose and walked over to her, putting a strong hand on each of her arms and locking onto her eyes. "We're partners in this, Lauren. Putting the two of us together was Jim's first mistake and probably his biggest. No offense meant, but you were once his mistress. I was once his student and his friend. Between us, we know this guy in every way possible, both personally and professionally."

Lauren opened her arms and put them around Kyle, hugging him close, with her face against his chest. There was warmth there. And safety. "What are you going to do?"

"I'm going to kick his ass and put him in the grave," Kyle said, returning the embrace and rocking her back and forth.

37

The CIA did not have the only computer in town, and many experts considered the system rather primitive. Lieutenant Commander Benton Freedman of Task Force Trident thought the Agency's Directorate of Intelligence was about five years behind the curve on hardware alone, and losing ground. They were barely in the game on software development.

Technology was constantly evolving, but the Agency was always slow to adapt. It was not unusual for public sector companies to ramp up new programs and tweak techniques faster than the Agency could follow. The CIA believed in keeping secrets, while the rest of the computerized world was dedicated to sharing as much knowledge as possible, as fast as possible. Just a routine task like moving an e-mail from an unclassified computer system over to a classified channel was tantamount to hard labor for a CIA worker. Swapping vital information with other government agencies did not work smoothly, and the entire World Wide Web was never really embraced at the Langley headquarters, because it could not be controlled.

Other intel agencies were doing only slightly better in stumbling around the secrecy problem: Anything put into a computer became prey for some dedicated hacker, and Freedman was a shadowy god to hackers everywhere. They were aware of his prowess but never discovered his identity. Bolstered by Top Secret clearances, the superhacker known as the Lizard trolled with ease through the CIA's internal system.

"What do you have, Liz?" asked General Brad Middleton when Freedman tapped on the open door of his Pentagon office. Middleton respected Freedman's electronic prowess but sometimes needed a translator when the Lizard lapsed into rapid-fire geek.

"Sir, you told me to follow the money, and I did." The brows behind the thick eyeglasses arched.

"And . . . ?"

"I can now prove for a fact that former agent Hall is a thief."

"That is excellent work, Lieutenant Commander Freedman. However, no one gives a healthy crap that he stole some money. We want to find him because he is a treacherous bastard and he set up Kyle Swanson to take a mass murder rap."

"He stole quite a bit, sir. Thought you would like to know."

Middleton felt his eyes beginning to cross as the Lizard ignored his comments and took a chair, uninvited, then opened his notebook. "You're going to tell me anyway, aren't you?"

"Why, yes, sir. Of course."

"I'm a general. I have rights."

"Sir, you are the very model of a modern major general, with information vegetable, animal, and mineral."

"Don't go there." If Freedman launched into *The Pirates of Penzance,* he might never shut up. "Stick with the money."

"Sir, Agent Carson, in her debrief before she left, gave me a list of former agent Hall's secret bank accounts that she had memorized. She has a remarkable ability of recall and, on instructions from Agent Hall, had not written them down anywhere. He believed that he alone had the codes, but she did, too. As I say, she is remarkable. And quite beautiful. Did you know that she was in the Miss America—"

"Back to the money, Liz."

"Sir. This is information that the CIA does not possess. The Agency still thinks the single account set up for the Pakistan operation was the only one Agent Hall looted, and he took the five million dollars that was left in it. That isn't even close."

"How much?"

"In total, sir, or in each individual account?"

"I have a pistol in my desk drawer, Lizard. I am going to take it out and shoot you in the head."

"One hundred and three million dollars and change, sir. Total. That's just rounding it off to the nearest million." He gave the general a printout with the names of the banks, the account numbers, and the amounts currently in each.

Middleton blew a low whistle as he studied the numbers. Coax the Lizard a little bit and eventually he would say something worthwhile. "Can you track all of these?"

"Oh, yes, certainly, sir. Money goes in, money goes out, and it's all routed through other banks. Former agent Hall cannot let it all just sit there, but false names on the accounts won't matter, just the numbers. For instance, his last electric bill at his apartment in Georgetown was for a hundred and thirty-eight dollars and twenty-six cents. It is now overdue. That is how we'll get him, sir."

"The electric company will send out a bill collector to find a CIA assassin?" General Middleton began to scratch the stubble of his short hair, a sure sign of impatience. *Liz has something important to say. He would not be in here otherwise.*

Freedman looked puzzled for a moment. "I don't think that would work very well . . ."

The general threw him a stern look. "Get back on track, *please*. Back on track, and stay there!"

"Umh. Yes, sir. Even traitors and sources and snitches have to pay their bills. Former agent Hall is going to have to dip into those accounts at some time, perhaps not for a million dollars, that would be unlikely, I think, but to pay a credit card or start a new checking account or rent a car or buy a dinner. Something cheap. When he does, the trap programs I have set in place will locate the banks involved and the billing source. When he moves money, I will see it."

Middleton tapped his pen against the desk a few times. Frustration was growing. "So has he paid some utility company a hundred and thirty-eight bucks?"

"And twenty-six cents, sir. Oh, no, sir. I would not expect him to start paying routine bills for some time. I, I doubt if he's ever going to pay that bill."

"Has he made any withdrawals at all?"

"No, sir. Not that I can tell. I would have known." The Lizard smiled like a college freshman who had finished a chemistry experiment.

General Middleton made a little spinning motion with his right index finger. "So, Lieutenant Commander Freedman, you are sitting here . . . why?"

"The *deposit,* sir, not the withdrawals! He hasn't taken any money out, but yesterday a wire transfer of funds was made into his Paris account from a casino in Monaco: fifty-seven thousand dollars."

"Son of a bitch went gambling. So he was in Monaco as of yesterday."

"And evidently won a substantial amount, too, sir. I can now backtrack and find the name he is using and where he is staying. He has already opened up for us, and I anticipate a lot of new information very soon as I become able to establish more specific criteria. Should I inform the CIA?"

"Oh, hell no. Keep this information within Trident for the time being. We're only a day behind him. Good job, Liz. Now get out of my office and go back to work."

At the age of four, in his home in Groton, Connecticut, Freedman stuck his right index finger into an empty light socket, and the electrical jolt threw him across the room. His nanny was listening to rock music on tape and never heard his cries. It stung! It burned! Eventually the pain eased, and the fright was replaced by curiosity. Benton Freedman had discovered electricity, and his world would never be the same.

At dinner that night, proudly wearing a Band-Aid on his injured finger, the little boy discussed the incident with his father, who took apart the offending lamp to show the boy how it worked. For months afterward, Benton roamed the two-story house with a screwdriver and needle-nosed pliers, disassembling toys, light switches on the walls, plugs at the ends of cords, and anything that remotely looked as if it ran on electricity. Within two years, he was devising simple programs on a basic Apple computer.

Freedman's father was an engineer who helped build submarines for the U.S. Navy, and he took Benton aboard one of the huge boats for a seventh birthday present. The Electric Boat yards on the Thames River was a howling seventeen acres of pure construction bedlam, where some twenty-five thousand workers worked with heavy machines performing some of the most intricate construction work in the world. Benton had often watched submarines gliding soundlessly up the smooth river with only part of the long black hull and the conning tower showing above the water. His dad took him across a rickety gangway in a huge dry dock, down a hatch, and into a new world. Lighted dials, pipes and valves, television screens and bundles of rubber-coated wires and sprawls of schematic diagrams. He was given a blue baseball cap with the sub's name woven in gold thread, and a birthday doughnut in the galley.

His father then showed him the most special part of

the boat, the space where a nuclear reactor was being installed to power this war beast. Benton quickly grasped the techniques, and the experience spurred his academic interest in science. He graduated from high school at fifteen, and took an associate's degree in mathematics at a state college while waiting to grow into the age limit for admittance to the U.S. Naval Academy. He was known among his classmates there as "the Wizard," graduated with honors, and went into the boats. Two undersea tours won him the coveted gold dolphins badge of a submarine officer. Then Freedman took a PhD in computer technology from the Massachusetts Institute of Technology and was swept up into the dark world of military special operations.

Despite his normal frazzled looks, Freedman never forgot the harrowing combat drills aboard the nukes, where he had honed his skills of working quickly and with total concentration in tight quarters, while under immense stress. Tons of ocean were just on the other side of the hull, waiting to crush you for a mistake. When General Middleton hand-picked the young genius for Task Force Trident, the lieutenant commander thought that it was the best thing that had happened to him since he stuck his finger in that light socket. Although the Trident Marines changed his nickname to "the Lizard," he tolerated the teasing because the organization's ultra clearances were the keys to the toy box, allowing him to draw from resources throughout the government to build a complex computer network that was secure, fast, and efficient.

For the present, his work was narrowed to supporting Kyle Swanson and Agent Lauren Carson and trying to track the renegade Jim Hall. With the financial sniffing programs in place on the secret accounts, the Lizard could spend more time patrolling the internal communications network of the CIA with his computer sweeps. The FBI was the prime agency hunting Kyle Swanson. The Lizard had plenty of access there, too.

There was also quite a bit on the Carson hunt, and much of the traffic seemed to be coming from the desk of a man named Jack Pathurst in the CIA Security Office. It was clear from the messages that her current whereabouts were unknown. That was as it should be, thought the Lizard, since he had worked with Major Summers to spirit the beautiful agent out of the country undetected and rendezvous with Sir Geoffrey Cornwell. Canadian passport, a wig of long, dark hair, a clean history, and presto, she was gone. Kyle was vectored in from another direction through Sir Geoffrey's extensive arrangements.

Now Freedman would build a protective information fence around the two fugitives. If anyone approached them, he would have plenty of tripwires in place.

38

Ridges of clouds with dark bottoms, pregnant with rain, had been gathering above the mountain towns of Umbria throughout the day, and the downpour broke about four o'clock, chasing Kyle and Lauren into the Tempio di S. Maria della Consolazione. It drummed ferociously on the weathered central dome and the four smaller hemispheric rooftops at each of the four corners, then slid harmlessly down the slabs of ancient stone.

"The only day in the past week that we decide to risk some time outside and it rains." Lauren shook her hair with her open fingers. It had been cut much shorter and colored a deep brown.

Kyle folded the umbrella and left it at the doorway. He had grown a mustache but not a beard. "I don't care. Being confined to the villa was reminding me of my old cell in Islamabad."

Lauren gave him a playful slap. "Being alone with me in a romantic Italian villa is like being in prison with those rats you told me about? Is that what you're saying?"

Swanson pulled her close and kissed her on the lips. She smelled good, tasted even better. "No. But that place is just two big shoe boxes stacked atop one another, with hardly any ventilation and a bathroom the size of a postcard." Turning her loose, he looked up at the intricate stonework, then wandered into one of the apses and back to the main entrance, his footsteps echoing. They were alone.

As he stared into the curtain of rain pelting the parking lot and grassy slope, she came up behind him, put her arms around his waist, and laid her cheek on his broad back. "We're leaving soon, aren't we?"

"Afraid so. Since I contacted the Lizard this morning to pass along your comment that Hall would have just gone to Monaco to play, we have to change positions again. Unfriendly intel people may track the cell phone towers and come up with the right country code." He had already destroyed the temporary cell phone and bought another. "We can move a little faster now."

"But why stay around here at all? This area has too many bad memories for me, Kyle. Jim Hall used to take me to his villa up in Tuscany for a weekend. I was so dumb."

Kyle paused to watch the gusting winds lash the paving stones on the approach road. He would not pass judgment on her. "Defense, Lauren. It is standard evasion and escape technique to think defensively in these situations." He took her hand, and they walked back deeper into the ornate church. "This place was perfect for a while. I did some training a few years ago with the

Gruppo Operativo Incursori, part of the Italian special forces, and one of the guys came from around here. He brought me down to the family farm for a weekend."

"So you milked a cow? So have I. It isn't a big deal."

Kyle laughed. "No. They grew olives. Anyway, I learned about Umbria that weekend, and how the residents of these mountain towns have been suspicious of each other for centuries. Every town was a fort unto itself, and they still compete in everything from who has the best wine to who turns out the best goat cheese. The original city walls still surround Todi."

"The people have been great to us," she replied.

"That's because we are a nice Canadian couple visiting on an out-of-season vacation. The Americans all go to Tuscany, to the north, just like Jim Hall did. So the Umbrians are pretty much left to themselves. Tourists are tolerated only as much as a rival merchant from another hill village. Strangers stand out and are treated differently."

"So if anybody was after us, we could spot them first?"

"It gave us a narrow edge while things developed. No more than that." He took her hand. "I don't like defense, Lauren. Never have. It's always better to be the hunter than the prey. Are you sure you are up to this next step? Might get messy."

"Can we go back to our place first? Dry off and wait for the storm to end?"

"Sounds good to me," he said.

"Yea," she said softly.

* * *

Just before dawn. Always the best time for an attack. Kyle threaded the little rental car through the curving mountain roads, little more than farming trails, outside of the mountain village of Pienza.

"Just ahead on the right, there's a small road leading to the north," Lauren said, using a small flashlight to illuminate the map. "If I remember right, that's the corner of the vineyard, and there is a water-pumping apparatus sticking out of the ground."

"Got it," replied Kyle, turning into the narrow driveway that unspooled down the hillside. The metal tanks in the backseat clanked together with dull thumps. In about a half mile they rolled onto the flat plateau, and he shut off the lights.

The old stone building had been around since the sixteenth century, beginning as a serf's cottage and growing, layer by layer, into a sturdy home with accompanying outbuildings to shelter farming equipment. Jim Hall owned the place through a false business name and leased the surrounding land, which was thick with neat rows of a vineyard that yielded fat purple grapes that were turned into a delicious wine. The entire place was dark.

They got out of the car, and Lauren walked purposefully up the steps, moved aside a pot of flowers on a ledge, and found the key to the front door. Without knocking, she opened the lock and went inside. "Nobody stays here but Jim, and a housekeeper comes in twice a week. Bastard likes to play lord of the feudal manor." She went from room to room, switching on lights, and the darkness gave way to light gold colors and white walls. A shudder ran through her as she remembered the time she had spent here as his lover. He had completely fooled and used her.

Kyle moved through the place to give it a quick search and clear. It was spacious and comfortable, with thick rugs on the floors and heavy European furniture. When he reached the rear bedroom, he saw Lauren furiously stripping black silk sheets from the king-sized bed, and then he silently followed her out into the backyard.

Without speaking, she flung the sheets over a clothesline and anchored them with a row of wooden pins. She stalked back to the house and snatched a large, sharp butcher's knife from the kitchen. Swanson stood aside and let her work, seeing her cheeks wet with tears of fury. Moonlight glinted on the knife blade as she plunged and stabbed and sliced through the soft cloth, ripping it to shreds until she ran out of breath and stood facing the tattered sheets, exhausted, breathing in big gulps. She dropped the knife, and ribbons of silk sheets flapped in a gentle predawn breeze.

By the time she turned around, Swanson was already lugging the heavy dark blue tanks of propane gas into the house. They had purchased the five ButanGas canisters over the past few days from different stores while still in Umbria, explaining that they were about to christen their new Spiedino stainless steel grill with some outdoor cooking at a picnic for friends.

Kyle found an expensive tie, a muted diamond design on lilac, on a closet rack, and a bottle of 80 proof brandy among the cluster of bottles on the marble-topped bar in the living room. He opened the bottle and stuffed the necktie deep inside, letting the rich alcoholic drink wick into the material. "Ready?" he asked.

She picked up a bottle of olive oil and threw it against the wall of the living room, then sailed a second one into the bathroom, where it shattered in the large multiple-head shower. Her face was red with anger. "You bet."

Swanson went to the bedroom of the villa and twisted the valve of the propane gas cylinder fully open, sniffing the air for the telltale odor. Lauren was doing the same thing in the second bedroom, and he leapfrogged into the hallway and opened the third of the bottles, each of which carried the emblem of a rearing white dragon on a blue shield. Lauren hurried past him to the kitchen and opened the fourth one. They met in the living room, and she opened the final tank.

"Go start the car," he said, and she dashed into the growing light of day, a smile coming to her face as she slid behind the wheel. Kyle was on the veranda, holding the bottle of brandy high and setting fire to the liquid-soaked tie with his lighter. The flame caught, tiny for only a flickering instant, then began to speed up as it ate into the accelerant. Kyle left the bottle sitting just inside the partially open door, with more of the expensive fuse disappearing every second.

Lauren already had the car turned around and rolling away when he dove inside. She stamped onto the accelerator. The little vehicle seemed to crawl, then gave a lurch, and the tires dug into the gravel.

Behind them, the propane gas had filled the entire house by the time the flaming Piero Tucci tie met the 40 percent alcohol brandy and the house erupted, its heavy stone walls funneling the blast upward in a rolling tower of flame and thunder.

39

"Gunnery Sergeant Kyle Swanson of the United States Marine Corps is charged with mass murder." The lawyer, a civilian representing the Central Intelligence Agency, was making a bland statement of fact, reading from a sheet of paper. "Specifically, the accused is to be court-martialed for violating Article 118 of the Uniform Code of Military Justice, by committing the unpremeditated murder of at least nineteen specific persons in Pakistan. The punishment will be something other than death, as directed by a court-martial, but may include dishonorable discharge, forfeiture of all pay and allowances, and confinement for life."

"Who?" Major Sybelle Summers gave away nothing. She adjusted the sleeves of her comfortable dark brown suit. The buttons of the jacket were undone to make it roomier for the pistol on her belt while she was seated. A beige blouse and flats and minimal accessories completed the understated outfit. Her black hair was styled short and swept back. Around her slender neck was a chain with various plastic cards that granted her entrance to quiet, private rooms in the Pentagon and other important places, such as this one. She had the highest security clearance possible.

The lawyer, Stephen Swinton, darted his eyes from the papers spread before him to the attractive woman seated across the table. It was difficult not to be impressed. "You are the operations officer of a special unit known as Task Force Trident, are you not, Major?"

"I know of no such organization. I work with the White House Military Office and sometimes carry the football, the briefcase containing nuclear codes the president may need in case of an emergency. I also help with the military side of advance work for presidential trips."

Swinton was smug, anxious to pierce the screens this woman was throwing up, and he continued his delivery. "And in your capacity as the Trident operations officer, you also were the commanding officer of Gunnery Sergeant Swanson at the time of the action in question, is that not so?"

"Someone has given you faulty information, Mr. Swinton. I don't know what you're talking about." Her voice was irritatingly precise and icily confident. Her calm, dark eyes betrayed no sign of nervousness.

Swinton, who had been a CIA attorney for three years, had dealt with difficult cases before. They always thought they could outsmart him, despite the knowledge that he had the resources of the entire Central Intelligence Agency to support him and build a case. He decided that an abrupt change of subject, a slightly veiled personal insult, might shake her confidence. "That is a designer suit you are wearing, Major. Very nice. Prada, if I am not mistaken. The shoes are Italian leather, and your purse is a small and stylish Gucci. Rather expensive attire for someone of your pay grade as a mere Marine major."

Not a ripple. She shrugged. "My daddy's rich and my mama's good-looking."

Jesus Christ. "Two weeks ago, you were in charge of a mission that inserted two snipers into Pakistan to take down separate Taliban targets simultaneously. But Swanson went on a rampage instead, and numerous Pakistani civilians are dead as a result."

"Sir," she replied, "on the dates in question, I was in Idaho, where the president was coming to make a campaign speech. Check the duty roster and the flight manifests. The Secret Service will vouch for me."

"Major Summers." The CIA lawyer, growing frustrated, spread his hand across a stack of folders filled with papers. "The Secret Service will not discuss presidential protection protocols."

"A wise decision, don't you think?" She smiled.

"I advise you to take this very seriously, Major Summers. We know all about you and Swanson and General Middleton and Task Force Trident."

"Boise was pretty. A little chilly this time of year."

"We know everything."

"About Boise? I imagine you would. The visit was widely publicized, and the new president is pretty popular. He gets a lot of press coverage."

"Why are you being so unhelpful, Major? We should be on the same side on this. We want to get Sergeant Swanson to safety in an American prison, and out of danger, as soon as possible."

"It's Gunnery Sergeant Swanson, not Sergeant. Please try to be accurate. Now. Is this meeting over? I need to get back to work. There's a party in the East Wing this afternoon, and the first lady wants me to be there."

The lawyer slapped his folders together in exasperation, turned off his little tape recorder, and stuffed it all into a leather briefcase. "Very well. I was hoping that you would be more cooperative in an informal setting. The next time we meet, it will be at CIA headquarters in Langley. I must advise you to bring your own lawyer. You will either answer my questions promptly and totally, or you may be charged as an accomplice, under UCMJ Article 107, for giving a false official statement. That could mean up to five years in prison."

"*Oooooh*. That's real scary." Sybelle Summers stood, buttoned her jacket, and went to the door. She turned around. She already knew the small room was not bugged, which was one of the reasons she chose to meet here. "Off the record?"

The attorney nodded. He also was standing, his briefcase on the table before him, his shield from harm.

"You think you know everything? Well, you don't. You know only what we choose to allow you to know. In other words, you don't know shit, and it's going to damned well stay that way. The Agency fucked this operation, not us, and now you have given your guy a pass. You don't want this to go public."

"Swanson is going down," snapped the CIA man. "Why are you risking a jail term yourself for this renegade?"

"You wouldn't understand."

"Try me."

"Simple. Kyle would do the same for me. We take care of our own."

"You are right. I don't understand why you Marines always want to lie down in traffic for each other."

"Of course you don't. Stephen, you are a desk jockey with no field experience. You would just leave your friends behind rather than risk your own ass."

"Anything else, Major?"

Sybelle's eyes suddenly became like dark stones. "Kyle didn't murder anybody. We already have sworn statements from Americans and Pakistanis who were on the scene, and they will destroy any case you try to bring. You people need to rethink this whole vendetta. Agent Carson also did nothing wrong, and we are thinking about giving the *Washington Post* an exclusive interview with her, pretty pictures and all. So you need to take care of this in a hurry, Stevie."

"Why?" The change in the woman had been remarkable; from a stubborn and stylish lady to a tigress protecting her cubs in the blink of an eye. The file said she was the only woman ever to complete the elite Marine Force Recon training and that she was known in the Corps as the Queen of Darkness. He had dismissed that as just the usual military hyperbole. The abrupt change made him a believer.

"If you don't, somebody might get hurt. That someone might be you. By bringing me in and threatening me, you have put yourself in the line of fire. Don't think your desk will protect you now, nor that stupid chocolate Lab at your home in Arlington, nor your weight-lifting buddy at the hideaway on the Eastern Shore. You have become part of the problem, and we solve problems."

The lawyer pulled protectively on the lapels of his suit and gave a nervous pat to his pale hair. "So you are trying to threaten me? Is that a threat?"

"A promise." Sybelle Summers smiled and left the room, closing the door softly behind her.

BERLIN
GERMANY

Selim Waleed of the Taliban stood outside a small hotel on Potsdamer Street, a quiet and midrange place favored by business executives, not far from the Landwehr Kanal that wove through the heart of Berlin. It was early morning, but all around him industrious Germans were already hustling to work. Selim pushed up the collar of his overcoat to keep the cold wind from his neck. He was of average size in most countries, but in Germany he often felt like a pygmy; the whole nation was full of large people who loved eating great portions of the filthy animal that no Muslim would ever touch. The diner at a table next to him last night had ordered *Eisbein* and *Salzkartoffeln,* which was a huge pickled knuckle of a pig, with the meat falling onto a bed of boiled potatoes. When the heavy tray appeared before the man, Selim fled from his own table and resorted to room service.

At precisely eight o'clock in the morning, an elegant silver-white Mercedes E63 AMG whispered to a stop before him, and a smiling Jim Hall waved from behind the steering wheel. The door on the passenger side clicked, and Selim opened it. The leathery new car smell was overwhelming as he slid into the seat, which fit as if it had been handmade just for him. "Howdy, partner," Hall sang out. "Let's go for a ride." The sedan accelerated rapidly into the traffic flowing toward the huge columns of the Brandenburg Tor.

"Like my new wheels?" asked Hall. "Zero to sixty miles per hour in four point five seconds. A 518-horsepower engine under the hood, and it flies like the wind. I thought about getting the Stirling Moss Roadster version, but that's really too much of a race car."

"Why are you doing this, Jim Hall? I thought you were to maintain a low profile until the job is done."

"Why, Selim, this *is* a low profile for me. I have always had expensive tastes. Got a discount on this baby, seventy-five grand, because I paid cash. Now I don't have to ride those damned trains anymore. I can take my time getting anywhere in Europe, and in comfort. Hand-stitched leather. Here, you're cold. I'll turn on the seat heater." He clicked a switch, then dropped his hand back to the gear lever, changing to a lower ratio as he found a route marker and turned a corner. Then the car leaped onto the *Bundesautobahn,* and when he spied a round road sign with the diagonal stripes, the speed limit came off. He opened up the big engine.

"This will only draw attention to yourself. It is madness. My father will not be pleased."

"He's your father, not mine. How is the old snake, anyway?"

"He is well. A bit anxious because the political center in Pakistan is still holding together. We had hoped the Islamabad attack might finish off the government."

The speedometer was pegging at 150 kilometers per hour. The car had been delivered with an electronic device that limited the top speed to that velocity, but Hall had a specialist remove the governor because he had not bought a hot car to only go 90 miles per hour. He pressed the pedal, and the sleek Mercedes leaped at the command. "Yeah, I hear you. Islamabad was a mess. I thought it would finish off the government, too."

"So now you have to complete the remaining task, the other option. Which is one reason you should still be under cover."

Hall kept a light grip on the wheel, letting the sensors in the driving avionics keep the car under control as he said without a care, "The assassination. Right. When and where?"

"The president is to meet with other regional leaders in a special conference in Istanbul next week. You take him out while he is there."

A vision of the Turkish city swam into Hall's mind. "I can do that. Then our deal is complete, right?" He was well over 100 miles per hour now and coming up fast on the bumper of an Alfa Romeo. Hall flashed his lights, and the Alfa moved over. He zipped past with a rush of air that rocked the smaller car.

"That is correct." Selim was holding on tight. "You must go back into your old ways, Jim Hall. This will not be an easy task for you. Get rid of this flashy car and those fancy clothes and the high-flying lifestyle until you finish."

There was a grump of a laugh. "I know how to go about my business, Selim. And the image doesn't matter because the CIA and I have a special arrangement. They won't bother me."

"You do not know everything, my friend."

"So I'm too busy these days to watch TV news. So what? You will get me the advance information I need to make the plan."

"So you are unaware that your friend Kyle Swanson not only has lived through the situation in Islamabad, but he also has escaped from prison. The CIA woman, Carson, also has disappeared."

Jim Hall froze for a second, then lifted his foot from the accelerator, tapped the brakes, and swerved out of the fast lane, all the way across the highway and onto the safety of the broad shoulder. By the time the car had stopped, his face was chalky. "Swanson is on the loose?"

"Yes. Nobody knows where he is," Selim told him, turning in the seat to face the assassin.

Hall sucked in some deep breaths. "He is coming after me."

"Perhaps."

"No fucking 'perhaps' about it." Already Hall's eyes were nervously surveying the countryside around him and the various mirrors. He pounded a fist on the cushioned steering wheel. "Shit. Double shit."

"It does not change our agreement. You still must go to Istanbul and kill the president next week."

Hall put the Mercedes back into gear and regained the highway, this time at an almost sedate pace, watching his mirrors and the passing vehicles. "Yeah. I'll do it. If Kyle lets me live that long."

They made the trip back into Berlin in silence. Hall dropped off Selim and drove back to the underground parking lot in the luxury hotel where he had booked a suite. Upstairs, with the door locked, he logged in to the laptop and began reviewing his private e-mail accounts. A little red exclamation point flashed by one from Italy, an urgent note from his property manager. Authorities were investigating an explosion and a fire that had destroyed Hall's little villa by the vineyards in Tuscany. Some bedsheets that had been sliced to pieces were still hanging outside on a clothesline. Arson was suspected; the agent had been questioned and was asking for instructions.

My villa! That bitch Lauren told Kyle about my villa! They were together and had gone active, removing his favorite place of refuge. Jim Hall fought to keep control of himself as he walked around the spacious hotel room. Things were not hopeless. Far from it. He knew Kyle too well. Additional countermeasures had to be put into place; then he could carry out the Istanbul hit. After that, he would take his time finding Lauren and Kyle and killing them both.

40

By the time Jim Hall received the e-mail about his
home in the Tuscan countryside, a tired Kyle Swanson
was handing a worn British passport to a customs agent
at Don Muang Airport. He had come in on a Thai Airways flight all the way from Rome, more than five
thousand miles, the trip made shorter by the customary
pampering of the excellent airline. Swanson had slept
most of the way.

Lauren had wanted to come, but as much as he wished
she could be with him, it would have been a terrible tactical decision. A single white man arriving alone in
Bangkok is expected to be drawn to the seedy parts of
the city, the massage parlors, bars, and whorehouses that
had made Patpong Road a destination for lonely men
since the Vietnam War. A *farang,* a foreigner, could find
sex of any sort there, for a small price. Prostitution was
a national industry. Kyle would be accepted with hardly
a glance, while Lauren's ivory beauty would have drawn
attention.

Also, she was being sought by the CIA and was

probably on watch lists around the world, while Swanson was apparently still being considered a fugitive but not a threat.

"Are you in Bangkok for business or pleasure, Mr. James?" asked the busy customs clerk, glancing at his face and the passport.

"A little of both, I hope," Swanson answered with a smirk.

The clerk sighed. The *farang* always gave that answer, an impolite joke that held the country up to ridicule. He stamped the passport for a five-day stay and let him go, hoping that the man caught some horrible disease from an unclean woman.

Kyle thanked him and walked through the international arrivals lounge, where uniformed car drivers waved names of their pickups on grease-board placards. Squadrons of other young men, drivers and freelance tourist guides, tugged at his shirt, promising to take him wherever he wanted to go.

A tall, gangly American with shaggy gray hair parted in the middle and falling over his ears caught his eye, turned, and shambled away. Kyle followed the man outside, to where a battered old Mercedes waited at the curb like a faithful horse. The man slipped a handful of baht to the cop who had kept an eye on the parked car, and they got in and drove away before ever saying anything to each other.

"Can't believe Jim Hall went over to the dark side." Tom Hodges had a voice like doom, naturally deep and made even more gravelly by years of smoking cigarettes. Originally from Iowa, he had prowled the Quang Tri mountains as a young Marine sniper during Vietnam and had trained under the legendary Carlos Hathcock himself. When Hodges had gone to Bangkok for a liberty pass, he emerged from his first visit to a classy steam-and-cream parlor with a smile on his face and a decision to make Thailand his home. It was not at all like Iowa. At the end of his tour, he spent a weekend in Des Moines at the home of his only sister, then flew back to Bangkok, bought a bar in partnership with a Thai politician, and never looked back.

"Believe it," said Swanson, leaning back in the seat. "How've you been, Tom?"

"Same old, same old. Too many girls, too many opium pipes, too much booze, and too many years." He grinned. The shiny teeth were false. "Somewhere along the line, I got old. Lucky for me, enough money keeps coming in to pay for my deviant lifestyle and bribes. Yourself?"

"Getting by. Tired."

"Rome is a long way from here."

"Yeah. And I've got to do this thing quick and get back there soon as possible."

"I have some pills that can help, little energy bombs that will take you way up, then a couple of pipes to bring you down again, oh so easy."

"No thanks. I've got to keep a clear head. What about the other stuff?"

"Middleton sent me your shopping list. I have it all at our apartment. Anything else, you just name it. Mary Kay and I are still the best fixers in town." Hodges had turned his links to the military into a lucrative side career, an efficient business that was guided by his wife, a beautiful Thai woman who came off a desolate farm in the country to become a bar dancer and then a respected entrepreneur. After peddling Mary Kay cosmetics to other bar girls, she made the company's totally American brand name her own and married the huge American. When U.S. covert operators, or anyone else, needed special assistance in Bangkok, Mary Kay and Tiny Tom Hodges were the go-to team, as long as the money was right. "Speaking of which, she is making you a curry dinner tonight. She won't let you go out to work without some solid food in your belly."

"You okay with helping out, Tom?" The traffic had grown steadily heavier and finally was humping along just a little faster than total gridlock. Stuttering *tuk-tuk* taxis squeezed between the halted cars and trucks. Nobody gave way, but somehow there was motion and slow progress.

"We'll break out of this in a half mile. Then I'll drive you past the place for a quick look-see. I've already taken some pictures and made a sketch. There's a map in the glove box. I circled the address in red marker. Not hard to find."

Swanson recognized some landmarks and saw the circle. "You didn't answer my question. You okay with this?"

"Actually, no, I'm not. If Hall is selling our covert operators to our enemies, then burning down his house ain't nowhere near enough punishment, Kyle. I'd rather shoot the bastard." Hodges pushed a hand through his hair to move it away from his face. His eyes were gleaming, excited, as if he were looking down a scope. "And since you don't know how to drive in Bangkok traffic, I will be going along tonight as your spotter. After we're done, I take you straight back to the airport, and you will be out of here by midnight. Sound like a deal?"

It was a nice, solid two-story home that would not have looked out of place in any upscale Middle America enclave, except for the lush tropical greenery and a thick seven-foot-high fence with broken glass imbedded along the top. A gate of ornamental iron was across the driveway, and a pair of concrete elephants stood sentinel at the corners of the front patio and steps. Lights were on over the entrance and inside.

"Hall has kept this place as a CIA safe house for more than ten years," said Tom Hodges, flat on his belly beside Kyle on the roof of an empty house two blocks to the south. He was peering through a spotting scope. "When the Agency had no further need for it because it had become too well known, our boy Jim sold it to himself in a sweetheart deal. A lot of us have been suspicious for a long time that he was letting terrorist types use it. I see one guard outside, just at the right side of the gate in that little shack. Looks Khmer. See the checkered scarf?"

"I see the guard," Kyle said.

"Now look inside at the big living room. Big-screen TV has a soccer match on. The guy in the chair with a beer is also Cambodian and is a big narcotics type. Ruthless bastard named Tea Duch."

"I see him." The man was obese, and his undershirt

bulged over his boxer shorts. "There's a girl on the sofa. And a woman servant back in the kitchen."

"So take your choice, pal."

"Assuming I can hit anything with this antique." He tightened the leather strap around his left arm and brought the smooth walnut stock of the old Model 70 Winchester .30-06 to his cheek. The long, slender weapon was a perfect fit, and the 10-power Unertl scope had no scratches.

"It was good enough for me in Vietnam, brother. If you can't shoot it, I can. Do the guard first. An inside shot would make the women scream and alert him." Hodges read off his data and did a final laser range check to the guard shack. The shot would be down, coming over the wall at a sharp angle. "Three hundred and seventy-eight yards, one-and-a-half-minute wind, right to left."

Kyle made final adjustments to the old rifle's scope and saw the lazy guard. His AK-47 was propped against a wall, and he rested against a tall stool, leafing through a girlie magazine. Lazy and ignorant, passing the time. Swanson exhaled quietly and tightened the pull on the trigger. "On target."

Hodges lifted his head and gave a quick look at the neighborhood. Quiet except for some passing traffic in the next block. "Fire."

The Winchester barked a single time, sounding more like a car's backfire than a gunshot, and the bullet drilled into the guard's chest before he could react to the sound. The impact knocked him from the stool and onto the floor, bleeding hard and in shock as his punctured heart slowed and stopped. The eyes never closed.

AN ACT OF TREASON

Swanson had already worked the bolt and reloaded
and was looking at the man inside. The big Cambodian
had not even twitched at the sound of the shot, probably because the sound was soaked up by the crowd
noise on the television set. There was no further need
for communication with Hodges, and Kyle simply cen-
tered his sight picture and fired again. This bullet had a
bigger target; it plunged into the enormous stomach of
the drug trafficker and tore through the kidneys and the
spine. The target jolted upright, his eyes wide with
surprise, and his bottle of Singha beer fell to the floor.
There was a howl of pain, and he grabbed for the
spurting wound. Kyle reloaded and pumped a second
round into the jittering big body, hitting the top of the
head and exploding the skull.

Kyle and Hodges were on the move immediately, and
as Hodges retrieved the car, Swanson ran to the gate. It
wasn't even locked, since the guard inside with the automatic weapon was believed to be more than enough security. In quick strides, Kyle was inside, where a slender,
pretty young girl with long and silky black hair stood in
the corner, fists to her lips in terror. The housekeeper, an
older woman, was standing beside her.

Swanson appeared as some dark and evil dragon,
face blackened and wearing black clothing that allowed him to blend into the night. He let them have a
good look at both his face and the big sniper rifle, then
handed the housekeeper a small envelope on which he
had printed the name JIM HALL. "Speak any English?"
he asked calmly, keeping any menace from his voice.

The woman nodded. "Yes."

"Make sure that note gets to the American that owns this place. Not the police."

She gripped the envelope tightly and nodded her head to show understanding, for she was used to seeing violent men come through this accursed home, and to doing what she was told without question.

"Now both of you get out of here. Tell anyone who asks what you have seen tonight. Go!" Inside the envelope was a piece of paper on which Swanson had written a single word: *HOG*. It would make no sense to anyone but a fellow Marine sniper, who would automatically recognize it as the acronym for their private, descriptive motto "Hunters of Gunmen."

As the women fled down the stairs and into the street, Swanson pulled the pin on an AN-M14 thermite grenade and tossed it onto the sofa.

He hustled back outside and found Hodges waiting at the end of the driveway, with the car door open. Inside the house, the grenade detonated, and for the next forty-five seconds, it spewed chemical droplets that burned fiercely at 2,200 degrees, setting fire to everything they touched. Within two minutes, the house was a raging inferno.

41

José Eduardo Bandeira remembered Lynn Cunningham well, for as manager of the Banco Português de Negócios, he had personally had the honor of assisting the American three years ago in opening a *depósito a prazo* for her company. It had proven to be a lucrative transaction for the troubled bank, for since that initial meeting, deposits were regularly wired in, and no withdrawals had been taken. He remembered her also for her beauty, and for her gracious smile. The *gerente* was smitten.

"I assume from these figures that your business has been successful, *sinhorita*," Bandeira said, forcing his eyes to focus on the figures on his computer screen and not on her lovely legs. "You have done well. How may I be of service today?"

Lauren Carson was using the name she'd used several years ago when opening the account with Jim Hall, who also had established a false identity for this stash of funds. She remembered the manager, too. A ladies' man. To deflect him from paying full attention to the account, she had dressed appropriately in a dark business suit with a short, tight skirt and a loose, scoop-necked blouse that showed too much when she leaned forward. She leaned forward, her eyes questioning. "I need to transfer some funds back to the United States," she said. "What is the total in the account at present?"

"Of course. It will be no problem." Oh! She was so stunning. "May I please examine your tax card?"

"Yes." Lauren sat back, crossed her legs, and wasted some time digging through her purse. She brought out a leather-bound business Day-Timer and removed the fiscal permission form that was in a plastic folder.

Bandeira found it to be current and proper. "Both you and Mr. Roger Petersen have access to this account. He is not with you today?"

"He is elsewhere on company business. Is that a problem? We are expanding quite nicely." She smiled. "It gives me a chance to spend some time alone in this lovely city. I am dying to visit the Berardo Museum."

"Ah, my favorite. Many prefer the Calouste Gulben-kian, but the Berardo is my personal favorite: a trea-sure house of modern art," the *gerente* agreed. "Perhaps I could host you for a luncheon and a personal tour."

Lauren cocked her head to one side, her eyes on him. "Should time permit, I would be delighted."

José Eduardo Bandeira adjusted his tie and uncon-sciously touched his small mustache. "Excellent. Now to business." He looked at the computer screen on his wide desk and tapped some keys. "This account shows about . . . one moment, let me get out of euros . . . twelve million dollars, U.S. Since it is a joint account, you have the necessary access."

"Very well." She opened her Day-Timer again and gave him two account numbers in the United States. "Mr. Petersen and I would like to transfer six million dollars to each of those accounts, as soon as possible."

"All of it?" The bank manager exhaled with a deep sigh. She was closing the entire account. He tried to think of some way to change her mind, but the order and tax forms were perfectly legal. Perhaps a veiled threat might work. "I must make certain that you are aware our bank goes to great lengths to prevent international money laundering, not that you would do such a thing, of course, but it is a requirement since we were nationalized. These transfers must be reported in accordance with the terms of the USA Patriot Act."

Lauren Carson recrossed her legs to give a flash of thigh. "We are counting on that," she said. "Our company certainly endorses the financial elements of the Patriot Act, if for no other reason than to keep our own policies ethical. We would insist the names of the recipients—Mr. Pathurst and Mrs. Glenda Swinton—be filed with the proper financial authorities within the American government and the Department of Homeland Security. In fact, we would insist on that even if there was no such requirement on your part."

He busily wrote out an instruction, stapled the paper with the new account numbers to it, and summoned an aide from an outer office to make the transactions. "It will take but a few minutes, Sinhorita Cunningham.

Perhaps we can have some tea and chat about the museum while they finish."

"*Muito obrigado,*" she replied in Portugese—thank you. "I would quite enjoy that. And I also regret closing the entire account, but such is the world of venture capitalism. We have found a unique opportunity and must act quickly."

"Such is the world," agreed the manager. It was only money, after all. Spending a few hours with Lynn Cunningham on his arm was worth much more.

WASHINGTON, D.C.

The Lizard had been paying careful attention to the time changes around the world. The day officially began when the sun broke for a new morning on the islands of the Pacific Ocean, so that meant that the banks in Asia were his first targets. He wanted the instructions to land with the first batch of business for the day, when the data load would be heavy clearing away the overnight transactions from America and Europe.

The Standard Chartered Private Bank of Singapore was a large and efficient operation, one of the anchors of the Pan-Asian banking system and very discreet, with miserly interest rates on deposits. Lim Hwee Liu, a sector manager, fielded the incoming wire transfer request, a rather standard transaction that would shift eight million U.S. dollars. He checked the password and authorization codes and scribbled a note that the eight million, split evenly between a pair of accounts in the United

States, would carry a higher than normal transfer and handling commission for the bank. Eight million dollars also was not enough to worry about. That figure would not even reach the middle range of the other interbank wire transfers that he would handle from all over the world during the long day to come. Liu then handed a printout of the instructions to one of his three assistants to finish and turned to thoughts of the Bank of China's new interest rate schedule. That country was awash with new money, and one of Liu's responsibilities was to examine ways in which the Standard Chartered Private Bank of Singapore could continue as a major player for a share of that wealth. Then there was an opening-hours flip in the direction of the Nikkei Index that measured the Japanese stock market. What was that about? Closing an account for a small and private American company with a routine transfer of funds did not raise an eyebrow for Lim Hwee Liu.

When the confirmation was made that the Singapore account had been eliminated, and the money gone, Lieutenant Commander Benton Freedman took his time bleaching the entire file. Not a scrap of electronic data would trace the source of the original order back to him.

Jack Pathurst of the CIA and Glenda Swinton, the owner of a small fashion boutique in Georgetown and wife of CIA attorney Stephen Swinton, were each richer by still another four million dollars.

Freedman then began stacking up the information he needed for later in the day, when he would do a similar morning blitz on Randall MacDavies, a senior vice president at the Royal Bank of Scotland in Edinburgh, where the Lizard would raid still another hidden account belonging to Jim Hall. He could do even more of the accounts, probably all of them, in a single work shift, but that was not the plan. Two was quite enough for one day, plus the one that Agent Carson had done in Portugal. Kyle had been very specific about the schedule.

42

Kyle Swanson came up smoothly from the depths of his slumber, rising from the busy REM state in which the brain fires up convoluted dreams through the vague fog just below the surface of sleep and then, pop, awake. He sensed peace and safety rather than any danger. His eyes took in the red numbers of the bedside alarm clock, and he allowed himself the luxury of a long, muscle-stretching yawn. Morning. Naked beneath smooth, clean sheets in a large bed. Totally recovered from the long round-trip flight from Italy to Thailand. Feeling good. Cell phone and pistol within reaching distance.

The hotel room was dark in the bedroom, with the heavy drapes closed, but beyond the door, daylight illuminated the adjacent sitting room. He could see a pair of bare feet, and he heard the buzz of a television set. Swanson threw aside the sheets and a lightweight duvet, pulled on his shorts, and padded silently toward the portal and leaned against it.

The room smelled like Dr. Frankenstein's laboratory. Lauren was on the sofa, wearing a white hotel robe loosely knotted at the waist. Her hair was wet. Her feet rested on a cushion, and she was slowly painting her nails while watching an English-language news program on the BBC. The nails were a pale pink; she was curling her fingers to get a getter look. Bottles and jars of cosmetics were strewn on a dressing table with a big mirror. He walked up behind her, leaned over, and kissed her wet hair, looking straight down into her cleavage. She stretched her head back for a full kiss, and he obliged, then slid his hands down her front, into the folds of the robe, and cupped her warm breasts.

"Mmmmm. You pick the strangest times to get amorous," she said. "At least let me finish my nails." She gave him another languid kiss and a big smile. "Welcome back, Kyle. You were a wreck last night when you got in."

"I was really tired."

"Being fugitives from justice can be exhausting," she agreed.

Kyle reluctantly moved away from her and went to the little kitchenette and put together a quick breakfast of apple slices and cheese on soft croissants, and strong coffee. "Not much longer, Lauren. Things should really be coming into play later today."

She glanced over. He seemed unfazed about their problems. "Why are you so certain? I'm scared to death."

Kyle swallowed a bit of breakfast and took a long hit of caffeine before responding. "How long have you been out here doing your girl stuff?"

Lauren dipped the little brush into the bottle and

stroked the liquid onto her left index fingernail. "I had the concierge round up all of these things early this morning, and they were delivered about an hour ago. I've been hard at work ever since then."

"The TV on the whole time, too? The BBC news readers?"

"Yes." She waggled her toes. Wads of tissue were stuffed between them, part of the process. "Just background noise to keep me company while you snored away in the next room."

"I don't snore." He poured a fresh cup of coffee, walked over, and sat on the table beside her feet. "Have you heard anything about us on the Beebs? Seen our pictures?" He slid his free hand onto an ankle and felt the smooth skin.

"Stop that! And no, we have not been on TV for the past hour." Lauren stretched her legs and shifted her feet to his lap.

"We won't be, either. Not only are we old news, but the authorities are not pushing anymore. Things have become static while Washington decides what to do next. Meanwhile, we increase the pressure on Jim Hall to force him out of his own hiding place."

"Jim's smart and dangerous," she warned.

"So are we," Kyle said, tracing a finger up her left leg to the edge of the robe, and then under it, loving the touch of her skin.

She used a foot to explore his lap further. "Not everything is static."

"And to hell with your fingernails."

ANTALYA
TURKEY

Jim Hall stared out at the incredibly blue waters of the Turkish Riviera from the balcony of the suite in the small but exclusive beachfront hotel and wondered if the CIA was fucking with him. They had a deal! Were they going to need another lesson?

He fixed a drink at the little bar and took a swallow, getting over the shock as he paced the soft rugs. Somebody was going to die for this.

Hall had come into the comfortable lobby, as he had done in a thousand other hotels, and automatically ran his eyes over the few people sitting and standing around. There was nothing suspicious, so he walked to the front desk and smiled at the neat young man behind the computer screen. There was no need to ask if the man spoke English, for most Turks speak several languages fluently, a gift from the wandering ancient Seljuks whose business was conquering other nations from the ports along this Mediterranean Sea coast. The Turks were merchants to their souls. Hall said he had a reservation and gave the false name of Roger Petersen, showed the false passport, then placed his platinum American Express card on the slick stone desktop.

The clerk pulled up the reservation, printed it out, then swiped the Amex through the card reader. He paused, then did it again. And a third time. When he spoke, it was with a lower voice, so as not to embarrass the guest. "I am sorry, Mr. Petersen, but this card seems to be invalid."

Jim Hall blinked in surprise. "Pardon me?"

"Sir, the card is not being accepted, for some reason. I'm sure it is nothing but an error at the bank, but would you care to put the room on another card?"

Hall recovered quickly. When he had last checked that account with the Banco Português de Negócios, it contained about twelve million dollars! He forced a smile, stayed calm. "Of course. These things happen. I will deal with it later." He dug a MasterCard from his wallet. Same name, different bank. It was processed flawlessly.

Once he had dismissed the bellhop and settled into the room, he opened his computer and, using the hotel's Wi-Fi network connection, went to a secure portal and called up a screen that automatically updated his accounts around the world. His palms were flat on the table on each side of the little laptop, sweating, as he scanned the accounts.

Portugal, Singapore, and Scotland all showed the same number in the balance column: a big fat zero. *What the fuck?* He clicked the screen to Transaction History and discovered that all three accounts had been closed. Twelve million from Portugal, eight from Singapore, and ten from Scotland had vanished. Somebody had stolen thirty million dollars from his retirement fund.

Hall's throat was dry, and he grabbed a bottle of water as he burrowed deeper into what had happened. All of the transfers had been split, half going to Mrs. Glenda Swinton in Virginia. He had no idea who the hell Glenda Swinton was. Never heard of her. But he knew the other name all too well. Jack Pathurst was in the Security Office of the CIA.

Pathurst made the agreement not to chase me but never said anything about not taking the money, Hall thought. *The little weasel knows the Agency has written off the funds, so he is doing some financial farming on the side. Probably figures that I will just write off the loss as the cost of doing business.* Hall closed down the screen. Thirty million was a lot of money, part of his plan to live the rest of his life in comfort and ease.

Hall finished off the drink and stood at the big window, letting his pulse return to normal. He had a job to do on the northern side of Turkey and could not leave until it was done. The financial loss was staggering, but he could absorb it, if Jack Pathurst did not get greedy and snap up any more.

He decided to let it go for the moment. Maybe a few months from now, maybe a few years, he would drop by to see Pathurst and explain how it was not nice to steal from your buddies. But who the hell was Glenda Swinton?

Hall had been so absorbed with the financial loss that he did not get around to checking his e-mail until after a light lunch on the terrace, followed by a nap. With all of the numbers running around in his head, sleep was impossible, but he had a good hour of rest, then a shower, and felt refreshed.

He booted up the computer again and went to a Gmail account subfolder. Two messages, one of them an obvious spam sales message that had automatically been blocked. The second was from the estate management agency in Bangkok, where he maintained a profitable safe house for people in the dark trades, a beautiful home in which he had stored treasures that he had gathered during his years of journeying around Asia.

Jim Hall gasped aloud as he read it. The house was attacked, and two guests murdered by gunshots that police said appeared to be the work of a sniper. Then the building was set afire by a hand grenade and was completely engulfed in flames by the time the firefighters arrived. The live-in maid actually saw the gunman, who came into the house after the murders and gave her a message for delivery to Jim Hall. The police had opened it instead. It contained a slip of paper with only one word on it, "HOG." The authorities, said the Gmail, would like to speak with the owner.

He lowered his head, closed his eyes, and buried his face in his hands. *Hunters of Gunmen.* Kyle again.

Swanson was trying to ruin him. It became clear that the Agency was not behind the financial losses. Swanson was working with Lauren to identify and shut down his secret accounts, and if Kyle did the Bangkok hit, then he also did the villa in Tuscany. *Well,* thought Jim Hall, *that shit has got to stop.*

He had five days before the scheduled job in Istanbul, and he would put them to good use. As he sat at the table, the assassination of the president of Pakistan became a lower priority for him than saving his wealth and getting rid of the bulldog tracker who was after him. If he had to choose, he would rather have the Taliban on his tail than Swanson. The Talibs moved like a herd of elephants, whereas Swanson ghosted about unseen unless he wanted to become visible, and then it was usually too late to stop him.

Yet Hall also felt a burst of confidence, and thought to himself, *I was your teacher, Kyle. I know everything you know. You want a hunt? I'll give you a goddam hunt, except I will be the one hunting you.*

The decision made, and some of the steam of anger gone from his thinking, Jim Hall used the hotel telephone to place a call to a number in the nearby city of Adana, the fifth-largest in Turkey and the home of the massive Incirlik Air Base. Incirlik was home to a wing of the Turkish air force but still had a population of some five thousand American military personnel. He knew people there.

43

Nicky Shaw vigorously pumped the hand of Jim Hall when they met at Pinky's, a gaudy little restaurant that was a painted cube of concrete blocks near the beach. "I almost had a bad case of the sads when I heard you got yourself killed," Shaw said, with a broad smile that flashed perfect teeth. "Thought, *Dang, should have had a life insurance policy on ol' Jim.*"

"Death is sometimes overrated." Hall took in the big man. "You still look like an NFL linebacker."

"Image, my man. Gots to sell the image. Big, bad muthas." Shaw was clean shaven, including his domed head, and had a jaw like a granite square. Muscles bulged at his neck, and his biceps pushed at his shirtsleeves. He wore all black except for a large chunk of turquoise and silver that had been made into a belt buckle. Nicky had grown up on the dangerous back streets of Washington, D.C., and become an Army Ranger and then a mercenary in Iraq. When he saw the money available for that sort of work, he started his own company.

"How's business?" asked Hall.

"Same shit, different day," replied Shaw. "I don't go out in the sandbox anymore unless I have to. Incirlik turned out to be a good location for my headquarters. I can run teams anywhere they are needed, and the gummint provides the air transport for free. Pay's awful good."

"I got a job for you. A hundred-thousand-dollar job."

Shaw did not lose his smile, and his eyes flicked over to a pair of pale girls walking by in skimpy bikinis. European tourists. "You still with the Company?"

"Nope. Retired. That's why I have to reach out when I need help. The Langley boys are no longer my best friends."

Nicky Shaw laughed. "Mine neither. Whatcha got?"

"Need some goons to take out a nerd back home. You don't need to know why. Interested?"

"A terminal kinda situation, then? That sorta thing?"

"Absolutely. But I want him banged up and hurt some first. At his home."

"Sounds like Jimmy-boy wants to send a message to somebody. This nerd got a wife and kids we need to worry about?"

"Yes. Wife and a daughter and a son. Collateral damage is fine by me."

Nicky Shaw watched two girls walk slowly down the beach, hips almost touching. "You know, Jim, the U.S. dollar ain't as strong as it used to be. You want me to broker a hit, well, okay, I can do that, but that hunnerd thousand needs to be in euros, not greenbacks." Shaw took a PDA from his pocket and found the information. "As of today, one euro goes for one-point-five-oh-eight-seven. Round it down to a buck and a half, so I can give a deal to an old friend."

"For that price, you guarantee the work. I want your personal confirmation when it's done. And you throw in a piece of equipment, a sniper rifle and fifty rounds."

"I always guarantee on a contract. Gimme a number I can call you at. On the second thing, the big gun, fine. Not a fifty-cal, though. You going to tell me what kind of mischief you up to, needin' that bit of gear? Need any help, a spotter?"

Jim Hall said, "Everything you need to know about the propeller-head is in an envelope under your place mat. I'll transfer half the money now to an account of your choice. Other half when you are done. Sniper rifle is for a friend."

"Fine," said Nicky. "Anything particular I need to tell my people?"

Jim Hall would not explain that the target, Lieutenant Commander Benton Freedman, was the resident computer genius for the dark black hunter-killer group known as Task Force Trident. Hall had studied dossiers on all of them in the past, and there wasn't a weak link in the bunch. Kyle Swanson would have made sure that Freedman would be leading the electronic attack on Hall's assets. The man was no physical commando, but he was a protected component of the Trident brotherhood. It was better if Nicky did not know that. "No. This guy is just a Navy computer geek who is nosing around places where he should not be involved. Works at the Pentagon and lives in the 'burbs. Piece of cake. Just do it fast, like day before yesterday."

"Know what I think? Sounds like an Agency black job reaching through you to me, sittin' here minding my own bidness in Turkey, to run a hit back in the States." He wrote a bank number on the back of a cream-colored business card and handed it across the table.

"I told you, Nicky. The Agency's not involved. This is personal."

"That's what you always say," Nicky Shaw said, standing up and sliding on a narrow pair of dark sunglasses. He put away the PDA, folded the envelope, and stuffed it in a pocket. "I'll get right on it."

ALEXANDRIA, VIRGINIA

Night brought the comfortable cover that the hit team needed for their home invasion, and the fantasy that nothing could stop three large armed and dangerous predators who viewed the coming attack as little more than an evening of fun and a nice paycheck. They had to stay alert, so limited themselves to one beer apiece and a shared marijuana joint as they waited for Lieutenant Commander Benton Freedman to come home.

"Glad it's finally dark," said the leader, Samuel Achmed Fox, his big frame slouched in the passenger seat of the little Nissan. "Get this over with. Little Jap cars ain't made for comfort. You shoulda stole an American, like a big Ford SUV." His hand rested on the butt of a pistol stuffed into the front of his pants.

"You tol' me to get something that wouldn't be noticed. There are more Jap cars in this neighborhood than in downtown Tokyo." Vincent Parma caught a strand of his long black hair and hooked it behind an ear as he sucked on the joint, catching the smoke in his lungs and holding it as long as possible.

He passed it up to the driver, LeGarret Shields, a nervous kid with shifty eyes, youngest of the three. All had served time together for various crimes, their bodies were painted with raw jailhouse tattoos, and they enjoyed inflicting violence on others. "Why not pay us the rest of the money now, Achmed?" LeGarret already had five thousand dollars in his pocket and was mentally counting the five thousand yet to come.

"After it's done, bro. After it's done. Don't worry. I'll hand it to you right when we get back in the car. Meanwhile, think about what might be worthwhile in the house that we can take. Could be some good shit." Parma and Shields each got ten thousand for the hit, and Fox would pocket the lion's share, twenty-five thousand. After all, he was the one who got the call from Nicky Shaw a few hours ago. He had made it to the bank in time to cash the wire transfer.

The car drove in loops and figure eights through the area, all three men low in their seats. Two black men and a dark-skinned Italian, all dressed in black, would draw the immediate attention of any passing police cruiser in this suburban neighborhood, so they roamed, centering their pattern on a corner house two blocks in from the nearest large street. A single porch light had automatically come on at dusk. The driveway remained empty. They circled. Had another joint. Stayed cool. Took time for a hamburger and bathroom break at McDonald's.

Their car climbed the hill once again, then nosed around a right-hand turn, and LeGarret pulled to the curb and shut off the lights. "Damn, there's the mutha, right there! He just got home."

Parma leaned forward between the guys in the front seat to get a better view. In the dim light from the porch and the light that popped on from inside the target's car, they made out the figure of a skinny man in the white uniform of a naval officer. "Got to be him. He's alone, too. No lights in the house, so the family ain't home."

"Damn," said Shields. "I wanted a piece of his wife."

The target unlocked his front door and went inside, and immediately a series of lights bloomed throughout the house. Living room, kitchen, bedroom, bath.

"Now?" asked LeGarret Shields, his tongue licking his dry lips.

"Not quite. Let him get settled for a minute. Probably taking a leak, then he'll make some food and turn on the TV. Get comfortable."

The figure came unexpectedly into view again, walking down the driveway, pulling a green plastic trash cart out for curbside pickup. He had a blue plastic carton of recycled cans under one arm, propped on his hip but resting on a little towel to protect his white uniform.

"Fuck waiting," hissed Parma. "This is the chance. If he's taking out the garbage, he's already off guard and getting comfortable. Soon as he goes back inside, we do it."

"Unh-hunh. You right. Get ready." Achmed Fox pulled his pistol free and rested it on his leg. "Go on up there now, LeGarret, soon as he's back inside." Fox felt the car drop into gear and slowly creep forward, sticking to the curb.

"Let's go on and do it," said Fox, his voice now tense, ready. He threw open the door of the car and climbed out, waiting only a moment for the others to form up beside him; then all three advanced rapidly up the walk and onto the porch. Parma reached up with his pistol and smashed the front porch light as Fox opened the screen door and kicked hard with his steel-toed boot at the lock on the wooden door.

It crashed open, and the three of them dashed inside, looking at the startled man across the room. Little dude in a white uniform. Calm. Fox had expected to see fear. He shouted, "Get your ass on the floor, muthafucka! Get down or I'll cap you where you stand."

LeGarret Shields closed the door and turned to look at their prisoner. "What you grinnin' at, muthafucka?" he yelled at the sailor, who was kneeling, hands locked behind his head.

Then all of the lights went out.

There was a muffled *crummpp* sound, and Vincent Parma screamed as a high-velocity bullet took out his right knee. He dropped to the wooden floor, and a second rip of bullets shredded the middle of his chest. Another cough from a different direction, and the back of LeGarret's head exploded.

Before Samuel Achmed Fox could react, an incredibly strong hand reached out in the blackness, closed around his pistol, and snatched it away at the same time a muscular arm wrapped in a tight V around his neck and tightened in a choke hold. The oxygen was cut off, and Fox tried to pry off the arm, but it was as if it were made of steel and concrete. His resistance faded; he could not breathe. The lights came back on, and as his sight faded, he saw four men in full battle gear watching him.

The little sailor spoke. "We've been expecting you," Freedman said. "Let's have a talk."

Then the arm turned Fox loose and he toppled over, gasping for breath as his lungs burned in pain. His neck felt broken.

44

"The money keeps rolling in, doesn't it, gentlemen?" Bartlett Geneen, the director of the Central Intelligence Agency, spread his hands over two neatly stacked piles of papers on his desk.

Jack Pathurst from the Office of Security kept a confident look on his face and remained calm. "I am apparently on my way to becoming as rich as the CEO of some state-owned utility company. What's my latest total, Mia?"

Mia Kim from the Financial Department said, "Two new deposits were wired in just before midnight. One from the Canary Islands, the second from Buenos Aires. You are each up to about forty million."

"You have it all tagged to be scraped up later?"

"Yes," Kim said.

"Good."

Stephen Swinton sighed loudly and looked at his folded hands, which were shaking. His face was ashen. "My wife has left me," he announced softly. "Glenda cashed out those first deposits in her account and departed, leaving a short note beneath a magnet on the refrigerator. She has gone to Reno to file for divorce."

Pathurst gave the lawyer a smirk. "Glenda is a smart girl. You owe the government some big bucks."

Bart Geneen stood up and stretched. "One of the neatest frames I have seen in a long time," he said. "Homeland Security is interested in both of you, which poses new problems. Bobby Richardson over at the White House is trying to distance himself from this entire episode. He has become a political liability for the president and will soon be dismissed as chief of staff, even if the media does not get a hint of this, as I fully expect them to do."

Pathurst held up his right palm and moved it slowly left to right. "'CIA Officials Caught Taking Bribes.' That catchy headline will be crawling across the bottom of TV screens for weeks. Smart."

Geneen moved to the tall American flag on a stand in one corner of his office, picked at the gold fringe, and rubbed the silk of a red stripe between his fingers. "That's not even half of it. Not even the worst. You two will be painted by the press as working with America's enemies, the Taliban. You are getting rich on bribes from a rogue agent, Jim Hall. According to the testimony of the soldiers who escaped, they watched Hall actually protecting the Taliban's people when Kyle Swanson pulled his gun on them. So, Hall equals Taliban equals the overthrow of the Pakistani government equals nuclear weapons in the hands of terrorists who hate America." He turned to face Pathurst and Swinton. "Is that about right?"

Pathurst said, "I wasn't involved in that."

"Neither was I," protested Swinton, looking up. His eyeglasses were dirty.

"Does not matter," responded the director. "We don't want to have to defend ourselves in public. Therefore, I am pulling the plug on the investigation of Agent Lauren Carson and restoring her to active status. It's pretty obvious to me that Jim Hall set her up. Similarly, I have already spoken with the FBI, Homeland Security, and General Middleton over at Task Force Trident. Gunnery Sergeant Swanson is off the hook for any and all charges. Again, it looks like that was Hall's doing."

Pathurst shifted in his chair. "Okay—but I think you may be moving too fast, Mr. Director. We still cannot get involved because we have to protect our deal not to chase Jim Hall. Son of a bitch will roll up more of our networks if he thinks that we are chasing him. Nothing to stop him from doing so in the future."

"I know, Jack. But for right now, it won't be us. Swanson and Carson are the leads, both now working through Task Force Trident. If they need some of our help, they will let us know through the Trident loop. Let them finish him off. We stay out of it. Hall probably has laid a trap or two that would alert him if we get involved. So we don't. No memos, no phone calls, no e-mails, no nothing."

Swinton blinked and caught his breath. "Trident? It's them! That Major Sybelle Summers threatened me, and this is their work. We can charge them all now—"

"Shut up, Swinton." Bartlett Geneen was growing red in the face and was tired of dealing with the whining lawyer. "Earlier tonight, a three-man hit squad hired by

Jim Hall tried to kill a naval officer who is part of Trident. They failed. Trident is in the clear, do you understand me? That case is over."

"Yes, sir."

"As of right now, I have to suspend you both from duty until further notice. And, Jack, because you are the watchdog around here, I cannot allow the Security Office to conduct the investigation. It cannot even be anyone within the Agency, so I will arrange for a sympathetic independent counsel to cover all of our asses."

Pathurst remained calm. "Understood." In a smooth move, he placed his CIA credentials on the director's desk. "I'll be home doing chores until this gets cleared up."

"Swinton?" The director's voice was harsh. "Go find your wife and get that money back. Contact Mia Kim every day, and don't consider trying to run away. You are not cut out for that sort of thing. This meeting is over. Everybody out."

The office emptied, and the director went to a cabinet and poured a stiff shot of icy vodka he kept in a small refrigerator. There were some sliced lemons in a little plastic bag, and he dropped one into the drink and took a long swallow. *What a mess this is,* he thought. The agreement with Hall was a deal with the devil, but time has a way of changing things.

The good part was that the Trident people had already flipped the hired thug into becoming an asset and forced him to send an e-mail of confirmation to the man in Turkey who had hired them. Geneen did not want to spend much time thinking about how they got that information so quickly, but the e-mail was being traced to an exact location.

INCIRLIK
TURKEY

For Nicky Shaw, the e-mail message spelled the end of days, and he trembled slightly as he read it. Sam Fox and Nicky went back a long time in the gangster life that thrived in Washington, D.C., even in the great shadow of the Supreme Court. As fast kids, they snatched handbags from tourists and headed back to the projects on the run. In their teens, they turned to mugging tourists, picking their victims in the crowds around Union Station. Armed robbery came next during the years they should have spent in high school; then Sam got snapped up by the cops when he and another brother tried to hold up a Vietnamese liquor store one night. The other kid was new to the game and had crossed in front of Sam's pistol, giving the owner just enough time to snatch a big Remington pump shotgun from beneath the counter and blow a hole in the robber's stomach, hurling the instantly dead body into Sam, knocking him down. When Fox had looked up again, he was staring up the big smoking barrel of the Remington. When Nicky heard about the botched robbery, he decided that it was time for him to join the U.S. Army and be all that he could be, far away from the gangs.

Sam should not have freelanced like that. He should have waited until Nicky could have done the job with him. They were a fearsome pair, because Nicky had brought brains to the party. He even devised a set of code words, like a quarterback in a huddle, meaningless to anyone but him and Sam. "Green Cat" meant everything was fine. "Grand Canyon" meant to proceed with caution. "Lowrider" meant to stop immediately and withdraw, while "Buffy" was their code word that the shit had hit the fan and to run like hell.

After assigning the hit, Nicky had been expecting a smooth "Green Cat" message of confirmation. Instead he got "Buffy," repeated three times in capital letters. He had no idea what had gone wrong, but Sam had managed to send the ultimate warning. The law was coming, and it was time to go. He did.

"All good things must come to an end," he said.

"Cut the bullshit philosophy. What the hell happened?" Jim Hall was in the passenger seat of Shaw's Land Rover, parked in an isolated little industrial park near the base. It was packed with layers of boxes and suitcases. Extra storage was in a container secured to the top of the rugged vehicle.

"Beats me. All I know is that my man sent me the code to get the hell out of Dodge. Been knowing him for thirty years and he's never crossed me. Not a dude to panic easily, either."

Jim Hall's mind was spinning with possibilities. Some shithead gangbangers failed to take down the Task Force Trident communications guy? The guy was a nerd, not a field operator. Hall felt a tingle along his spine. Trident had expected something to happen and had pulled an ambush. *Swanson. Thinking like me.* "I hope you don't think I'm paying the rest of the fee," he said.

"Nope. Just wanted to meet and give you a heads-up. We known each other a long time." Shaw slid his right hand up inside his jacket and grasped the stock of a pistol. "By the way, don't even think of trying anything, old man. You ain't no match for me. Gimme the gun in your belt, fingertips. Flip it into the back."

Hall lifted the Glock from the nylon holster and tossed it over the seat. He put his palms on the dashboard without being asked. "Okay. I'm just thinking. So, the job failed and you're on your way out. Tough luck all around. But I still have work to do. Did you bring the sniper rifle?"

"Yep. You still owe me for that stuff. See that key on the floor mat between your feet? It opens up that storage shed over there, 18-A printed on it. Your stuff is in there. Plenty of other toys, too. Help yourself. Ten thousand for my going-out-of-business sale."

"Let me reach for my wallet?"

"Careful, Jim Hall. Just give me the money and go on about your business. We both walk away. Never see each other again."

Hall slowly removed a long, flat wallet of brown leather from his inside jacket pocket, and handed it over, using his left. "Here, just take it all. Eleven thousand, close enough."

"You a good man, Jim." Nicky Shaw flashed his Grade A smile and reached for the soft leather wallet with his right hand, having to briefly remove his fingers from the shoulder gun.

Jim Hall had known all along that he would have to be quick, because Nicky was a big guy, a warrior. There would be no second chance, and he could not win in a brawl. The narrow knife with the four-inch blade fell into his palm from the rear, hidden side of the wallet, unseen in the dim light. When Shaw reached for the money, Hall grabbed his right wrist to hold it still, counted on the steering wheel to delay the left coming over, and plunged the knife upward into Nicky's throat.

Hall threw himself atop the bigger man, the weight of his whole body pinning the muscle-pumped right arm and shoving Nicky tight into the driver's seat. Nicky cursed in surprise, and his left arm broke free and a big fist thundered down on Hall's right shoulder. Hall took the pain and dug into the throat again and again, ripping and tearing at the larynx and arteries. Jets of crimson blood flooded from the thrashing man's throat. Nicky Shaw was extraordinarily strong, and Hall panted with exertion to keep him from breaking free. Thank God the man was wearing a seat belt that helped hold him in place. The legs were useless, trapped in the space beneath the dashboard.

The fist lost some of its power, and the right arm softened. Hall pulled away just enough to remove the knife from the neck and go to work on the stomach, slicing more veins and wrecking internal organs. Nicky's cursing turned to grunts of pain, and finally to sighs of surrender and a gurgle of life puffing from him.

Jim Hall did not stop cutting until he was sure the huge mercenary, once a friend, was nothing more than a piece of dead meat.

45

The noon sunlight reflected mirror-bright off the snow-covered sharp peaks of the Bernese Alps that marched off into the distance outside the city. It was crisp but not too cold, and Kyle wore a lightweight bomber jacket, while Lauren was in a belted tan trench coat, with apples and carrots in her deep pockets and the collar turned up. She held his arm as they strolled beside the River Aare; gentle swells pushed the dark, swift-flowing waters to within inches of the wide walkway.

"I can't believe that we are somewhere that you have never been before." Lauren playfully pushed against him.

"The Swiss have been neutral for seven hundred years." He pushed her back. "Not much call for my specialized services. Anyway, they have some pretty tough guys in their armed services to meet their needs. Do a lot more than guard the pope."

Near the Nydegg Bridge, Kyle saw the spire of the cathedral, and they slowly climbed a long set of sharply angling stone steps that took them upward toward the center of the ancient city. At the top, he checked his tourist map, orienting himself, then they moved on.

The attractive couple seemed to be something they were not. Instead of being a pair of love-struck tourists, Kyle and Lauren were making an in-depth reconnaissance of Bern, readying for the time, coming soon, when Jim Hall would have to break cover.

It was a meandering stroll, and Kyle constantly was on the lookout for places in which death might hide, might even be hiding at the moment. He would not discount the possibility that Hall had hired a counter-surveillance team of his own. Moves and counter-moves, the eternal survival game of life and death. *Where are you, Jim? What are you thinking?*

"It looks like a fairy tale," Lauren said as they moved through the winding streets, with brightly colored statues on every corner. A small crowd had gathered before the fifteenth-century clock tower, and exactly at one o'clock a parade of carved animals, jesters, knights, and bears made their noisy journey about the clock face. She watched the clock. Swanson watched the crowd. Tourists of every shape and size, many with phone cameras and video recorders, making pictures of this Aesop's Fables wonderland to show their friends. That worried him, but nothing could be done.

In a few minutes more, they were waiting at the Bear Pit. Lauren started tossing carrots to the three large and shaggy beasts, who ignored her treats. Two were sound asleep, and the third just sat there, digesting. The pit was littered with the uneaten food from earlier tourists.

A small, compact man in a gray business suit leaned his arms on the railing beside Kyle. His longish hair was swept back, and he had eyes like steel marbles. "They are treated like animal royalty. It is a long and boring story. My name is Commander Stefan Glamer, and today, I represent the Federal Criminal Police." He let them glimpse the badge on his belt, then extended his hand, and both Lauren and Kyle shook it. It was a strong, firm grip. "The cantonment police asked for our help in this matter that you have brought to their attention. Fortunately, our base is at Worblaufen, which is not far from here."

"We're more than happy to have your guys handle it," Kyle said. "We will just be along to assist the identification."

As the plan had come together, General Middleton of Task Force Trident in Washington had put in a call to his counterpart with Einsatzgruppe (Task Force) TIGRIS in Switzerland. The existence of the special covert unit had been totally unknown to even the Swiss for many years. The press called them Supercops.

"Then let us go get some coffee and have a look at the bank plaza," said Glamer, and they headed toward the bank. Glamer was one of the rare men who seemed unfazed by Lauren's looks. Like Kyle, he looked like nothing was going on, but he was already hard at work, visually checking the dark shadows beneath the covered walkways. He led them to a little restaurant and, speaking German to the waitress, ordered some pastries and coffee.

"We have heard of you, Gunny Swanson. When this is over, I hope you will come out to the camp and talk to our sniper teams."

Swanson raised his eyebrows. "I thought you guys might be hunting us."

Glamer laughed softly. "That is old news. You and Agent Carson are no longer wanted by anyone for anything. You have not gone to the CIA with this?"

Lauren lifted the dainty cup of coffee and sipped. Strong, with a bite of liquor and an aroma that dazzled the senses. "I have an appointment to go meet with them at the American Legation and reestablish contact this evening. When I am satisfied about my reinstatement, I will advise them what is going on but insist that they stay out of your way. It will remain your operation, Commander Glamer."

Kyle added a lump of sugar and stirred it in with a little spoon. "General Middleton thought it best to keep things unofficial to avoid any perception of a breach of neutrality. We consider this to be strictly an internal criminal matter for the Swiss to handle as they see fit. There are no American national interests involved, although the terrorist himself is an American."

Glamer said, "I read his file. Former Marine and ex-CIA. And once a friend to you both."

Lauren answered through gritted teeth. "Yes."

Kyle put his own history out for the commander's view. "He was even my instructor before he was my friend. I did not know what a crook he was until he retired and went rogue. Make no mistake, Commander

Glamer, Jim Hall is still a dangerous man, a stone cold killer. Your people must take care."

Glamer absently scratched an ear. "We have yet to have to fire a shot in any of the cases we have encountered and resolved. We will be prepared, of course, but it will be a nonlethal capture. How do you see things unfolding?"

Kyle pointed across the street, where a monolithic bank stood. It looked like a fortress at the far end of the narrow stone plaza. Traffic was minimal on the street that ran in front of it. "You scatter some people around outside, and Lauren will be in an overwatch position with them. I will be inside to confirm when he walks through the front door. You take him down."

"When will this happen?"

"Soon. Maybe even tomorrow," Kyle said, pushing away his coffee cup and saucer. "This is the last of his money, and it is at the one bank where he placed it beyond our reach, perhaps anticipating an emergency. He has about five million dollars in cash in their safe."

"Did the bank tell you this?"

"No," said Lauren. "I helped him stack it in there several years ago. It was left over from a covert project in Iraq and is in various currencies and denominations."

Stefan Glamer's face did not register any surprise. "Won't he take it out by a banker's draft or a certified check?"

"That is very doubtful," she said. "We think he wants the money in his hands, so he will probably need help carrying it away. You should be prepared for several other men who would do the actual lifting."

"Yes, of course." The Supercop's expression changed slightly. "It could be difficult if not handled properly."

Kyle said, "Use overwhelming force, Commander. Jim Hall will fight to the death, and you will only get one chance to take him. Surprise must be total, and your men cannot hesitate to pull their triggers if necessary."

Glamer wrote his private cell phone number on the back of a business card and put it on the table. Lauren wrote out a number for him. The TIGRIS commando rose and gave them a slight but rather Prussian bow. "We will stay in close touch, then, and if you do not hear from me, I shall meet you at this place tomorrow at noon. You have my permission to launch the mission. But, Gunny Swanson, you will not be permitted to carry a firearm. Understood?"

Kyle nodded. He waited until Glamer left the restaurant, then waved to the waitress and ordered another pot of coffee.

"Never fired a shot in any of their operations?" said Lauren. "Not good."

"Maybe they are that good," Kyle said. "Better be." He dialed his cell phone and was connected over a secure link with Lieutenant Commander Benton Freedman in the Pentagon.

"We're on deck in the land of the cuckoo clock, and I'm looking at the bank," Kyle Swanson said.

"Can you bring me back a real Swiss Army knife?"

"No. Tell the general that his friends over here are ready."

"Or a nice watch. A Swiss military watch."

"Lizard, shut down those other two accounts right now. Hear me?"

"Can't do it, Gunny," Freedman said, a little piqued, knowing his answer would guarantee that he was not going to be getting any presents. "We waited too long. Agent Hall beat us to the punch on them and wired the money out with encrypted transactions that he apparently had set up some time ago. They slipped through the net. About eight million total. Sorry about that."

ISTANBUL
TURKEY

Jim Hall was staying at the Four Seasons hotel in Istanbul, with a view of the Blue Mosque on the far side of the river. The assembly of dignitaries would be held at the Anadolu Auditorium of the Istanbul Convention and Exhibition Center, a world-class facility that could handle the international affair with ease in the center of the bustling city. Security was a standard item in such a place that was frequented by world leaders, and police would be out in force, inside and on the streets.

Even presidents have to sleep and walk around in their underwear sometime, and the chief executive would be staying overnight in one of the Palace Roof Suites of the Four Seasons on the European side of the Bosphorus Strait. The rest of the Pakistani delegation would share the other rooftop suites. Jim Hall was in a one-bedroom suite five stories below in the same hotel. Meetings of national leaders happened all the time, and in an elite hotel, they could be accommodated while regular paying guests would not be disturbed. It was almost too easy. Hall had already figured out three different ways to kill the man and successfully escape. Security off-site from the convention center was not much stronger than a team of rent-a-cops, and he also had an inside guy.

A million-dollar payday from the Taliban and head for the cabin, which was fully stocked and ready in the Bavarian Alps, where he would remain hidden until springtime, when he could shake off the snow and begin his new life. Jim Hall did not kid himself. He suddenly needed this money, badly, because Kyle Swanson, Lauren Carson, and that electronics geek at Trident had raped and pillaged his secret accounts. There was no sign that the CIA had helped, so he would still abide by the earlier deal to leave the Agency alone if they would leave him alone. Best deal he had ever made.

He had only three open accounts left—one in Havana under his French pseudonym, one in Sydney under a British identity, and his fail-safe stack of real money in a big vault in Bern. He had always believed in diversification, and if the authorities did not know of a bank account, then they could not hit it. Lauren knew some, but not all, of the locations. It was all a matter of timing now, careful planning, and he had laid it out carefully. Pull the trigger on the Paki dude, and only then transfer all of the remaining funds to Switzerland, to be put into cash into a separate vault that was already waiting for it. After the hit, he had reservations for Switzerland, where he would collect the cash and vanish.

The disturbing buzzing in his brain was Kyle Swanson, who would probably be figuring the same way and planning some way to turn it to his own advantage. That was why Jim Hall, at the same time he had hired the late Nicky Shaw, had also contacted a burly, bald German freelancer to organize some extra muscle and place a surveillance team in Bern. That was the best bet for Kyle to set an ambush.

Hall had taken dinner in his room, had a few drinks, and was watching the plasma TV screen as darkness came over the city that separates Europe from Asia. It was the German.

"We found them," said the German. "Our watchers spotted them at the clock tower in the middle of town and took some pictures. I enhanced the images, and they match the photos you sent."

Hall smiled to himself and made a vigorous *yes* pumping action with his right arm. "Both of them?"

"Yah. They met some civilian for coffee right across from the bank."

"You have somebody on them now?"

"Yah." The deep voice had a sinister rumble.

"Kill him. Take the girl. I have one more item of business to take care of tomorrow, but barring any unforeseen problems on this end, I will be there on schedule." With Kyle dead and Lauren captured, the CIA still on the sidelines, what could go wrong? *Checkmate, Swanson, ole buddy.*

"Yah."

46

Selim Waleed was seated on a silk-covered cushion, with his legs crossed, modestly basking in being so publicly displayed at his father's right hand. The entire leadership of the Bright Path Party was gathered in a spacious room to officially launch the Taliban's candidate for the presidency of Pakistan, and everyone was aware that it was the son who had engineered bringing his father to power.

Only a day earlier, Selim had been in the remote mountain hideaway of the legendary warlord Muhammed Waleed and had spoken the words that both men had wanted and had waited for so long to hear. "My father, it is time," said the young man. "Allah, praise be unto him, has given us everything we have asked. You can now arise from the wildness of our mountains and move into the city to prepare for the final event."

The older man paused, never one to act in haste. "You are certain of my safety?"

The son nodded and stroked his mustache lightly. "Absolutely. I would never put you at risk. I am in constant contact with our ally General Nawaz Zaman of the ISI, who assures me that all is ready. He has cast his lot with us in exchange for the promise that he will be appointed minister of defense in your new government, giving him control of the army. As the head of the secret police, he is even now starting to crack down on the political opposition. Our own men are assisting in the population centers throughout the country."

A large white cloud that had drifted through the blue sky opened, as if in a heavenly sign, and sunshine flooded their home. Every window seemed to leap with the sudden illumination. Surely a sign from Allah! "The election is to be announced for next month?"

"Yes, Father. Not that it will matter. When the president is assassinated in Istanbul by Jim Hall, you will be the only candidate in position with a functioning and powerful political movement, and the backing of brokers such as General Zaman and the other tribal warlords. When the president falls, we—*you, Father!*—will step forward and assume the leadership. The public will demand that it be so because of the destruction in Islamabad by our bomb and the killing of the president. You will be the only one who can bring stability. The election will become a mere formality. Once in power, you will never surrender it."

So they came out of the mountains, surrounded by a ragged convoy of media vehicles that shielded them from the Americans' hungry Predator drones and missiles. The caravan grew ever larger as it drove through the villages, trucks and automobiles and tractors, and they arrived in Islamabad as if leading a parade. Crowds jostled along the streets for a view of the famous guerrilla leader who would bring Pakistan back to its rightful position in the community of nations. Then, with his hand on Pakistan's nuclear missiles, silent but ominous for now, he would have a guarantee that other countries would listen to him.

In the meeting room, the bearded leader was greeted as if he had already taken office. In his humble robes, he moved with ease among the rich supporters, the experienced political teams, and the powerful men who recognized the wave of the future and were clambering aboard his golden train. The conference was called to order by none other than General Nazam, who pledged his loyalty and spoke in glowing terms of young Selim Waleed, hailing him as a patriotic young man who had almost single-handedly transformed the Taliban into a legitimate political organization, the Bright Path Party, with the respected Muhammed Waleed as its presidential candidate.

The general hugged the smiling, bearded warlord as the international film crews buzzed around them. The audience erupted in sustained applause that shook the squares of the soundproofed ceiling. As arranged by Selim, General Nawaz then quietly departed from the platform and left the room so as not to distract any further from the attention being lavished upon Muhammed Waleed. Also on Selim's instructions, the general was handling a final task of weakening the president's personal protective services for the Istanbul conference by infiltrating men loyal to him into the inner security ranks. There was much work to do.

General Nawaz was back behind his desk within fifteen minutes, and he immediately placed a scrambled, secure call overseas. When a voice answered, Nawaz asked, "Football?"

"Soccer! Good to hear from you." CIA Director Geneen was in a sealed communication cubicle adjacent to his office. He had been expecting the call.

"And you. By any chance are you watching television?"

"Why, yes, I am. One of the news channels."

"Hold on for a second, would you, Football? I have to make another call. Will only take a moment." General Nazam pulled open the right-hand drawer of his polished desk and picked up a cell phone. He dialed. The signal was received by a little phone, and the battery sparked a detonator embedded in blocks of plastic explosives that were hidden in the false ceiling directly above the speaker's platform at the headquarters of the Bright Path Party just as Muhammed Waleed was making his acceptance address.

The general strolled to his large window and looked out over the city and saw a mushrooming cloud of smoke and debris rising into the afternoon sky. He went back to the phone. "Football? I fear that something terrible has happened that will be requiring my attention. It seems to be a car bomb or some such thing."

"Yes, Soccer. I understand that you must tend to your duties."

"Oh, before we go, I also mentioned our friend Jim Hall to the Turkish police handling the security for our president's appearance tomorrow. They will deal with it. No trace of your company's involvement."

"Best of luck, my friend."

Both men hung up at the same time. Waleed went back to his window to watch and heard the first sirens of the emergency responders heading toward the scene. In the United States, Bart Geneen made no notes about the brief conversation. He just smiled.

ISTANBUL
TURKEY

Jim Hall also had been watching an all-news channel on television while building a bomb of his own. Wires, battery, detonator, and four powerful blocks of C-4 imbedded with hundreds of marbles were being fashioned into a makeshift claymore mine that he would place at the head of the president's bed. A pressure switch would be stuffed into the mattress, and when the man lay down to sleep, the circuit would snap shut and the explosion would result. One of Selim's henchmen on the security team was to allow him entrance to the room. He worked slowly and carefully.

The irritating little news banner crawling along the bottom of the CNN broadcast caught his attention.

NEW EXPLOSION ROCKS PAKISTAN . . . ISTANBUL POLITICAL MEET-ING TARGET . . . POLICE CLAIM TALIBAN LEADERSHIP KILLED . . . NEW EXPLOSION ROCKS PAKISTAN

Ten minutes later, a Turkish tactical police antiterrorist team rushed into the Four Seasons Hotel in Istanbul, sealed off an entire floor, and breached the door to a small suite. The bed was covered with the makings of a bomb, and explosives experts moved in to secure it.

Jim Hall was gone.

BERN
SWITZERLAND

Kyle and Lauren had spent much of the afternoon resting and making love in their hotel room and now lay beneath the light duvet. They had fallen asleep with her head on his arm and her free hand resting on his chest, registering his strong heartbeat. It was a struggle to come awake again and hit the shower, but Lauren's appointment was at seven o'clock for dinner with the CIA assistant station chief who was driving in from Zurich to reinstate her to duty and return her credentials. Basically, the man was apologizing for the CIA's hurried investigation, which had leaped to an incorrect conclusion about Agent Carson. Those words would never be spoken.

"What are you going to do while I'm at dinner?" she asked, clipping on a new set of earrings that she had bought earlier that day. Little silver bears.

"I'm going to do some more walking around, try to get a better feel for the area around the bank and check out how things look when it gets dark."

"You never stop, do you?" She gave him a bright smile. "The Swiss Gestapo or Cheesemakers or whoever they are will handle this now, Kyle. We're done except for pointing a finger at Jim when we see him tomorrow."

"I'm concerned that they want to just catch him without firing a shot. It could still all go to hell."

"Kyle, the Swiss guard the pope. They were Europe's best mercenaries for hundreds of years. Trust them."

"I do, but they don't know Jim like we do. He will have a good plan, which is why I want you to get an armed CIA escort tonight. The assistant station chief can arrange that. Also he gives you a ride back to the hotel in a company car."

"Yes, teacher. You know best, teacher. Anything you say, teacher." She somehow smiled and frowned at the same time. "Tonight, I get my creds back and can start legally carrying a weapon again. I can take care of myself, Kyle. Don't worry. I will be the one of us with a gun. C'mon." She moved toward the door.

Swanson picked up his jacket and walked out behind her, locking the door. She waited beside the elevator, and when she turned to look at him, he was again struck by the beauty of the woman. From hair to eyes to toes, everything seemed to just fit her perfectly. He gave her a slight kiss and was scolded for risking the makeup job.

Downstairs, he led the way out of the elevator into the busy lobby, which had the look and feeling of normalcy. Two female clerks behind the front desk, a young couple talking with the woman concierge about affordable restaurants, a uniformed bellman pushing a hand-cart stacked with luggage. Then out the door, Kyle first, looking both ways. The front of their hotel was easy to identify, not because of its own signage, or the set of columns beside the door, but because some unhappy tagger had written YANKEE GO HOME in red paint on one of the cornerstones. Traffic was flowing smoothly, and he told the green-uniformed doorman to get a cab. Behind them, the young couple emerged, chattering in French, and waited their turn. A little Nova Taxi with its distinctive red sides and yellow top swung out of the flow and pulled to a stop.

As the hotel doorman reached for the handle, a dirty painter's van swerved out of the traffic and slammed into the rear of the taxi, throwing it forward and knocking the doorman to the ground. Everyone automatically took a step back at the moment of grinding impact, with Kyle already changing into combat mode. He grabbed Lauren's arm as the side door of the van opened and a huge man lumbered out. He was totally bald but for a mustache and goatee and wore a black leather jacket and biker boots. He had a knife in his right hand. "Back inside! Quick," yelled Kyle.

The young couple behind them slammed into Lauren like a pair of charging linebackers, sweeping her away from Kyle's grasp and pushing her in a single motion into the van, where more hands gripped her. The man with the knife lashed out at Kyle, who danced to the side, reaching for Lauren but seeing the door already closing. He could hear the van's engine roar and her scream.

The man with the knife stood easily, dominating the space between Swanson and the vehicle, with his mouth curved down into an evil smile. When the young hotel doorman struggled to his feet, he was slashed on the arm and kicked by the thug with a hard karate-style thrust of his right foot, the leg fully extended in a practiced move. It was a moment Kyle would not let pass. The guy had been watching too much television.

Using the side kick had left the thug standing for an instant on one foot, tilting his body to the other side for balance and his attention drawn to the newest threat, the doorman. Kyle took a single step forward and delivered a powerful kick to the totally exposed groin, grabbed the knife hand itself to take it out of play, and delivered a flat-hand punch into the assailant's throat. The big man staggered back, choking and hurting and suddenly uncertain of his strength. Kyle followed with a single, flowing right-side attack—a right cross deep into the gut, then bringing his elbow up hard into the man's chin, which rocked the head back. Swanson's fist was now cocked right beside his own ear, and he finished the combination with a downward hammer strike that crushed the man's nose. The thug was staggering, so it was easy to snatch the knife from him, which Kyle did, then flipped it and slashed him across the stomach. The man grabbed for the cut as he toppled like a fat tree. Kyle moved aside to let him fall and then made two more quick cuts that severed the Achilles tendons behind both ankles. The man wasn't going anywhere.

When the frenzy of the fight cleared, Kyle turned to

the street as his breathing returned to normal. The white van was nowhere to be seen. Lauren had been professionally kidnapped, slickly taken right out of his arms. *Damn it all!*

47

Commander Stefan Glamer of Einsatzgruppe TIGRIS was on his cell, looking nothing like the suave civilian that Kyle had met at the bear pit. The commander was in a black jumpsuit with the legs tucked into the tops of flat black jump boots. His Kevlar helmet, flak jacket, and submachine gun were stacked on a table. "This man Jim Hall is a monster," he said. The icy eyes betrayed no real emotion. It was a statement of fact.

Glamer, CIA Assistant Chief of Station Mark Brand, and a ranking team of civilian detectives had interviewed Swanson for hours in a private room at the canton police headquarters, prying for details of the attack. Kyle had tried every trick in the book to increase the memories of those moments, draining his thoughts into words. Colors, smells, invisible hunches, anything that might help. There was not much.

"The fellow you took down has been identified as nothing more than a contract hit man paid to kill you. Ignorant beyond what he was told and did not know who hired him. The van was abandoned a kilometer away from the hotel. It had been stolen, and the forensic people are going through it for evidence." One of the detectives was drinking coffee, the sort of beefy, seen-it-all investigator who is found in almost any city in the world. He didn't know about terrorism, but kidnapping was a serious crime. With every passing hour, the chances of solving it became less and less.

Mark Brand was almost an invisible man, average in every external way, which was why he was the chief administrator in the CIA office in Switzerland. The country had been the safe haven where spies came to meet for hundreds of years, and the goal here was to conduct intelligence work without rocking the neutral boat. He might as well not have been in the room at all.

"You people are going to continue to sit on the sidelines while one of your agents has been abducted by another one of your agents." Swanson felt like spitting on the American.

"Technically, neither of them works for the Central Intelligence Agency. Ms. Carson had not yet been reinstated to duty, and Mr. Hall left some time ago. Also, our hands are bound due to an issue that I cannot discuss here." Brand's movements, even with his fingers, were precise and birdlike, and Kyle considered him to be a born pencil-pusher.

Swanson shook his head slowly. "You mean the deal you made with Hall to leave each other alone. You think that's a secret?"

Brand shrugged. "The danger to a single agent must be weighted against potential damage."

"So why don't you just get the fuck out of here and

let us work? Go back to your desk before your suit gets dirty."

"I was instructed to help the Swiss police in any way possible." Brand did not seem perturbed, and Kyle knew the CIA man was really in the room to hobble anything that might bring harm to the Agency.

Commander Glamer looked at the detectives, and they spoke in a rapid German dialect. One looked over at Mark Brand and snorted in derision. "All kidnappings have a reason, Gunny Swanson. Most of them involve a ransom, and that requires the kidnappers to make contact. Agent Carson has no family here, so the contact will come either to you or to Mr. Brand. Is that right?"

Swanson took out his wallet and extracted a single U.S. dollar. "That's the reason," he said. "Hall is after the cash in the bank. He will want to make a trade. If we keep watching the money, he will turn up. He is playing for millions of dollars." Kyle fought to keep his thoughts on an even keel, worried about how long the routine logic of a law enforcement situation would apply to Jim Hall. Kyle had come to the conclusion that there would be a killing at the end of the road, and either Jim or Kyle would lie dead. Lauren was a pawn in the game.

The commander stood before a map taped to a cardboard backing propped on a tripod. He pointed to the business district of Bern, then used a fingertip to trace the perimeter where his men were already in positions. Police throughout the city were on alert, and more federal agents had been dispatched to support them. "He cannot possibly hope to get away. Our borders are sealed tight all around the country, and we have the area around the bank saturated. We are missing something."

The room lapsed into thoughtful silence, and when a cell tone started to chime, all four of them reached for their own phones. It was the phone in Kyle's pocket that was chirping, and he jumped to his feet when he saw the incoming number on the small screen. Lauren!

He pressed the TALK button and heard the hard voice of Jim Hall on the other end say, "Hello, buddy-boy."

The instructions were as precise as they were absurd, and Hall delivered it all with rapid-fire intensity. "Your number was on the phone in her purse. Listen up and don't even think about negotiating. You want to see the bitch alive again, this is what you and your cop friends are going to do."

There was a wave of steps to his plan. Each would have to be completed before the next could be initiated. First, he had something for the police, he said. His team had planted half a dozen small bombs throughout the city, and the detonators were attached to timing devices. As proof, he gave the location of the first one as being in the ancient clock tower in the middle of the old city. "Tell them that now, Kyle, and I will call you back in ten minutes. They need to know that I am serious." He hung up.

Stefan Glamer and the two detectives went into action as soon as Kyle gave them the information. A terrorist attack against Switzerland, the most neutral country in the world, and being conducted by a former American spy, not a Muslim fanatic, was almost too much for them to comprehend. Glamer had a team at the clock tower within three minutes, and they found the brick of C-4 plastic explosive, attached to a timer detonator, exactly where Jim Hall had said it would be. Instantly, emergency calls were made to get every cop in the city out on the streets and searching for bombs.

"So they found it okay?" The opening words of the next call were menacingly humorous. "I would have hated to see that beautiful piece of art turned into a bunch of really old splinters, but, hey, that's the game."

"Let me speak to Lauren," Swanson demanded, some power in his own voice.

"She's not available right now, Kyle. The poor girl has had a rough time over the past few hours. You will see her soon." Hall let the silence extend for a few seconds. "Now back to work. In four hours, at exactly nine o'clock this morning, a black SUV will pull up in front of the bank. Police will have a parking spot ready for it. The driver will remain at the wheel, and three other men will go inside the bank to meet a bank official with access to my safe deposit boxes. When the meeting takes place, my representative will tell the police the location of the second bomb, which is set to explode at nine thirty."

"How many bombs are there, asshole?"

"Enough," replied Hall. "My people will empty the boxes and take the cash in duffel bags to the SUV. By then, the cops will have found the second bomb, and I will give further instructions. There will be safe conduct all the way through the border at a point of my choosing."

Kyle was jotting down the information on a white legal pad, with Glamer reading over his shoulder and making notes of his own. The commander wrote *Keep him talking* on the pad, and Swanson nodded. The police were tracing the call. "You aren't going to be at the bank?"

"Shut up," Hall barked. "We are out of time for this call. While that exchange is happening at the bank, you will be meeting me somewhere else, and I'll swap Lauren for the cash and safe passage. Until I am out of danger, the bombs will only be disclosed one by one. Arrest anybody and I will turn this city to cinders. Remind them of what happened in Islamabad. Call you later with the address." Hall laughed distantly and hung up and destroyed the cell phone. He had several spares.

Stunned silence engulfed the room. Commander Glamer leaned forward, hand on the table, and stared at each of them in turn. "He is leaving no room for negotiations. Just issuing orders for us to do this and do that and then the promise that something else will happen."

Strangely, it was Mark Brand of the CIA who broke the silence this time. He knew a lot about making detailed plans that reached too far into the future, and was ruled by the old saying that the best plan never survives longer than the first gunshot. "Too much choreography on the part of Hall. It leaves too many chances for things to go wrong for him, as well as for us."

"But we have no choice but to lock the bank down and erect concentric circles of protection while we continue the bomb searches. Getting across the border will be impossible, for even if we agree, none of the surrounding countries would. He has no leverage with them. It makes no sense." Glamer slapped the tabletop. "I will make the arrangements, Gunny. You stay here and keep us informed of any new calls."

The commander left the room, and the two Americans were alone. "What's on your mind?" Kyle asked the CIA man. The guy was fully involved now, showing a background that he had kept well hidden in front of the police.

"I think it is a dodge. Hall has laid out a plan so complicated that it collapses beneath its own weight. How about if his car has a flat tire on its way to the bank? Or the bank manager panics and refuses to give up the cash? A dozen things like that could derail it all. Therefore, I believe that Jim Hall does not care if his plan succeeds, and *that* leads me to believe that probably there are no other bombs. He is looking for a way out."

Swanson walked over to the coffeepot. In other places, the coffee would be old and tired after several hours. Here it always seemed freshly brewed, and someone had just put on a new pot. It held a scent of chocolate. He poured a cup and regarded Mark Brand again. Perhaps not such a pencil-pusher after all. It made sense. Hall shifted the eight million from those other two accounts, plus whatever else he had stashed away. Maybe he was ready to sacrifice the Swiss account. "He still has Lauren. I've got to go and get her."

The analyst's background in the CIA officer was perking right along with the fresh coffee. "That's the other half of the distraction. The police will be tied up at the bank and are combing the city looking for nonexistent explosives. You will be busy rescuing Agent Carson. All of his enemies will be distracted long enough for him to get away."

"Hiding, blending, and deceiving," Kyle said. "Basic sniper tactics."

"Yes. And the CIA still cannot be involved. Hall would still ruin a lot of networks if he thinks we are in the game."

"He doesn't want to do that. He knows you guys have no control over me, which is why he has not been leaning on you to stop me. And if he plans on living a long and happy life, he definitely does not want to ruin such a good insurance policy. You guys would be all over his ass in a blink to limit the damage." Swanson looked at him steadily. "The Swiss won't let me have a gun. Will you give me yours?"

"Absolutely not." Then Brand brought a small box out of his briefcase and pushed it across the table. "However, you can do me a great favor. I was to give this material to Agent Carson at our dinner that never took place. Perhaps you could deliver it for me when you see her again."

Swanson put down his ceramic coffee mug and opened the lid. Inside the box was the small leather wallet with Lauren's badge and credentials, and resting on a cushion of white foam was her pistol, with a full clip of ammunition.

"Good luck, Gunny," Mark Brand said and extended his hand.

Kyle shook it, and his lips curled into a smile. "Thanks. Things just got a lot better."

48

Lauren Carson hovered just below consciousness, in a dull black drug haze that had begun when she was pulled into the van and held down while someone popped a needle into a vein. A few heartbeats later, the drug had circulated throughout her body and she was down and out. Now she was coming to the surface, being brought up slowly and expertly by the woman who had helped kidnap her. She was thirsty beyond belief, her mouth cottony and her body dehydrated. She sighed aloud when she saw light for the first time, but her eyes were still unfocused. She worked her jaw slightly and said, "Water . . ." A paper cup was lifted to her lips, and a hand held the back of her head to help her drink a few swallows. Then it was taken away. Jim Hall watched, then nodded to his woman helper, who had been chosen for the kidnap mission because of her training as a military nurse. Her portion of the job was almost done, and she would walk away with ten thousand euros. The nurse picked up a filled syringe off a clean towel, found a vein in Lauren's arm, and put in the needle, slowly pushing in a drug to speed the recovery.

Lauren sensed feeling returning to her arms and legs, which she still could not move. She lifted up slowly from worse to bad to better and heard a familiar gentle voice say, "Come on, Lauren, girl. Time to get up."

Her memory was scrambled because the drug still had her in its strong grip, just not as tightly. A woman's hands worked around her. *A nurse? Am I in a hospital?* Her clothes were being adjusted, shoes wiggled onto her feet. The nurse's and stronger hands, those of a man, helped her into a sitting position. Nausea swept over her momentarily, and she gagged the fluid back down. She was given more water.

The calm voice again. "Okay, Lauren. It's almost over. We're going to see Kyle now."

Kyle! Yes. Kyle would take care of her. The mention of his name brought hope, and she strained to stand, helped by the guiding hands. The tendrils of the drug still held her back from fully functioning.

The man and the woman took her weight as they guided her through a short, dark hallway and into an elevator, which took them all down. Even at the slow rate, Lauren had to struggle not to throw up. It clanked to a halt, and she heard the male voice say, "Go on down and get the car ready. I've got her now." Flat heels made sharp snapping noises in the hallway.

Light. A lot of light, shining on Lauren, *a spotlight?* She waddled closer, held gently by the man. "A few more steps, Lauren. Be strong. Kyle's just on the other side of the door." She blinked several times and ran her tongue across her dry lips. There was a shadow in the light, a silhouette forming, something familiar about the solid shape. *Kyle?* Kyle had come to take her out of the hospital? *I'm not wearing makeup. What will he think when he sees me like this? My hair is a mess. Will he still love me?* Tears began to well in her eyes and roll onto her cheeks.

"Wait here for a minute, Lauren, and get some strength. Just another minute. I promise."

She knew the voice now and leaned against the man. "Okay, Jim. Thank you."

The address that Jim Hall had given was an apartment house in the Herrengasse section of Bern, a stone building surrounded by a thick wall, with knotted brown vines climbing over it at some points. Swanson walked all the way around the place. The wall was merely decorative, with no gates. A wide entrance at the rear opened into an alleyway to facilitate off-street, underground parking for the tenants. The front was a spacious, well-maintained walkway rising to a single line of stone steps up to a set of doors. Carved stone bears flanked the entranceway, and polished steel banisters extended down the stairs for assistance during the bitter winters. He closed his right hand around the pistol in his jacket pocket and went up past the bears and cautiously pushed open the door.

It was a weather portal, an air lock that helped hold in the heat, a seven-by-seven sanctuary from the weather. The floor was of well-worn marble with a rubber mat on which to wipe shoes and boots. A cheap painting was on one white wall, and on the opposite side was a brass line of call buttons for the individual residents and a set of mailboxes. In front of him was another pair of doors, tall and heavy with a rectangle of thick glass in each. The doors were secured by heavy interior bolts that could be activated by a tenant. There were no knobs. It reeked of Swiss solidity, dependability, and safety. Kyle thought those doors, which seemed so inviting to visitors, could probably stop a cruise missile. The glass certainly was not bulletproof but was made up of several thick layers, even more protection from the weather.

He peered through, using his hand as a shade, and saw three figures step from a small elevator and into the hallway. Two women, one man, all in enough shadow to distort their images. One of the women walked away, and the other two people turned to face him.

Jim Hall was holding Lauren tightly around the waist, supporting her weight. She seemed dazed, hardly able to walk, but Kyle saw no blood. That was good. He took his pistol from the pocket, racked in a cartridge, and held it by his left side, out of sight beneath the glass. He saw Hall say something to Lauren but could not hear the words.

Hall extended his right arm and touched a button, and the hum of an intercom hissed in the entranceway. He then leaned down and gave her a slight kiss on the cheek. "Here she is, Kyle. A deal is a deal."

Hall threw Lauren against the door so hard that she hit it and bounced back; then there was a clap of thunder and she slammed into the door a second time. Her eyes flew wide in surprise and shock, then hurt and pain. As she slid down, Jim Hall pulled the trigger again and put a bullet into her upper right shoulder. A spray of crimson smeared the window, and Kyle watched her slide to the floor.

He screamed and fired a shot through the glass, which webbed out to absorb the impact but did not shatter. It *was* bulletproof! "I'm coming, Lauren!" he yelled, then began punching every buzzer on the call board, shouting in English, German, and French for somebody to unlock the damned door. A girl is dying in the foyer. Open the door and call the police.

It seemed an eternity before a few responses came, residents asking for more detail before they unlocked the portal for a stranger. Finally one person upstairs hit the button and the lock buzzed and slid back. Kyle pushed on the door, but Lauren's body was in the way. He put his shoulder to it and managed to open it enough to squeeze through, weapon first, shifting his eyes to the hallway in case Hall decided to snap off more shots. He heard footsteps pounding down the stairs, Jim Hall escaping.

Adrenaline surged through Kyle, telling the warrior to go after the target, to take down the threat no matter what. Finish what you start. Finish Jim Hall now, because you might never get another chance. But this was Lauren lying at his feet, with a couple of terrible bullet wounds that were bleeding profusely, silently weeping and trying to eat the pain. He dropped the gun.

On his knees, Swanson felt for a pulse and found a weak one. He gripped her hand, and somehow she smiled. He ran his hands over the wounds, front and back. The first bullet had struck her in the thigh, the second in the back. He knew from his own past that the two bullets had done a lot of damage, too much for any first aid to mend. She needed a hospital and a surgeon. He would not leave her to die alone on a cold marble floor in Switzerland. He ripped off his jacket and tied the sleeves around the thigh wound, which was spilling dark blood like a waterfall. Kyle bit his lower lip, knowing the sign that her femoral artery was hit. His shirt became a bandage for the back wound. No exit wound meant the bullet was still in there. *Shit!*

The hiccupping sirens of approaching police and ambulances could be heard, but in his heart, Kyle knew they might lose this race. He wrapped his arms around Lauren, sat back against the wall, and pulled her close, pressing the makeshift bandages. "It's okay, sweetheart. I've got you now," he whispered. He was at a loss to do any more and felt hot tears of his own. He stroked her hair and looked deep into the beautiful eyes that were growing dim. "Hey, did I ever tell you about a place called Flo's Hot Dogs, back in Maine? I'll take you there soon." And he explained to her the mysteries of making a great hot dog.

BAVARIA

The gloves came off after the shooting of Agent Lauren Carson and even the CIA joined the hunt—only in a support role, but it furnished a ton of support. The orders from the president were explicit: Find Jim Hall.

Every alphabet agency in the U.S. government, and their counterparts overseas, put him at number one on the international list of active terrorists. Any country knowingly providing him aid and comfort could expect harsh retribution and a cutoff of all financial aid from the United States.

Still, it took five months before the German police talked to a woman in a small Bavarian village.

She was angry, she said, because a friend worked as a housekeeper for a rich American man up at that house in the mountains and he paid her too much money. She was nothing but a showoff, throwing that money in everybody's face with her new clothes and the new car. Nobody else could make that kind of money as housekeepers, and it was unfair. A police visit to the friend's place turned up a few hundred-dollar bills with sequential serial numbers.

Technology then came into play, with the isolated house, a large cabin that was perfect for withstanding a winter in the Alps, targeted by satellites and drones. The German intelligence service contacted Switzerland, where this suspect had made such an imprint, and asked Commander Stefan Glamer for any ideas.

Glamer gave them one. He knew a man admirably equipped to handle the situation, he said, a specialist, the best there was at this sort of thing, and it would be kept quiet. The Germans liked the idea. Glamer placed a call to General Brad Middleton in Washington.

Four nights later, in cold and frigid darkness, Kyle Swanson was dropped off by helicopter in a touch-and-go two miles from the cabin. He humped in overnight, nearly invisible in his winter white combat gear, using a GPS system that led him right to a ridge from which he could see the house. He came to a stop in a tree line five hundred yards from the cabin. New snow veiled the rocks and underbrush.

Jim Hall obviously knew that Kyle would be coming after him, sooner or later, but the months had passed quietly since Bern, and the harsh winter had clamped onto the Alps, providing an extra barrier of protection.

Kyle studied the place through his binos from the tall trees that shadowed him from the bright starlight illuminating a cloudless sky. There were no lights in the windows. After so much secure time, Hall had let his guard slip. *Hell,* Kyle thought, *the guy can't stay up and alert all night, every night.* He edged closer, into a thicket only about three hundred yards away.

A little dark shape darted nearby, a curious fox that smelled the strange scent but did not follow it. Kyle was glad to see him. Abundant wildlife meant that motion detection sensors would have been useless as a defense mechanism. This time, his binos showed cameras perched at all four corners of the cabin, but he believed the harsh weather had likely corrupted their lenses over the past few months. The dustings of snow and ice would blur his image anyway.

Using a laser rangefinder, he studied the cabin from all sides, charting it with precision in his notebook. A driveway was clogged with snow all the way to the garage, and a snowmobile bulged beneath a blue tarp next to the front deck. Beside one wall were twin white tanks of propane gas for indoor heating. No smoke came from the brick chimney, telling him that the fireplace had been doused for the night and not yet relit. A small covered porch ended at one edge with an adjacent shed that was empty, indicating that the nearest supply of dry cut logs had been used. These days, Hall would have to trek out about ten yards from the steps to the secondary, larger stack. Kyle estimated that more than a cord of split wood was left. A path had been worn in the snow with the routine of bringing the logs inside. Everything seemed in place, and matched precisely with the information that the cleaning woman had provided the police.

As a precaution, Swanson slowly turned and scanned in a circle all about him, comfortable that he was invisible and alone, but checking nonetheless. This was an omnidirectional target, so there should be no one scouting behind him. The silence of the mountain was almost tangible. Kyle continued forward, ever more cautiously, and closed to within a hundred yards, then followed a snow ridge into a swell created by the blowing snow, only seventy yards from the house. That would do it.

He crawled forward to come in directly behind the two-foot-high mound, then quietly began to tunnel into the back side, out of sight of the windows and cameras. The new snow was soft and gave way easily to the small entrenching tool and his busy hands and feet. Kyle constantly estimated the depth of his burrowing, and finally his fingers punched through the outer crust and he stopped. He could see the front porch through the hole, which he carefully widened to become a small window at the front of his snow cave. He pulled a square of white cloth from his pack and secured it across the mouth of the hole, with a little space left at the top. It resembled the veil of a burka worn by a Muslim woman, covering everything but for the eyes.

Kyle squirmed backward. He would leave the rifle in its drag bag to protect it from the weather for now, but when it came time to work, he would be able to sight over the top edge of the cloth and fire through the sheer white material. He had become part of the landscape, and the only possibly visible element was the scope, which was also cammed out. In addition, the rising sun would be at his back and shining into the eyes of anyone on the porch. It would be impossible to spot his hide site.

Out of the wind and the weather, comfortable in the insulated suit and secure in his small igloo, he broke out some rations and calmly munched a bar of chocolate and drank some water. For Kyle, time simply stopped. He could stay there as long as need be, and the only mild concern was whether his trapped body heat might melt the tunnel.

Forty-eight hours ago he had been with Lauren at a hospital run by the CIA. She had survived the attack in Bern, but barely. The major artery in her leg had only been nicked, and skilled Swiss doctors managed to suture it before she bled to death. The bullet in the back had chipped the collarbone and sent fragments tearing deep into her, perforating a lung. The doctors had to cut deeper than they wanted, leaving behind a heavy lacework of scars that were requiring plastic surgery. The flawless beauty of her face remained intact, which only amplified the torn places in her back and leg. She was visited each afternoon by a Company psychiatrist.

Kyle did not care how she looked; she was alive, and he would be her guide back to full health. Lauren was strong and was getting through the process as well as could be expected. He knew she would.

She had burst into tears unexpectedly when he told her he had to leave for a little while. One more mission. He would make it quick, then come right back. She asked, How many more missions would there be? Having come so close to death herself, she looked at life differently now. When he could not answer the question, Lauren closed her eyes in disappointment and kept them closed. He did not know what that meant. Kyle kissed her softly, then left the room.

He pushed those thoughts aside because he could not dwell on that now, or any other things in the past, or future. This moment, this instant in time, was sucking up all of his concentration until the only thing he was thinking about was the shot to come. All of his senses were alive and vibrant. It would have to be exact, because he did not want to kill Jim Hall immediately, only to incapacitate him.

In fact, it was so important not to kill him with the first shot that Kyle had chosen a little rifle that fired a small .22 caliber long bullet for the job. He had finished the computations, figured the angle of the dangle, as his pals called the mathematics of the sniper's job, and was listing the likely damage that would be caused by such a gut shot when lights began coming on in the windows. Swanson readied the rifle and peered through the scope over the veil. Wisps of smoke came from the chimney. The door of the house opened.

Jim Hall appeared at the top of the stairs in a worn blue parka and unlaced boots. A puff of exhaled air came from him, and he looked around. A new light snow was falling. The days were already getting longer, and soon he would be able to leave this place. The sunshine was calling his name.

Kyle Swanson slowed his breathing. Nothing else in the world existed but the target below. Hall slowly gathered an armload of wood, balancing it on one arm, then two, and turned back toward the house. Swanson gently squeezed the trigger and the rifle fired, not much more than a loud snapping noise.

The little bullet hit Jim Hall low in the abdomen and drilled deep before smashing to a stop against a bone in his left leg. His arms flew wide, the logs dropped with a clatter, and Hall fell with a yowl of pain into the snow, face-first. The sudden pain had been excruciating and was intensified by the extremely cold weather. Hall was down and hurt and disoriented.

The initial shock would last about thirty-five to forty seconds, and Kyle had no time to waste. He dropped the rifle, drew his 9mm pistol, and erupted out of the snow-pack, charging to reach the stunned Hall and yelling, "If you fucking reach for a weapon, I'll shoot you right in the ass!" It was not a joke, for a bullet in the butt also would be tremendously painful.

Swanson stomped a boot into Hall's back to hold him down and made a quick search. There were no weapons. He peeled a few plastic zip-ties from the batch in a vest pocket and jerked Hall's arms back so he could bind him. There was a trickle of blood coming from the stomach wound, and it stained the crust of snow. He rolled him onto his back, and Hall stared up at the sky, moaning in shock and pain. A flash of recognition cut through the pain. "Kyle," he said.

Unable to grasp his wound, Jim Hall tried to curl into a fetal position. That wouldn't do. Swanson grabbed the collar of the thick jacket and hauled him over to a tree, leaned him against it, and used lengths of duct tape to secure the ankles to some smaller stumps. "I'll be right back, Jim. Don't go anywhere."

He was certain the cabin was clear; even so, he kept his pistol at his side as he walked in. The place was small but warm, and Kyle saw that the main heating source was a baseboard system that was fed by the big propane tank outside. Pale wood-paneled walls gleamed with polish and were dappled with reflections of the flames dancing in the fireplace. First thing in the morning, and Hall already had it burning at a comfortable size. A sofa, a small television set, and a low table littered with magazines dominated the living room. Another TV set showed the views from the outside cameras, all fuzzy and useless. He could barely make out the bound shape of Jim Hall.

Through one door was a small dining table surrounded by a few straight-back chairs. A modest kitchen was directly through the far doorway, and he smelled fresh coffee and saw the makings for a breakfast of eggs and wurst. Toast had been made and buttered, and Kyle picked up a slice and nibbled it while he strolled into the bedroom. The thick blankets had been kicked aside this morning. Swanson slowly ransacked the place until, in the garage, he found two large brass-bound steamer trunks filled with banded stacks of hundred-dollar bills and other currencies. He scooped up an overflowing armful of cash and went back outside.

Some of the shock had worn off Jim Hall. His stomach seemed on fire, and it felt like some animal was clawing at his insides. "Kill me, Kyle," Hall said. "Please."

"Shut up," Swanson snapped and dumped the money at Hall's feet. The paper currency thudded and fluttered and spun into an irregular pyramid. Kyle went back and got another load and tossed that onto the pile to make it larger. Then he grunted, satisfied.

Hall had regained some of his edge and said with a sneer, "You win, so shoot me. Go ahead and shoot me now."

"I've already shot you, but whatever." Swanson smoothly pulled the pistol, aimed, and squeezed the trigger. A loud crack jarred the forest stillness, followed by a primal scream as the bullet tore into Hall's right thigh. "Gee, I hope that didn't hit your femoral artery, Jim, because then you would bleed to death too soon."

He holstered the pistol and walked back into the house, leaving Hall screaming. In the kitchen, he emptied his thermos and refilled it with the warm brew. There was a partially used block of cheese set out on the table, and he cut off a large slice. He grabbed a blanket from the bedroom and a chair from the dining area, then returned outside.

The pool of blood had increased around the sprawled body of Jim Hall and was caking fast in the cold. Hall's eyes were rolling in torment. "My legs are gone, man. I can't feel them." He sucked in the cold morning mountain air. "God, this hurts. Take me back to the States and put me on trial. Put me in the SuperMax in Colorado. I'll plead guilty to everything!"

Kyle did not reply. He put the chair beside the money, wrapped himself in the blanket, and sat down facing Hall. "This is what it was all about for you. Always was. You were always talking money, money, money."

"We were friends," Hall groaned.

Swanson barked a harsh laugh. "My friend Jim Hall died years ago. You're just another asshole terrorist. You had everything, but even that wasn't enough. You turned traitor to your country and worked to give nuclear weapons to the Taliban."

"Yeah, yeah, yeah. Okay, I admit it. Put me on trial, dude. One of those Gitmo tribunals, so it can be kept out of sight." He sucked in more air, twisting in the snow, the pain from his stomach joining in increased agony with the pain in his thigh. He twisted at the flex-ties on his wrists and the ropes on his ankles.

Swanson continued as if he had not heard a word. "You betrayed me, and worst of all, you damned near killed my Lauren. You did not have to do that, but you did it anyway, and shot her in ways that you fucking *knew* would prevent me from chasing you. That girl had loved and respected you at one time, and you shot her down like a stray dog and didn't care if she died."

Hall just stared at Kyle. Swanson fumbled in a deep pocket and came up with a yellow can of lighter fluid, flipped open the little red nozzle, and squeezed. A liquid stream squirted onto the mound of money. He kept squeezing, saturating the paper. When the can was empty, Kyle put it back in the pocket, swapping it for a plastic cigarette lighter.

"You want a trial? You had it the day you shot Lauren. I was your judge and jury, and I decided right then to show you the same amount of kindness you allowed her."

"Mercy shot, man." Jim Hall's eyes were glazed in pain. "Gimme a mercy shot."

Swanson clicked the lighter, and when the little flame popped up, he touched it to the soaked pile of money, which erupted with a loud *whoosh*. Streams of flame immediately whipped out in paths created by the flammable fuel, and the money caught fire and burned brightly.

Hall whimpered, "Kyle. Please. Take all the money. I have more. Millions. It's all yours. Just let me go."

"I sentenced you then to a slow and painful death." Swanson took a sip of coffee from his thermos, then bit into the sharp cheese. He sat, chewing, and stared at Jim Hall, the fire warm on his face.

Hall whimpered, "I'll do whatever you want, Kyle. Just let me live." He began to cry.

"I'm all out of words, Jim." He took another sip of

coffee, another bite of cheese, and wrapped the blanket tighter around him, his empty eyes watching the burning cash. Kyle Swanson felt nothing for the man bleeding to death in the snow. He adjusted the hood of his parka. The snow was starting to fall heavier, and a stiff breeze was picking up.

He waited as more blood oozed out of the wounds with every heartbeat, and new snow kept covering the angry crimson stain, as if trying to erase what was happening. Within minutes, Jim Hall's eyes fluttered and closed as he fell unconscious. Kyle waited a while longer before standing up, moving to the body, and kneeling beside it. He removed a glove and felt for a pulse, finding none.

Standing up, he took out the heavy pistol once again, aimed carefully, and put a 9 mm bullet right between the eyes. The body jumped with the impact. The job was done, his pledge fulfilled.

Kyle Swanson looked straight up into the falling snow. He just wanted the flakes to wash over him and the cold wind to take him away, to fly him through that steel-gray sky. The pistol in his hand was the ticket that could take him away from all of this. One more squeeze of the trigger was all that would be required. He stood like a statue, not a muscle moving, for several minutes, and eventually a fragment of the Robert Frost poem swam into his thoughts: *The woods are lovely, dark and deep, but I have promises to keep, and miles to go before I sleep.*

He sighed heavily. *No. I won't be dying here, and not today.* He holstered the weapon and immediately switched his thoughts back to the routine of finishing the job. He had to burn the body beyond recognition and torch the cabin and hike out to the landing zone for helicopter pickup. Miles to go.

Read on for an excerpt from the next book by
Gunnery Sgt. Jack Coughlin, USMC (Ret.),
with Donald A. Davis

RUNNING
THE MAZE

Coming soon in hardcover from St. Martin's Press

1

Five-minute break. Doctor Joey Ledford sat on the
shaky remnants of a wooden chair, smoking a Marl-
boro, and sweating while monsoon rains slammed the
tin roof of the makeshift medical clinic of United Nations' Refugee Camp Five. Somewhere, doctors and
nurses were performing surgeries in antiseptic, air-
conditioned rooms that were packed with every con-
ceivable device of the medical arts, with storage areas
nearby bulging with vital, life-saving medicines. They
were listening to Bach or Norah Jones or Latin jazz as
they performed meticulous cuts and closed wounds
with care, taking all the time they needed to do it right.
Somewhere, the magical art of medicine was a smooth
choreography conducted by well-educated profession-

als in offices and clinics and hospitals. Somewhere, but not here.

Ledford exhaled and twin streams of cigarette smoke flowed from his nostrils. The rain was not a gentle and sweet thundershower like back in Iowa. Instead of giving life to crops, this was unrelenting and fell in great sheets, as if some angry demon had ripped open the bellies of the fat, black clouds. He looked out at the sprawl of the camp, where thousands of people were hiding under whatever shelter they could find. Armed guards were at the clinic door to keep them out. They had been driven out of their homes by overflowing rivers and leaking dams and were still being pursued by water. Poor creatures, Ledford thought. Poor, damned souls.

Sweat caked his T-shirt and khakis, and when he dropped the cigarette and ground it out, he noticed the bloodstains on his black rubber boots had become deep, splotchy layers during the day, and he could not recall the individual patients from which they had come. He would wash it off later. Break over, Ledford ducked back into the tent, back into the world of misery.

He sloshed his hands in a basin, slid gloves on and put on a surgical mask and a fresh apron, then walked over to what had once been someone's kitchen table, but now served a higher purpose as an operating room surface and was covered by squares of disposable white paper on which a baby girl lay screaming as a nurse inserted an IV needle in her arm to start a drip. The mother shrieked nearby, echoing and amplifying the suffering of her one surviving child.

"It looks like another cholera," a nurse replied. "Once

you set the broken arm and leg, we will begin the antibiotics."

Ledford nodded. "We have any patient history or
X-rays for her?"

"No. She's about six months old, has a 101 fever and
coughing. Cries are weak. The mother just arrived this
morning and said a big rock banged into the child during
a mudslide two days ago."

The doctor wasted no time complaining about what
they didn't have, because they could only work with
what was available. He was thirty-one, an even six-feet
tall, had longish dark hair that reached his collar, and
possessed impeccable credentials: University of Iowa
for pre-med, then the Carver College of Medicine there,
followed by a three-year internal medicine residency at
the Mayo Clinic in Minnesota, and was ready for the
next step toward a successful career when he decided to
take a holiday from his studies and go see the world. He
did not like what he found out there. He had a rugged,
handsome face, but the eyes were those of a combat veteran, for he had seen horror after horror in refugee
camps from Haiti to Africa. The emergency calls for
help from Pakistan as the floods struck had come as he
was wrapping up an assignment in Bangladesh, and he
did not hesitate. This was who he was now, at least for as
long as he could stand it.

"OK," Ledford nodded to the anesthesiologist,
David Foley, an irreverent Canadian from Ottawa.
"Let's put the kid to sleep so we can move her on
down the assembly line. We've got a lot of other customers waiting. Raining like hell and the drinking

water is filthy because we can't store it. No excuse for water-borne diseases here."

There was a soft hiss in a plastic mask over the baby's mouth and nose, and she immediately began to calm. "Hey, Joey?" asked the gas-passer.

"What, David?"

"Five years from now you will be doing nip-and-tucks for rich ladies in your own fancy clinic. I will be driving a red convertible. We will Tweet and play Fantasy Football and date supermodels." He looked at his instruments. All good. "OK. She's down."

Ledford let his fingers gently probe the left arm of the infant and explore the fracture. "Stay focused, Dr. Foley."

"Joey?"

"Be quiet. I'm trying to concentrate." He found the break and tried to picture in his mind how it looked. With luck and a few years, if the child beat the odds and lived that long, her limbs might one day be strong again. Babies were resilient.

"Doc Yao says we can have some time off. Sort of."

Ledford's hands were working smoothly now, and the nurse stayed with him, putting another damaged little human being back together. He let her do as much of the work as possible to improve her skills. "What's the catch?"

"We go up north and visit some of the flooded villages where the water is receding. Pick a site for a new UN facility upcountry. I think we can carve out some serious down time in the process. Actually get some rest. We about done with this kid?"

"Just a few more minutes." As the nurse finished the bandaging, he gave the rest of the body a quick examination. No other breaks, but she was malnourished from being sick and unable to feed. He could clearly see the rib cage. He gently pinched, and the skin did not quickly resume its shape. "The arm will be fine, but the cholera is going to kick her little butt." He made a note to admit the child as a patient and try to get her cleaned up, inside and outside. If she survived all of that, then all she would have to worry about would be measles and malaria and land mines and machine guns and mortars and a long menu of infectious diseases and the questionable privilege of growing up in a third-world country in which women were second-class citizens. Thankfully, Ledford thought, the strict Islamic religious zealots had not invaded the camp yet, or he would not have been allowed to touch or even look at the naked female baby.

"What did you tell Dr. Yao?"

"I volunteered us."

"Humph," Ledford grunted. Might be interesting.

The team of nine medical workers headed out the following morning, in a convoy of three United Nations trucks, carrying just enough supplies to establish a base camp that could expand rapidly to help meet the flood emergency. Fifteen hours later, after grinding through brutal, washed-out roads, they reached a camp that was run by Doctors Without Borders, where they spent the night before pushing on deeper into the wasteland in the dusty gold of the new dawn.

"My ass is completely broken," complained David

Foley as the sun reached its zenith. He was in the third truck, and Ledford was riding as the only passenger in the lead vehicle.

"Take two aspirin, put it in a sling, and call me in the morning," Ledford joked.

"Better idea would be to just stop and have some lunch. Get our bearings," Foley replied.

Ledford thought that was a good idea, for the road had smoothed out a bit for the last few kilometers as it moved through some small hills. A side road branched off to the right and downward, and he told the driver to follow it to a spot where they could have a break. In a moment, they were on the back side of the hills and following an old road that sloped down into a valley, edging onto a flat plateau. "Here," he said. The trucks pulled up, nose to tailgate, and the team got out and stretched.

Foley walked up to join Ledford. "Why the grin? This place looks like the dark side of the moon." The flood had laid waste high up the banks before receding.

"I think we can set up the camp here," Ledford said. "Water is down quite a bit, and there is plenty of room to spread out. And look up at the other end of the valley, Dave. That big bridge is new; hell, they're still working on it. Traffic, people, and supplies could feed over it and down to us without a problem. And the valley is perfect for air resupply drops. Maybe the bridge people could lend us a bulldozer to carve an airstrip."

Foley had a pair of binoculars. "There are big machines at work up there, but I see trucks, too. So maybe it is in operation. You're right."

They joined the others, who had spread some blankets under stunted trees and laid out a lunch. Having some time off from the misery of the camps was reinvigorating. Afterward, some of them stretched out in the shade for quick naps, while Ledford took a walk farther down the road, alone. Although the driver, who carried a pistol, was the only member of the team with a weapon, they felt safe; medical workers helping people in need, no matter what their politics, were usually immune from any severe threat.

"Well, I'll be damned," he said with a loud laugh. He had come across an old steel trestle bridge that had been taken out by the flood, and the eastern end was canted down into the water. It reminded him of home, of an almost identical bridge where he and his sister Beth once played. He found his cellphone, snapped a picture, added the text message "REMEMBER THIS?" and sent it to her.

The group was stirring again when he got back. "Come on, everybody. Let's go for a walk and get a feel for the valley as our possible refugee camp site, then pay a visit to the big bridge at the other end. They will be our new neighbors, so we might as well pay our respects to whoever is in charge." There was a path along the western side of the river, and they followed in line. The afternoon was sunny, and a wind pushing through the valley cut the heat. This could be a good place.